One Hell of A Shipmate

A COLLECTION OF SEA STORIES

T. MATT RYAN

KITSAP PUBLISHING

One Hell of a Shipmate
First edition, published 2019

By T. Matt Ryan
Cover illustration: Annalise Lyon,
Cover Photo: Arron Choi-at Unsplash.com

Copyright © 2019, T. Matt Ryan

ISBN-13: 978-1-942661-49-8

Published by Kitsap Publishing
Poulsbo, WA 98370
www.KitsapPublishing.com

ACKNOWLEDGMENTS

Brian Roberts for editing this manuscript

Publisher Ingemar Anderson

Nick Johnson and Analise Lyon for creating the book's cover

Bob Schumacher and the Saturday Writer's Group:
having faith in me to carry this project to completion.

Classmate Jim Bruso, critic and supporter

My wife Pat Ryan for her help when I was sick
and her editorial wisdom when I was well.

My Eldest Son, Eric for his daily help and care.
My younger Sons: Scott, Carl, and David
for being there when needed

FOREWORD

"Do the right thing even if it means ending your career."

– Vice Admiral James Stockdale, USN

This is a collection of sea stories. While it is fiction, the author wove actual events which happened to some officers in the U.S. Navy during the Cold War. The setting is the fictitious heavy cruiser Beaverton, based in Long Beach, California. It's the summer of 1956 - a time unlike today. For example, today a single DUI will end a naval officer's career. But back then, the attitude toward booze was more liberal. Attendance at "Happy Hour" was expected. Every ship had its Liquor Officer whose duty it was to guide the purchase, delivery, and passage through Customs for each crew member of two cases plus a wine gallon of tax-free alcoholic beverages. Regulations defined a wine gallon to be any alcoholic beverage. If any officer failed to handle his alcohol or preserve decorum in port, the commanding officer would note it on his fitness report. Be it officer or enlisted, he could deem him a "liberty risk" and restrict his liberty, such as after dark in every port, until the end of a cruise or enlistment.

The Navy in 1956 was a decade past the time when it was the largest fleet in world history, but it was still a formidable force. The Cold War brought major crises that year that kept the fleet on high alert: a revolt in Hungary; and conflict over the Suez Canal between Israel, aligned with Britain and France, versus Egypt, backed by the Soviet Union. Against this tense backdrop, even placid Melbourne, Australia, becomes a front line of the Cold War when the Beaverton is among the flotilla of Navy ships whose visit coincides with the Summer Olympics held in the fall of 1956.

The protagonist, Ensign Joseph Aristotle Xylos, is labeled "The Original Liberty Risk" by a very prejudiced Senior Watch Officer, whose imaginings will follow Joe through the pages of this novel.

CHAPTER 1

Reporting Aboard

"Heavy cruiser in sight, sir. Should be the *Beaverton*. Yes, it's her!"

A minute ago, U.S. Navy Ensign Joe Xylos's world had been the Long Beach harbor seawall in the distance and the grey steel mooring buoy his motorboat was circling on that hot August afternoon. It all changed in an instant when his coxswain called that he had the USS *Beaverton* in sight beyond the breakwater.

Straining to see between the fingers of smog, Joe for a moment saw clearly a majestic work of art. Ever so briefly, a bright sun highlighted the imposing man-of-war from the radar directors atop its superstructure to the batteries of nine- and five-inch guns before the big ship disappeared again into the Southern California haze.

The next time she came into view, all he saw was her bow turning toward them through a gap in the breakwater. Spread out abeam on each side was a huge bow wave. *She can't stop in time. She'll swamp us!* thought Joe, in spite of the cloud of smoke rushing from the two stacks, as he mentally gauged the ship's speed relative to the breakwater. Much to his surprise, the coxswain nonchalantly steered their little boat right between the fast-approaching ship and the buoy. "Sailor, get us the hell out of here before we're run down!"

The coxswain gave him a puzzled look. "Aye, aye, sir. My instructions are to bring you to the port accommodation ladder by the quarterdeck as soon as we moor."

"Faster! Faster, damn it! Get us out of here!" The words no sooner escaped his mouth than Joe realized he knew next to nothing about the Navy and ship handling. Maybe this guy at the helm knew what he was doing. It was at moments like this that Joe fervently wished he had spent the last years of his father's life tapping into his wisdom about going to sea as master of merchant ships, rather than spending those long days reading the Greek classics to him.

"Don't worry, sir," said the coxswain, "there's plenty of time to stand clear."

"Sailor, I don't know much about what it takes to stop that cruiser, but I prefer to be a living witness who's laughed at. Steer away from that buoy."

"Sir, you need to have faith in the Captain. He's a fantastic ship handler. You ought to let me bring you alongside early. Otherwise, you just watch. We'll be floating around out here until they grant the crew liberty."

"What are you talking about?"

"I've said way too much, sir." The coxswain pushed the throttle all the way open and sped away, two hundred yards off the cruiser's beam.

Frightening minutes for Joe passed. He saw the cruiser's huge bow waves dissipate and splash harmlessly on the breakwater as the ship's backing bell sounded and white water roiled astern. The ship was barely moving forward when he saw a motor whaleboat touch down. It swiftly cleared its boat falls and made its way toward the bow. Moments later, seamen in whites and orange life jackets scrambled onto the buoy. Soon a line was passed from the ship and the anchor chain was paid out until the end of the chain rested on the buoy.

As the whaleboat lay close by the buoy, a man in a khaki uniform shouted up to the deck, "Where's the damn mooring shackle?"

From above, an angry voice answered, "In the friggin' whaleboat, of course!"

A big dark-featured man with the insignia of a Boatswain's Mate First Class shouted upward, " Like hell it is! Check the Second Division gear locker! Get that mother down here!"

The coxswain laughed. "'Friggin''? You can bet the Chaplain is out of earshot when they use language like that."

Joe pointed at the buoy and asked the coxswain, "Is there anything we can do to help, like lend them a spare shackle?"

The coxswain laughed and shook his head. "We don't carry one, this is an officer's motorboat. Nobody can save the Second Division fuckups from their fate. Let me see if we can bring you alongside, sir."

Joe squinted into the putrid brown haze that hung like a curtain beyond the breakwater. Even the blue waters of the Pacific Ocean were dulled by the ever-present mucky smog. He watched every maneuver the coxswain made until they were aiming for the just-lowered port accommodation ladder. Then he dropped down into the cabin, opened the briefcase his father left him, and confirmed that the envelope of orders and records was on top. *I wish you were alive, Dad, so I could write you about today.*

The coxswain goosed the throttle to head the boat toward the ladder. As Joe moved his two suitcases and the briefcase topside, he heard the same angry, disembodied voice shout from above, "Coxswain, stand clear until the Admiral's barge clears the side."

"Aye, aye, sir! " was the coxswain's loud reply. In hushed tones, he muttered to Joe, "Just our luck, the Officer of the Deck is good old Lieutenant Harry Leach. It will take two watches to unscrew his watch as OOD. The barge isn't even in the water yet." In a voice meant to be heard, he continued, "It looks like we're going to have a little wait. I'm sorry, sir. I got you here in plenty of time. I'll give you the four-bit tour, sir."

He eased the throttle farther open and turned hard, making a smooth semicircle in the water with his wake. By the time the motorboat circled back to the bow, a large gleaming shackle was being lowered by light line to the buoy.

The coxswain remarked, "Sir, I can understand why you reacted like you did. This is one big cruiser. Don't worry. Captain Slaxman is the best ship handler I've ever seen. Right now, we have about a ten-knot wind blowing, and still he's held this ship right on top of the buoy until those screwups found the shackle. I'd go to hell and back for that man. He's fantastic!"

While they waited, Joe took advantage of the tour being offered. He was most impressed by the obvious pride these young sailors had in this aging World War II ship, the *Beaverton*. Even close up, she was graceful and majestic with colorful flags and pennants flapping. The paint was fresh and clean. Joe pointed to the line marking where the black boot-topping paint began and the Navy-gray paint ended. "I've never seen such a beautifully kept ship. Before my father died, he was a master of World War II cargo ships. Not only is the line straight that marks the boot topping, but everybody I've seen looks so shipshape that they could stand in for recruiting posters. What's up? Why so spiffy?"

The coxswain smiled. "Officially it's because we're a flagship for Cruiser Division Nine. You know the old-school saying, 'Shine she must, work she may.' The reality of it is that we'll be going to the Olympics in Melbourne in December."

"How do you know?"

Nodding, the coxswain pointed out the white "E"s for excellence, emblazoned on turrets one and two. "If anybody goes, we go. We earned it. We have the best gun crews in the Pacific Fleet, and we're the best in Cruiser Division Nine."

By the time they were abeam of Number Three turret, the young officer was duly impressed with all the awards and accomplishments of his first ship, from a Presidential Unit Citation for service in Korea (which the coxswain proudly bragged about) to the weathered big red "E" for Engineering Excellence on the forward stack.

Sounds of water splashing from the ship's overboard discharges mixed with the many sounds of shipboard life as the motorboat leisurely glided through the smooth water close by the *Beaverton*. As they cleared the stern, a work party was swinging out boat booms and a black motorboat was underway after being lowered from the hook of the huge crane on the stern.

As the black boat approached the accommodation ladder, pairs of bells sounded over the announcing system and a gravelly voice called out, "Cruiser Division Nine, departing." The high-pitched call of a boatswain's pipe cut through the ambient noise and hung over the water as a tall man with golden shoulder boards—the Admiral--scrambled down the ladder toward the waiting boat. Above, on the cruiser's mainmast, his absentee pennant--the signal that the Admiral had left the ship--snapped open and caught the breeze.

After the Admiral's barge was well clear, the coxswain brought the motorboat alongside. "Careful stepping onto the platform, sir. They're still working to stay on top of the buoy."

⊶⊷

A seaman put Joe's two suitcases on the lowered platform while Joe carried the large leather briefcase. It wasn't until he stepped across that he realized how little space the platform had to stand on. Lieutenant Leach, who was now visible, barked on his megaphone, "Coxswain, shove off. You, mister, clear the forward accommodation ladder."

Joe's attention was entirely on the water; wave after wave was working its way down the side of the ship, with the crests passing ever closer to the platform he stood on. *Holy smoke, what is this bastard doing? I could lose everything over the side.* Joe looked up at the top of the ladder where stood the rotund Lieutenant glowering down at him.

What is it with that fat guy? Joe wondered. *If this is his way of breaking me in, I fail to see the humor. I just paid for all these uniforms, and I'm broke. Oh, what the hell.*

He hoisted the briefcase onto the third step and the suitcases to the first and second steps. From his place on the platform, he shouted, "Excuse me, sir, I have more luggage than I can carry. Please, I need help. My new uniforms, I can't afford to lose them. Could you send someone down to give me a hand on these stairs?"

"This is an accommodation ladder. Didn't they teach you anything in the knife and fork school? Mister, you are a disgrace. Your uniform is a size and a half too large. Stand tall! Your shoulder boards are drooping, thanks to your round shoulders."

Now what does my uniform size have to do with anything? For a minute, Joe stood frozen until he heard Lieutenant Leach mutter in a voice that carried down the ladder, "One more greaser Reserve, just what we need!"

Another voice followed Leach's. "Harry, what the hell are you up to? Call the officer's motorboat back alongside. I've got to deliver these job orders to the shipyard today."

Leach barked at Joe through the megaphone, "Move your damn bags, mister. You're interfering with those who have shore leave."

"Harry, you son of a bitch, that's our new Ensign. Of all the harebrained crap. Call that boat alongside and send your messenger down to help him or I call the XO."

"You should have been awaiting your boat. This is my watch, my quarterdeck, Mister Kane."

"He's my shipmate--a snipe. You, seaman, go down ahead of me and give the Ensign a hand."

"This is my quarterdeck," repeated Leach.

The messenger stood frozen, looking from one officer to the other, until the Boatswain gave him a hand signal. The other officer snapped, "Harry, you're interfering with my time ashore. I will make an issue of this. I'll fetch his luggage. You, messenger, turn to."

Minutes later, Joe watched his first suitcase proceed upward in the hands of the messenger, followed by the second in the hands of the officer who'd been arguing with Leach. He introduced himself as Lieutenant Milt Kane, the Main Engines Officer. "I apologize for the way you were treated when you were reporting aboard," he said. "Trust me, the rest of the officers aboard aren't like The Hairy Leech. Let me apologize in advance for his garbage. Don't make an issue of the crap with your suitcases. He's a horse's ass."

Lieutenant Leach's gruff greeting was no surprise as Joe stepped onto the platform at the top of the ladder. "Show me your orders, mister."

As Joe took a step onto the deck and bent over to open his briefcase, his back was sternward, toward the Lieutenant. Leach's sarcastic voice bellowed, "Now that you have your sorry ass on my quarterdeck, the other way! Always, you salute the ensign at the stern, not the jack at the bow, mister."

Joe felt a flush of embarrassment as he stood up, rotated, and gave a smart salute to the rotund OOD. He sang out, "Request permission to come aboard, sir."

Leach returned the salute and repeated, "Show me your orders, mister."

"Orders are in my briefcase, sir." Joe squatted and opened the briefcase.

"You should have those in hand when you step onto my quarterdeck." Leach read the mimeographed copy of Joe's orders. He studied them for some moments before he looked up. "X-elost, what kind of name is that?"

I've put up with enough crap from this clown. "Xylos. An honorable name, a proud name, solid as oak." Joe peered at the Lieutenant's name tag: LT Leach, OOD. "And what sort of name is Leee-aach, sir?"

Taken aback, the Lieutenant took a step toward Joe and looked down his nose at the short, dark, and round-shouldered young man standing rigidly at attention. "Look, Ensign, I don't need the comedy. You'd be smart to pick an American name that people can pronounce."

"People who stayed awake in grade school until all the sounds of the alphabet were covered have no difficulty because they know that X, when used as the first letter of a word, is pronounced as a Z. People who can handle 'xylophone' find Xylos a snap, sir." Joe's dark, laughing eyes met Leach's.

Leach's knuckles grew white as he pushed into his armpit the OOD's long glass that he carried.

"Ensign Zilyus, do you know who I am?"

"Yes, sir. You're the OOD, Officer of the Deck. To whom do I report for duty?"

"Give me a copy of your damn orders so we can spell your name correctly in the log."

"You have a copy in your hand, sir."

Leach glared at him. "The messenger will take you to Officer Personnel. Boatswain, have a steward remove this officer's luggage from the quarterdeck. Zilch, you'd be wise to show respect to your seniors. I am the senior Lieutenant on this ship and I make up the in-port watch bill."

"The name is Xylos, Ensign Joseph Xylos, sir. United States Navy . . . Reserve. Certainly, I will show you the same respect that you show to me, sir."

While the Quartermaster made entries in his log and Joe waited for his copy of the orders and the messenger to take him to the office, Lieutenant Leach was called to the phone.

Watching Leach stride across the quarterdeck, Joe thought, *This will be a long two years if they're all like this Leach. He looks more like a sponge in a khaki uniform than anything else; needs a shave and a haircut. His brown shoes are well shined but badly cracked, and the heels are worn down. His cap looks like an aviator's with a fifty-mission crush. Beside him, I don't look too bad.*

Leach shouted into the phone, "I don't understand. I am the Main

Battery Officer. It's the First Lieutenant's job to take care of the mooring tackle. . . . Yes, I know that Second Division has those responsibilities. I'll talk to Outside White personally when I get off watch. Yes, Commander, I fully understand why the Captain was upset. . . . How was I to know the mooring shackle was missing? The Admiral didn't notice when he departed. The new Ensign you were expecting was on the officer's motorboat. He's a wise ass. . . . Ensign Zilchloss. . . . Yeah, that's his name. Starts with X, but he pronounces the X like a Z."

A pimply-faced seaman in an immaculate set of whites tapped the newly arrived Ensign Xylos on the arm. Minutes later, he found himself in the overly warm Officer Personnel Office. Four desks were crammed between file cabinets. Crowded into the space were the Personnel Officer and two yeomen. Joe felt relieved when the Personnel Officer, a tall man in his thirties with a small paunch and a receding hairline, extended his pudgy hand, first to introduce himself as Lieutenant Barry Tumwater and then to take the packet of records and orders. He pushed forms and papers into Joe's hands and seated the young officer at the only empty desk in the office.

While Joe filled out the paperwork, he heard in the corridor a loud, somewhat high-pitched voice with a very strong Southern drawl. "Damn it, the Old Man is embarrassed about the way sea detail went this afternoon. If we had any kind of weather today, we would have had the makings of a disaster. You're the department head and I want you to get to the bottom of this. You've got two officers who don't talk to one another, Leach and the First Lieutenant. I'm not as much interested in making bloody examples as I am in correcting what went wrong. Keep me posted. I know you can handle it." The other officer's voice was low and muted, so Joe didn't understand the reply.

Once Joe was finished with the forms, he was handed a packet of instructions and told to read them. He had just taken off his khaki blouse and begun to work his way through the material when Tumwater announced, "The XO will see you now. Go forward and take the first right."

The young officer slowly pulled his blouse back on and buttoned it up. He turned the corner and stepped into the office of the Executive Officer (XO) to find the Chaplain, a Lieutenant Commander, waiting in front of the intake desk with a short, red-eyed seaman in tow.

The Chaplain was tall and handsome, with a youthful, athletic build that made him look from a distance as if he were in his twenties. However, his wrinkled hands and the deep lines in his face were more accurate measures of his age. He leaned over the yeoman at the desk, thrusting his hands in jabbing gestures. "This is of the utmost importance. I need to see Commander Longstreet right now. This time that savage has gone too far. He's not the kind of man who should be in the modern Navy."

It wasn't until the XO stepped into the small office that Joe identified him as the disembodied voice he'd overheard from the Personnel Office. The XO was a short man with a red face and a pale white forehead. His small blue eyes were widely set on either side of a large, crooked nose. Framing the sides were large red cauliflower ears, made all the more prominent by dark, thinning hair streaked with gray and cropped very close. He stood ramrod straight with an annoyed look as he listened to the Chaplain. "Father, what's all this commotion about?"

The Chaplain put a hand to his forehead as if about to cross himself. "Boatswain Tallfeathers! Commander, we've been over this ground before. Now he's taken upon himself to restrict this man to the ship indefinitely. Not even the Captain has that kind of power. Look at this poor boy! Frightened, fearful! How can we give these youngsters confidence to succeed if they're browbeaten like this?"

The XO turned to the young man and rested a hand on the youngster's shoulder. "What's your name, boy?"

"Pickens. Seaman Apprentice Lyle Pickens, sir."

"You're up in Second Division with Boatswain Tallfeathers, aren't you?"

"Yes, sir."

"And did the Boatswain tell you that you were restricted to the ship indefinitely?"

"Not exactly, sir. He took my liberty card and he's never going to give it back."

"Did you see him destroy it?"

"No, sir."

"Then what prompts you to believe he'll never give it back?"

By now tears had filled the youngster's eyes to overflowing and he was sniffling loudly. "He keeps his word. He told me when I give him the mooring shackle, he'll give me my liberty card. I'll never get liberty . . . ever!"

"Why do you say that?"

"Because I threw the shackle over the side after he told me he never wanted to see it looking so cruddy ever again."

"Oho!" The XO pulled his large earlobe and grinned, revealing nicotine-yellowed teeth that stood unevenly like the stones of a druid temple. "Boy, I don't think you should say any more to me about this. It could be used against you. I'm afraid that rather than redressing what you believed was a wrong, you may have committed a violation of the UCMJ—the Uniform Code of Military Justice. I want you to report back to your division. Father Bill, I appreciate the care you have for our young men and certainly hope you won't take offense. Keep the lines open and let me know when you find something."

Father Bill blew through his fist and coughed before weakly smiling. "Stan, I had no idea. I never in a month of Sundays thought I'd be the one to solve the mystery of the lost mooring shackle. Still, that Boatswain had no authority to restrict this man to the ship. You'll look into it, won't you?"

"The question will be raised. But don't think for a single minute I'm going to deny my petty officers the power to hold liberty cards. You ought to know by now, Father, that liberty is a privilege."

The seaman fled the room as soon as the XO dismissed him. As the Chaplain turned to go, he extended a sweaty hand to Joe, who had stood quietly against the bulkhead while the exchange went on. "I'm Father Finn, the ship's Chaplain."

"Ensign Joe Xylos, sir."

"Xylos. You're Greek, correct?"

"Yes, sir!"

"Xylos, that means 'woods' in English."

"Yes, sir."

"Save the sirs for the officers you report to. Call me Father or Father Bill. It's not often I get to use my Jesuit language training here. Μιλάτε Ελληνικά?" No response. "Do you speak Greek?"

"Oh! Sorry, Father. No, hardly a word."

As the Chaplain followed his errant charge out the door, the XO introduced himself as Commander Stanley Longstreet, USN. Joe shook his hand vigorously. "Ensign Joe Xylos, sir."

As the XO guided the Ensign into his office, he repeated, "Xylos . . . Xylos. Lieutenant Leach pronounced it differently, more with a zil____."

"Leach is an ass."

"He may be that and more, but he is your senior and a member of the wardroom. Not for one minute will I tolerate disrespect toward members of the wardroom. Lieutenant Leach has some days that are better than others. What happened between you and Mr. Leach for him to have such a poor initial impression of you?"

"He obviously doesn't like my looks. When I got on the platform, before I set foot on board, he called me a 'greaser reservist.' He's laid on one insult after another. He advised me to change my name to some American one. He's overbearing."

"You have to admit that Xylos isn't too common a name. Was your father an immigrant?"

"No sir. My father's people have been here since the Civil War. My great-grandfather sailed blockade runners out of the Carolinas."

"A Southern boy! Son, you don't talk like you're from the South."

"I was born in New York. My dad was in the Merchant Marine. We moved to Missouri, where I grew up."

"I see here that you're a graduate of the University of Colorado with a degree in industrial engineering and got your commission through Navy ROTC. Have you given any thought as to what kind of duty you'd prefer on the *Beaverton*?"

"I want to get qualified as an OOD Underway. I'd prefer the Gunnery Department. I need the qualification to get into Submarine School."

"Fine. Fine. That's what I like to see, a young officer who comes aboard with a career map laid out. You sound like a man who's made a long-term commitment to his country . . . a potential career man."

"I have given it some serious thought, yes. I think nuclear power is the wave of the future."

"Certainly, my boy. A good attitude! You've got your course set. I'm pleased to see that. Report to the Chief Engineer. You'll be the new

Assistant B Division Officer."

"Engineering? B Division? Why? Will I get to qualify as an OOD Underway?"

"All Engineering watch officers stand at least six indoctrination watches on the bridge. Don't look on an assignment to Engineering as being second class. You have the educational background we need in the Engineering Department. You'll have your own division far earlier, and your own watch as well. You'll be working for one of the most professional engineers in the Pacific Fleet. If you're a superior performer in Engineering, in a year or so, we'll look at rotating you into Gunnery."

The XO spent the next twenty minutes on what Joe recognized as a standard welcoming lecture for new Ensigns. Twice the young officer tried to change the subject back to his assignment, but without success.

It was a dejected young Ensign who returned to Officer Personnel. Joe groused to Tumwater about his assignment as a snipe (Engineering crewman) and the loss of an early opportunity to go to Submarine School.

Tumwater pulled a faded green cloth-covered three-ring binder from the metal shelf above his desk. He licked his thumb and turned the pages until he read aloud, "'Qualification as an Officer of the Deck Underway or Engineering Watch Officer Underway is required . . .' Joe, you stand a far better chance of making it to Submarine School in Engineering because we have Lieutenants (junior grade), in line for Lieutenant, who still haven't qualified as OOD Underway. And you'd be in line behind them. Come on, I'll show you where your bunk is."

Joe read and reread the newly issued instruction before closing the cover and handing the book back to Tumwater. "Thank you, sir, for showing me the instruction. I feel a lot better--a hell of a lot better!"

They passed through the wardroom, where Tumwater introduced him to more people than he had the ability to absorb names.

Harry Leach followed along. Although Tumwater correctly introduced Joe as ZY-lohss, Leach kept "correcting" him loudly, braying "Ensign Zilch," followed by giggles and guffaws. Joe noticed that Tumwater turned his back on Leach and made no attempt to engage him. He too chose to ignore Leach. Following the brief introductions, the pair exited the space through the forward door.

Once they were clear of the closing door, Tumwater said, "You did the right thing by ignoring Leach. Most of us do. He's been passed over a second time for Lieutenant Commander and will be leaving the Navy next June."

Joe smiled broadly. "Mister Leach and I met on the quarterdeck. He's hung up on 'zilch,' like a child with a new toy. People like him fail to realize that failure to pronounce a word correctly is not a reflection on the bearer, but on them. I imagine he'll give me ample opportunities to help him acquire a liberal education."

"Careful now! You'll be pissing up a rope. He may be wounded, but he can do you serious harm if you give him an opening. Come on in here. This is your stateroom. It's called Boys' Town because it's where Jay Ohs—junior ."

The young officer was led into a room that had six bunks lining its sides. Interspaced between them were tall gray clothes lockers, and along one wall were four desks. Sitting in a chair, with stacks of paper on the desk before him, was a muscular young blond man adding columns of figures and shuffling invoices from one stack to another as he worked. The man rubbed his lantern jaw while his brown eyes scanned from sheet to sheet.

He only broke his concentration when the Lieutenant said, "Larry, this is Joe Xylos, who just reported aboard. He's been assigned to Boys' Town with you. Joe, this is Larry White, better known as Inside White. He's a fellow snipe, the A Division Officer."

While they were shaking hands, Tumwater continued, "Larry is a graduate of the trade school in Annapolis, Maryland.

"Trade school?"

"That's what we call the Naval Academy. Don't worry, he's a good man. Let's see, Larry, you ought to be making Lieutenant (junior grade) in December. Does that make you Bull Ensign?"

"Naw. Lawyer Sawyer is the most senior. He was commissioned three weeks before me. Anyway, we still keep the power here in Boys' Town."

"Where is Sawyer?"

"On the first liberty boat, where else?"

"What keeps you on board? Duty?"

"Yes, I've got to get the mess bills out and get the books ready to turn over to Rob Swenson after he wins the election. Lucky guy, he's a shoo-in to succeed me as the next Mess Treasurer. Joe, I'll need $29.51 from you to join the mess."

"Oh, yeah, I remember. You have to put money into the wardroom kitty to join. Can I write you a check?"

"Sure."

"Besides you and Sawyer, who else lives here?"

"Lieutenant (junior grade) Cyrus Penelton. Cy is away at some school in San Diego. I think it's Air Controller's School. He's the Assistant Combat Information Center Officer."

"Then we have two empties?"

"Most of the time we run that way. Although during the last deployment we were full for about half the trip. Usually we get the two-week Reserve officers and staff overflow."

Tumwater went back out, after Joe shook his hand and thanked him for his help, leaving the two Ensigns to get acquainted.

CHAPTER 2

First Underway

Late Monday afternoon, with the ship underway since early that morning, Joe finished his first day of duty in Engineering. This was the first opportunity since Joe came aboard for the four occupants of Boys' Town to be together at the same time. The roar of an axial fan and the rush of air in the ventilation trunk in the after end of the room created a constant background noise that was louder the farther one ventured in from the door, which was forward. Thus the four Ensigns all tended to congregate around the forward end, near the door and the desks.

Carter "Lawyer" Sawyer sat at one of the desks and peered through thick glasses at an open file atop a small stack of folders before him. He had a lazy eye, the left, whose lid drooped. His large mouth, along with his slow Southern drawl, left the appearance that his mental elevator didn't reach the top floor. His pale skin was the result of keeping out of the sun, so much so that people ashore would often ask him when he arrived in Southern California. Although in his early twenties, he had the paunch and somewhat stooped posture of a middle-aged man.

Carter was a good roommate, according to Inside White, because he never made any noise either aboard or ashore; in fact, White called him "Ensign Enigma." Intrigued, Joe started a conversation with Sawyer, if it could be called that. Joe felt like he was cross-examining a reluctant witness. "Where are you from?

"Florida."

"Where in Florida?"

"Panama City."

"How is it down there?"

"It's home."

"Did you join the Navy right after you graduated from college?"

"No."

After a very long pause, Joe asked, "Well, what did you do?"

"I passed the bar and lawyered for awhile."

Inside White had just returned to the room from jogging around the ship half a dozen times. He was wearing dark blue shorts with a thin white stripe running down the outside seam. Tufts of reddish-blonde hair on his chest glistened with sweat. He stood in front of the mirror and admired his physique, then dropped to the floor and did his daily fifty sit-ups. When he was done, he grabbed the flat of an I-beam running across the overhead and did half a dozen modified chin-ups, being careful not to bang his head against the metal ceiling.

Joe placed the middle of his back against the chair and his butt almost at the edge of the seat to form an "S" posture while he watched his new roommate. "Larry, you don't need to do all this on my account. I feel tired enough after a full day of climbing up and down ladders."

"It's for me. Life is too easy on this floating palace. It's too easy to forget this is a warship. It's too easy to let yourself become the weak link in the chain. It's too easy to forget that our business is to go to war. You've got to get in shape and stay in shape. Come on up and join me tomorrow afternoon."

"I don't want to rush into something like that. I might get the bends from too much fresh air."

"Come on, Xylos, you haven't been a snipe long enough to talk like that!"

White left the room to take a shower. Moments later, the fourth man walked through the door: Cyrus Penelton, a Lieutenant (junior grade) ("Jay Gee" or JG for short). He had to duck slightly to keep his cap from being swept off his head by the top of the door jamb. Once inside, he tossed the cap on his bed and ran his fingers through his rather long, dark, wavy hair.

Cy wore an air of confidence. He had the looks of a matinee idol, blue eyes, perfectly clear complexion, a measured smile, very straight white teeth, and a square chin. Inside White had told Joe that Cy was a native of Beverly Hills and the son of a producer at Paramount Studios. He never wanted for money, and he drove a pink Cadillac convertible, a gift from his father.

Cy laid a big hand on Joe's shoulder and said, "Back from the black hole of Engineering, I see."

"Yep, I survived the first day underway, no sweat."

"What do you think of the good ship *Beaverton*?"

"Big! They tell me she's 673 feet stem to stern, with 61 officers and more than 1,000 enlisted men. I never dreamed you could put so many compartments inside a space this size. I think I spent half the day lost."

"Learn how they're numbered and it's easy."

"I still get turned around."

"To change the subject, I take it that you had a run-in with the infamous Lieutenant Leach."

"Not really. He had the deck when I came aboard and couldn't pronounce my name properly. Boy, that guy was impossible! He hasn't mastered the alphabet past "W.""

"They don't waste time indoctrinating you down there in Engineering, do they? Harry isn't exactly loved there—or topside either. He came to us last year after he was relieved of command of a landing ship, the USS *Fusillade*. He failed to get underway with his ship when his formation sortied to avoid a typhoon. I heard he was still in Beppu harbor when the eye of the storm passed through. Yeah, Harry is an exception to the normally congenial officers of this wardroom. Actually this is a very unique wardroom. I don't think you'd find a wardroom outside Long Beach like this one."

"What does Long Beach have to do with it?"

"Proximity to Hollywood and central casting. Start with the Captain—skipper, CO, Old Man—whatever you call him, Sam Slaxman. He could be a stand-in for James Cagney: short . . . swaggers . . . terrific sense of humor, very, very quick mentally."

Joe gave a thumbs-up. "The Chief Engineer says the Captain skippered a sub in the war . . . decorated with the Navy Cross. The way he brought the ship in last Thursday when I came aboard was impressive. I thought he was going to overrun the buoy."

"He is an outstanding ship handler. His one weakness is that he does it all. The result is that very few officers get qualified as OOD Underway. I've just about given up hope myself. I'll be in Combat forever."

"So I've heard."

"And the XO is straight out of 'Looney Tunes.' Every time they show a cartoon with that crazy rooster, the crew just howls. 'Foghorn Leghorn,' that's what they call the XO behind his back. Then there's my boss, the Operations Officer, Commander Wyman. He's an underweight Fredric March."

"Tell me about the Chief Engineer."

"He's a hard one to peg. I'd say he's a combination of Red Skelton and W. C. Fields. That's when he's ashore . . . and any number of characters underway. Did you know he was the Naval Attache in Venezuela until they overthrew the dictator?"

"No."

"Get him to talk about it after he's had a few, which is just about every day in port. He'll keep you laughing for hours."

"Don't tell me about Leach . . . I think I saw him in a dog food commercial."

Penelton laughed. "You've got him pegged. His bark is far worse than his bite. He's straight out of a 'Road Runner' cartoon."

⇥⊶◉ ◉⊷⇤

Joe witnessed the wardroom election where the chore of running the wardroom mess was passed to two Lieutenants (junior grade). As Inside White had predicted, Lieutenant (junior grade) Swenson was the new Mess Treasurer. The entire election process was very casual. A number of people had been nominated, but it was obvious that the two senior tables had caucused, at least informally, since they seemed to vote in a bloc. Joe counted the number of Ensigns and Lieutenants (junior grade) and noted that together they were a majority of the wardroom.

Just after the last vote was counted, Joe rose and in a loud voice called out, "Point of information."

XO Longstreet, who had presided over the meeting, went on talking to the Operations Officer. After a few moments, Joe tapped on his glass and said again, "Mr. Chairman . . . Mr. Chairman. Point of information."

Longstreet looked up and bellowed, "Are you talking to me, boy?"

"Yes, sir. I have a question to ask."

"If you're going to talk to me, boy, I'm no chairman. I'm president of this here mess. Now what is your question?"

"Mr. President, just so I understand how the meetings are run, what parliamentary rules do you use?"

The XO was slow to answer. "Par-lay-mentary rules? Sir, I'll have you know we run fair, democratic elections here."

"I'm sure you do, sir. Then you abide by *Robert's Rules of Order*, as do most organizations?"

Red-faced, Longstreet sipped his cup of coffee and looked around the table where he sat.

A voice far down the table said, "That's right, XO. Everybody follows Robert's Rules when they run meetings."

By that time all conversation had been interrupted. All eyes followed the give-and-take back and forth as the short, red-faced XO stood up and shouted, "Certainly we run this mess's meetings with only proper parlay-men-tary procedures. Of course we follow Robert's Rules. Certainly, my boy. Why do you ask?"

"I'd like to make the motion that we adjourn the meeting and get on with our lunch."

There were a few muffled laughs followed by a pause, then an anonymous "Second."

Longstreet rolled up his napkin into a cylinder and stared at Xylos for a long moment until Ensign Sawyer volunteered, "Commander, a motion to adjourn calls for a vote. No debate."

At last the older man caught the drift of what he was supposed to do. "All in favor of adjourning the meeting, say 'aye.'"

A chorus of loud "ayes" was followed by more subdued laughter, which drifted into the hum of conversation as the stewards moved from table to table.

The XO stared at Joe for almost half the meal. When he was finished, he walked over to where Joe was sitting and in an almost subdued manner said, "I took what you were about today as an attempt to be helpful. Thank you, Ensign. However, I'm more than capable of running this mess."

⸺◉⸺

That evening, Lawyer Sawyer found Joe lying on his bunk studying a technical manual. "Joe, what was all that stuff about *Robert's Rules of Order*?"

"I needed to know the ground rules. Did you know that the Ensigns and Jay Gees constitute a majority in this wardroom?"

"No. Come to think of it, you're right. What are you thinking about?"

"If we all vote together, we could let the senior people get stuck with running the wardroom."

"Yeah, but that could cut two ways. You'd be making some pretty powerful people mad."

"Maybe, but it would be fun to pull off . . . starting with Harry Leach."

Joe's life fell into step with the shipboard routine. For several weeks the ship got underway each Monday--to break in the new crewmen like Joe and get all systems running smoothly--and returned to Long Beach on the weekend. The B Division Officer, Lieutenant (junior grade) Todd Morgan, assigned him the less pleasant administrative chores and made him his commissioned 'gopher,' or errand boy. Between watches and the usual workday, Joe took it upon himself to learn the major engineering systems as quickly as possible. He wasn't seen in the wardroom in the daytime except for meals and an occasional movie, either in port or at sea. The Chief Engineer, Commander Henry Moran, kept hearing that Joe was seen in this space or that, continually asking questions. He was pleased.

In mid-August Joe received an invitation to a reception ashore in honor of Commander First Fleet, Admiral Gilbert. Moran called Joe aside and confirmed that he had received the invitation. He told Joe this was a "command performance" and suggested that, if he knew any young ladies, he bring a date because the price included an open bar and heavy hors d'oeuvres. Joe shrugged his shoulders and promised that he would attend.

The appointed Friday evening found a large number of officers and their ladies from the ships in port standing around the party room, clustered in groups according to ship. A small Navy band provided live background music from a bandstand while shafts of late afternoon sun cut through the smoke to illuminate a very well waxed dance floor. The last of the guests were filtering through the receiving line headed by the white-haired Admiral, wearing a blue blazer with a gold patch on the pocket, and his wife.

Commander Longstreet had taken an informal muster and had but one sheep missing from the fold, Joe Xylos. He was on his way to talk to the Chief Engineer when he heard subdued voices nearby,

"How did that runt talk that tall honey into a date?"

"Sayyy, isn't that Lola Getz from the Body Shop?"

"Look at the way that dress fits! I don't think she has a stitch on under it."

One by one, conversations faded and the staccato hammer of high heels on hardwood rose above the din. Walking beside the short, round-shouldered Ensign Joe Xylos, who was wearing a dark brown business suit and a light tan tie, was a statuesque brunette, made even taller by her spike heels. Her white knit dress hugged every curve as snugly as a layer of spray paint. Patterns of colored sequins caught the sun, shivering and moving with every step she took. The deep vee in front exposed the tops and sides of high, firm breasts.

Joe and his spectacular date walked through a gauntlet of stares toward the Admiral. All the while the brunette was chewing and very audibly popping gum between her teeth. She walked with a flowing gait that rolled her hips. The more the heads turned, the more obviously accentuated became the walk.

Harry Leach moved from his wife's side to stand behind the XO and whisper in his ear, "Commander, that greaser has no common sense, bringing her here. He looks like he's her pimp. Mark my words, sir, you have the original liberty risk in our wardroom."

With a slight bow and flourish, Joe said, "Admiral, sir, I'd like you to meet my friend Pam Lifshifski. Pam, Admiral John Gilbert."

"Hello, Pam. I didn't catch your name, young man."

"Ensign Joe Xylos of the USS *Beaverton*, sir."

Pam extended a hand whose long red-tipped nails grazed the Admiral's lapel. "Please don't blame Joe for being late. I got lost twice . . . first in Long Beach finding the fleet landing and then on the way here. I'm always getting lost in L.A."

"Then you must be new to the area?"

"Oh no. I've played L.A. at least twice a year for the last two years."

"Ah, you're in show business. Movies? Hollywood?"

"I'm an exotic dancer."

The Admiral's wife, a graying woman standing behind him, snorted, "Exotic dancer! You mean stripper?"

Pam shimmied and with a big smile and sparkling dark eyes, exhaled, "I take it off and turn 'em on! Whatever Lola wants . . . Lola gets! Lola Getz—that's me!"

Admiral Gilbert looked out of the corner of his eyes at his wife as she sharply asked, "Tell me, Ensign Silos, how did you become acquainted with Miss Getz?"

"She's the one who's like a silo . . . so round . . . so firm . . . so fully packed. I'm like the smooth sound of a zither; it's Zzzzylos, ma'am, as in xylophone."

"Thank you, Mr. Xylos," The Admiral smiled ever so slightly, followed by his aide and finally two or three of the senior officers around him.

Pam stuck a cigarette in the corner of her mouth, "He got me my first job at the Casbah Club outside of Denver. That was about two and a half years ago. Right, Joe?"

"Right. Remember, you almost didn't get the job because, like tonight, you were trying to chew gum and smoke a cigarette at the same time. They thought it was part of your act to pop gum bubbles with the burning tip."

She smiled. "Joe was the emcee, the stand-up comic. I had just flunked out of the University of Colorado when he talked me into auditioning. I was the last act of the show and all night he told one funny story after another about his little sister. After every laugh, he'd say, 'You've got to meet her sometime.' Then in the break right before I came on, he really warmed up the audience. This guy is one of the best I've ever worked with. He waltzed me around the floor before introducing me as his little sister. I had a tall headdress on that made me look even taller. I was laughing so hard, I almost forgot my act. A month later I had top billing, and it's been all uphill ever since."

Raising a brow, the Admiral turned to Joe. "Emcee? How did that fit into a Naval ROTC program?"

"I worked my way through college, sir--five nights a week, first as a busboy and later on stage. Twice I ran out of money and had to quit for a term to keep going."

"Worked your way through, eh? You are to be commended."

Mrs. Gilbert, with arms folded below her ample bosom, wrinkled her nose. "Isn't this kind of work full of temptation and immorality?"

Joe shrugged. "It can be. There are cities where the clubs are fronts for prostitution and worse. My big temptation at the Casbah was gluttony, pure and simple. There was always more food there than I could handle. Working there was like a school lunch program for starving college students."

"How did you become the emcee?" she asked.

Pam waved the lighted cigarette like a pointer. "The guy before Joe was a dud. Joe was getting more laughs clearing tables than that guy was with a microphone. One night he started heckling Joe. Joe turned the guy into mincemeat."

"He drank on the job," continued Joe. "He was like a bowl of hot chili and jello . . . full of beans and shaking all over. When I faced him down, he lost his temper. The boss called me into the office, and I thought I was going to get fired. Instead he offered me the job. It was fun; finding new material was always a challenge. The part I enjoyed most was the give-and-take with the audience. As I was telling Pam, it was an exciting chapter of my life, but now it's over. I'm on the next chapter that I hope will be longer and more rewarding."

The admiral shook his hand. "I'm pleased to meet you, Ensign, and your . . . ah . . . lady."

CHAPTER 3

Lola Getz and Harry

Joe and Pam moved to the hors d'oeuvres. Both filled their plates until a conical mound of edibles rose well above the surface. Then, balancing the plates and their drinks, the couple strolled over to the contingent from the *Beaverton*. The introductions were stiff and formal. Conversation petered out. Male stares mentally undressed Pam while the wives' eyes condemned her.

The attention of the senior officers was drawn to the frequency with which the white sleeve of the admiral's Filipino steward offered his tray of beer and whiskey to the Chief Engineer, Henry Moran. Each time, Moran would lift a shot glass of whiskey between his thumb and index finger with little finger fully extended, tilt his head back, and down the double shot in one gulp. He would then carefully place the empty on the tray, pick up the schooner of beer, fill up a mug, and pour the whole mugful down his throat in one great swallow.

Pam raised her arm in a thumbs-up salute to Moran. "Well, all right! That's class! At least there's one good man in the crowd tonight!"

Filling his mug again, Moran raised it in a toast toward her. "We engineers all have class and are connoisseurs of the best things in life." Then he drained the mug to the accompaniment of scattered "Hear! Hear!"

Smatterings of conversation began again in the group as the band began to play a tango. Pam looked at Joe, and both laughed. Moments later they were among the handful of couples dancing on the nearly deserted floor. The first few turns around the floor, they looked like (as Leach snidely remarked) a teenager teaching her grade-school-age brother to dance.

There was one major difference: whenever they dipped, Joe's face disappeared into Pam's cleavage, at which time his partner would roll her shoulders in time to the music and giggle. He emerged from each encounter with a broader and broader grin.

By the time they began to draw an audience, the Admiral's aide was whispering into the ear of the bandleader. The number was cut off midway through and, after a short hesitation, the band began a foxtrot. Joe finished the dance with a deep dip, in his usual position with his face between Pam's breasts. They caught the beat of the next number and began as if in a ballroom dancing competition. The lithe brunette moved with the practiced grace of a professional dancer. The spangled knit dress accentuated her movements. The more she danced, the more the dress seemed to reveal, teasingly yet not indecently.

When the dance was over, there was scattered applause. Pam curtseyed, bending enough at the waist to give those in front of her a nearly full view. Joe took an exaggerated bow. The band, which had only played two numbers, took a break. One or two of them clapped and cheered as they left their instruments.

The couple rejoined the group from the *Beaverton*. The same aide who had been talking to the bandleader whispered in Captain Slaxman's ear. The Captain, while trying hard to keep a straight face, nodded in acknowledgment of the message. He in turn crooked his finger toward the XO, Stan Longstreet.

After a whispered message from the Captain, the XO solemnly motioned for Joe to follow him out of the room. Leaving Pam next to the Chief Engineer, Joe fell in beside the older man until they were around the corner.

Longstreet pulled on the short end of his tie and snugged it closer to his collar before clearing his throat. "Boy, I don't want to know how you came to ask this broad to this reception or who taught you to dance with your nose between her tits. The pair of you put on one hell of a floor show. You embarrassed the Admiral. The band is going to start playing again and you two *aren't* going to dance. Is that clear?"

"Yes, sir."

When they returned, the *Beaverton* wardroom and their ladies were part of an oval in whose center stood the Admiral. The steward skirted the edge of the group, carrying a small tray with a shot glass and a mug of beer. He thrust the tray between the ranks toward Henry Moran's elbow. The Chief Engineer performed his ritual of downing the shot followed by a large swallow of beer. The Admiral was recounting some part of the Battle of the Philippine Sea, where he had commanded a destroyer. In mid-sentence he stopped and focused his gaze on the drinker.

Moran raised his glass. "Go on, Admiral. It's okay. I'm Irish, I can drink anything."

"You mean everything. Not that I'm concerned about that, but what I am curious about, Commander, is how you've managed to nearly monopolize my steward this evening."

"Old shipmates, Admiral. Santos was my steward when I was Naval Attache in Caracas."

"Wait a minute . . . Santos has told me stories about that. So *you're* the one that the dictator demanded to be assigned there and screamed for your tour to be extended."

"The same, sir. And I was on the next plane out of the country right behind him after the coup."

When the band started playing another set, Joe sat this one out as ordered. Pam danced, but only with Henry Moran. He was a little wobbly but still decorous, keeping his head high and his face away from her chest. The Admiral and his entourage left as the last rays of the sun were reflected on the clouds beyond San Pedro. The band packed up, and finally the free bar closed. The number of attendees diminished quickly except for one or two groups. One was the *Beaverton* contingent.

The *Beaverton* wardroom, minus the Captain and the XO, moved into the club's restaurant. As luck would have it, Joe and Pam found themselves sitting across from Harry Leach and his wife Leah, who sat on an upholstered bench between two other couples. Like Harry, she was overweight. She had a small mouth and thin lips that turned down on the corners, giving her a careworn appearance.

There was a long silence. Leah squirmed in her seat, staring all the while at Pam. Finally, while smoothing her dress over her girdle, she asked, "Pam, that is an awfully . . . er . . . striking dress. Where did you get it?"

Drawing deeply on her cigarette, Pam exhaled as she replied, "Neiman Marcus in Dallas, cost eight-hundred-twenty dollars."

Leah's eyes bulged from inhaling a huge gulp of air. "Eight hundred and twenty dollars! That's more than my husband draws in a month."

"That's not so bad. I've got six costumes that cost more."

"You wear this when you work?" asked an incredulous Leah.

"No, this is my special party dress."

Conversation at the table bypassed Lieutenant Leach, who sat silently staring at a point just below Pam's chin. His eyelids for a time drooped to half-open, then widened as a full cocktail glass was placed in front of him. His focus dropped to the bottom of the vee between her breasts. He scooped an ice cube from the glass and, in a single motion, stood and shoved the little ice block inside the dress between Pam's breasts. The frozen cube made a lump just over her stomach.

Pam jumped to her feet, toppling her chair in surprise, and spit through clenched teeth, "Asshole!"

Leach began to laugh. "It was too good to resist. Anybody who wears a dress like that deserves an ice cube to cool it off."

The tall brunette remained on her feet. For a moment, she began working the cube upward until Joe said, "The other way is easier."

Their eyes met and she nodded. He smiled. Holding her right hand over the cube, she reached under her skirt with the other, baring most of her well-proportioned legs almost to the tops of her stockings. After some wiping and fumbling motions beneath the skirt, the errant ice cube appeared in her left hand.

Leach's smile faded as his eyes met Pam's angry gaze. Her husky voice dripped sarcasm. "Suck on this, hotshot! It's the closest you'll ever get to the real thing." She broke eye contact only long enough to drop the ice cube into his glass.

But she misdirected it. "Hey! That's my glass!" shouted Leah, startling Pam.

Joe had already risen. He leaned across the table, scooped a couple of cubes out of Leah's glass, and dumped them into her husband's glass. Stirring the drink with his finger, Joe did a passable imitation of W.C. Fields. "There, there, madam. No harm done. Come, my dear, it is time to be on our way. There is a reason the drinks are so cheap here. You have to put up with uncouth bores."

Leach broke his gaze from the glass in front of him and halfway began to stand. He was reaching for Joe's retreating arm when Leah hit him with her purse. "Harry! How could you! You've embarrassed the life out of me. Now sit down!"

Blocked in by people on either side of him, the chubby Lieutenant dropped heavily to his seat, sloshing drinks on the table. "Zilch, I won't forget this! I'll make life interesting for you."

There was a spate of comments from the others at the table, all directed toward Leach. He glowered at them and at the backs of the couple walking out of the room. He started to take a sip from his glass, then roughly pushed it across the table, bellowing, "Waiter, I need a drink!"

⟵⟶

The following Monday, Joe was assigned as Junior Officer of the Deck (JOOD) on the quarterdeck watch from four to eight in the morning. Supervising him was Lieutenant Leach, who again was the OOD.

Leach paced up and down along the shoreward side of the ship, keeping an eye on the accommodation ladder. Joe stood back near the athwartships passageway that led to the small compartment where the Quartermaster kept his log and the Boatswain's Mate made announcements over the ship's public address system.

Joe watched as Leach paced the quarterdeck. Neither man said a word for almost half an hour.

The Lieutenant looked out of the corner of his eye and talked out of the corner of his mouth as he began, "That was quite an ex-e-bee-she-oon you put on at the reception Friday evening, Ensign. I understand the XO spoke to you about that dress."

"It was about the dancing, sir. Yes, he spoke to me. I didn't see anything wrong with the dress. It was undoubtedly the most expensive dress in the room."

"Nothing wrong, you say! Look, Zilch, if my wife can't wear shorts to shop in the commissary, that floozy can't show the crack of her ass through the material at the Officers' Club."

"Lieutenant, you are the only member of this wardroom who makes a practice of insulting me. I can't recall meeting you before I came aboard and am at a loss as to what I've done. Could you tell me?"

"Tell you! I'll tell you. The Navy is going to hell in a handbasket, commissioning just anybody who stumbles in off the street. And after what you put that slut up to . . . wiped herself with that ice cube and then she tossed it in my wife's glass."

"Lieutenant, it was your ice cube! I thought I would have heard an apology from you by now for what you did to Pam. If you're trying to bait me with petty insults and childish stunts, can it! I've made a living dealing with obnoxious drunks. If pushed enough, I don't get mad, I call the bouncer. I'm sorry the ice cube ended up in your wife's glass. Please give her my apologies." He extended his right hand. "Sir, could we start this over and bury the hatchet?"

"Aw, Leah's all right. She was pissed off Friday night, but she got over it by the next day. She even came aboard for the movie last night, but fortunately didn't run into you. I'm glad you chose to turn in early."

"I was tracing systems in Number Four boiler room, sir."

"Be that as it may. Mister, I'd like to go out to that nightclub where that smart-mouthed bitch works and give her a lesson. That whore!"

Joe dropped his hand; clearly a restart wasn't about to happen. "Lieutenant," he said, "Just for the record, Pam isn't like the little dancing girl who first dances on one foot and then the other and in between them makes a living. She is a talented professional dancer. She opens in Harrah's at Lake Tahoe next week and plays through Labor Day. By the way, in most places I've worked, that game you're playing would get you--at a minimum--a lecture out on the sidewalk from the bouncer. At a maximum, you could have your hair parted with a baseball bat."

"Now you look here! Shrimpy, undersized, and undernourished Ensigns don't threaten or even try to intimidate Harry Leach. Get off my quarterdeck! Go stand your watch in the Quartermaster's shack."

Joe strolled through the athwartships passageway and into the small Quartermaster's compartment, where a young Quartermaster of the Watch was seated at the desk. Once inside, he remarked to himself, *At least it's warmer in here than out there.* Leach paced from one side of the ship to the other, regularly passing in front of the door to the shack and glowering at Joe.

After some minutes, the Quartermaster of the Watch asked Joe, "Pardon me, sir, but there's a word in the plan of the day that I've never seen before . . . 'heraldry.' What do they mean?"

Joe picked up the mimeographed sheet and read,

The insignia of the USS Beaverton, *which features a cartoon character destroying Japanese ships and planes, is an affront to our postwar ally and beneath the dignity of a ship of the line. A contest will be held to select a new emblem, which will be along the traditional lines of naval heraldry. Entries containing cartoon characters will be disqualified. The winner will be given a $25 U.S. Savings Bond from the ship's recreation fund. Submit your entries to the Chaplain's office by Friday, August 24, 1956.*

Joe replied, "Heraldry has to do with the shields and banners from medieval days."

The young man at the desk tossed down the sheet and said, "How do I know what sort of shield they want?"

"Look, Beaverton is a city in Oregon. Maybe you could tie it to what they do up there . . . to the state's flag or whatever."

"Yeah, but what is a heraldry?"

Joe dug into his front pants pocket for a moment and drew out a square red condom box, which he tossed on the table. "Here's a sample: 'Shields' from the Shield Rubber Company."

"That's great, sir. Can I have this box?"

"Sure, but I'll need the contents."

The sailor handed him the two foil-wrapped rubbers and studied the box earnestly.

Joe continued, "I would imagine that the quality of the submission is very important. If you neatly draw it on some heavy posterboard and ink in the colors carefully, you'd improve your chances of winning."

The Boatswain, who had been listening, volunteered, "The Old Man probably saw the insignia on the *St. Paul,* Seventh Fleet's old flagship. Anything is better than that dumb-looking beaver with a Zero in his teeth and swatting a Jap ship with his tail over a rising sun flag background. I like that rubber idea."

⋅⋗▭⦿ ⦿▭⋖⋅

Joe watched the black of night pass into the brilliant hues of sunrise from his place in the Quartermaster's shack. Soon Reveille sounded and the seamen were topside washing down the teak decks. At fifteen past seven, Joe penned into the smooth log, *04-08. Anchored as before.* It had been an uneventful watch.

When Leach was relieved at 7:30, he raged, "Zilch, who told you to write this log? I want you to rewrite the mid-watch entry, have it signed, then bring me the log and I will make the entry for this watch."

"Is there anything wrong with what I did, sir?"

Leach cracked his knuckles. "That is beside the point. I'll tell you to write the log when I want you to."

Joe said, "Lieutenant, if my work is unacceptable, I'll redo it. In fact, I'll rewrite the log for the whole day if the Navigator says I did it wrong. If not, I stand by it."

Then, harking back to what Leach told him when he first came aboard, Joe addressed the Lieutenant in his role as the officer charged with making up the in-port watch list. "One last thing, Mr. Senior In-Port Watch Officer, sir . . . It is readily apparent that there is a serious personality conflict between me and Lieutenant Leach. He insults me by mispronouncing my name. He has performed a debasing act to my date in front of my fellow officers and not only refused to apologize, but he has defamed her virtue when I sought his apology. Verbally I am requesting that in the future I be assigned watches with OODs other than Lieutenant Leach."

"You don't seem to be listening to me. I said . . . rewrite the log for the mid-watch."

"I'm not saying I won't. I'm just saying I intend to bring this whole thing to a head if you insist. Before you make a federal case out of it, think for a moment, sir. I wrote the smooth log for you just as I was instructed by every other OOD with whom I have stood a watch. I did it without being told. If what's written on any watch doesn't meet your gold standard, I'll rewrite it for that watch's signature. The Chief Engineer has made it clear that he expects me to use my best judgment in deciding what is the appropriate use of initiative. I'm confused. Now you are saying I had no authority because you didn't specifically tell me?"

Joe watched Leach's face turn red while he fumbled with the large deck log folder until he had within his grasp the stack of completed deck logs. Out of it, he extracted one day's completed log, snapping, "Initiative! Initiative! Ensign, this is the log for last Thursday when we came into port. It's riddled with errors. Before you leave this quarterdeck, find them, write a corrected log, and bring it to me for my inspection. I've been commanding officer of a ship, and I know my logs. I want you to become competent as a log writer to help you qualify as an OOD in port. That's within bounds . . . right?"

Tentatively taking the sheet in his hand, Joe asked, "Sir, are you asking me to agree that you are an authority on deck logs, or do you want me to start writing?"

The Quartermaster of the Watch snickered, stopping when Leach glared at him.

Shoving the folder into Joe's gut, Leach growled, "Start writing, mister!" He hitched up his pants over the expansive girth of his middle and marched off the quarterdeck.

The Quartermaster said, when Leach was out of earshot, "I've never seen anybody stand up to him the way you did."

"Tell me . . . did I write the log correctly?"

"'Zero four to zero eight' . . . 'Anchored as before.' Lieutenant Leach forgot to sign the log. The Navigator will be all over his butt again."

"I'll never get this done by quarters. Damn! I'm hungry as a bear!"

"I'll call the mess and tell them to save you a ration, sir. I'll call the Chief Engineer too, and tell him you've been delayed on watch."

With help from the Leading Quartermaster, who took him through the Quartermaster's notebook and the sample entries, Joe was finished with the assignment by half-past eight. He went to the wardroom, where he ate a breakfast of soggy French toast and crisp sausage.

Leach walked in and bellowed, "Ensign Zilch, why can't you eat at the same time everyone else does? I'm going to ask the President of the Mess how you rate such privileges. What do you have to say to that?"

"Mr. Leach, the log you ordered me to copy at the end of my watch is ready for your inspection, sir. If you want to tell the XO, fine; I want to tell the XO where you willfully shoved an ice cube Friday evening. I want to tell the XO that you continually call me Ensign Zilch in front of enlisted men and my fellow officers. That's for starters. The ball in is your court, sir."

The Lieutenant balled his pudgy fingers into a fist. He raised it over Joe's head and as he lowered it under his nose, he extended his index finger. "You'd damn well have better written that log correctly."

As Joe was finishing the last dregs of his coffee, he received a call from the quarterdeck. It was the Quartermaster of the Watch. "From Mr. Leach, sir. He signed the log for the 04-08. He accepts your request for future in-port watch assignments. He says you caught the errors that were in the Quartermaster's notebook."

Joe hung up the phone and grinned from ear to ear. "Gotcha!"

CHAPTER 4

Labor Day Weekend in Tijuana

Joe accepted an invitation to join Cy Penelton and the newly reported ship's doctor, Lieutenant Rufus Johnson, on a trip to San Diego for Labor Day weekend. Their Friday evening destination was Imperial Beach for a party at the house of an airline stewardess, Lyla Reeves, whom Rufus had met on his flight to L.A.

Cy wheeled his new pink Cadillac Eldorado convertible south into the swelling horde of travelers after short stops on base for beer, booze, and a full tank of gas. The pace on Route 101 was slow, so the heat of the sun more than canceled out the breeze with the top down. Sitting alone in the back seat, Joe polished off the better part of a case of beer by the time they stopped for dinner.

In spite of his years working in night clubs, drinking was something Joe had done very little of because he had found it necessary to remain sober to do his job. Thus the beer quickly took its toll. Well before they reached San Diego, he was fast asleep in the back seat. He barely stirred when they arrived in Imperial Beach, despite the cool evening breezes and serious attempts by his pals to rouse him.

Perhaps an hour or two later, Cy made friends with Tammy Nuslund, a sloe-eyed blonde of magnificent proportions, who extolled the virtues of Rosarita Beach, a resort south of Tijuana. Rufus didn't take long to convince Lyla that all of them ought to go there with Cy and Tammy.

Joe didn't stir until the first holdup in traffic after they crossed the border. Cy, on seeing Joe awake, said, "See, girls, I told you he wasn't dead. Joe, this is Tammy Nuslund and sitting next to you is Rufus' date, Lyla Reeves. Girls, this is our very own Greek Ensign, Joe Xylos."

By degrees, Joe focused his eyes on the female form sitting next to him. Lyla wore her short hair in a pageboy cut and had a very slim figure. Her smile was bright and revealed a perfect mouth. She reached out a hand to Joe. "Pleased to meet you, Mr. Greek Ensign."

Joe took her hand and grunted. He sat up fully and looked at the passing scenery for a moment before saying, "Cy, I thought you said Imperial Beach was a good place. I've seen better neighborhoods in East St. Louis."

Lyla answered, "We've just crossed the border into Mexico. This is Tijuana."

"Tijuana! What happened to Imperial Beach?"

"Joe," said Lyla, "you were sleeping so soundly, we left you in the car. We're on the way to Rosarita Beach. But first we're going to stop for a drink or two before heading on down there. Maybe you might find a girl . . . if you know what I mean." She smiled and nodded her head toward a pair of well-painted women standing at the side of the road, eyeing the traffic. Cy made a beckoning motion with his hand.

Joe studied the women out of the corner of his eye. One stepped down from the curb, her upper torso bouncing with each step. He held up his hand and waved her away as the traffic began to move. "No, thanks," he said, "I wouldn't want to do anything that would endanger my opportunity to be in the Olympics."

Tammy laughed. "Olympics, you? What sport?"

"I haven't decided, but I want to keep my amateur standing intact."

"You silly boy, it's the girls who are the pros."

"Now just a minute. If you play in the National Football League, you're a pro, because you get paid to perform, right?"

"Well, yes. But what does that have to do with picking up a whore?"

"And the players on both sides are pros, do you agree?"

"Yes."

"If I enter the field of play with a professional, a paid performer, then I have played as a professional."

"To be a professional, you have to be paid. You won't be paid, you'll be paying."

"You assume that the only reward for entering the field of play with a professional is monetary. There are certain psychic rewards. And if I receive them, I could be declared a professional."

Lyla chimed in, "You're nuts. And probably too cheap to buy a girl a drink."

"Ah, my dear, there are some amateur leagues to which I am open to a draft. Are you?"

Lyla ran her hand along Rufus Johnson's inner thigh. "Goodness, no! Why would I want to trade this handsome hunk of a doctor for a skinny little runt?" She turned to the doctor, opened her mouth, and deeply kissed him. Then, nodding toward Joe, she whispered, "I don't know if I want to spend a whole weekend with him around."

Rufus asked, "Cy, what are we going to do with Joe here?"

Joe said, "Perhaps you ought to let me out at the bus station and I'll find my way North."

Cy answered, "The natives down here are downright friendly, Joe. I'm sure we'll turn up something once we get to Rosarita Beach."

"Like I said, I don't play with pros."

Tammy laughed. "Well, Joe, it looks like you ought to have stayed on the other side of the border, because that's all you're going to see down here. Cy, darling, let's get a taco from that wagon. I'm hungry."

While Rufus was buying the tacos, Joe studied the wagon through his beer-induced haze. "Now that looks like an interesting business. I'll bet that would be a lot more fun than being the odd man out here."

Cy laughed. "Joe Taco! I tell you what, shipmate, I'll buy you the wagon and you pay me back with interest, okay?"

"Okay," said Joe, " But you have to get the wagon back to the ship because I don't have room to put it under my bunk."

Less than five minutes later, Joe watched the taillights of the Caddy disappear in the dark while the old taco vendor shambled into the nearest bar with three crisp hundred-dollar bills. The others had agreed to rendezvous with Joe on "late Sunday afternoon," but if that seemed a bit hazy, it didn't bother the young businessman.

Joe opened the metal-covered trays and saw the taco shells, lettuce, and all the makings. On the far end was an ice-filled box stocked with Mexican beer and American soft drinks.

Moments later, a car pulled up and a voice shouted, "Hey, you! What you selling?"

"The best tacos in Tijuana. How many?"

"Three. Kid, you speak good English."

"Thanks . . . Here you are, that'll be three dollars."

"Three bucks! Are you crazy?"

"Well, how about three for a dollar?"

"Make it a dollar and a half?"

"A dollar and a quarter."

"Two dollars and I'll throw in a free Coke." Joe held up a Coke.

Pulling a dollar bill and three quarters from his pocket, the man said, "Okay, for a dollar seventy-five. Take it or leave it."

Joe said, "Thank you, sir! Have a good evening."

"You're no Mexican. What the hell are you doing here?"

"Let's just say I'm working on a wager. Have a good evening."

The customer drove off laughing. Others arrived. Mexicans laughed at his prices and walked away, but he bargained with the tourists with jokes and small talk, selling taco after taco until the cart was all but empty. Through sign language and slowly repeating himself, he learned from another taco vendor where he could get a resupply. The vendor guided him down back streets to a not-so-clean kitchen where a middle-aged Mexican woman, Juanita, sold him another cartload of tortillas and taco fillings. Juanita charged him just over twenty dollars. He was then guided to the back door of a small warehouse where, for another twenty-five dollars, he restocked ice, beer, and pop. He had grossed just under $145. Even in his somewhat hung-over state, Joe sensed that this was a money-making venture.

The hour was approaching midnight when he rolled back toward the streets near the border. The people kept coming and going. He ran out of the makings about three in the morning. Not knowing where he could leave the cart, Joe parked it outside Juanita's house and slept under it until it grew light. Then with a fresh load, he returned to the streets.

So went Saturday and on into Sunday afternoon, when finally the twenty-hour days, the lack of a shave, and sleeping on the ground took their toll. Joe looked like one of the less reputable taco men, and the success he'd had the first day in extracting premium prices was waning. Yet he continued to work, selling almost by rote.

As the sun closed on the western horizon, he worked the main road right by the border crossing, keeping an eye out for Cy's Eldorado. As the lines of cars backed up, he hit his stride again. People insisted on paying in pesos, whose value he still wasn't sure of, but there were few arguments.

As he worked alongside a row of cars close to the inspection station, a deeply tanned U.S. Border Patrolman walked quickly toward him, waving his arms in a pushing motion. "Hey! Hey, you! Vaminos! Git!"

While taking money from a lady in a car, Joe said, "What's the problem, officer?"

"Oh, good. You speak English. You can't come here. You're on the U.S. side of the border."

"Are you saying that if I were an American citizen, I would be welcome?"

"Not necessarily."

Joe pulled his wallet from his pocket and handed the man his driver's license.

The agent took it. "So you have a Colorado driver's license, Señor Exlos."

"It's ZZZylos and I'm an American citizen. Okay?"

"You don't look like much of one. Now get out of here!"

"So you're saying that private enterprise isn't allowed on this side of border?"

"Look you, I'll call the Tijuana cops and they'll toss you into their jail."

"What for? I'm an American citizen and on my side of the border. How can I be interfering with you when I'm selling to people who are waiting to go through your inspection? Have a heart, I'm looking for my friends to give me a ride back to Long Beach."

Squinting, the agent asked, "Where did you get the cart?"

"I bought it from a guy Friday night."

"So you're going to bring that roach coach across the border? It's a dutiable item. Come on, I'll get the book out and figure what the duty comes to."

Turning the wagon toward Mexico, Joe said, "I'm not ready to cross yet."

"Well, when you do, you'd better have plenty of identification because I'm not all that sure you really are a U.S. citizen."

"Oh, dry up!"

"And keep that filthy wagon in Tijuana, Zzzzylos."

Joe worked up to the border, slipping across a few car lengths, then fading back until the afternoon rush was over. The pink Caddy never showed, but Joe didn't worry about it. He was on a roll.

Late in the afternoon, he noticed the old Mexican man who had sold him the wagon. He stood silently some distance away and watched as Joe sold tacos. The man was lean, with cold black eyes. He was rumpled, his hair was disheveled, and the corners of his mouth were turned down. His shirt was beer stained and the collar, sweat stained. He disappeared by the time Joe returned to Juanita's yard for the night.

* * *

Early Monday morning, Joe returned to his place close to the border. By noon, he was getting concerned about what he was going to do with the taco wagon and even more concerned that he had missed his shipmates.

Through the days, Joe couldn't avoid rubbing elbows with the terribly poverty-stricken people with whom he shared the streets. The adventure of selling the tacos and matching wits with the tourists had worn off. He was tired, dirty, and looking forward to a hot shower and his bunk on the *Beaverton*.

Just short of 2:00, Joe saw the previous owner again, looking just as rumpled as the day before. Then, one by one, others joined the man. First was a woman made shapeless by childbirth and age. Clutching her right hand were three small children in a line like paper cutout dolls. Unlike the man, she was clean, and the children were dressed in worn but neat dresses and short pants. Next to come were other taco vendors with whom he had competed. Finally the group was joined by a tall Mexican policeman with a pencil-thin mustache and his hat pulled down until it almost entirely covered his eyes.

There was an animated conference, with the woman gesticulating and shoving the old man while the vendors added comments. All of it was in Spanish. At last the man slowly walked from the group with the policeman just behind him.

He stopped about five feet from Joe, who had just made another sale, and said, "I want buy back wagon."

Joe said, "How much?"

"Same price, tres hunnred dolar, okay?"

Joe looked from the policeman, with his Sam Browne belt and a big pistol on his hip, and back to the man. "It's a deal."

The man pulled an envelope from inside his shirt and, almost as if his joints were hurting, took the last steps and placed it in Joe's hand. "Gracias, señor. I tell my amigos that this best wagon in all Tijuana. Anybody sell tacos from it, even you, a gringo, must make big money. Is true? I must have it back to feed my family."

Joe said, "I understand," as he looked into the envelope, which was filled with a number of fives, tens, and twenties and one new, crisp hundred-dollar bill. He looked at the woman, whose eyes were filled with tears, and back to the policeman. He asked the buyer, "Where are the other two hundred-dollar bills? What did you do with the money?"

The policeman, whose voice was deep and heavily accented, said, "He spent it on the whores and too much drink. He did not come home until yesterday. That's when Angela told him to go out and buy it back. His friends lent him this money."

Joe reached into the envelope and counted out its contents--$150, which he carried over to the woman and placed in her hand. "Here," he said, "Let's say I rented it for the weekend at $50 a day. Fair enough?"

"Gracias! Gracias!" said Angela.

Joe replied, "It's all yours. Thanks, it was fun while it lasted." Then he returned to the cart and scooped up the money he'd earned, pulling it out from under a pan where he'd stored it.

The policeman said, "Señor, you are a true diplomat. Mateo had to buy it back because in his heart, this is the best taco wagon in all Tijuana. And now you tell her that you rented it. You gave him back his dignity. I was called to arrest you because you are working in Mexico without authorization."

"Oh, no."

Raising his hand, he said, "But I was very touched by your fairness to Mateo Jiminez. I couldn't arrest a visitor who showed such generosity. Of course, if you come down here again to sell tacos, you won't be a visitor. Es verdad?"

Joe looked at him blankly for a moment, then softly said, "One weekend like this is enough, thank you."

"May I escort you back to the border? I know that you have had a very successful three days in our country. The other men have complained that you sell more tacos at higher prices than they do. They are afraid that you will give Tijuana a bad name, selling as you do. I believe you Americans call it 'scalping.'"

"Scalping! No, I hadn't the faintest idea how much to charge, so I made a game of it. Yes, it was a good weekend, but I've got a problem. My friends went to Rosarita Beach Friday night and were supposed to pick me up yesterday and take me back to Long Beach. They're riding in a pink Cadillac convertible."

"Rosarita Beach? Do you mean the resort?"

"Yes. I think so."

"Did you not hear? There was a predawn raid by the National Police. Everyone at the resort was arrested, and they are all in the Tijuana jail. I am sure your friends are there because the commandante arrived in Tijuana Saturday noon, driving the car you described."

Joe laughed. "Arrested! Do you mean they've been in jail all weekend?"

"Yes."

"Why did they arrest everybody?"

The policeman half-smiled. "The officials in Mexico City frown on open gambling. And, of course, this is an election year."

"Is there a way to bail them out?"

"Perhaps. Would you care to visit them? What are their names?"

"Lieutenant y (junior grade) Cyrus Penelton and Lieutenant Rufus Johnson. We're all in the Navy and have to be back on board before the ship sails tomorrow."

"You are in the American Navy too?"

"Yes."

Raising his visor slightly, the officer studied Joe's face. "You look more like one of us."

"I'm Greek. There were two women with them--Lyla--and the other was something like Terry."

◦◦►━◉ ◉━◄◦◦

Joe followed the officer into the crowded lobby of the jail. There was a babble of voices speaking in Spanish and English. The officer pushed through the crowd at the counter and spoke to the man behind it. Then, pointing to a door on the side, he said to Joe, "Go through that door."

Once on the other side of the door, Joe found himself in a foul-smelling room with closely spaced bars down the center. There were two other people talking to a single prisoner at the far end of the room.

The officer soon appeared behind him. "The jail is very crowded, but they have located your friends from the ship. Without last names, I cannot locate the two women."

Extending his hand, Joe smiled and said, "Thanks. I appreciate everything you've done for me. You never introduced yourself. I'm Ensign Joe Xylos."

"Yes, the Border Patrol told me. My name is of no importance. Good luck."

Fifteen minutes later, Cy and Rufus walked into the other side of the room escorted by a guard. Both were dirty and unshaven, wearing clothes they had obviously slept in.

The doctor exclaimed, "Praise the Lord! It's Joe Xylos! Thank heaven you found us!"

Cy said, "Joe, you are a sight for sore eyes. You look almost as bad as we do. Are you in here too?"

"No, I avoided arrest by paying some money. Not a bribe, though—anyway, it's a long story. But what happened to you guys?"

Rufus said, "I'm not all that sure. The Federales—that's what they call the national police—came in the middle of the night and grabbed us. Lyla and I were in bed asleep. It's something about gambling."

Cy said, "They arrested everybody in the resort. Nobody ever told me that gambling was illegal. Tammy and I were still at the tables. I lost a bundle, and I don't have enough left to get us out of here. Did you see my car?"

"No."

"Damn, I paid one of the cops a hundred bucks to drive it back to Tijuana."

"It's here somewhere," said Joe, "because the policeman who told me about you said it was here in town. What does it take to get you out?"

Rufus said, "Two hundred fifty bucks each, give or take a few dollars."

Cy said, "What happened to that taco cart? I've been kicking my butt for buying that damn thing."

Joe said, "I sold it back to the guy for a hundred fifty bucks."

"One hundred and fifty dollars! Damn you, Xylos!"

"Hell, yes, but look, you'll get your full three hundred. And there's just over three hundred in profit remaining after that."

"You cleared six hundred? That's one hell of a lot of tacos!"

"You're telling me. There are people out there who'll buy tacos at all hours of the day and night. I haven't been to bed other than to nap under that blasted cart. I cashed a check for fifty before we left. So with that, there's about five fifty in the kitty. That takes care of two of you." Turning to Rufus, Joe asked, "What do you have?"

Rufus whispered, "Twenty-five dollars and thirty-six cents."

Cy smiled ruefully. "The Federales took a hundred and seven dollars from me."

Joe said, "Well, that takes care of three of you. I wonder if the girls have enough to make up the difference?"

Rufus said, "I doubt it. Lyla had a little. I think the guy who busted us stole it. How are we going to work this? I'd hate to have to leave either of them down here."

Cy said, "Tammy went broke real quick. And she lost every cent I gave her. Rufus, this isn't the time for chivalry. The *Beaverton* gets underway tomorrow morning and if we're not on board, we'll miss movement. And you know with Captain Sam, missing movement is a hanging offense."

"Yeah, but what are we going to do?" said Rufus.

Joe pulled a coin from his pocket and said, "Heads we leave Lyla and tails, Tammy. Okay?"

Rufus shrugged his shoulders and looked at the floor. "Maybe we ought to ask them. Oh, hell, what difference does it make? Go ahead and flip the coin."

Joe flipped the coin and leaned over to read it. "Tails. Sorry, Tammy. Well, when we get across the border, we'll raise some money and come back and bail her out. Or maybe Lyla can do it while we get back to the ship."

Cy said, "That's the way it will have to be. I can tell you that this is the last time I ever set foot in this rotten country. I still don't understand why they picked this weekend to pull this stunt."

Joe said, "The cop who found you for me said that apparently they're having an election and the politicos are using this to get a few more votes. At two hundred fifty a head, I'd say it's nothing more than a shakedown."

Joe returned to the lobby and the tumult. It took him another four hours to make his way to the head of the line, wait, and bargain. When a clerk hinted that he could speed the process with a bribe, Joe pleaded that he didn't even have enough to bail everyone out. In the end, it was a whisper to a jailer by the same policeman who had guided him there that finally brought their freedom. He showed them the way back to the Eldorado, which was red with road dust.

Close to seven in the evening, they turned toward the border with Joe sitting in the front seat next to Cy. In the back, Rufus sat in one corner and Lyla in the other. Other than asking Joe why he wouldn't bail Tammy out and a shrug of the shoulders when he said there wasn't enough money, she said nothing.

When they reached the head of the line at the border, the agent asked if everyone was a U.S. citizen and where they were born. It was the same agent who had confronted Joe on Sunday.

Cy replied, "Los Angeles, California."

Joe said, "Staten Island, New York."

The agent asked, "May I see identification?" Joe produced his Colorado driver's license.

The agent scanned it, then turned beet red. "You again! The scrounge with the roach coach! Like I told you the other day, I'm not sure this is isn't a fake. Do you have other identification?"

"Here's my Navy I.D. card."

The agent scanned it and said, "Are you aware that it is a federal offense to impersonate a commissioned officer?"

Cy snapped, "Look, Jocko, he may not look like it, but he is a real live United States naval officer."

Pointing over to the side, the agent said, "Pull this pink dreamboat over to the side, we're going to give you a thorough search. And when you get over there, Jocko, go inside for a personal search."

Joe rose up partway in the seat, saying, "Come on! If you have a gripe with me, fine, but leave them out of it. They've just been through two days of hell. We had to leave Cy's date in the Tijuana jail."

"Oh, sure, wise guy. You've been haunting the gate for the last two days peddling tacos and who knows what else. Now you come through here in a brand-new Cadillac."

"They're giving me a ride back to the ship. Is there anything wrong with spending the weekend selling tacos?"

"No self-respecting naval officer is going to spend the weekend selling tacos. Especially not the way you did. And you sure as hell don't look like a naval officer!"

"Should I have worn full dress and sword?"

"You heard me. You're holding up the line. Get over there before I have you all arrested."

Lyla put a hand on Cy's shoulder and said in an almost frantic voice, "Do what he says. We don't need any more trouble. I've got to get to L.A. in time to make my flight!"

Once they were inside, an older man wearing brass-colored oak leaves on his collar said, "Go into the dressing rooms and take off your clothes for a body search."

Lyla began crying. "Why are you doing this to me? I haven't done anything. You're just as bad as those Federales. Are you going to stand one of your guards right in front of me while I take my clothes off? Maybe it would speed things along if I just took my dress off right here because I don't have anything else on."

The agent said, "There will be a woman agent in the room. The quicker you go, the sooner this will be over with."

"I don't want to. Why can't you leave me alone?"

"We have the duty to conduct inspections to prevent the smuggling of contraband into the United States. And this agent's suspicions"—he nodded toward the agent Cy had called "Jocko"—"were aroused."

Joe asked, "What contraband? What specifically are we supposed to be smuggling?"

The first agent stepped in front of Joe, stopping a nose length away.

"You've been playing games with this station for the past three days. Now you show up with a disreputable-looking bunch of people in a brand-new car. I say you don't have the means to keep it on the road, never mind owning it."

Joe shrugged his shoulders. "You're right, I don't make enough to buy a spare tire for it. And it's not my car, it belongs to the guy driving it; he gave me a ride down. Please hurry this up because we have to be on the *Beaverton* or we'll miss movement."

Cy raised his voice. "Hey, Jocko, I resent that. Have you ever heard of Penelton Productions or the Hollywood Special Effects Company? My family owns them. And as for cars, this is the cheap one. We own a Bentley and a Mercedes too."

Rufus pulled on Joe's and Cy's arms. "Come on, you two! Giving this guy a bunch of lip is going to buy us nothing but trouble. He's just doing his job."

The agent smiled, clapping his hands. "I'm glad that there's one among you who has some sense left."

With Rufus's words fresh in their exhausted heads, they stood close by and watched the agent examine each and every item. A first he found nothing but a collection of fuzz and dirt out of the cuffs of Joe's pants; but then he called out, "Tammy Nuslund?"

Cy replied, "Yes, that's my date. We didn't have enough to make her bail. She's still in the Tijuana jail. Can you help us?"

Instead of answering, the agent brought out a glass jar labeled "Tammy Nuslund" (from which he had read the name) and dumped out a collection of small dried objects onto a plastic sheet. He played around with the pile until he sorted out a single dried green leaf and a single nearly-round object. He studied them closely. "This could be a blade and this could be a seed."

Joe looked over his shoulder. "Just like my cuffs. Kentucky fescue or Bermuda grass?"

"How about marijuana? Tammy, whoever she is, played courier for you."

"Bull!" Joe exploded. "A little shakedown is one thing, but don't put yourself out on a limb. I don't even smoke cigarettes. There is no way that could be marijuana, and you know it!"

The agent held a small object in his tweezers. "Speaking of limbs, how about this?"

"It looks like a little twig to me," said Joe.

"We shall see. We shall see." Walking to an intercom, he said, "Okay, Mike. I have slight indications of possible marijuana. Search the car."

A new agent appeared. He demanded access to Joe's and Tammy's suitcases. Cy was barely able to control himself as everything that could be collected and moved was collected and moved. Joe observed this new agent as he performed a second, more thorough search. The agent removed each item, shaking open every folded garment. He squeezed the toothpaste tube after tasting it, and felt the sides and bottom of it. After he paused for a doughnut and a cup of coffee, he made a second long inspection as if he had missed something.

Finally he smiled, pushing the pile of clothes across the table toward Joe, saying, "Looks like the luggage is clean this time."

Joe slowly folded each and every item, then carefully put them back into the suitcase. He snapped it shut and carried it back to where his friends stood. The car was up on a hoist while Mike, the agent, inspected and poked into recesses and wheel wells.

Finally, when it sat with every panel pulled that could be removed, and the trunk open so that the gas pedal was in plain view from behind the car, the senior agent with the oak leaves on his collar said, "It looks like you're clean. You can go now."

Cy fumed, "Put this car back together or I'll sue!"

Rufus said, "Calm down, old buddy. Look, officer, I'm a doctor and I know how to cut and remove organs, but I don't know much about cars. You can't expect us to drive away from here with the seats loose. How about it?"

The agents did put the car back together, but it was almost 10:30 at night before the adventurers could resume their journey. The final delay occurred when the convertible top froze halfway up. One of the agents made an adjustment, and it lurched the rest of the way up with a teeth-jarring grinding sound. Muttering obscenities through his teeth, Cy almost peeled rubber as he sped out of the Border Patrol garage, heading North at last.

CHAPTER 5

Back to Long Beach

Joe was asleep in the front seat before the top was fixed. He slept through Lyla's nagging Cy to drive her to the L.A. airport because she had missed her flight from San Diego. He missed Rufus and Cy grousing about having to drive the extra distance and, finally, their begrudging agreement. He didn't know it when they stopped in Imperial Beach so the trim blonde could change into her stewardess uniform. Or when Cy stopped at a drive-in to wolf down sandwiches and coffee.

Joe was finally startled awake by the sound of the tires biting gravel and a swerve as Cy got the car back onto the pavement. "What was that?" he exclaimed.

Cy replied, sounding almost drugged despite the coffee, "I almost fell asleep. I don't think I can go any farther."

"Well, pull over then," said Joe, "before you get us all killed!"

Lyla's voice came from the back, as tight as a fiddle string, "We can't stop now! I've got to get to the airport. We can make it if we keep going. Let me drive."

Cy pulled over and traded places with Lyla. She gritted her teeth as she slid into the driver's seat and eased herself slowly behind the wheel. Sitting tall, she grimaced as she adjusted the seat so her feet could reach the pedals, then slowly eased herself down before steering the big Caddy back onto the road.

Joe was now wide awake, charged with adrenaline after the close call. He looked into the back seat where both Cy and Rufus slouched uncomfortably in slumber.

After a short time, Lyla said, "Sunday night, for the first time since I was a girl, I prayed that somehow I would be set free. And Joe, thank you for picking me. You saved my life. I'm going to church next Sunday and thank God for hearing my prayer."

Joe raised himself off the seat while he fished in his front pocket, then holding a palm full of change close to the dim dashboard lights, he picked out a coin and gave it to her. "I don't know if this counts as a prayer, but here it is: the coin I flipped. A five-peso piece--I don't even know exactly how much that's worth. Would you like it as a souvenir of this momentous Labor Day weekend?"

She glanced at the coin in her hand before she dropped it into her breast pocket. "Thank you, Señor Taco. Now don't conk out on me. I need company to stay awake."

"Okay. Then let's start with questions. Do you live down there and commute up here for work?"

"I used to, but I've been transferred to Chicago. My girl friend let me use her place for the past week while I was on stand-down."

"And you came all the way back here to have a weekend with Doc Johnson?"

She looked in the rear-view mirror before answering, "Yes. And I'd say I blew it."

"Lyla, we've given a new meaning to the cliche, 'lost weekend.' It will be one weekend none of us will ever forget. And he can't blame you for what happened."

She bit her lip, then paused, shifting uncomfortably in her seat, before she said, "No, but he's seen me at my worst. My very worst! First in the hotel, with those cops gawking at us when we were naked as the day we were born. Then at that damn police station. And again tonight. I've been a shrew. I saw the look on Rufus's face. This has been hell! I'm not sure I'll be out of the woods even if I make my flight from LAX. If United finds out about this weekend, I'll lose my job for sure."

"Come on, what they did down there was an old-fashioned shakedown. Nobody gets fired for being put upon."

"You don't understand. Those papers we signed back in Tijuana . . . I had to admit to an act of . . . prostitution with Rufus. And he had to admit that we did it for money. They kept my money as evidence. It was the only way they would let us go. I feel so dirty . . . so used."

"Wait, I thought I was posting bail. Had I known that, maybe there would have been enough to spring Tammy."

"It wouldn't have been enough, even if I could get it back. I had fifty dollars in my purse, which was sitting on the night table next to the bed. I can still see those five bills floating to the floor, almost in slow motion after the guy turned my purse over."

"Turned your purse over?"

"Yes, they barged into our room in the middle of the night. I've never been so scared in my life--two cops pointing guns at us, giving orders in Spanish. I didn't know what they were saying. The guy who flipped my purse picked up the money and stuck it in his pocket before pulling the covers off. He called me a 'puta,' a whore. Rufus and I were both naked. I was scared as hell! I put my dress on and was going to grab my undies when he handcuffed my hands behind my back. The others were taken to the jail in buses. I rode in a paddy wagon with the other . . . whores."

"Ah, the more things are different, the more they're the same."

"Meaning . . . ?"

"That's the way it works in the States. I worked a club in East St. Louis. I think the owner forgot to pay his protection. Sure, the girls did a little freelancing with the audience. It went with the territory. The cops raided the place and cuffed all the girls in a daisy chain and took them in."

"Were you arrested?"

"No, I only tell bad jokes. And nobody appreciated my humor when there was no ebony flesh to admire."

"Ebony? They were black?"

"Yeah. The owner and I were the only palefaces working there."

"You're a hoot! After we let you off in T-town Friday evening, I think we laughed all the way to the hotel about you selling tacos. Rufus and Cy told some awfully funny stories about you too. Did you really invite a stripper to the Fleet Admiral's party?"

"Sure did. Pam Lifshifski, who peels under the name of Lola Getz. She's an old friend. I got her her first job after she flunked out of Colorado U. I don't why they made such a big deal of it. She didn't do her act for them."

"Apparently you're not like any other green Ensign they've ever seen."

"No, I'm not. I didn't go through on some scholarship and have it all handed to me on a silver plate. I earned the degree in every sense of the word, and I asked to be commissioned on my merit. But enough about me . . . Lyla, the one person we haven't talked about is Tammy. I feel real bad about not being able to get her out too."

"Don't feel real bad. Maybe a *little* bad--but not *real* bad. If anyone deserved to be left behind, she's the one. Believe me, she's no charmer."

"Sounds like the two of you didn't hit it off."

"To put it mildly. All the other women in the paddy wagon with me were out by Saturday noon. The guards and everybody in the jail called me 'La Puta Gringa,' and Tammy rubbed it in, making a big thing of my being charged with prostitution. And this morning, she made fun of me because their doctor examined me for venereal disease. That was an ordeal, and I'm still sore. I can hardly sit!"

Looking over his shoulder toward the sleeping Navy doctor, Joe said, "Now I understand why you sat down the way you did. Did you tell Rufus?"

"No. I don't know why I'm telling you. It's not the kind of thing you tell a man. I just couldn't ask Rufus. If it's still bothering me after the flight, I'll drop by the hospital emergency room on my way home. About the trouble at the border . . . Joe, were you selling something more than tacos that made you so much money?"

"No, I just kept at it. Fools and their money are soon parted. I found out that if somebody wouldn't pay a dollar for a taco, they'd pay the equivalent in pesos . . . or we'd settle at a price well above what everybody else was selling."

"Don't you feel a little guilty for rooking people that way?"

"No, I gave them more than the other guys and a few laughs besides. If they didn't like it, they could always walk . . . and some did."

"Well, when the guard told me I was going to be let go, Tammy asked why. I told her my pimp finally came through. I assumed they would come for her next. And when they didn't and the matron told her that you, Señor Jose Hee-los, had decided to purchase only my release, she blew her top."

"I don't blame her. I wanted to talk to her, but by the time all the paperwork was done, they said I'd have to come back tomorrow. No way I could wait."

The remainder of the trip to the airport was uneventful as they moved through light late-night traffic. Rufus barely awakened to receive a goodbye kiss from Lyla. She kissed Joe on the cheek and trotted into the terminal with her single suitcase trailing behind her on a small dolly.

⇥▬◉ ◉▬⇤

The *Beaverton* weighed anchor in Long Beach harbor at eight o'clock sharp Tuesday morning and turned her bow to sea for two weeks of exercises. Joe, Cy, and Rufus were onboard, having made it with two hours to spare.

As Cy and Rufus told and retold their adventure, Joe became known in the wardroom as "Joe Taco" or "Señor Taco." On payday, he felt a certain pride as Cy counted out fifteen crisp twenty-dollar bills to augment his meager one-hundred-and-eleven-dollar wages.

Much to Joe's surprise, the Chief Engineer bragged about his resourceful new Ensign, who could make more in a weekend selling tacos than he could in a month aboard. Privately, he let Joe know that the extra time he'd been spending learning the ship had not gone unnoticed. He informed him that, thanks to his hard work and initiative, he would be moved to the Main Engine Division (M Division for short), with plans to fleet him up to Division Officer when Lieutenant Kane left the ship in November.

On return to port, Joe stayed aboard that Friday doing reports and paperwork that his new boss Lieutenant Kane had not done for the past two months. He continued working over the weekend between watches.

On Monday they were underway again for the week. Joe was standing watches with Kane, whom the crew greatly respected for his tremendous knowledge of the ship's engineering system. However, they held him almost in contempt as an officer. Milt Kane was a Merchant Marine officer who had been drafted into the Navy. A slightly overweight man of heavy build, he wore his uniform more like the uniform of a steamship company than a military service.

As Joe immersed himself in his new job, he found that Kane had kept letter-perfect records where they pertained to the actual operation and maintenance of the plant. However, if a record pertained to the shipboard organization or anything military, it had been either ignored or discarded.

Joe sensed that he'd been given a rare opportunity because there were officers in the Gunnery Department, for instance, who had been aboard over eighteen months and were still junior division officers. He worked close to eighteen-hour days, and with his efforts came results. By October, Milt Kane was slapping his back and praising his abilities as a watch officer in front of Chief Engineer Moran. Moran in turn shared with Joe the notes he got from the Personnel Office, thanking him both for timely submission of data and for meeting deadlines. Each note stated that this was a first for M Division.

⊰═◉═⊱

Kane invited Joe to his standard Friday first-night-in-port bash at what he called his "snake ranch" in Belmont Shore. Joe ate onboard and got a ride with Larry White, who was meeting his wife at the party.

Enroute, Larry explained that an invitation to one of Kane's parties was a sure way to make out. Kane had a leased house across the road from the Belmont Shore beach, sharing a driveway and a palm-shaded patio with a two-story apartment house occupied mostly by young, single women. Plenty of free booze would be consumed because a case was pledged by each *Beaverton* officer invited who'd been onboard long enough to get a liquor ration. That amounted to about 39 cases of prime booze.

Even before Larry parked his car across the street, the deep thump of a bass viol ionized the warm night air. They walked toward the driveway, which was flanked by a cement block fence festooned with tangled vines that looked almost plastic in the glow of strategically placed floodlamps. Visible from the street was a wrought-iron-fenced lanai with all its facing doors open. People in all states of dress, from business suits and dresses to shorts and even one rather fat brunette in a cotton bathrobe, stood around or leaned against the rail.

Once Joe and Larry stepped through the fence, the pure tones of the speakers were muffled by the din of conversation. Larry guided him into the middle of the crowd. *These are all what you call "fashionable people,"* thought Joe. All the smiles were toothpaste-commercial perfect. Some figures were spectacular, and almost none were fat or dumpy. The men were for the most part tanned, muscular, and blue-eyed.

In the center of the patio was a table that Joe estimated was about six feet in diameter, in whose center was a huge stainless-steel bowl of ice. Covering nearly every inch of its surface, almost to the edge, were bottles of almost every kind imaginable.

With a glass in hand, Kane met him and said, "Well, if isn't my Jay Oh. What's your poison, friend?"

Joe said, "How about a glass of Metaxa?"

"I have hundreds of bottles here and you have to ask for some damn Mexican stuff. Are you still playing the Joe Taco role?"

"No, it's Greek, a brandy."

"Brandy! That's a lady's drink. How about a glass of scotch?"

"How about a plain soda?"

"Joe, you've got to do better than that. I can't drink this whole table alone."

Scanning his eyes over the crowd and up to the second floor, Joe replied, "I think you've called out a big enough work party."

Putting a hand on his shoulder, the Lieutenant said, "Maybe they have something that will wet your whistle upstairs. I think it's time you had the opportunity to meet some of my very friendly neighbors. You deserve it after all the time you've put in. Too bad you're wasting yourself in the Navy. Like I told you yesterday, when you get tired of the BS and the dumb paperwork, look me up and I'll find you a berth where technical competence is appreciated . . . and you get paid for it! Joe, the girl I'm about to introduce you to is . . . different. Don't let first impressions mislead you. Trust me."

Threading through the crowded lanai, they stepped onto the second-floor balcony. Joe saw a large, lone goldfish lazily swimming in a small backlighted turquoise pool that was nestled between the building and a single palm whose trunk and fronds were painted the warm hues of blue and green landscape lighting.

Kane led him to a second-floor apartment that was as overflowing with people as the lanai below. They squeezed between bodies until they were in the living room, where three young women sat like queens at court. One of them stood out. She had peroxide-blonde hair, piled high on her head in a bouffant style. Otherwise she was very thin, almost skinny, light-featured, with very large breasts. The cleavage moved with every breath she took. Joe focused on the bare expanse of satin-smooth flesh between her neck and the top of her off-the-shoulder dress, where it marked a demarcation line just barely on the side of propriety. When she smiled, Joe thought she could be a stand-in for Marilyn Monroe, if Marilyn had dark brown eyes.

Kane said, "Felina, this is my shipmate, Joe Xylos, that I told you about. Joe, Felina Hoskins. I think you two will hit it off very well."

As Joe took her hand, his boss said, "Please excuse me, I've got to get back downstairs and play host."

Her smile revealed a mouthful of perfectly even, sparkling white teeth. Her voice had the high-pitched tonal quality of a twelve-year-old as she said, "Milt is my friend. He says that you are his friend. And he says that we could be good friends. The sofa is comfortable. Please sit on the sofa."

"Thank you, Felina." Although he was charmed, Joe thought, *She's different, all right. She talks like a child's first reader.*

Joe slid into the space between Felina and another blonde named Rhonda. A cup of punch that had the minty bouquet of crème de menthe and froth of champagne was pushed into his hand.

After taking a sip, he asked, "Felina, what do you do here?"

"I teach school. I teach kindergarten. I teach at Holy Names Academy. Holy Names is a parochial school."

"A parochial school. Then we have something in common. I'm in the Navy for the love of my country. And you must love to teach, because they don't pay much at private schools." *I guess that explains it; she talks like the pupils she's with every day.*

"I love children. I don't do anything for the money. I do everything for the pleasure. I like fun and parties, don't you?"

"Sure. It's good to get away from the ship and mix with people."

About an hour and a half later, while Joe and Felina were standing at the punchbowl, a disembodied voice came through the wall that said, "You may sound the backing signal."

There was a pause of perhaps fifteen seconds, then the deep-throated blast of a ship's whistle, "BBBBBRRRRRROOOOOOOOPPPPP!!!"

The volume built to the point he felt a twinge of pain in his ears. Before him, waves spread from the sides of the punchbowl in concentric rings to a splashing little geyser in the center.

No sooner had the whistle stopped than the voice again said, "Give me the backing signal!"

"BBBROOOP! BBBROOOP! BBBROOOP!"

Turning to his companion, Joe said, "It sounds like there's a ship right outside. What is that?"

Laughing, she said, "Oh, that! Milt has a stereo. He has very big speakers."

Faintly the official voice said, "I don't like his intentions. Sound the danger signal."

"BBBROOOP! BBBROOOP! BBBROOOP! BBBROOOP! BB-BROOOP! BBBROOOP!"

With the last echo of the whistle, loud cheers and laughter washed in behind the ear-piercing sound.

Joe said, "That thing is loud enough to vibrate the nails out of coffins. I'll bet it's making waves in the coffee cups down at police headquarters!"

Felina took a sip from her glass and said, "Well, it just wouldn't be one of Milt's parties if the cops didn't come once or twice. That's why he always invites the neighbors. The police are nice. Some policemen are handsome. The station is across town. They have a long way to go to come here. Don't worry about them."

She had hardly said her last word when there was a high-pitched click of a phonograph needle touching a record and another long twelve seconds of the whistle, even louder than the previous one. Joe watched the punchbowl again, fascinated by the effect the sound was having on it.

Joe took her by the arm. "Felina, let's get out of here. I don't want to be around when the cops come."

"Oh, they never do much. They were here earlier. I saw them talking to Milt. They wanted the people to move their cars, I think. Besides, it's early. It's not even ten o'clock yet."

"Why don't we go for a walk on the beach? That thing is just too loud for me."

She smiled. "I like to go to the beach. It's fun on the beach at night. It's all dark now. We could have fun in the dark. Would you like to have some fun?"

"Sure, Felina, that's what life is all about."

The couple threaded their way past the booze table and through the crowd on the lanai. She carried a rolled-up cotton bedspread, while he carried an unopened champagne bottle and two glasses. As they passed the door to Kane's place, Joe heard the familiar voice of his roommate, Cy Penelton. "Here we go, Milt . . . the sound effects record of the carillon and the cannons from the *1812 Overture*."

Joe and Felina were on the far side of the street when the first cannon blasts boomed out into the night. Joe felt the echo. Beyond them the fog that had hung offshore during the day had descended as an opaque curtain just beyond the beach. The night had cooled, and lights along the shore in both directions faded in the haze. As they walked across the broad beach toward the waves gently lapping the shore, the sounds of cannons and bells seemed to bounce and echo off invisible walls.

Ahead of them a man was pointing seaward, saying, "There must be one of those Navy ships having trouble. First there were all those whistle signals and now, explosions."

Joe and Felina heard people talking and shouting all around them. Just as it seemed they had moved into a vacant part of the beach, more people appeared. They also were looking seaward and talking about the strange noises, which they all thought were coming from the harbor.

For about ten minutes, the sound effects were quiet and faint bars of big-band music mixed with gentle lap of the water on the beach. All the while, the fog spread its opaque fingers around them. Behind the vapor curtain, they sank onto the bedspread. Her lips and hands told of urgent needs.

When the next round of sound effects began, Joe was vaguely aware of the thump of what sounded like the guns on the *Beaverton* firing. Felina pressed hard against him and demanded his full attention. The cannonade built up in intensity and was punctuated by explosions. Although the volume wasn't nearly what it had been in the house, the sound of large naval guns wasn't music to make love by. Cy would later tell him this was the soundtrack from a newsreel of the Battle of San

Bernardino Strait.

Next there was the drone of diving aircraft, more gunfire, and explosions, pulled from footage of the invasion of Okinawa. Nearby, a high-pitched male voice, sounding almost as if its owner was in the grip of a shark, screamed, "It's the Russians! They're attacking the Navy ships in the harbor! We've got to get out of here! It's the end of the world!"

At this point, their privacy was interrupted by sounds of feet running down the beach and a woman screaming, "Oh, God save us! The Russians are coming! The Russians are coming!" Felina and the Ensign rolled themselves up in the bedspread like a cocoon.

Soon more feet approached. The first two people who happened upon them jumped over them. The third was a preteen boy who attempted to hurdle the bundle only to snag his toe, giving Joe a sharp kick in the ribs before tumbling to the sand, where he began crying as if he'd been shot.

In the darkness, a woman's voice called, "Ryan! Ryan! Where are you? Ryan!" Soon she came into view. She snatched the boy up in her arms and, after she gave him a few words of comfort, kicked sand toward the couple while shouting, "Disgusting! Simply disgusting! And in front of children! How can you do that when the world is ending?" She pulled the youngster to his feet. In a shrieking voice, she screamed, "Run, Ryan, run!"

Joe shouted after her, "Relax, lady! It's only sound effects."

Just after the mother and child disappeared into the black ether, the war sounds stopped. For a few minutes, there was some more shouting and some people's feet crunching the sand, but they remained hidden. The ambient sounds dropped to the night sounds of traffic mixed with water lapping the shore, punctuated by buoy bells and the distant growl of the foghorn on the Long Beach breakwater.

In time, Joe lay beside Felina, half asleep. In the distance, he heard a bullhorn-powered voice order, "Okay, let's get them on the buses."

As the couple were taking the first sips of champagne, the hiss of air brakes and the acceleration of a diesel bus engine drowned out the ting of their glasses. Wearing the bedspread like a double shawl, they walked arm in arm silently toward the street.

Through the haze, they saw two men carrying armloads of bottles to the back end of a pickup that was parked in the driveway of the totally darkened apartment building. Sitting at the curb was a white sedan with its trunk open. Two police officers, each with his arms full of bottles, returned to the car.

Felina said, "Joe, the lights are out. It is quiet. Where is everyone?"

He slowed his pace, whispering, "I think the inevitable has happened. You've been raided."

"What are they doing?"

"Taking the booze, it looks like."

"But that's our booze!"

"Probably evidence. Let's be quiet."

"But they can't do that! It's our booze! We paid for it!"

"Felina, we're scot-free right now. And I don't want to get run in. Let's just walk past them, but don't let them know you live there. Okay?"

Pouting, she said, "Well, okay. But they have no right."

"They're cops. Maybe they're collecting it as evidence. If there is talking to do, let me do it. Just in case these are robbers in uniform, let's get their license plate numbers."

Two men in civilian attire carried a few bottles in their hands and placed them in with the others. A uniformed officer followed, saying, "That's all there is, let's get going."

The officer laughed. "Boy, the feds are going to love us! What a haul! I don't know how these Navy guys can afford to buy so much booze, even if they got it duty free."

Joe and Felina crossed the street, arriving at the far curb about a house length away from the apartment. They waited on the sidewalk while the pickup backed into the street and continued past the police car. Two officers sat inside the car, where one was talking on the radio.

Felina said, "There is a cross street up ahead. We can walk down it. It will take us to the other side. I park my car there. And the green truck's plate is GT 1054. The police car's number is C-21334."

"Do you have your car keys?"

"No, silly. I keep my keys in my purse. My purse is in the apartment."

"Then how are we going to get into the apartment?

"There is a secret key. We hid the secret key. I will find it."

After they turned the corner, Joe caught the blur of the police car out of the corner of his eye as it slipped away into the night.

Joe mused, "Maybe I should have asked where they took everybody. We ought to get down there and try to bail them out."

"Joe, we don't have to worry about them. They'll book them and then let everyone go. We've got some unfinished business. And we've got plenty of time. Nobody is here . . . just you and me. You are still interested, aren't you?"

"Well . . . sure, I'm interested."

She giggled. "See, you like fun. And stop worrying. They'll all be back in time for breakfast."

"Are you sure?"

"Darling, that's the way they do it here."

CHAPTER 6

"War of the Worlds" Aftermath

The ringing of the phone and Felina's voice brought Joe back from a very deep, exhausted sleep, "Rhonda, why are you calling me at this hour? . . . I'm very tired. I want to go back to sleep. I went to sleep very, very late."

He could hear the modulations of a voice emanating from the earpiece because the bleached blonde was holding it away from her head.

"Well, you don't have to shout. Of course I was! Do you think I'm an old maid? . . . What do you mean, you have to post bail? . . . Well, of course I'll be there."

Then, looking over at Joe, she laughed. "Of course. It was a wonderful night."

As she placed the phone back in its cradle, Felina fell back onto her pillow. "They're all in jail. They have to post bail! Can you imagine?"

"Doesn't surprise me one bit. I couldn't imagine any place where somebody wouldn't call the cops with a noise machine like that in the neighborhood."

"Is it that you're smart or just lucky?"

"What do you mean?"

"Last night, I thought you were very fast."

"Fast?"

"Yes, that was a good line about the place being too noisy. We were at the end of the bedroom line. I thought you were extra horny. Admit it, you couldn't wait until our turn."

Joe smiled and traced a gentle line along her cheek. "Call it serendipity. Yes, it was a good evening. You're somebody special, Felina. We ought to plan to pick up later from where we left off last night."

He moved her hand out from under the covers. "The business at hand is our friends. Are they all still in jail? Everyone who was here last night?"

"Yes."

"They don't fool around in this town! What were the charges? Drunk and disorderly? Disturbing the peace?"

"I don't know. She said something about illegal hooch. I don't understand. There must be some sort of misunderstanding. We all kicked in for the champagne. Rhonda and I bought it at the supermarket. I'm over twenty-one. I don't understand."

◦┼▄▄◉ ◉▄▄┼◦

Joe looked at his watch and noted that it was just after four a.m. as Felina parked her rusting 1950 Studebaker coupe close to the Long Beach Police station. The inside was calm compared to his recent experience in Tijuana. A sleepy officer behind the desk pointed them to an office door.

Inside, a sun-tanned man in civilian clothes, who appeared to be in his early fifties, looked up from a report he was writing when Felina in her high-pitched voice said, "Mr. Policeman, why are you keeping my roommates and our friends in your jail?"

"Pardon me, ma'am, who are your roommates? And who are you?"

"Rhonda Hamlin and Beverly Winthrop. They're very good girls. And I'm Felina Hoskins."

He picked up a clipboard and began flipping through pages. He stopped, put a paper clip on a page, then continued for another five pages. After he studied the pages, he said, "These charges are all going to have to be sorted out. Let's see . . . Drunk and disorderly. Disturbing the peace. Maintaining a disorderly house. Violations of the California Code under Section—ah, that means possession of untaxed alcoholic beverages. There may be federal charges as well. The quantities could compound into a felony." He checked a separate lined pad, "Felina . . . Felina U. Hoskins. Is that correct?"

"Yes."

"Since you live there too, you could be implicated. By the way, where were you last night?"

Joe said, "Felina, don't answer!"

Raising his eyebrows, the officer said, "And who are you, her lawyer?"

"No. I'm Ensign Joe Xylos and I'm here to get my shipmates released."

The officer scanned the list, then ran his finger from name to name before saying, "I have no information on you specifically, but you were at the party too, weren't you?"

Joe waved his hand. "I'm not going to bite that baited hook. My reason for coming here is to get my shipmates out of jail. I know at least one of them has duty starting at eight a.m. How do we go about it?"

"Miss Hoskins, there could be some serious charges facing you regarding untaxed alcoholic beverages—"

Joe cut him short. "Officer, do you have any evidence that specifically implicates us?"

"Well, I just wanted to talk to you first—"

"We're not here to talk. We're here to get people out of the lockup. How do we go about it?"

Pointing a pencil at the Ensign, the policeman snapped, "I think I could establish probable cause—"

"If you're planning to book me, you'd damn well better have all your ducks in line. Arbitrarily threatening people who come to help others is the basest form of intimidation. I resent the implication that either Felina or I had anything to do with this mess. In other states, posting of bail is commonly used to allow freedom until time to go to court. I assume California has a similar law."

The man stood up, towering over Joe. He poked a finger in Joe's direction and spoke out of the corner of his mouth, "For a little round-shouldered twerp, you have a damn big mouth. And you damn Navy officers are the biggest pain I've had in weeks. So don't come in here, Endswine Zilops, and tell me about 'ducks in a line' or how to run this station."

Joe smiled, extending his right hand. "I didn't catch your name, officer. My name is Xylos, as in xylophone, and I am an Ensign."

The officer studied the Ensign's hand for a moment before hesitantly shaking it. "I'm Lieutenant Conrad Cruse. I guess I was off base. Thanks to these clowns, it's been too long a night. I've been on overtime since midnight." He looked Joe in the eye and sniffed, "I guess you couldn't be part of that bunch. You're too damn sober. What ship?"

"*Beaverton*, pleased to meet you, Lieutenant."

"*Beaverton*! You travel in bad company. It's not often we haul in so many officers. And these charges could be serious."

"Well, you can't choose your shipmates. But overall, they're a good bunch."

"These Lieutenants Kane and Penelton seem to have dug themselves a deep hole."

"I hope it isn't too deep. One is my boss and the other my roommate. I don't think anybody got hurt by their sound effects even though it was awfully loud."

"So you *were* there?"

"Close enough to hear it. We were walking on the beach. And it was loud."

"Yes. Even the Coast Guard is involved. There are rules about sounding false navigational signals. They dispatched cutters. There was a panic in the Belmont Shore area. Some people reported that Seal Beach blew up. There were calls in here that the Russians were attacking the Navy ships in the harbor. You were damn smart to leave when you did. This isn't the first time Lieutenant Milton Kane has cranked up his doomsday machine. Labor Day weekend, we warned him to turn it down. And before that, in July."

"Well, that takes care of my boss and Cy. Now how about Larry White? He has the duty today."

The officer twirled a yellow wooden pencil like a miniature baton. "That complex has become a focus of too many complaints for too long. Loud parties. Loud cars. And too much hijinks. It spills over onto the beach. Last night was a regular bacchanal. Hell, whorehouses don't wear out mattresses as fast as they do in that place. The chief said to haul in everyone this time. And with all that untaxed booze, we've got a hammer."

Felina's face reddened, but she got no further than uttering the first syllable, "Off—," when Joe interrupted, "Officer, I'm sure you have good cause to act as you did. I don't want to waste any more of your time, so why don't you let me check over your blotter so I can find out who is here and figure out what it will take to get these officers and their ladies released so you can fill those cells with the real criminals."

As Joe pulled a sheet of paper from his pocket, the policeman eyed him. "Ladies? The way the word rolls off your tongue, I get the feeling that you've had some experience springing people out of jail. Are you an attorney . . . or a pimp?"

Joe smiled, "Is there a difference?"

"Well . . ."

"The answer to both, is no. Let's say that necessity demands we learn unique skills. And it's only a coincidence that the word 'ladies' is applied both to officers' escorts, because officers are gentlemen by act of Congress, and also to those damsels who toil on their backs to earn their way in life."

Felina kicked Joe in the shins. "I resent that!"

She started for the door, but stopped when Joe asked, "Are you going to leave your roommates in the pokey?"

Over the next half-hour, Joe collected names and totaled the tab. There had been sixty-seven people arrested. Thirty-three, who lived in the neighborhood, had been released with the equivalent of parking tickets. The residents of the complex, plus those who didn't live nearby, were still in custody. Eleven of the number were from the *Beaverton*; seven were officers from other ships. Two were civilian males who lived in the complex, and the remaining fourteen were single females, most of whom lived in the apartments. All were charged with felonies for possession and consumption of untaxed alcoholic beverages, plus a laundry list of misdemeanor charges. Bail recommendations would require $400 cash for each of them except Milt Kane and Cy Penelton, who were pegged at an even $1,000 each.

Joe made a request that the *Beaverton* officers be released into his custody for return to the ship, but he was turned down flat. While he was there, five of the women were released when their parents made bail, leaving all the males in custody, plus seven women. In a brief visit with these remaining prisoners, Joe found out that they carried an average of about $100 each among them. Two of the *Beaverton* officers had Saturday duty, Angus Adams and Larry White. Angus had enough cash—if someone could get it from his safe on board—but Larry had just over $100. Angus gave Joe his combination, and Felina, with a little coaxing, drove Joe to the ship to get Angus's bail money and try to raise another $300 for Larry.

⋅∗⊨⊙ ⊙⊨∗⋅

Todd Morgan, the B Division Officer, sat up with a start and bumped his head when Joe roused him by asking, "How much are you willing to spring for to save Larry's bacon and get yourself relieved on time this morning?"

After another ten minutes of coaxing in B Division, Morgan gave him just over $70. With $30 here and $20 there and making up the difference from his own pocket, Joe filled an envelope with bills and carried it back to the blonde awaiting him on the pier. By then, it was after seven a.m. It took another ten minutes to convince Felina of the importance of releasing the officers before her roommates. Even then, as he watched her drive back to the jail with the money, he wasn't sure she would keep her word and do as he asked.

Short of sleep and more than a little angry, Joe gobbled breakfast, shaved, and relieved the JOOD, sparing Larry "Inside" White from being marked absent from his forenoon watch. Chief Engineer Moran, who was the off-going Command Duty Officer, gave him oral pats on the back for covering for his shipmate, and promised to go by the jail on his way home.

Close to ten a.m., Joe had just been relieved when XO Longstreet came aboard, vowing that "heads would roll or worse" for the early Saturday morning calls to his house from both the police and the Long Beach Shore Patrol. He left a list of names of those who would remain aboard until Monday, when he would sort out the mess. The last name on the alphabetical list of thirteen was Xylos.

By noon, all the *Beaverton* contingent were released without having to post bail after all. The understanding was that they would remain on the ship until the first hearing Monday morning. All the civilians were also released on their own recognizance.

Larry handed Joe back the cash-filled envelope and thanked him for his efforts. Joe called the station and confirmed that his shipmates were released and that he had never been charged. Puzzled at why his name was nevertheless on the XO's list, he tried to call the XO. Longstreet refused to even take his call, but relayed a message through his wife to remain aboard.

⋅→⫶⊚⫶←⋅

Late Sunday morning, the partygoers sat glumly around the wardroom table. At its head, Lieutenant Harry Leach, who was Command Duty Officer for the day, sat with his feet propped up on a chair with the Sunday edition of the Los Angeles *Times* strewn around his end of the table in a disorderly fan.

He tapped the front of section B, followed by a loud chuckle as he put his pudgy finger on the left column. He read for another minute and then, chortling, looked down the table at his miserable shipmates. He smiled and his eyes danced. "My, my, Mr. Kane, it looks like the irregular Navy made the front page. Listen to this . . . . Under the headline, 'War of the Worlds Threatens Belmont Shore,' it reads,

'Friday evening, beach visitors and residents from Long Beach to Belmont Shore and Huntington Beach reacted in panic to what to them sounded like a major naval battle going on in the thick fog off the southern part of Long Beach harbor. The Coast Guard received reports of a large ship aground just south of the Long Beach breakwater. For a time it was thought that there had been a major accident at the Navy's Seal Beach Depot. Media switchboards were swamped with calls not just in Belmont Shore but also in nearby Huntington Beach. Law officers knew they were dealing with sound skipping from an undetermined source. Professor Benjamin Northwood of the USC School of Atmospheric Physics said in a phone interview that the phenomenon of sound skipping and being heard miles away from its source is common during temperature inversions, which the area experienced Friday evening . . ."

"Wait, it gets better." Leach took a sip from his coffee cup before continuing, *"'Coincidentally, Long Beach Police Lieutenant Conrad Cruse was organizing a group of officers to raid a very large and boisterous party in Belmont Shore at which an officer earlier in the evening had reported seeing large numbers of untaxed alcoholic beverages being consumed. The residents of the house and neighboring apartment complex had been given numerous warnings over the past six months. . . . Lieutenant Cruse reported that the sound from the huge speakers mounted in the house window of Milton Kane, a naval officer stationed aboard the Navy cruiser* Beaverton, *was so loud that his ears hurt. The power was so intense that he could feel the air vibrating. Arrested with Kane was Cyrus Penelton, Jr., son of Cyrus Penelton, the renowned producer from Paramount Studios and founder of Penelton Special Effects. Young Penelton is also an officer on the* Beaverton. . . . *Nine other* Beaverton *officers were among sixty-seven persons booked following the incident.'"*

Leach pulled a typed list from his pocket and counted the names. "There are thirteen names on the list and the paper says eleven were arrested. Did they make a mistake?"

Milt Kane pulled the list out of Leach's hand. "Joe Xylos and Doc Johnson weren't arrested. In fact, the doc wasn't even anywhere near there."

Leach grabbed the list back, saying, "It's all academic anyway. The quack left on Friday and won't be back until tomorrow morning." He smiled and slicked back his hair as he poked Kane in the ribs. "But you, you non-reg SOB, are finally going to get a ride down the iron-shod tubes. I'll bet they throw you to the wolves and when you get out of jail, they'll run you out of the Navy on a rail."

"Harry, if they run me out of the Navy on a rail, it will be bent from having first carried your obese carcass to the gate. How many times have they passed you over for incompetence?"

Leach lurched for Kane, but missed, then said, "Well, I'll get the last laugh on this one. Captain Sam may look and sound like James Cagney, but he's one tough old boy. And he doesn't like his ship's name splashed all over the papers. That goes for the whole bunch of you— from Adams to Zilch."

Larry said, "I don't why Joe is on the list. He kept his nose clean. He was smart enough to leave the party as soon as Milt lit off the doomsday machine. In fact, there isn't a one of us who were in that jail who isn't indebted to him for being the first one there to bail us out. We called the ship, but only good old Joe showed up. He's one hell of a shipmate. He even stood my first watch to cover for me."

Leach leaned over the table and in a low voice, almost a whisper, growled, "Listen, that little greaseball should never have had a commission in the first place. I've set Stan Longstreet straight on him. Ensign Zilch doesn't look like an officer. He doesn't talk like an officer. And he sure as hell doesn't act like one either."

Kane asked, "Harry, you're an officer, aren't you?"

"Yes. Why? That's a dumb question from a dumb draftee!"

"Let me share one small observation with you. I've had my belly full of dilettante naval officers. Shoveling paper, kissing ass, and enjoying the easy life on this showboat is just about all you do. But that man learns how the equipment runs. Joe Xylos is better qualified as an engineering watch officer in—what has it been, two months?—than half the people standing watches. Since he's been my assistant, he's kept the Chief Engineer and the XO off my back about all those stupid reports. He puts in the time! The man is a worker. Harry, even as fat as you are, you get lost in his shadow."

The obese lieutenant rose to his full height and wagged a finger. "Kane, you're always baiting me. Well, I'm going to enjoy the next few weeks while you get accustomed to the four walls of your stateroom. And for the lot of you, who've had your share of laughs at my expense today, I'll have the last laugh when the escorts for the Miss Universe contest are announced."

Kane held both arms out at shoulder level and turned both thumbs down. "Harry, that's exactly what I mean. This ship is getting ready for a deployment and possibly combat duty, if things get out of hand in the Middle East. And what are you, the Main Battery Officer, preoccupied with? Naval escorts for a bunch of beauty queens!"

Harry's jowls quivered as he tilted his head back and looked down his nose. "You belittle me, sir. As the Public Affairs Officer aboard Cruiser Division Nine's flagship, I have been given the responsibility of selecting a suitable cadre of junior officers to escort the contestants during the formal portion of the contest. The entire program will be carried on prime-time television and give a nationwide audience the opportunity to see these fine naval officers at their best."

Kane exhaled a lungful of cigarette smoke in Leach's direction as he said, "The nationwide audience is going to be looking at the depth of cleavage exposed and the sparkle of Colgate smiles, not the shining gold stripes of your gaggle of hormone-rich college boys in blue suits."

"See here, Kane, you're full of sour grapes. By the time you get out of hack and set foot on dry land, you'll do it as a civilian. You thought you were so smart, fixing it so you could get yourself a free ride to see the Olympics in Melbourne."

"Harry, Harry, do you think I'd want to ride all the way to Melbourne to see some silly sports contests? The real reason I shipped aboard the *Beaverton* is that I found out that you're a lowly Polliwog . . . and as a Trusty Shellback, I couldn't delegate the serious responsibility of initiating your fat ass into the Mysteries of the Deep when we cross the Equator."

From the far door, Joe, who had just entered, said in tones laced with laughter, "Sir, do you mean that Lieutenant Harry Leach, USN, USNA, former commanding officer of a United States Navy ship, has never been across the Equator? The denizens of the deep will await your pleasure, sir."

Kane's smile grew broader with his every word as he exclaimed, "Well said, Trusty Shellback!"

Harry screwed his neck around to look at Joe, then spat, "Him? That's impossible!"

"I beg your pardon, sir," said Joe. "On the one midshipman cruise that was allowed in NROTC, I sailed from Charleston, South Carolina, through the Panama Canal to Guayaquil, Ecuador. And was on that voyage initiated into the Mysteries of the Deep."

"How did you find out— that I'm not—?

Kane smirked. "Harry, we've started our search for key players in the drama. And frankly, with your great seniority, demeanor, and reputation, we were disappointed that we couldn't ask you to accept a role as a key player in the line crossing ceremony."

"You mean, King Neptune."

Joe laughed. "No, sir, the Royal Baby!"

"Zilch," fumed Leach, "you're disrupting the decorum of the wardroom. Leave and don't come back until no earlier than five minutes before the next meal."

Milt Kane stood up, putting his hands on his hips. "Leach, you are the worst excuse I have ever seen for an authority figure. What you just did is the equivalent of kicking the dog. This is as much his—"

Joe, who had just filled a coffee cup and was carrying it toward the door, said, "Mr. Kane, don't bother with him. It's just been one of those days."

"What else happened, Joe?"

"I called Felina to invite her down for dinner and the movie, but she's already got herself another boyfriend."

"Fickle Felina. That's the story of her life. You're not the first and, whoever he is, he won't be the last."

"I'll say one thing for her. She's got a sense of humor."

"Oh?"

"She told me she could never get serious with me because if we married, she'd have a dirty name. Now, get this. Her initials would be F. U. X."

"She ought to adopt the acronym. It's Felina; it describes her very essence. But Joe, about this marriage business. What kind of a line did you feed her?"

"Honest, boss, I never mentioned the word or even hinted at it. To think of spending my life trying to understand a mind that only under the most emotional stresses can express itself above the level of a second-grade reader is more than I could comprehend. It's just as well to have the distraction removed. We have more than enough to do before deployment."

Lieutenant Leach, as he rose from his chair, tilted his head back and said, "Mr. Xylos, leave, get out of my sight."

⊰⊱⊰⊱

Monday morning brought good news for most of the partygoers. Cy Penelton's attorney's brief conference with the prosecutor resulted in all charges relating to liquor violations, drunk and disorderly, etc., being dropped. The evidence that carried the day was the pile of Customs declarations, each listing two cases plus a wine gallon. The total exceeded by some twelve bottles the number confiscated. The Coast Guard withdrew the federal charges with the understanding that the Navy would take action under the UCMJ.

Only Cy Penelton and Milt Kane were charged at the arraignment Monday morning, on a series of misdemeanor charges that centered on the chaos caused by the sound effects. Lunch in the wardroom was a noisy affair, with more laughter and conversation than had been heard in days.

CHAPTER 7

Tijuana Jail Aftermath

Early that afternoon, Joe answered the call to report to the XO's office. Already waiting in the grey steel-walled room were his roommates, Carter Sawyer and Cy Penelton. Then Joe's boss, Lieutenant Milton Kane, and lastly, Doc Rufus Johnson added to the crowd. The Doc looked everyone over one by one before he posed the question, "What is all this about?"

Lawyer Sawyer, the ship's Legal Officer, gained eye-to-eye contact with his sad, half-open eyes and replied, "Doc, you ought not to hang out with these boys. They tend to get into trouble."

"One weekend in Tijuana was enough! Besides, I wasn't at Milt's blast Friday. I was enjoying the high life in Redondo Beach with one of my civilian colleagues from medical school days. We spent the weekend sailing off Santa Barbara."

Cy said, "Yeah, Carter, what *is* this about? Joe wasn't arrested either. Faithful as a Saint Bernard, he was the first one to come down and try to bail us out. As always, covering for his shipmates. He even took Inside White's watch Saturday morning. Surely he's not in trouble for covering for him?"

Carter shrugged his shoulders. "Cy, there's more than last weekend. You know that. The XO has material that goes back to early summer."

Joe said, "Early summer! I wasn't even here!"

"I don't have the particulars, but I understand that the XO feels you've been in the thick of things. And I've been instructed to give each of you a warning about self-incrimination, from Article 31 of the UCMJ."

Ten minutes later, they were standing in a row at attention in front of XO Longstreet''s desk. Joe watched the XO's face change to a darker shade of red with each puff of his cigar while Carter laid out files on the cluttered desk. "Lieutenant Kane," said Longstreet, "I get damn short of patience wasting my time with your damn snipes, who get in brawls on the Strip and all the other crap they can manage to step in. But when I have to disrupt my days to deal with moral decadence and immature college pranks by my wardroom, I want to let you know that I intend to make some bloody examples." He looked from one to the other. "And I mean bloody! Every time the lot of you sets foot ashore, you cause this command embarrassment."

Doc Johnson, looking thoroughly puzzled, said, "Commander, I believe you owe me an apology. I had nothing—"

"Poppycock! Let's go back to Labor Day weekend when you engaged the services of one Lyla Reeves for the sum of fifty dollars for a night of fun and games at the Rosarita Beach Hotel."

"Wait! That's absolutely preposterous!"

The XO held up a dark brown stack of thermofaxed papers. "Come now, doctor . . . These reports are translations of the documents that you and the whore signed before your release by the Mexican authorities. And I might add, they are well publicized in the San Diego *Union*!"

"Commander, you have no right to slander Lyla. I demand that—"

Joe raised a hand. "Sir, please, just a minute, there has been a misunderstanding."

The XO's voice went up half an octave, "Xylos! Misunderstanding! I'll say! Selling tacos, my ass! You were her pimp. I saw these two paying you off on payday, counting out twenties. If you weren't so cheap as to have left Tamara Nuslund, a lovely young woman, to rot in the Tijuana jail, this whole thing wouldn't have blown up in your faces."

Cy said, "Sir, I don't know where you're getting your information, but Joe Xylos is no pimp. A pain at times, but not a pimp. Even after we dumped him in Tijuana, he used every cent he had to bail us out so we could be back on time. There simply wasn't enough money to release all four of us. We flipped a coin and Tammy lost. It may not have been chivalrous to leave her, but neither of the women would have been in trouble with the law if they didn't get back Monday night."

"I read you from Miss Reeves' statement, 'The fifty dollars found loose in my purse was given to me by Rufus . . . .'" The XO flung the thermofaxed sheets on the desk in front of the doctor.

Joe said, "Commander, Lyla Reeves is no prostitute. She is a stewardess for United. She had to get back to work or she would have lost her job. She signed those papers under duress. There was no trial. And I know from the conversation we had on the way back, that she was crushed that the weekend ended as it did. She's quite fond of Rufus."

Doc Johnson's dour look brightened to a smile momentarily. "Do you think so? I haven't had the courage to even write her after that weekend."

Stan Longstreet pushed his finger into the letterhead on the desk until the digit bent in an arc. "And not one of you bothered about the fifth person in your party. Don't any of you know who Tamara Nuslund is?"

Cy said, "I think she said she's a schoolteacher somewhere in the San Diego area. She spent my money like it was going out of style. If she hadn't been such a big player, I would have had more than enough to bail all of us out. From what Lyla said, I gather that she was somewhat of a spoiled bitch."

"And for that, you left her to rot in the Tijuana jail! Mr. Penelton, you obviously have an independent income beyond your Navy pay. On a Commander's pay, not even I can afford both a Cadillac and to support my family. Why didn't you have the decency to seek her release after you got back?"

"Well, there wasn't time. We barely made it back before the ship got underway. We left a note about her in the apartment in Imperial Beach. We had just met that night before we were arrested. And I never got her home phone number. I called the Imperial Beach number after we tied up, but no one answered. I figured she had to be out by the time we got back. Commander, she was my date and I more or less forgot." He looked down at his shoes. "I guess I owe her an apology."

Longstreet gripped his cigar so tightly that the stogie bent. "Damn, boy! Owe her an apology, hell yes! She was fired from her job as a schoolteacher! Obviously by your replies, you are unaware that her father has the Captain's ear. Captain Ole Nuslund and Captain Slaxman commanded submarines in the same squadron during the war. Need I describe the pain her parents suffered for over two weeks while she was missing? And her humiliation to be forgotten in the Tijuana jail with God only knows what riffraff?"

He gathered up the letter and the thermofax copies and aligned their edges carefully before placing them in a folder, which he carelessly tossed into a box marked "OUT." He reached for the fat files in Carter Sawyer's hands and flipped through the pages. He went through them a second time, then said, "Where the hell is the stuff on Xylos from Kane's party?"

Carter replied, "He wasn't arrested."

The XO rose from his chair and leaned across the desk. He blew smoke in Joe's face. "He wasn't arrested? And why not? What did you do, Mr. Xylos, hide in a closet until the coast was clear? Or did you sneak out the back door just one step ahead of the cops?"

Milt Kane pointed at Joe. "He wasn't there. He left with one of the girls and went out on the beach. He was the only smart one Friday night."

"What were you doing, Mr. Xylos? Screwing out on the beach while your shipmates were being arrested?"

Joe's face colored. His mouth moved slightly, but he didn't say a word.

Carter Sawyer drawled, "Commander, like I told you, Ensign Xylos wasn't arrested either time. In fact, he used his own money both times to help get people out of jail. If ever I got in trouble, I'd like to have a shipmate like him around."

Longstreet snapped, "Sawyer, I figured you'd say something like that. After all, you live with him."

Lieutenant Kane countered, "Frankly, I don't even know why Joe is here unless you're looking for him as a witness against us. Don't step on him like he's a cockroach. Commander, he's one of the few good Ensigns you've got."

"Not according to Lieutenant Leach. And not according to Agent Jawrulski."

Joe wrinkled his brow as he asked, "Agent Jawrulski? Never heard of him."

"U.S. Border Patrol at the crossing on U.S. 101."

"Oh, him! The feeling is mutual. That guy has to use an enema nozzle as a cigarette holder. If he hadn't held us up at the border and torn Cy's car up, Terry Nasmon might not have been left to rot. We told him she was there. Obviously he didn't do a thing either."

"It's Tamara Nuslund, mister. He reported you to the Navy for impersonating a naval officer, along with voicing suspicions that you either use or are involved in smuggling marijuana."

"Marijuana? That guy is a petty tyrant. He's sore because I was selling tacos to the people waiting to cross the border. I think he expected me to give him a taco. If the way he treated me is the same way he treats Mexicans, the good neighbor policy ended when they hired him. Let me ask you, Commander, would you go back to a place where they try to pin crimes on you that you didn't commit? And hold you up while they tear your car apart? I'm sorry about what happened to the Captain's daughter, but you couldn't get me to go through that border again for all the tacos in Mexico."

Cy chimed in, "Damn right! I had to have over fifty dollars' work done to fix the front seats and straighten some of the trim. And after that shakedown in Mexico, Dad won't be going on location down there without some ironclad guarantees. That's what he said."

Milt Kane pointed to the folder in the XO's hand as he rolled his lips back from his teeth in a pained smile. "Commander, that problem in Belmont Shore was all my doing. I threw the party. I rounded up the duty-free booze. I invited the neighborhood. It was my stereo and I was the one who turned it up. Give Cy a break. Just because he lent me his sound effects records, that doesn't mean he should be responsible for the way I played them."

The XO said, "Bull! He was in the apartment with you when the law arrived."

"Commander, I never dreamed I had built such a powerful system. When those cops got me down to the station and told me about all the reports they'd received, I guess I shouldn't have laughed so hard and so long. But what the hell, I created my own little "war of the worlds" right there in Belmont Shore. Hell, I even laughed when I read the story in the L.A. paper Sunday. Sober and in the light of another day, I can understand the trouble I caused. And I will accept whatever the Old Man dishes out."

Kane pointed first to Joe and then to Cy. "Like I said, it would be totally unfair to either of them—especially Xylos. He has grown into one outstanding snipe."

Longstreet squashed his cigar out in the nearby ashtray. He studied the report for some time, looked up, cleared his throat, and spoke in a very flat voice, "Very well, gentlemen—and I use the term advisedly—I'll convey your sentiments to the Commanding Officer . . . along with my report. You, Mr. Cyrus Penelton, of course, are at the head of the line here today. I want to hear from each of my bad baker's dozen. Don't any of you even think of requesting shore leave until after you've met with the Commanding Officer."

⟶▬◉ ◉▬⟵

Joe waited with his twelve shipmates until Thursday, when they were singly called to the Commanding Officer's in-port cabin. The seven who had been arrested but not charged received letters of reprimand. Cy Penelton and Milt Kane were given three weeks "in hack," confinement to quarters. Both were declared charter members of the "Sundowner's Club" (Captain Sam's designation), whose members would not be granted shore leave that extended beyond daylight until the following May when the deployment would end. Since Lieutenant Kane was leaving the ship for discharge on arrival in Australia and Lieutenant (junior grade) Penelton was leaving in January, the action was partly symbolic. However, it certainly sent a message to the enlisted "liberty risks."

Doc Johnson got off without a penalty, but the Old Man chewed him verbally for not making sure Tammy Nuslund had been freed and for letting himself get into trouble in a foreign country.

Early Friday afternoon, Carter Sawyer opened the cabin door and summoned Ensign Xylos. Joe entered with his stomach pressing against his throat and palms so sweaty he could barely grip the brass doorknob. Lawyer Sawyer stood to one side with a copy of the Uniform Code of Military Justice tucked under one arm and fat manila folders in his hand.

After the preliminaries, Captain Slaxman leaned back in his chair. "Mr. Xylos, twelve officers pleaded your case yesterday. The Chief Engineer even wrote me a memo, which is something he seldom does." The Captain held up a sheet of lined pad paper upon which was scrawled, *No man should be punished for being a good shipmate.* He folded the sheet and placed it in Joe's file. Joe watched the Old Man pull a single cigarette out of a pack, tap it on his desk, and put the end in his mouth. After he lit it and drew in a lungful of smoke, he began speaking as smoke floated out of his mouth, "I find that at no time was your conduct in violation of the Uniform Code of Military Justice."

"Thank you, Captain."

"After I talked to Miss Nuslund on the phone last night, I confirmed that I had been operating on a false premise. When she returned, her father reported that yours was the only name she mentioned for the first two days. Logically, he concluded that you were with Tammy and had thoughtlessly left her behind. However, she couldn't even describe you, other than you're short and slept all the way to Tijuana. In the end, her only accusation was that you couldn't have put together $750 honestly in one weekend selling tacos. She still believes you must have been a pimp or involved in some illegal activity."

"I didn't come up with the full amount, Captain. Cy—Mr. Penelton— and Doc—Mr. Johnson—supplied the rest."

"I know, I know, but why did you choose to go into the taco business?"

Joe rubbed the back of his neck and inhaled deeply. "Well, Captain, I had no date, and I don't like whores. Cy bought the wagon, and what else was there to do? I was committed at that point. And after I got started, it was fun."

"Fun? Charging a dollar for a two-bit taco?"

"I didn't know how much to charge. I had never even eaten a taco, let alone made one. I didn't even know what a peso was worth. I figured people would complain if it was too much. Their culture expects that there will be bargaining before arriving at a price. There's a challenge to matching wits, and I like being tested. Whatever the price, they got their money's worth."

"How can you justify that?"

"Captain, you drive a prewar coupe and Cy, a Cadillac. Both are cars, transportation, isn't that correct, sir?"

"Well, yes, but what has that got to do with tacos?"

"Yours is worth maybe five hundred and his, eight to ten thousand?"

"Yes."

"And both will take you from point A to B?"

"And?"

"Captain, one man is happy with an inexpensive car and the other has to have all the chrome and comfort he can find. Well, sir, the gringo tourists got the fattest tacos on the street from somebody who spoke their language. They got free jokes and respect. If my tacos cost too much, there were plenty of other wagons to buy from."

"And you made more in one weekend, I hear, selling tacos than you do in a month as an Ensign?"

"Yes, sir. I didn't sleep much, either."

"I'll bet you didn't. Mr. Xylos, Commander Longstreet urged me to burn your ears. He feels that working as a street vendor is beneath the dignity of a commissioned officer. He senses that something is wrong when anyone is so close to these tar spills but doesn't even get splashed."

"I beg your pardon, sir. Not being able to go ashore since Saturday, I do feel well splashed."

The Captain laughed. "If you had sold tacos in uniform or used your rank to effect the sale, that would be misconduct. But, as Mr. Sawyer pointed out, you acted in such a convincing way that the Border Patrol wouldn't accept your identification as a naval officer when you crossed the border. It would certainly not be my choice of the way to spend a Labor Day weekend. It speaks loudly about the extent to which junior officers are underpaid that you can earn more from a taco wagon in a weekend than you can in a month as an Ensign. You say that you like being tested, Mr. Xylos. Well, I hope you find more productive ways to direct your considerable energy. I don't ever want to see you under these circumstances again."

"Thank you, Captain. You won't."

He stood and reached for Joe's right hand. As he shook it, he said, "You've got the kind of grit I like to see in a young officer. Be careful in what you do ashore."

"Aye, aye, sir."

When they were almost all the way back to their stateroom, Carter broke the silence, drawling, "Joe, I don't know how you do it, boy. Last Friday night, I thought he was ready to keelhaul you. But after he held mast on the playboys, he started coming around. Like he said, every one of them stuck up for you, especially Milt Kane and Cy Penelton. This morning, it was the XO who was ready to hang you, but it was Captain Sam who defended you. About the XO—be advised, he has little use for you. I would suggest you keep a very low profile."

"Thanks, Carter. I will."

Joe and Carter were surprised to find the Chaplain pacing up and down just inside the door to Boys' Town. His brow was furrowed and his hands made jerky moves as he focused on the two. "Carter! Am I glad to see you. Commander Longstreet suggested I talk to you. I don't know what to do. I'm in a mess."

The Legal Officer put a hand on the older man's shoulder. "Well, Father, I've always wondered what a preacher does when he needs somebody to talk to. Like everybody else, he finds a lawyer. But you know, I'm not the one most people on this vessel confess to."

"No, this is serious. My car was just stolen from the lot at the fleet landing while I was out at a meeting on the *Toledo*."

"You mean that pretty yellow Chrysler Imperial you inherited from your dad?

"Yes. And if it were just stolen, I'd leave it in the Lord's hands and let it all be settled on Judgment Day. But I can't, because I sold the car and bought another."

"Now why would you sell that beautiful Imperial? It's as good as new."

"Carter, Joe, I'm a priest, a Jesuit. I took a vow of poverty when I entered the priesthood. And driving that ostentatious luxury car was coming between me and God."

"But Father, why would you trade it in right before a deployment?"

He looked down at the deck between his shoes and answered in a wavering voice, "I sinned. I was taken in by this world's greed. I had planned to sell the car and then on our return buy something more modest. I went out to J.J. Carruthers, the Chrysler dealer who advertises on television, with the idea of selling it to them. The salesman offered me a deal that just seemed too good to be true. He offered me four thousand five hundred dollars for it, if I bought their last 1956 Plymouth Belvedere for two thousand dollars. That was better by eight hundred dollars than the best cash offer I had. Of course I accepted."

Carter half-smiled, "You went out there yesterday to pick up the new car. After you signed over the Imperial to them and gave them the keys, a mechanic came in and said that when they were prepping the new Plymouth, they found some sort of problem that would take until the next day to fix. The salesman then handed you the keys to your old car and said to come back the next day."

"Yes! How did you know?"

Pulling his ear, Carter said, "You're not the first one on the *Beaverton* to have a problem of this sort. Chief Dilpikil in Fox Division had the same thing happen to him. Let me guess what happened next . . . Good old J.J. said that without the trade-in, he'd fix you up with a nice installment plan over the next twenty-four months. You bought the car and he is going to deliver."

"Well, yes. They were awfully nice about it. He even offered free storage while we're deployed."

"Think back a minute. When you were making arrangements about picking up the new car, did you mention where you'd be keeping the old car?"

"Why, yes. I told them I'd drive out in the early afternoon after the conference. Carter, you don't think they could have . . .? That's a Big Three dealer!"

"I've talked to the L.A. County District Attorney. They don't know who's pulling this off, whether it's J.J. himself or one of his people, but this stunt has been pulled with enough regularity that the D.A. is anxious for it to stop."

Joe said, "There must be something we can do. Did you report it to the police?"

"To the Long Beach police."

Lawyer Sawyer opined, "That won't do much good. I can tell you now that they will be clean—or at least, so it will seem. Anyway, you'll get something from the insurance."

"It wasn't covered for theft."

Cy Penelton raised himself up from his bunk and said, "I have an idea. Paramount is shooting a new detective series on location west of Las Vegas. They're always wrecking cars. And need them on short notice. Carter, call my Dad and ask that Property call them up and buy—ah, what was it?—a yellow Chrysler Imperial to be delivered on location or somewhere nearby. Carruthers is used to high-priority orders from the studios. Like they needed it yesterday because they have to shoot a retake and people are standing around collecting overtime."

Carter snapped his fingers. "And if they deliver it in Nevada, it's interstate transportation of stolen goods. How are we going to know if they'll ship the Padre's car? And where are we going to come up with the money?"

Cy said, "Easy. The studio normally pays on a bill. Ask them to offer to pay on a voucher on delivery. That will require the sellers to furnish serials and full ID. Carter, all you have to do is take delivery and the whole thing is wrapped up."

"Not me! They know my face from when the Chief's car was stolen."

All eyes turned to Joe, who held up two open hands. "Wait a minute! I've just returned from wading in the river Styx. And only minutes ago, I promised the Captain I would stay away from trouble. I enjoy my freedom and more importantly, I don't want to further reduce my chances of going to Submarine School."

Father Finn laid a hand on his round shoulder. "Joe, of all the officers on this ship, I think you would best fill this role. You have a presence that's believable. You've been in show business and would arouse the least attention. If I clear it with both the Captain and the XO, would you do it?"

"Well, okay. Why can't the Paramount people sign for it?"

Cy said, "I can't visualize anybody at Paramount going out on a limb for such a scheme. It'll be up to you, Joe."

"And what if they bring the wrong car?"

"You'll know in advance from the numbers they give you. It's just a matter of checking the numbers. If it's a different car, call the thing off; say that it's the wrong color or the director decided not to use the scene. You've got balls . . . Fake it."

Joe held up his hand. "Wait! This thing is full of holes! These guys will be expecting a check. If Paramount won't send a body, they won't send money either. What am I supposed to do? Jump in the car and execute one of those made-for-TV chase scenes? We've got to be better prepared than that."

"I can't believe my ears. This is the man who sold dollar tacos and you're worried about a little play-acting. Look, Joe, when they ask for the money, sign for the car. Tell them the studio will send a check to J.J."

"Yeah, but what if the dealership isn't involved? I wouldn't sell a hot car on credit."

"Well, ask my Dad. Maybe he can get them to issue a check. After all, they can put a stop payment order on it."

Carter noted, "The FBI and the U.S. Marshal's Office have an interest in this case already, because I convinced them that these cars had to be moved out of the area to be sold. Let me see what I can do."

Father Finn said, "Carter, how do you know so much about this sort of thing?"

"Well, Padre, before I answered my nation's call to arms, I used to go after crooks for a living. It's nice to keep my hand in the trade, if you know what I mean."

⋯⊷⊶⋯

Saturday afternoon late, Joe wheeled Cy's pink Cadillac convertible into the parking lot of the small combination gas station and restaurant at Jean, Nevada. With him was Paul Mellon, a federal marshal, who sat with a long filter-tip cigarette resting on his thin lips. His skin was wrinkled and dry as old saddle leather. They had taken a detour via Wilson Pass and arrived from the north. The road had been rough and the pink sides of the car faded into the browns of the dust that marked their journey.

As they pulled in, a pair of men were hunkered around the rear license plate of the yellow Chrysler Imperial. Fixed in the bracket was a New York plate. As they stood up, the shorter of the two, a lean acne-faced man in his mid-twenties, looked at them with wide, surprised eyes. He held California dealer's plates in his hand.

Joe said, "Mr. Flint? I'm Joe Xylos of Paramount."

The man shifted the plates to his left hand and shook Joe's hand. "I'm Lee Flint. This here is Raul Lopez. You must be desperate to pay $6,000 for a used Imperial just to wreck it."

"I don't make the money decisions. They screwed up my weekend.

I had to hand-carry the damn check out here. I don't know why your company couldn't bill us. We're good for it."

"Hey, you tell us you're going to buy a car to wreck it and then send us a check! What if you don't follow through? It's not like we could repo the car. The cost of going through the courts would exceed our margin."

"We use lots of cars. And I mean lots. Maybe we can work something out for the next time. Here, lift the hood. We've got to check the numbers against the paperwork."

Lopez pointed into the shadows beneath the hood. "These are the same ones we gave you over the phone. You're lucky you called when you did. We were ready to sell it to a dealer in Phoenix."

Joe handed the paperwork to Mellon, saying, "Here, you check the numbers against the invoice."

Mellon put a finger beneath each digit as if he had difficulty reading them. Once he was done, he asked, "I winter in Phoenix. Who do you wholesale to?"

"Van Pappen Motors. We usually sell through their auction."

"Aren't they the guys west of town on the road to Yuma?"

"Maybe. It's on the west side."

Mellon tugged on the fan belt and touched the distributor wires, then said, "Okay, start her up. I want to see how she sounds."

Flint said, "It drives okay. Take my word, it's got years of life left in that engine."

"Look, I gotta drive this damn thing! And the reason we're doing the retake is that the last piece of Mr. Chrysler's iron broke up before we got to the end of the road. It may have years left driving grandpa to the golf club, but it could blow up before I get it over a hundred."

As Flint slid behind the wheel, he said, "Chrysler makes damn good cars. Especially at the top of the line."

As soon as the engine dropped to an even idle, Joe said, "For crying out loud, Paul! Do we accept it or not? You know there'll be hell to pay. The whole cast is stuck out there on time and a half, and you're acting like you're going to drive it a hundred thousand miles. If this picture goes over budget because of you, they'll be looking for a new driver."

Mellon said, "Xylos, you are a royal pain. Give him the check."

Lopez spoke with a slight accent. "So you like big, heavy cars? We can provide anything you want."

"I like what the script calls for me to drive."

Joe said to Mellon, "Say, buddy, you've got to take care of the custody stuff before I turn over the check. You're the one who has to run this beast through the system."

As Mellon was signing the documents, the pimply-faced man said, "You're right, that guy is a royal pain. He didn't even introduce you. I'm Lee Flint."

"I'm Paul Mellon, head stunt driver. Yeah, Mr. Smart Ass there from corporate . . . I think his father owns part of the studio." The masquerading marshal gave Joe a thumbs-up sign. "Mr. Xylos, you can give the man the check."

As the two men from the dealership focused on the check, the marshal drew his gun and announced, "I want the two of you to face the car and put your hands on the fender. I'm United States Marshal Paul Mellon. You're under arrest for the interstate transportation of stolen property."

Lopez shook his hands up in the air. "Lee, I told you this was too good to be true. I felt it in my bones. I told you it was a setup."

"Fuck you."

The two men had hardly been handcuffed when a sheriff's car pulled up and the driver leaned out. "Paul, so these are the two. How did it go?"

"According to script. And an Oscar performance by Mr. Xylos of the United States Navy. I think he's missed his calling. He ought to be in the movies."

CHAPTER 8

Harry's Follies

Mid-October came and went. Talk in the wardroom concentrated on the recent Miss Universe contest. The Belmont Shore bachelors, whom Lieutenant Harry Leach left out of the festivities, mostly sat with arms folded across their chests and scowled as Leach held court. He bragged about the beauty of the contestants and basked in his new-found popularity, both on the *Beaverton* and ashore.

Leach was the talk of the ship. Depending on your point of view, he was either a heel or a slick operator, or both. Early in the contest, he began going with Miss Finland, whose Scandinavian beauty had turned most heads. For reasons only the judges knew, she was eliminated in the early rounds.

Through ruses, Leach concealed his dallying from his wife. First, he told her he had been sent to a three-day school in San Diego. When he went on leave, he told her the ship was getting underway for a pre-deployment shakedown cruise. Then, with leave papers in hand, he disappeared in Cy Penelton's Cadillac with the Finnish beauty at his side.

Meanwhile, events on the far side of the world overtook everyone's plans. The Hungarian Revolution began on 26 October. Knots of officers bunched around the newly installed wardroom television at every news broadcast.

Thanks to the burgeoning international crisis, the arrest of J.J. Carruthers and seven of his employees, along with the revelation of his unique car theft and fraud ring that had preyed on more than one hundred car buyers over a three-year period, was hardly noticed in the media.

⊷⊷ ◉═⊷

Deployment date was moved from 6 November to 2 November. The day after the invasion began, a Saturday, the *Beaverton* moved to an explosives anchorage where ammunition for the trip was loaded. With all of the Gunnery Department involved in the loading, Joe and Inside White were assigned the first quarterdeck watch.

Late that morning, an officer's motorboat arrived with Leah Leach standing in the back. Her first words on stepping aboard were, "Tell Harry I'm here. I want to talk to him . . . now!"

Joe said, "Mrs. Leach, he's not on board."

"Of course he is. They don't move the ship without him. He's the Special Sea Detail OOD."

Larry announced, "Mr. Xylos is correct, ma'am. He's ashore."

She folded her well-fleshed arms beneath her ample bosom. "Then I want an escort to the wardroom. I will await his return from his business ashore."

"Mrs. Leach, Leah," stammered Joe, "I don't think that would be appropriate. Lieutenant Leach is on leave."

"He can't be. He told me—Oh, that two-timing, lying SOB. He's off with one of those . . . those . . . Isn't he?"

Joe grimaced. "I'm sorry, Mrs. Leach. I don't know where your husband is or what he's doing."

Tilting her head slightly toward the rail, she asked, "When is that boat going back to the beach?"

"In about twenty minutes. Would you care to go down to the wardroom for a cup of coffee? We'll make sure you're called."

Dabbing her eye with the back of her hand, she took a step toward the door leading off the quarterdeck and then froze. Almost mumbling, she said, "No. No, I'd rather stay here. I'd be too embarrassed sitting there with everyone looking at me and knowing that they know. How could he do this to me right before a cruise?"

⋯━◉ ◉━⋯

Harry Leach returned from leave on Monday the 29th, concurrent with the news that Israel had invaded Egypt. The ship, which had seemed to swarm with yard workers before, was awash with them and the din of their tools around the clock. Deployment date was moved to the afternoon of 31 October.

Late that afternoon, although the band played and the flags snapped in a fresh breeze, the wives and children standing on the pier, as well as many of those aboard, were somber as the *Beaverton* backed clear of her berth at the shipyard. The cause of the tension was the news reports saying that President Eisenhower opposed the invasion of Suez by French and British forces. The *Beaverton* could be sailing directly into harm's way.

Although no word was passed as to any change of schedule, the potential for involvement was made clear when the cruiser returned to the explosives anchorage, where lighters retrieved the ammunition so recently put aboard and new rounds were loaded through the night. No liberty was allowed, and the only boat runs allowed were to go to the fleet landing to pick up some forty enlisted men who had missed the move from the shipyard to the anchorage.

Before the first rays of sun on 30 October heated the smog and lifted the shroud from the harbor, the *Beaverton* and the other ships of Cruiser Division Nine, plus their destroyer escorts, slipped away. Final repairs and testing of Number Three boiler were completed by the end of the next day by a small cadre of shipyard workers who had remained aboard and would go ashore in Hawaii.

A brief note in the plan of the day stated that the *Beaverton*'s visit to Melbourne and the Olympics was contingent on events along the Suez Canal. No word was passed as to where she would be headed, but a change of plans was rumored because of the ammunition reload. The rumors were confirmed when Harry Leach made the careless comment that the magazines were full of shore bombardment ammunition.

The trip to Pearl Harbor, Hawaii, was filled with drills and hours of exercises at General Quarters. The *Beaverton* passed Buoy PH, "Papa Hotel," two nautical miles from Pearl, during the early hours of the morning watch on 4 November; and workers from the Pearl shipyard were streaming aboard that afternoon, even before the sea detail was secured.

Like all the other engineers, Joe worked straight through until early evening, when his boss Milt Kane told him to go ashore for one last liberty because they would be getting underway the next morning. Earlier in the day, he had been topside long enough to see a dark gray submarine pass by en route to the submarine base across the harbor. This gave him an idea for how to spend his liberty.

Thus early the next morning at breakfast, where the others bragged of their evening exploits at Waikiki Beach, Joe reported that he'd spent until almost midnight aboard the USS *Bocaccio,* SS 223, keeping the duty officer company during a battery charge. He explained that the sub was an old "thin skin" boat that had been fitted specially with a large passive sonar array in its bow and was essentially a killer submarine that hunted other subs. He told of a very relaxed atmosphere and a quarterdeck manned by a young seaman.

Harry Leach, who sat at the next table, turned around and bellowed, "I think you could find a home in the underwater Navy. After all, you are already a sub mariner, aren't you, Zilch?"

Joe said, "They call themselves submaREENers, emphasis on the third syllable. Lieutenant, I'd like to join your team for the upcoming wardroom election."

"My team?"

"Yes, sir, there is a grass-roots movement to elect you to the exalted office of Mess Caterer. I'd like to sign on as your campaign manager. I'm sure that working together, we could put you over the top."

"Thank you, Mr. Xylos, but I'm not interested in pursuing the position."

"Think of the prestige it would bring to the wardroom when we entertain the Australians to have you—the . . . sixth . . . most . . . senior . . . lieutenant . . . in the Navy—at the helm."

Harry's face reddened. "You need not remind me of this. And I've heard about you talking to the Jay Ohs, asking them to vote for me. They're not dumb. They know that if I'm Caterer, I'll make frequent inspections to assure that they keep their rooms in top shape."

"Splendid, we're all for having Officer's Country set the standard for cleanliness throughout the ship, sir. This is my first election. Would it be appropriate to mimeograph some campaign literature? Perhaps some catchy phrase like, 'Leach Leads the Way.' I'm sure everyone would vote for you if they knew what high standards you have."

"Zilch! I don't want the damn job. Stop bugging me."

"Lieutenant, like all great leaders, you are indeed humble. And like them, I know that if called, you will serve with pride. Wasn't it General Grant, later President of the United States, who said, `Although I have been in two wars, I never entered the army without regret, and never left it without pleasure?'"

Leach coughed, then pushed his coffee cup away, stood, and squinted his eyes before marching heavily out of the room.

Carter Sawyer asked, in a heavier-than-usual Southern accent, "Wheah the hayell did yew get that quote?"

"From the Dale Carnegie book on Lincoln in the wardroom library. See, I didn't waste the week we waited to see the Old Man."

"Joe, you lucked out the last time, boy. But this is different. Friend, you are the only Jay Oh in the wardroom that baits Harry. What you did just now was equivalent to poking an angry bear with a stick. What do you hope to gain from it anyway?"

"Actually I think Harry was touched by the comparison to Grant. What do I hope to gain? Begrudging respect. He never has missed an opportunity to take a cheap shot since the minute he laid his eyes on me. Getting him elected Caterer ought to be a piece of cake."

"How?"

"Simple mathematics. There are more Ensigns and Jay Gees than all the other ranks. If we vote as a bloc, we control the mess. Carter, has Cy talked to you about getting a proxy?"

"Oh, sure. The trouble with Harry is that he's been nominated but never elected."

Joe smiled. "And Harry Leach never had Joe Xylos running his campaign before. Nor has he had thirteen eager campaign workers in the past."

"Then that's what all this talking and meeting is about. Cy kept saying that if I went along, there would be a guarantee that none of us will be Treasurer either. He said the choice is between Sean Perkins, Third Division, and the First Lieutenant, George Speed. I thought we were going to protect our own."

"Sean won't join. And I think it will be easier for Milt Kane to convince some of his table to support him. Sean is a good man, and I'm not sure I can hold everyone together, proxies or no."

"Joe, the XO said I've got to be Parliamentarian. And I don't know beans about it."

"Don't worry. Just look up the answers in that book he gave you."

"I have a feeling that lunch today is going to be long remembered. Where does it say you can have proxies?"

"Look up Article Six and then go to the commentary in the back. There is a section that speaks to important matters such as elections."

Lawyer Sawyer thumbed through the pages. "Well, yes, here it is. Joe Xylos, you're always full of surprises. And when did you become an expert? Another day's reading while waiting to see the Captain?"

"Not quite. I've acted as parliamentarian at meetings in college. Once I was even paid ten bucks."

"Does the XO know this?"

"No. And let's not tell him just yet, either. Okay?"

Carter scratched his head. "I suppose he ought to know, but there won't be much chance to talk before lunch because he's going to be tied up in a meeting with the Admiral's staff all morning after sea detail."

⊷∙━◉ ◉━∙⊶

Joe returned to Boys' Town full of good spirits because it was the first time he had the Engineering watch since leaving port. As he moved toward the far end of the room where his bunk was, he saw the back of a new man, which all but filled the space between the bunks like a door. Piled on the only open bunk in Boys' Town were a pair of jungle-green suit bags and a large leather briefcase. As the man turned, his silver Lieutenant's bars, known as "railroad tracks," flashed. In silhouette, Joe's first impression was of an uncommonly handsome man who looked like he had stepped out of a recruiting poster. He had the build of a football lineman and biceps that bulged in his shirt as he moved a suit bag around.

On hearing the Ensign say, "Good morning, sir. Are you sure this will be your stateroom? This is the Jay Oh bunkroom," the big man turned to face him and put on a pair of wire-rimmed glasses.

Focusing his blue eyes on Joe, he said in a New England accent, "When you come aboard just as they remove the gangplank, you can't be too choosy. I turned down the last room because I have no desire to spend this cruise with 'Roman Candle.' My name is Francois Villerouge. My friends call me Frenchy."

Joe was a bit startled by the big man's pure French name, which didn't seem to go with the accent. He extended his hand and tried not to wince as it was squeezed in a huge paw.

"I'm Ensign Xylos, Joe Xylos, sir."

"Pleased to meet you, Joe. In here, please call me Frenchy. Now which of these lockers are mine?"

"The left one, those drawers, and the after drawer under the bed. There's more space in the hanging closet in the central area. Out of curiosity, who is Roman Candle?'

"You have a Lieutenant on board who used to command an LSMR. That's a Landing Ship Medium Rocket. That was their call sign. Let's say that the acquaintance wasn't pleasant."

"Lieutenant Harry Leach, right?"

"I'd rather leave it at that."

"Have you joined the mess yet?

"No."

"Ensign Swenson, down at that desk there, is the Mess Treasurer and can sign you up. If you pay now, you can vote in the election at lunch."

Shrugging his shoulders, Frenchy replied, "That's okay. I don't know anyone."

"Yes, you do. We're supporting Leach for Caterer. And we want your vote."

Frenchy rubbed his jaw, squeezing the dimple into prominence. "You know, I don't have a grudge against the man. I just don't want the displeasure of associating with him any more than I have to."

Joe held up his stack of proxies. "That's okay. I have more than enough votes here to go over the top. It's just that I would like to give Harry a true mandate."

"Proxies? I've never heard of a wardroom election with proxies. What are you up to?"

Joe smiled. "Make Lieutenant Leach the Mess Caterer."

"Is he campaigning for the job?"

"No. But I am . . . on his behalf."

"Are you nuts?"

"Slightly crazy, perhaps."

"There's an old saying that you can't piss up a rope. Leach can make life interesting for you."

"I don't know what more he can do. I'm scheduled for duty the first day in port for most of the cruise and seem to be the first one called as Boat Officer whenever it starts getting foggy. He has selected me to supervise so many working parties that he has to get clearance from the Chief Engineer to use me. He hardly misses an opportunity to pass along another uncalled-for insult. Even if by some chance he doesn't win, today is this dog's day."

Following lunch, the stewards rolled in a blackboard on wheels and parked it next to the bulkhead behind the head table. Commander Longstreet rose from his seat and lit a fresh cigar. As the first cloud of smoke swirled over the head table in the center of the wardroom, he bellowed, "All right, gentlemen, may I have your attention? Let's get on with the election of a Mess Caterer and Mess Treasurer. Anybody got any nominations for Mess Caterer?"

A voice on the far side of the room said, "Lieutenant Barry Tumwater."

"Outside White," came another.

There was a pause and the XO said, "Anybody else?"

Joe rose. "Mr. Chairman, I would like—"

"Boy, if you're going to talk to me, I'm the President of this here mess."

"I beg your pardon, sir, but under Robert's Rule of Order, the individual presiding over a meeting is the chairman unless it is a religious assembly, at which time he would be called 'moderator.'"

"Xylos!"

There was a ripple of subdued laughter.

"In the absence of any bylaws to the contrary, I will bow to wishes of the chair. Mr. President, it is a great honor for me today to place into nomination the name of an officer who is known by us all to have an experienced palate, as is so amply evidenced by a waist of epicurean diameter. A man, who with every step he takes, carries with him evidence of more capacity for consumption than most active-duty officers. A man bound to lift the morale of every cook because there never has been a dish placed before him that he didn't consume. A man of considerable stature, both vertically and horizontally. A man whose frequent presence in the wardroom will exemplify that old Southern adage that 'The finest fertilizer is the master's footprint upon the sod' . . . to bring to reality his promise to make the wardroom and Officer's Country the place where the highest standards exist . . . to serve as an example to all aboard the *Beaverton*. It is a great honor to place into nomination . . . Lieutenant . . . Harry . . . Leach . . . The sixth most senior Lieutenant in the United States Navy!"

His voice rising above what was now sustained laughter, Leach turned around in his chair, raised his beefy arm, and extended his index finger like a drawn pistol. "Zilch! I have a long memory. And I shall never forget this!"

Milt Kane, who was still applauding, volunteered, "Harry, that's the most accurate description of you I've ever heard. And you've got my vote."

The candidate gulped almost half a cup of coffee as the nominations were closed and the XO called for the vote.

Joe rose again. "Point of order, Mr. President."

"See here, Mr. Xylos, I am in the midst of voting and this is no time for silly games."

"I beg your pardon, sir, but Article Six allows the appointment of tellers, typically two, one from each side. Since we are having an election, such a procedure would remove the President from a position where partisanship could be implied."

Turning to the ship's Legal Officer and newly minted Parliamentarian, Lawyer Sawyer, who was noisily turning the pages of his book, Longstreet snapped, "What the hell is he talking about? We never had tellers before."

Carter studied the book for a long pause and finally said, "XO, it's here in the book like he said."

"Fine, fine, I say . . ."

Joe, who was still standing, said, "Mr. President, may I recommend that the outgoing Mess Caterer and Treasurer act as tellers today?"

"Mr. Xylos, you're just full of good advice. Certainly! Certainly, anything to get this farce over with and stop this infernal wasting of time."

The two officers rose as Joe nodded his head, and stepped to the sides of the room. The XO called, "All those in favor of Lieutenant Barry Tumwater."

There were twenty-six votes, mostly from the head table.

"For Outside White."

There were eight votes.

"For Lieutenant Harry Leach."

Five hands went up, and Joe stood with his hand raised. "Mr. President, acting on the proxies of all Ensigns and Lieutenants Junior Grade, and under the unit voting rule, I hereby place in the hands of the tellers thirty-seven votes for Lieutenant Harry Leach . . . our next Mess Caterer."

Leach bounced to his feet, sending his chair over backward. "He can't do that!"

The XO turned to Carter, whose nose was down as he searched the pages.

Joe smiled as he raised his hand with the index finger extended. "Point of order, sir."

Leach bellowed, "You shut up!"

"Mr. Leach," said Joe calmly, "a call for a point of order is a privileged motion and must be heard."

Leach shook his fist at Joe. "I've had enough of your insubordination."

Carter said, "XO, he's right. A point of order is a privileged motion."

The XO nodded toward Joe while pointing his cigar at the fat Lieutenant. "Leach, shut your mouth and sit down! Make your point, Mr. Xylos."

"Mr. President, in furthering your desire to complete this balloting in an expeditious manner, I would suggest that the chair consider that since there are no bylaws that prohibit it, and that the use of proxies is mentioned in the commentary that supplements the rules, I would beg that you consider that whenever we hold an election, someone is going to be missing because watches must be stood . . . and that the use of proxies would avoid unintentional disenfranchisement of any member of this mess. The alternative, of course, is to have another showing of hands. In light of the broad lead enjoyed by Lieutenant Leach, such an exercise may mollify the candidate, but the outcome would be unchanged."

The XO pointed toward Leach and said, "You're it, Lieutenant. And don't say another word. Now who's going to be Mess Treasurer?"

A voice at the Ensigns' table said, "I nominate Mr. Sean Perkins."

Commander Wyman leaned back and said to Leach, "I'll nominate Xylos, if you want."

"No! No! I have enough on me without having him directly under my feet."

The wardroom fell silent except for the sounds of the ship and chatter from the galley. The XO stood and stared at the chalkboard, burning his cigar down by half, before he closed the nominations. He accepted Joe's motion to cast a unanimous vote for Mr. Sean Perkins as Treasurer.

With the voting completed, the meeting was adjourned. Many of the victorious junior officers crowded around Joe, slapping him on the back or shaking his hand. Smiling and feeling good about his victory, Joe returned to Boys' Town.

Frenchy came in and drew him aside. "That was quite a performance you put on, mister. I've been riding ships for more years than I care to remember, and this is the first time I've ever seen such a show. There was one fatal flaw to your plan."

"What was that?"

"You made the XO look like a fool. And you may hold the field after today's skirmish, but you've all but guaranteed the loss of the war."

"Do you think so?"

"Hell, yes! Where did you learn all this stuff about parliamentary procedure?"

"I'm a registered parliamentarian. I took a course on it at Colorado University and passed the test."

"I don't regret voting with you. That was the smoothest railroad I have ever seen. That it was put together by one Ensign makes it almost frightening."

"Frightening? I didn't intimidate anyone. The votes were freely given. To change the subject, what are you doing on board? Are you getting a free ride to the Olympics?"

"If the men in the pin-striped coats succeed in their deliberations, yes. If not, I'm officer of charge of a special communications unit embarked to enhance the flagship's capability."

"And you speak French just like the guys who invaded Suez?"

He put a finger to his lips. "Yes. But we don't advertise things like that."

Just then, a steward came in and announced that the XO wanted to see Joe in his stateroom.

⊶⊷

Stan Longstreet looked up from his copy of *Robert's Rules of Order* as Joe sounded off in front his desk, "Ensign Xylos reporting as directed, sir."

He placed the book on the table. "Mr. Xylos, you nicely pulled yourself out of the hole by helping the Chaplain and next getting yourself qualified in record time as an Engineering Watch Officer Underay. Then, at my expense, you orchestrated this stunt today."

"I beg your pardon, sir. I came away with the feeling that you have a fine sense of fairness and made your decisions well within the bounds of parliamentary rules. I mean that in every way as a compliment."

"Thank you, Mr. Xylos. However, I came away from the election with the distinct feeling that you ran that meeting, not me."

"Commander, Lieutenant Villerouge said I had embarrassed you. If you feel that way, I'm sorry. I came away with a good feeling that you had done as any good chairman would. You allowed the rules to serve the will of the assembly."

"I'm not all that sure that they did."

"The majority elected Harry Leach . . . and he predestined that when he left most of the *Beaverton*'s bachelors out of the Miss Universe contest festivities."

"Except for screwing Miss Finland, Lieutenant Leach did nothing more than carry out my instructions."

"I don't believe it was your intention to have our collective noses rubbed in it."

Longstreet smiled slightly for the first time. "That's something I'm sure Harry would do. But what concerns me most is the running battle between the two of you. Ensigns don't win wars with Lieutenants."

"I agree, sir. I hope this is the end of it."

"Good, good, that's what I like to hear. Mr. Xylos, I felt that you took advantage of me today. I felt that you flummoxed me, and I didn't like it one bit. To memorize this Robert's book on parliamentary procedure just to get back at Harry Leach strikes me as being extreme."

"I am a registered parliamentarian with the American Institute. I did nothing more than fully exercise my rights as a member at a meeting. If I offended you, sir, please accept my apologies. It was not my intent."

"Certainly, apologies accepted. Now I understand. Mr. Xylos, the custom on this ship to hold elections is well established and although I have regretted some of the choices, it has worked well. The wardroom has yet to elect anyone who was an embarrassment. Harry Leach may not have too many qualities that endear him to you, but he is not incompetent. My concern is the precedent you set today. I've read enough of this book to know that we ought to have some bylaws to keep people like you from running amok. And I'm smart enough to know that I need some help. They say, 'If you can't beat 'em, join 'em.' I want to see a set of bylaws, and I want it understood that nobody will ever again hand me a stack of proxies. I want you to write these bylaws. And hereafter, I will appoint you as Parliamentarian for our wardroom meetings."

"Thank you, Commander. I would be honored. And I accept, so long as I can effectively serve in an objective and impartial manner."

"Mr. Xylos, I'm learning that when you qualify something, there is more to it than meets the eye. What would interfere with your impartiality?"

"Being nominated."

He laughed. "You are an artful dodger, sir. Go ahead and draw up your bylaws. Let's see if you can slip that one past your shipmates. I'll put them to a vote of the wardroom after I've gone over them."

When Joe returned to the wardroom, Frenchy handed him a fresh cup of coffee. "Well? Are you in hack?"

"No. But I've got to draw up a set of bylaws for the wardroom."

"A fitting punishment if I ever saw one. Old Stan is ever the Southern gentleman. Meanwhile, I've got some good news: the Suez crisis is over. The British and French agreed to a ceasefire and apparently will withdraw. Melbourne, here we come!"

CHAPTER 9

Crossing the Line

The *Beaverton*, accompanied by a squadron of destroyers, sailed south until she approached the Equator. There were two groups aboard the ships, those who had crossed the line before, called Trusty Shellbacks, and those who had not, called Lowly Pollywogs.

The ceremony to "celebrate" crew members crossing the Equator for the first time is steeped in tradition. Individuals who have crossed during earlier cruises are appointed to positions in King Neptune's Court, whose role is to conduct the initiation that lifts the newbies from the misery of being Lowly Pollywogs to the esteemed estate of Trusty Shellbacks.

The XO exerted considerable control for the purpose of making sure no one would get carried away and allow the hazing to get out of control. He essentially approved each individual appointed to King Neptune's Court, as well as the lines through which the Pollywogs had to pass.

Joe was the youngest member of the court and was asked to be the Court Jester. Among the other members was his boss Lieutenant Kane, who fed items to the Royal Prosecutor to charge people with. Part of Joe's role was to read the charges. He was surprised at the number of charges against Harry Leach.

While the court was going over the schedule with Captain Slaxman on the afternoon of the day before the crossing, one event was included that wasn't on the list approved by the XO, a "surprise" mutiny by a band of Pollywogs.

The band captured Lieutenant Leach at the end of his watch as he descended the ladder from the bridge. Initially he took the prank in fun, proclaiming that he too was a Pollywog. The young sailors, most of whom were from the Engineering Department, led the Lieutenant to the fantail, where they tied him on a wire stretcher and hoisted him high above the main deck. There he twisted slowly in the air for close to an hour until the Royal Sheriff released him and added the "mutiny" charge to be heard by King Neptune.

The next day the Pollywogs lined up and passed through a gauntlet that took them through a series of mild hazings, including a crawl through a canvas tubing partly filled with garbage, a very mild jolt in an "electric chair," a hosing-down with salt water to remove the garbage, and a final lineup in King Neptune's Court, where they had to kiss the Royal Baby. The Royal Baby was an overweight Shellback whose navel was covered with mustard; the Pollywogs had to kiss his belly. All through the gauntlet, the Polliwogs' butts were smacked with wooden paddles. The high point of the day for Joe was when he read the charges against Harry Leach to the court.

⋆⊨◉ ◉⊨⋆

Following the ceremonies, Leach came into the wardroom and poured himself a glass of iced tea. The fat Lieutenant started to sit down, but changed his mind and chose to stand next to a bulkhead. Across the room, Lieutenant Kane, between guffaws, recited again the charges that Joe had proclaimed:
"When it came time to escort the beauty queen,
Leach left out the Trusty Shellbacks so clean.
Masquerading as a Trusty Shellback, he hid so well,
That even lowly Pollywogs gave him hell.
To become Caterer he begged for every vote and won,
Hoping for power over mighty Neptune's domain when done.
Even he visualized himself as our mighty king,
When all can see he is a plebeian thing.
Always eating to emulate the Royal Baby so fat
Will guarantee him more than a gentle pat.
Leach, bloodsucker of a worm,
Now is the time to get your turn.
Hear the King's judgment and for it, your bloated bottom will burn."
As Joe listened to Kane re-read the long poem, he saw that Lieu-

tenant Leach wasn't taking it at all well. Joe took a few steps, bowed the same way he had as Court Jester, and began clapping. "Well done, Lieutenant Leach, sir, you earned your stripes today as a Trusty Shellback."

Leach turned to face Joe. "You, Zilch, Mr. Court Jester, and that jackass of a Royal Prosecutor did it all at my expense." He lightly touched his sore butt and glared. "Damn you, Kane! And that Zilch! Never have I seen an officer who painted himself like a harlequin and danced around like Puck."

The Operations Officer, one of the Shellbacks, said, "Yeah, Xylos, thought you did a bang-up job as the Royal Jester. You sure kept me laughing."

Still rubbing his wounded cheeks, Leach grumbled, "I'm not laughing about his wooden sword. I don't think I'll ever be able to sit. Why were they allowed to keep hitting me after I got stuck in the garbage chute?"

"How big around the waist are you, Harry? " asked Kane.

Patting the flesh just above his belt, Leach answered, "Forty-six . . . maybe forty-eight inches."

"The chute was cut at an even sixty inches."

"Well, it was twisted and greasy as hell. I got tangled up with that new guy on the staff. And whoever put those rotten watermelons in there didn't help either."

"Harry, you're lucky you got stuck."

"Lucky! I'm black and blue!"

Lieutenant Kane replied, "Yes, lucky, because we planned to send you through a second time."

Leach walked across the room and seized the pad on which the poem was written. He held it out to focus his somewhat farsighted vision, then said, "I'd know this handwriting anywhere. Zilch wrote this, didn't he?"

"Harry, it was all in fun. It's just a custom. Take it easy. We all contributed to it."

His chubby fingers wrapped around the page and tore it from the pad. "Leach, a blood-sucking worm! Some fun! That damn punk! You dismiss his slander to my name . . . his continual challenges to my authority . . . as being nothing. If I ran this Navy, scum like him would not be sleeping in officer's country."

Milt Kane raised his coffee cup. "Harry, we can all sleep a little better knowing that you won't ever be running the Navy . . . at least not after next June."

The chunky Lieutenant walked stiffly, wincing with every footfall as he headed for the door. He paused by Joe's chair and leaned close long enough to whisper, "I will have your ass."

⭑

The *Beaverton*, which was built during World War Two, didn't have air conditioning outside of the spaces where cooling was necessary to keep electronic equipment running. In those days there were no solid-state circuits, only heat-generating vacuum tubes. Temperatures in the Engineering spaces stayed over one hundred degrees Fahrenheit.

Propulsion for the cruiser, state of the art for that era, was the system whose details Joe learned in order to become a qualified watch officer. One detail, a major weakness of the system, was the accumulation of combustion products on the boiler water tubes, which heated water to superhigh temperatures. This accumulation had to be regularly removed by scrubbing the tubes with steam in a process called "blowing the tubes." The gunky residue collected was drawn upward, out the smokestacks, and into the atmosphere. Where it went from there depended on the relative speed of the wind. It could fall into the sea or, if it came straight down, coat the decks with filth.

In the Southern Hemisphere, the *Beaverton*'s tubes were not getting blown because the ship was set on a course and speed that were the same as the wind. Captain Slaxman chose to hold off the process rather than have the gunk expelled all over the ship. This decision prompted Lieutenant Milt Kane's soliloquy, replayed in the main control room, in the log room, and around the table in the wardroom, about the poor care given Navy ships by line officers who abused their commands and by Admirals who allowed a whole formation to wear out their boilers. His pet peeve was that Captain Slaxman, as a former diesel submarine skipper, did not, in his opinion, understand how to maintain a steamship.

Kane went on and on about the longer the time between blows, the greater the harm caused by the buildup of combustion residue, the harder it would be to remove, and the greater the amount of fuel needed to heat the oil. Upkeep periods during time alongside would necessitate the crew working around the clock when most others were on liberty. He always finished up with his declaration that he was looking forward to the day they arrived in Melbourne, when he would be discharged. He would fly out to sign on under Merchant Marine masters who treated their ship's powerplant with care and respect.

It was a pleasant surprise to Joe when Lieutenant Kane arrived in main control and relieved him half an hour early at fifteen after three in the afternoon or 1515 Navy time. Joe made the necessary entries in the log, including two requests (from Kane) to blow tubes. When Joe offered to follow up with a call to Lieutenant Leach, the OOD, Kane waved him off and said he would take care of it.

Joe was in the log room when he heard the distinct sound of steam being admitted to the pipes that, through a series of nozzles, scoured the collection of soot, ash, and combustion byproducts from the fire side of the boiler. He looked at his watch and saw it was twenty minutes of four or 1540 Navy time. That surprised him because he knew how long it would take to bring the ship to a heading where the soupy residue would fall harmlessly into the ocean.

The high-pitched sound filled the air for several minutes, then stopped, and another fire room began its routine. Within a minute of the second blow starting, the office phone rang. It was Leach, who bellowed, "Secure blowing tubes, Zilch! You were ordered by sound-powered phone and telephone to stop blowing tubes at least twenty minutes ago. You chose to ignore me! Of all the dumb stunts you could have pulled! Your timing was impeccable. I saw the Admiral running for cover. First Lieutenant Speed and just about every man in the divisions forward of amidships are after your hide. Globs of that black garbage are all over the forward half of the ship. You can hardly read the hull number atop turret Number Two."

"Sir, sir, get a hold of yourself. Calm down, yours is a simple error, you forgot I'd been relieved, and the watch here didn't divine you weren't calling me. This is the log room; are you having trouble contacting main control? What can I do?"

"Damn you, Zilch! Why aren't you in main control?"

"Lieutenant Kane relieved me early. I heard the talker use his phone to relay the relief to the bridge."

"Bullshit! The Captain wants to see the Chief Engineer in his stateroom."

⋅⊶⊷⋅

Chief Engineer Henry Moran's hands shook as if he was coming off a two-week drunk as he entered the log room and focused on Joe. "I just had a reaming the likes of which I'll long remember. The Old Man told me I have one more unauthorized blowing of tubes between me and an unsatisfactory fitness report. What could have possessed Lieutenant Kane? Every horizontal surface from the stacks forward will have to be cleaned. On top of that, he told Captain Slaxman he should stick to command of diesel-powered vessels. Yes, he's in hack and relieved of all duties. You are now the Main Engines Officer, a week or so early."

Joe leaped out of his chair and extended his right hand. "Thank you, sir. I'll put my full energy into the job."

"I have every confidence you will. Xylos, you have made a very favorable first impression. Don't be afraid of asking for help. Listen to the Chiefs and your warrant machinist.

⋅⊶⊷⋅

Joe was sitting in the wardroom reading and drinking his second tall glass of iced tea when a carbon-stained and sweat-soaked Lieutenant Leach pushed the door open hard enough that it bounced off the rubber stop on the bulkhead. "Zilch, you damn snipes really did it this time."

"Boy, you look a sight. A bit hot on the bridge, was it?

"I am the senior Lieutenant assigned to this vessel. It's 'yes, sir' and 'no, sir.' If you wish to communicate with me directly, you will use my name, ending sentences with 'yes, sir' or 'no, sir.'"

Joe continued to drink his iced tea until he finished, tilting the glass back to get the last dregs from beneath the cubes.

"Mister! I'm talking to you! Don't sit there and ignore me! You and that draftee dilettante Kane may think it was a good laugh to screw up my watch . . ."

Joe continued to look ahead as if Leach wasn't present. Leach walked around the table and leaned over it so he faced toward Joe. "You, boy!

I'm talking to you, mister! I say you've stood your last watch as Engineering watch officer for a long time. Your disrespect will be added to the list."

Joe put the glass down on the table. *How did I manage this? The fat son of a bitch is on the ropes.* He wiped his mouth with the back of his hand, then looked up. "You're right, sir. Treating one another with respect ought to be second nature. But before you make a federal case of it, consider the reaction of Captain Slaxman when I tell him you have never called me by my correct name. That's because I'm Greek and you don't think I'm good enough to eat in the same room as you do."

Joe watched the fat Lieutenant stand tall and look around the room to see who else was there before replying, "You little wise ass. Zilch, I am your senior. It's 'yes, sir' and 'no, sir.' I am Loo-ten-nant Leach to you, mister."

Joe stood up, extended his right hand, and spoke in a quiet voice. "Yes, sir, I am your junior, sir. Lieutenant Leach, give me the small courtesy of correctly calling me by my name. Or is it that you've forgotten my name already? My name is Joe Xylos, or Mr. Xylos, sir."

Harry Leach stood looking at Joe's hand for a moment, then smiled as he shook it. "You little bastard . . . Main Engines Officer, eh? You earned it, mister. Good luck with your division."

"Thank you, Mr. Leach, sir. I still have way too much to learn."

On return to Boys' Town following the evening meal, Frenchy said, "Joe it's one thing to poke a stick at a tiger in his cage. It's another to poke him in the jungle. I have never seen an Ensign get away with what you did with Mr. Leach."

"He always goes off half-cocked. The guy sets himself up for trouble. At the end of it all today, he mellowed, said I had earned taking M Division. Who knows, he may come around."

"Don't count on it. He was Zilching you at dinner, taking bragging rights over who shut Lieutenant Kane down, serious time on the range."

Joe concluded, "I'm going to ignore it. I've got the biggest responsibilities in this new job. I'll limit my time out on the range, just stay off my back."

"You're winning all the battles, but you're going to lose the war."

"Oh, I don't know about that. Apparently because I flunked the Charles Atlas fitness course and my complexion is darker than his, I am supposedly unfit to be in the wardroom. My name isn't all that hard to remember. What do you suggest I do?"

"For starters, meet with him privately and apologize. Let him know your feelings about your name. Personally I have little use for Harry Leach, and I can well afford to keep him at arm's length. But you're in no position to keep twisting his tail. Isn't there a saying in show business about meeting the same people on the way down that you met on the way up?"

"Yeah, I suppose you're right."

"Of course I am. We live in a small world in this man's Navy. Always treat people like you're going to work with them later. It wouldn't hurt to practice on Harry. From what he *didn't* say at dinner tonight, I would gather that you have his attention and, probably begrudgingly, his respect. It would be a good time to heal the breach. That's why I say apologize. Eat a little humble pie. Without intervention, he's just waiting for you to stumble. And we all make mistakes. I'm not asking you to be his best friend, just show him the respect due his rank."

"Frenchy, you're a good sea father."

CHAPTER 10

Olympic Village

Joe, clean from his first shower since the *Beaverton* moored, came topside to see the scenery and breathe Melbourne's fresh air before going ashore. In the sunlight, he brushed dust from the sleeve of his light tan sports coat and his dark brown trousers.

He had been delayed for the time it took the XO to hold a meeting in the wardroom, during which he announced that all officers were expected to attend social functions that were scheduled for their benefit. The first function to which Joe was "invited" was a cocktail party that evening, hosted by the Australian-American Friendship Society. The XO hinted that there would be a number of young, single Australian women at the party.

As agreed, Joe stood by the rail opposite Number One turret awaiting his roommate Frenchy, who was to meet him after he finished going through the official mail sent to his detachment. Joe examined his brown Navy shoes and shined them on the backs of his pants legs. Since it was early afternoon, the first crowd of visitors filled the decks, making them look more like busy downtown sidewalks than the decks of a cruiser.

As always, Joe let his gaze follow the girls who passed by. There were some return glances, but none that interested him. Through the din, he heard Frenchy's voice but could not understand what he was saying. He looked over by the turret and saw Frenchy talking to two men. One was almost as short as Joe and looked to be in his late thirties, with a receding hairline and a slight paunch. The other was tall, blond, and very muscular, with a pockmarked face and rather thin lips. Joe figured he was probably in his late twenties or early thirties. Both looked flushed. The blond looked up and down the deck nervously, as if uneasy about being on an American ship.

As Joe approached, he heard the older man say to Frenchy, "You startled me, sir. I didn't think I'd meet an American who spoke fluent Russian. I am Piotr Waluski, official interpreter for the Polish Olympic team. This is Colonel Rapishinski, coach of our decathlon team. We were just admiring your fine ship."

Frenchy adjusted the earpiece on his glasses and said, "Piotr, I'm Lieutenant Villerouge and if they've sent you all the way from Poland to find out how thick the armor is on our turrets, it would have been cheaper to look it up in *Jane's Fighting Ships.*"

"*Jane's Fighting Ships?* I don't understand. Please don't take offense, we weren't spying. Just curious. What is this *Jane's Fighting Ships?*"

"It's a book published by the British. You might call it private-enterprise intelligence. It's available in the better libraries."

Joe felt the Colonel's pale blue eyes staring at him as he volunteered, "In fact, we have one in our wardroom. Would you like to find out about the ships in your navy?" Immediately Joe felt he had taken a step too far when he saw white all the way around the Colonel's irises. The man's eyes were now darting to and fro, almost as if he had a tic. Frenchy gave Joe a very dark look after the muscular Pole said in very broken English, "Certainly, yes."

The older Pole extended his hand toward Joe, who shook his hand and the Colonel's. The Colonel smiled, displaying crooked, gold-capped teeth, but said nothing. He removed his cloth cap and wiped his forehead. At Frenchy's invitation, the four of them went below to the wardroom.

⊷▬◉▬⊶

After the stewards served coffee, Frenchy pulled the heavy blue-bound book out of a metal locker and thumbed through it until the pages on the Polish Navy turned up. He laid the book in front of the Colonel and said, "This is what a private book publisher in the free world knows about your navy."

The Colonel's face turned red to the hairline. He studied the pictures and text, then, jabbing his finger on some of the data, began muttering in Polish. Interpreter Piotr said a word or two in Polish, and the Colonel fell silent.

After a few more minutes of turning pages, the Colonel closed the book. "I cannot believe, "translated Piotr, "that some capitalist book publisher could have access to information that is classified in my country. How can this be? You take great liberty showing us this data. This is joke, no?"

Frenchy smiled. "It's called freedom of the press. We thrive on it. Here, take a look at the rest of this book."

The Lieutenant turned to the section on the U.S. Navy and showed him the picture of the *Beaverton*. The two visitors spent almost twenty minutes flipping through the pages while their hosts sipped their coffee.

As Piotr closed the book and handed it back, he said, "Your hospitality and friendship are wonderful. We would like to respond. Please join us for tour of Olympic Village. Do you have tickets to any of the events today?"

"No, we don't," answered Frenchy.

"Please come with us. There will be a historic match between Hungary and the Soviet Union in water polo. I believe we could find you very fine seats."

Frenchy leaned back in his chair and folded his arms across his chest.

Piotr raised his arms, extending his palms upward. "We are here to be friends. I knew many American friends in the war. I fought with the free Poles in Italy. Please say yes."

Joe said, "It sounds good to me. What do you say, Lieutenant?"

"I don't know if we should."

"It's certainly a better way to spend the afternoon than sitting in some pub. Piotr, how much will the tickets cost?"

"You will be seated in participants' seating area as guests of Polish Olympic Team. There will be no cost."

Frenchy pushed his wire-rimmed glasses back up the bridge of his long nose. "Well, the price is right. Sure."

Just over half an hour later, they pulled through the gate of the Olympic Village, where the guard handed passes to Joe and Frenchy.

Piotr said, "These passes allow you to be in Olympic Village. Without fail, you must turn them in when you leave."

From a parking place near a newly built brick building, Piotr led them into a conference room. Joe found himself surrounded by three of the six members of the Polish Olympic Committee. All of them were heavyset, middle-aged men wearing slightly oversized business suits. Joe noted the bulges of shoulder holsters on three of them. He decided they looked more like Mafia dons than sports officials.

The oldest of the group, whose suit looked new and hand tailored, spoke in Polish and Piotr translated. He spoke of Polish-American friendship before ordering glasses to be passed around.

As Piotr filled Joe's glass, he said, "This is real Polish vodka, not vile Russian stuff. Please enjoy it."

The leader made a toast, which Piotr translated as, "To peace forever between our great countries."

The Poles and Frenchy tilted their heads back and swallowed the shot. Joe took a sip. Then, embarrassed, he followed suit. The Poles clapped.

There followed three more rounds. The Colonel, as well as two or three of the committee, attempted to draw Frenchy into conversation in Russian or Polish. He either didn't answer them or replied in English.

When they refilled the glasses for the fourth time, Frenchy raised his glass and loudly proclaimed, "To a free Poland!"

The drinks were downed, but afterward the leader frowned as Piotr translated the toast. This ended the liquid hospitality.

Piotr ushered them onto the tour. As they were walking toward a workout area, he said, "Lieutenant, your toast struck some tender nerves. There was an inference that my country is not free."

"It was meant that way. There is no reason for the Soviets to keep your country under occupation."

"This is true, but all you Americans do is talk. The foolish Hungarians listened to you, and look what good it did them. We must live with the Russians."

"Well said. I just like to let people know how I feel. Please apologize for me if I offended anyone."

The interpreter slapped Frenchy lightly on the back. "Certainly, certainly. We Poles are too smart to suffer what Hungary has just been through. Come, let's not talk of our differences."

True to his word, Piotr gave them a Cook's tour of the facility. He pointed out athletes who had won medals, most of whom were Russian. At one point Joe attempted to introduce himself to a young Russian woman. She backed away from him with fear-filled eyes.

The Pole whispered, "The Russians still think Stalin lives. Perhaps in cafeteria we could find some of your countrymen who have finished their events."

As they walked into the cafeteria, they saw one of the beefy Poles with whom they had been drinking. He was drawing away from a table where an athletic-looking blonde sat. Joe's first impression of her was that she was somewhat of an ordinary young woman. That is, she wasn't extraordinarily beautiful, but she wasn't homely either. She had a rather wide mouth and lips that were neither too full nor too thin. Her dark eyes had a haunting, almost sad look to them. If there was any quality about her that was star quality, it was her long, thick blonde hair that cascaded in ringlets long enough to hide the swell of her breasts.

Initially Joe thought she was looking at him, but as they approached the table, it was obvious her gaze was fixed on Frenchy. The sadness, or maybe it was fatigue, vanished from her face and a slight smile curved her lips as she motioned to Piotr to join her.

She said to the Pole in English, "Piotr, who are these handsome strangers with you?"

Before he could reply, Frenchy said something in Russian. Piotr mumbled a reply.

She showed surprise (feigned, thought Joe) and paused before saying in a very flat Midwest accent, "Please don't talk to me in Russian. I am Eva Atvar, a Hungarian. I speak English very well."

It was only when she pronounced "Hungarian" that a strong flavor of a Russian accent marinated the syllables. She smiled, still with her eyes fixed on Frenchy's. In that instant, Joe noticed a transformation. The blonde was a knockout. The plainness of her light tan skirt, white long-sleeved cotton blouse, and cloth running shoes disappeared beneath the glow.

Frenchy stood across from her, holding her right hand in a frozen handshake. He gurgled and cleared his throat.

Piotr said, "Eva, I am pleased to introduce you to two very fine

Americans who extended very fine hospitality to us when we visited their ship today. This is Lieutenant Frank Villerouge and Ensign Joseph Xylos of American cruiser *Beaverton.* I am repaying their kindness and open American hospitality."

Joe offered his hand. "I'm Joe, and we call him Frenchy."

She signaled for them to sit down, lightly touching Joe's right hand with her left. Frenchy released her hand and eased himself into the cafeteria chair.

Piotr said, "I am pleased to find you here. I understand you are the person to see for passes to the water polo match this afternoon."

She nodded. "Yes. It will be an afternoon to remember. The Russians can't use their tanks in a swimming pool. We will win!"

She leaned over, opened a briefcase, and extracted three passes. "Here you are, Piotr. These passes are for the Hungarian participants' section."

"Thank you, Eva."

She pushed her coffee cup toward Piotr. "Why don't you and your friend get us something to drink? Frank, would you like coffee?"

After a pause, Frenchy said, "Well, yes. I'll go."

"No. Please. Let them go. I don't like to sit here alone."

Frenchy gave Joe a nod. He pushed his glasses back up his nose and settled his full weight into the chair. Again his eyes locked on Eva's.

Once they were clear of the table, Joe asked Piotr, "Does she have any girl friends?"

"Oh, you like her? Maybe we could find someone who has finished her events. It would be difficult. The rules are very strict for the athletes. Their coaches must keep them in training. We'll ask Eva when we return."

"What does Eva do?"

"She is a trainer and administrator for the Hungarian gymnastics team. She is also an interpreter. That's how I came to know her."

"How about the Poles?"

"Impossible. None of them speak English."

Just after the two men passed through the line, the same tough-looking, overweight Pole walked up to Piotr and barked a few words in Polish at him. He gestured toward the door and grumbled another sentence before he turned on his heel and left.

With coffee cups in hand, Piotr nudged Joe. "There is some sort of problem over at the wrestling match. I am needed. I don't know if you'll be able to see the water polo without an Olympic escort. It's too bad, because it will be one of the highlights of the games. Maybe Eva can find someone."

As they approached the table, Joe heard Eva saying something in French. Frenchy replied in the same language, but again most of the words were lost in the din of the cafeteria.

She turned to Piotr and said, "Comrade interpreter, you have met your match! This man has the gift of tongues. He speaks four different and difficult languages!"

Frenchy held the steaming cup of coffee in his hands as if warming them before saying very quietly, "I grew up speaking French and English. I took German in high school and used it during the war. I don't know, language has always come easy to me."

"And the Russian?" queried Eva. "How do you come to speak it so well?"

Frenchy smiled and narrowed his eyes. "Let's say I'm an avid student. Maybe you could teach me Hungarian."

Piotr waved his hand as if it were a paddle. "Eva, we have complications. I have been called to work. It is an emergency. I don't think the Americans can get into stadium without an escort. Could you find someone?"

Eva paused and looked at Frenchy out of the corner of her eye, then back at the Pole, and finally took a sip of coffee. She answered in very measured tones, "I think I could spare the time."

"Good. After the game, you'll have to arrange for transportation to take them back to Melbourne."

She looked into her coffee cup. "Then it's settled. Piotr, I'll need the passes!"

With an expression like a child who's been caught in mischief, Piotr fumbled around in his coat pocket for the passes. Before handing them over, the Pole said, "Remember, Eva they are your responsibility."

The trio finished their coffee and left for the natatorium. When Eva stood, Joe found that, even in her low-heeled running shoes, she towered over him. He felt like a fifth wheel as Eva made it plain, in language both spoken and body, that she wanted Frenchy.

Once they were seated in the second row of the stadium with the excitement of the spectacle unfolding before them, Joe quickly forgot how he was being left out. The match was full of surprises. The crowd soundly booed the Russians when they were introduced. The Hungarians were in no way bashful in this regard. Joe had never seen a water polo match before, so he was surprised at how rough the play was. Time and again, when the Russian player nearest Joe's side of the pool maneuvered in front of his opponent, the Hungarian would direct a well-timed underwater chop or kick into the Soviet's kidneys. It seemed that play everywhere in the pool was equally vicious. This was clearly no sport for the faint of heart.

During a lull in the action, he looked over and saw Eva whispering in Frenchy's ear. His friend nodded, with a very serious expression on his face. When Joe caught her eye, he saw a look of fear cross her face for a moment. But just then, the referee blew his whistle, and she stood up and began screaming.

The Hungarians around them were on their feet en masse, pressed against the railing and hanging over it. By the time Joe got to his feet, he saw why: the hard-hitting Hungarian player was holding a bloody nose. The referee signaled for the Russian to leave the pool.

The Russian player—big boned, with the well-developed muscles of a competition swimmer—pulled himself to his feet and angrily gestured at his bloodied opponent. As he did so, Eva leaned over the people in the first row to scream verbal volley after volley at the man in Russian. Frenchy later told Joe that he'd never heard a woman swear so eloquently. By the time the Russian turned to face her, Eva had pushed down to the railing, where she leaned across and spit in his face. He first scowled and then, obviously recognizing Eva, half-smiled and pointed a finger at her. He shook a fist toward the crowd before strutting to the penalty area.

Frenchy and a couple of the others around Eva grabbed her and pulled her back to her second-row seat. Her countrymen admonished her in tones of warning and concern. As their words rained down on the blonde, the color drained from her face and she sat down quietly.

As the action moved to the far side of the pool, she said, "Please forgive me. I am not normally this way. I can't get over what they did to my country. I should be quiet or I will get into trouble, I know. They're watching, always watching."

Joe turned to acknowledge her words and saw that she was lightly running her hand up and down Frenchy's thigh.

Frenchy replied, "Eva, I'd be mad as hell too, if some commie bastard blasted my home town the way they hit Budapest. Maybe the way people are treating the Russians here will send a message to the Kremlin. I just don't think you ought to tease the bear too much."

She pushed herself tall in her seat, squaring her shoulders, and her eyes somberly focused on the ball soaring over the turbulent swimming pool.

After Hungary won the match, she was hugging the players and laughing as they wrung out their helmets over her. More than one kissed her on the mouth. The dark mood that had held her for the latter part of the game disappeared like a quick summer storm. The front of her dress was dampened so that it clung to the curves of her small, high breasts.

Once they were clear of the stadium, Eva led them on another tour of the village, following almost identically the route Piotr had taken. Frenchy was close by her side, their shoulders touching as they walked. Eva fell silent after pointing out the same landmarks Piotr had, and the din of the crowds died until it was so quiet that they could hear their footfalls on the sidewalk.

At length Frenchy spoke, his first words sounding like a frog struggling for breath. "Eva, would you join us for dinner? There is a party being thrown by some Australians afterward."

"I have to work tonight. It is very difficult to get away. There is much security. Please don't think I am not wanting to go. Please don't forget me. I would like to see you again . . . very much. But it is difficult. I have my duties."

Frenchy said, "As a consolation prize, could I treat you to dinner here?"

She pressed her hand into his and whispered, "It would be very nice, but my time of day to work comes now after the competition. Perhaps there is time for a Coke or a cup of coffee. I'll call a taxi for you." She kept her grip on his hand, saying, "Now don't look at this paper, just put your hand into your pocket. It's my phone number. I am owed some favors. Maybe something can be done. During the afternoon, I have time off."

Once they were in the cafeteria, Frenchy leaned over and said in a barely audible voice, "She wants to defect. She's asking for help. What do you think?"

Joe nodded and after a pause replied, "I don't know. She's hot for your body. It could be a setup. Say, I think you're really taken by her."

The Lieutenant colored slightly, saying, "I swore after the divorce that I had been permanently inoculated against ever falling for another blonde. But there is something about Eva that's magnetic. When she touched me, I couldn't think straight. Is there such as thing as love at first sight?"

"Frenchy, there's something about this whole thing that doesn't ring true. Let's give her the benefit of the doubt. If she really wants to take off, then we need to figure out how to smuggle her out when we leave tonight. If she gets a sudden case of cold feet, then we'll know it's all a game."

"Joe, I detect a little jealousy in your voice. You would have had a different attitude if she had brought along a friend."

"Well, maybe. Those fat guys in the oversized suits could be a challenge. Here she comes."

Eva slid into her seat. "I ordered a taxi. It will be at the gate in about fifteen minutes."

After they left the cafeteria, Frenchy whispered, "Eva, are you serious about not going back?"

"Well, yes."

"Then come with us when we leave."

"Now? How can I? There are many risks. I would not want to fail. You know I don't even have a pass to get through the gate."

Joe handed her his pass. "We have a saying. It's from *Julius Caesar.* `*There is a tide in the affairs of men. Which, taken at the flood, leads on to fortune; omitted, all the voyage of their life is bound in shallows and in miseries. On such a full sea are we now afloat, and we must take the current when it serves, or lose our ventures.'"*

"Shakespeare, yes? But how will you get out?"

"Don't worry about me. I'm a professional screwup. I lost it. Besides, I'm an American naval officer. Nobody's going to get too upset."

"But what if they recognize me?" Eva stared at the pass in her hands.

Frenchy said, "Then run like hell. If they try to grab you, I'll pitch in."

Joe shook his head. "Wait a minute. The best way is to go out as if you own the place. If they ask for identification, just tell them that you're Frenchy's wife and you left your passport at the hotel. Your English is good enough that you can pull it off. Frenchy has a Navy ID and can vouch for you."

Eva wiped her hands on her skirt as if drying sweaty palms. "It is very risky. There is no plan, no time to think."

Frenchy said, "Eva, this is your decision. We'll help you if you want to go. Look, you don't have to commit yourself until you present the pass to the guard. If it looks okay, say you're my wife like Joe suggested. If not, hand them the pass and say that it belongs to Joe, who somehow got separated from you. The people on the gate this afternoon were Aussies. They aren't about to play jailer for the communists. How about it?"

"But there is security. The teams are being watched."

They walked perhaps another ten yards in the gathering twilight. The sun was shining for the last time that day as it descended between the clouds and the horizon. The windows on a nearby building seemed aflame in its reflection. Eva looked around, studying each person they approached. Joe noticed that in the sunlight, her eyes were more green than they were brown.

Almost as if talking to herself, she said, "There may never be another good opportunity. Yes, I'm ready."

Joe rubbed his thumb on his fingers. "Frenchy, I'll need some props. Can you spare a ten-spot?"

"What?"

"There's a man with a bowler. I want to buy it. Trust me, I need something to make a diversion." Joe fished a twenty-dollar bill out of Frenchy's wallet. "Trust me, I'll give you the change."

"Trust you? Damn, but you've got nerve!"

Joe dropped back, leaving Frenchy standing there with wallet in hand. After a few steps, Joe bent over and retied the shoelaces on both his feet. When he stood up, he began retracing his steps toward the cafeteria quite slowly, looking at the ground.

Frenchy and Eva went through the gate without incident, together with a tour group whose bus stood just beyond the checkpoint. The uniformed Australian guard took the passes and stuffed them into a box. A powerfully built man in mufti, an Eastern European security agent, joined him, and they walked swiftly past the bus as the agent scanned faces. One couple was locked in an embrace so that they couldn't see the woman's face. Not seeing anything amiss, they strolled on, and the tourists boarded the bus—except for the amorous couple, who slipped behind the bus to a taxi as soon as their backs were turned.

As they walked back toward the guard shack, the security agent nodded in agreement when the Aussie guard remarked, "Bloody Yanks are a cheeky lot! Carrying on in public view . . . No sense of propriety, eh?"

CHAPTER 11

Escape

"You are really Ensign Joseph Xylos, United States Naval Reserve?" The middle-aged man shifted his gaze from the ID card to lock on Joe's eyes. "Why on earth do you want this old bowler?"

Oh my gosh, listen to that guy's accent. He's no Aussie. What the heck, I like the shade of green. Let's see if I can bargain him out of his hat. All I'm looking for, is something to stall enough to give Eva and Frenchy a good head start.

Joe twirled the green hat on his index finger, held it in both hands, and carefully placed it on his head. "It's a perfect fit for my act. I've mimed Charlie Chaplin before and need a new hat, especially one that's mint green. How much, five dollars U.S.? "

"That's a deal."

Wow, how did that happen so quickly? No sooner had he handed the stranger a five-dollar bill than Joe saw two of the Polish drinkers come into the crowded room. As he returned their waves, Joe could feel the acid flooding his stomach. *Holy smoke, I've had it now.* Much to his surprise and relief, they dashed into the men's room. He decided he could wait to use the facilities, and fled the scene.

Joe was surprised how quickly the hall filled by the time he left and how empty the entrance plaza was. In fact, he felt it was too empty when the biggest one of the Polish threesome waved to him from outside the fence line. Joe waved back. *I'm not blending into the crowd. What on earth ever possessed me to volunteer to hand over my pass? What if they arrest me? I'll be in hack, and my next liberty will be in Long Beach.*

The muscular Pole stopped and leaned against a metal post. The man repeated what Joe had watched him do between vodka shots: he snapped open a metal case and removed one cigarette. He tapped the tip on the case, then stuck it into the corner of his mouth and struck a match. He drew in a lungful of smoke and began exhaling smoke rings. *I can picture him blowing that smoke in my face as he interrogates me.*

Joe looked ahead to the gate. The uniformed Australian guard was settled back onto his stool with a smoke in his hand. *Well, here goes my first Charlie Chaplin act in Australia. Can I sell him before the big Pole gets back?*

Joe stopped some five yards from the booth. He set the mint green bowler down over his right eye as he reached into his left inner jacket pocket. Then his right. One by one, he searched each pocket. He looked into his wallet, which he clamped in his teeth. He turned each pocket inside out. He turned his back on the guard and looked back in the direction he'd come from.

At last, Joe dropped the wallet from his teeth into the bowler and approached the booth very slowly with a very worried look on his face. In his posture he tried to emphasize his skinny frame and sloping shoulders. He coughed a couple of times and said, "I know I'm supposed to return my pass to you, but I—I'm afraid I've lost it. I was invited out for a tour of the facilities. I hope I'm not in big trouble. I didn't mean to lose the pass."

"I figured as much, watching you going through your pockets. I don't believe it's an insurmountable problem, sir. You're an American visitor, then? Who was your host?"

"I'm not sure. He was visiting my ship today and invited my shipmate and me out. I'm not too sure just what country he was from. I had a really hard time understanding him."

"Don't I know it. And where is your friend now?"

Joe watched the muscular Pole approach the gate from the outside and stare at him. Behind him, the short Ensign heard other feet walking quickly toward the gate from the shadows.

This doesn't look good. I'm surrounded. Joe continued, his eyes focused on the approaching man, "We were separated when he was called away. I got to watch some gymnasts work out, but they quit for dinner. I'm late. I was told he had to go to a party you Aussies are throwing. I think he already left. I thought they were going to give me a ride back to town. Damn! Some days, nothing goes right. Where can I catch a cab back to Melbourne?"

"Highly unusual. The teams have been very good about following the rules. Do you have any identification?"

Joe pulled out his wallet and handed the guard his Navy ID card. "Ensign Joe Xylos. See, I'm with the American Navy. I don't want to cause any trouble."

The big Pole, now standing just outside the gate, bellowed, "Who is this fellow?"

"All the visitor passes are here," said the guard to the big Pole. "He's not one of yours. Just rest easy."

The Pole stepped aside as the guard continued, "I tell you what, mate . . . Maybe you slipped in without the proper clearance and maybe you had a pass. I don't know. You don't seem the sort to cause trouble. Go along now. And I don't want to see you around here again without a proper pass. All right?"

Wow, he just saved my ass. Thank you, thank you! Joe smiled and made an effort to look the guard in the eye as he touched the brim of his bowler. "You're most kind."

"About the cab, just walk down this road to the second intersection. Turn right and you'll see the main entrance area. There'll be a taxi there or, if your timing is right, a motor bus."

After walking some distance, Joe looked back and there, in the light immediately in front of the gate, he saw that the big Pole had been joined by the other two. Joe increased his pace until he was just short of a trot.

Joe had just turned toward the entrance area when he heard brakes and looked across the road to see a sailor stick his head out the window of a Morris Major. The sailor yelled, "Mr. Xylos! Can we give you a ride?"

Joe thrust a thumb up and shouted, "You bet! Thanks!"

As he crossed the street, he recognized two men from B Division, but he couldn't remember their names. Both were third-class boiler tenders. Joe squeezed into the back seat next to the larger sailor, whom he now recognized as Alex Frisch, a very muscular six-footer. The other, sitting in the front seat, was Murray Allen, who had the lean, almost undernourished look of Appalachia and spoke with a nasal twang. At the wheel was an older brunette who could have passed for a stand-in for a pit bull terrier. The corners of her mouth turned down, and there were well-established crow's feet around her eyes. They introduced her as Felicity Freeman.

Felicity said, "Where are you headed, Joe?"

"I'm supposed to go to a party tonight. I'll have to call the ship to get the correct address. First, I'd like to stop somewhere and get something to eat."

"We're headed to a good pub. They have very good sandwiches. It's not like the big hotels downtown, and neither are the prices. All right?"

"Sure."

"I like the hat, gives you a local flavor, Yank."

Joe touched the hat's brim and smiled. The car lurched into gear and took off with a roar. They careened down the road and--to Joe's relief—pulled up just over five minutes later in front of a plain white building. A barely illuminated sign over the door identified the place as The Boar's Keeper. The interior was decorated in linoleum table-tops and asphalt tile floors with bare light bulbs reflecting off yellowed ceilings. Joe took one look at the reddened faces and bloodshot eyes that silently sized him up and told himself that this place could get interesting.

The bartender said, "Felicity, my girl, who have you here? Yanks?"

"Right. Yanks. They're from the cruiser *Beaverton*."

"Well, lads, step right up. The first day ashore, the first round is on the house. You're among friends here. Isn't that right, mates?"

There were a few groans and feeble "ayes."

Felicity guided them to a table where a pair of Aussies sat. From the greetings, it was obvious they had all met earlier in the day at one of the games.

One look at them, and the first word that came to Joe's mind was *tough*, followed by *trouble*. Both were at least six feet tall and had large, heavily calloused hands with numerous scars on their faces to match. Dark stubbles deepened the shadows on their jowls and beneath their chins. Felicity introduced them as Mike and Bill.

In contrast to their threatening appearance, both men's voices were mellow baritones and they were quite friendly. The Ensign sat back in his seat and relaxed for the first time since Frenchy told him that Eva wanted out.

Joe ordered a corned beef sandwich and washed it down with a mug of Swan Lager while the others struck to strictly liquid refreshments. He sat half listening to their banter and half wondering if Frenchy and Eva had pulled off the escape. He felt a bit envious of his roommate's luck with Eva.

Felicity waved a hand in front of his face. "Joe, you don't seem to be here."

"Oh. I guess I'm a little tired. We did a lot of running today."

"You were coming from the road to the Olympic Village. Do you have some friends on the American team?"

"No, a friend and I were given a tour of the village. He and I got—got separated after he met this girl."

"Ho! You yanks don't waste a moment! Where's she from?"

"Hungary."

"Hungary, eh? They keep a close check on them. He'll get to look and not feel."

Joe smiled. "Well, I suppose they do. But some fish do escape the net. In fact, I don't know where they are."

Bill asked, "Not in the village? That took some doing. Is she defecting?"

Joe shrugged his shoulders. "There was some talk of it. Frankly, I don't know what to make of it. Could be."

Murray exclaimed, "Golly, Mr. Xylos, you might be involved in an international incident. After what the Russians did to Hungary, I'll bet the newspaper people are looking for stories about that."

The bartender volunteered, "In fact, there was a story on the telly about that team yesterday. It was part of the buildup to today's water polo match. They showed the guys in the water, but the reporters didn't get to talk to any of the athletes. There was just a tough-looking old man and a woman interpreter. Perfect English . . . she sounded like one of you Yanks. . . . said things are fine in Hungary and not anything like the Western press has been saying."

Joe asked, "Was she a blonde with dark eyes . . . a bit taller than I am?"

The bartender nodded.

"Damn! I hope he knows what he's doing."

"Who?" asked Alex. "Who were you with?"

"Lieutenant Villerouge."

"Who's he?"

"One of the riders from CINCPAC Fleet staff."

They drank quietly for a few minutes, then Bill pointed to Joe's smooth hands. "I've never seen a man who went to sea who had such smooth hands. What do you do on the ship?"

Joe examined his own fingers for a moment before replying, "I'm the M Division Officer, in charge of the main engines. You're right, I only have one callus . . . . right here on my right middle finger, from pushing a pencil."

"You must have a whole bunch of education to hold that job."

"Some, a degree in industrial engineering. The main qualification for the job is to do what I'm told to do."

Murray said, "He's pretty modest. He was my assistant division officer until he took over M Division. He's the only officer who ever came down and took a serious interest in everything we did. He used to write down what we were doing and how long it took. He may not do much work with a wrench, but he really knows how to organize work. I was sorry to see him go."

Bill sipped his beer, then asked, "Is that what industrial engineering is all about?"

"That's part of it. I took courses on work measurement in college. I'm pleased to put some of my schooling to practical use."

"How do you engineer industries?"

"It's a way of analyzing work and how it's done, so you can make changes that cause it to go faster and more efficiently. For a simple job, though, you do your own industrial engineering. Haven't you ever changed how you did something after the first time you did it?"

"Who hasn't?"

"Well, for complicated jobs like you find in manufacturing, you need to plan in advance. Industrial engineering works best when there are repetitive jobs."

"Repetitive? What kind of work is that?"

"One that you do over and over. Take that picket fence across the street. Suppose that was a moving assembly line and your job was to pull the pickets off the fence and put them in stacks of ten each. Then someone else wraps them and tosses them on a truck. You can measure how long it takes to do each part of the job, from the few seconds it takes to pull the picket off to stacking and tying them. You can figure where they can stand and how big a stack to put them in to do the job most efficiently."

"Then I suppose blokes like you would stand around with your clipboard and make sure blokes like me do it exactly like you want?"

"Ideally, yes."

"What a damn bore."

"Bill, that's why work on an assembly line is so killing. But that doesn't mean you can't use the same principles to make people think and look for ways to do a better job. Oh, look at the time! I've really enjoyed talking with you folks. You're the first live Aussies I've met and you're damn fine company. I'd like to stay, but I've been told I have to go to a cocktail party this evening."

"Cocktail party! Oh, my! And who's throwing this bash?"

"I don't know. Ever heard of the Australian-American Friendship Society?"

"Never knew we needed one. Look, mate, if you find the high life too stuffy, come on back here. The Boar's Keeper is, one of—no, it's *the* most friendly pub in Melbourne."

After Joe first called the ship to confirm the location of the party and then called for a taxi, he returned to the table. He could hear the voices of the two sailors, Murray Allen and Alex Frisch, mixed with laughter from the Australians.

Murray said, "I say you ought to be able to take a picket off every twelve seconds."

"I don't know," replied Alex. "I think you do that at the start, but it couldn't be sustained."

Murray waved a hand to get Joe's attention. "Mr. Xylos, we're having a discussion here about picket fences. Remember you were talking about a picket fence assembly line. I say you couldn't handle a job like that in less than fifteen seconds a picket. What do you say?"

Joe lifted his mug and drained the dregs before replying, "Frankly, Murray, I don't know. For something I didn't know anything about, I'd have to do some thinking and perhaps just rely on sampling. Bartender, another round for my friends. Bill, to change the subject, where is the best place to find single women?"

"Thanks, mate, for the suds. Oh, I don't know. You might hang out around the pubs downtown during the five o'clock swill. A Yank like you shouldn't have much trouble."

Felicity said, "That's right after work when everybody stops for a toddy on the way home. Oh, my, aren't you the lucky one? There's your hack now. They take forever when I call one."

⋅→═◉ ◉═←⋅

The taxi let Joe off in front of a huge brick house with a large porch. Cars lined the street and choked the driveway. From within, the beat of a bass fiddle and snatches of a saxophone and trombone drifted through the din of laughter and conversation. He bounded up the steps to the open door.

From the shadows, he heard the unmistaken drawl of the XO, Stanley Longstreet. "Boy, you're late. You'd a-come here much later and you'd be helping them pick up the empty glasses."

"Yes, sir."

"We're here on a goodwill cruise. Officers from the *Beaverton* will be good guests, gentlemen, punctual and properly attired. That combination you're wearing is barely appropriate for this evening. Don't be bashful about wearing your uniform."

"Aye, aye, sir. Have you seen Lieutenant Villerouge?"

"He was here earlier. He asked my approval to sign out on leave for the duration of our stay. He was escorting a very pretty young woman, an American girl . . . Amy, from Ames, Iowa. I don't recall seeing him go; I think they're still here. The hostess is Mrs. Lionel Collings-Cartwright. I'll take you in to meet her."

Joe joined the party, finding some single Australian women, but not as many as there were single Navy officers. Between trips to the bar and the hors d'oeuvres, he asked each shipmate if he knew where

Frenchy was.

All said that they had seen Frenchy with "Amy," but none knew where they were. The hostess gave him a Mona Lisa smile before saying no also.

Joe downed perhaps two more drinks before the affair began to wind down. One of the older Australian couples gave him and Larry White a ride back to the ship. Sitting back in their stateroom, Joe noticed that the time was just past ten thirty. Both the quarterdeck and Larry would confirm the hour later, when events unfolding in Melbourne would make it important.

⟶◦⟵

The picket fence across from The Boar's Keeper was the subject of conversation the whole evening. First the two boiler tenders hashed it out, then dropped the subject when Felicity's girl friends came. The thread of the puzzle of how long it would take to pull every picket from the fence passed from table to table and back to the bar.

The fence that was the object of all this theoretical attention was shrouded in shadows and barely backlit by the dim light cast from the living room of the house it surrounded. They were still chewing on the subject when the lights in the house blinked off.

Twice during the evening there were two brief fights between the Aussie patrons, one of whom was Felicity's friend Bill. Afterward, Bill picked up the fellow off the floor and bought him a drink.

After quaffing another beer, Bill said, "Alex, we've been talking about Fred Phinney's fence all night. There are a goodly number of people here who have money that says you can't pull off all 129 pickets in less than thirty minutes. I say you can, mate."

"Gee, I don't know. That guy could call the cops."

"Old Fred? Call a constable? Not likely, because we'll talk to him. Come on, lad! Win or lose, we'll help you nail the pickets back."

"Bill, what if the cops or the Shore Patrol stops me short of the end?"

"Look, lad, I've got a hundred pounds riding on this. I've got bets at two and four to one. There's a good two to four hundred to be made if you're man enough. Tell you what, mate, I'll make it worth your while. Win, and I'll split the kitty down the middle. And if you lose, I'll buy you a round tomorrow night."

They shook hands just before the call for the last drink was made. Quickly, with much commotion, the crowd poured onto the street. Alex took off his jumper and handed it to Murray. The big sailor walked up to the left end of the fence and grabbed the first picket just below the upper stringer. In one swift move, the wooden slat was separated from the fence with a loud *riiip.*

Felicity shouted, "The time is ten fifty-one! Alex has to finish by eleven twenty-one."

The crowd fell silent as successive pickets flew. Murray noted that the time between pickets was fourteen seconds for the first three, but after the first five had fallen, the pace settled at a steady one every nine to eleven seconds.

With each rude yank, the nails screamed a protest, *riiip*! Alex was now into a rhythm. He crouched with knees bent, grabbing each picket just inside the stringer and straightening his legs with a springing motion. The thin pine boards leaped from their places as if being handled by a machine. He yanked some so hard that he left the nails in the stringers.

Just over five minutes passed and one-quarter of the fence was gone when Fred Phinney came to the window and shouted, " Hey! Get away from my fence! Stop that!"

Moments later, he burst through his front door carrying an ax handle and wearing only an undershirt and pair of oversized trousers. He was a tall man in his sixties whose muscles were withered with age.

Bill shouted, "Fred, stand your ground! We have a wager going on here and can't have you interfering. We'll make it right on the morrow. We promise."

The old man started down the steps shouting, "Damn you drunks! Get away and leave my place be!"

He swung the ax handle as Alex pulled another picket free. The handle missed the young sailor and took the top off the third picket down the line. Mike leaped over the fence and pulled the handle out of his hand, shoving the old man to the ground.

Fred scrambled back to his front steps in crablike motions as his wife shouted from the window, "The lot of you are in for it. I've called the coppers."

Alex continued his labors. *Riiip . . . riiip . . . riiip . . . riiip.* Over the next ten minutes, the sailor averaged one picket every eleven seconds. His undershirt was soaked with sweat. By the end of the fifteenth minute, seventy-nine pickets lay on the ground. The siren of a police car, distant at first, grew closer as the crowd cheered him on. The noise brought three or four of the neighbors out of their homes. One of them was a middle-aged woman who time and again begged Alex to stop tearing up Phinney's fence.

When the police car stopped, the crowd pushed around it, keeping the law officer inside. Threats shouted from within were lost in the din of the drunken spectators. The officer, seeing Murray in uniform standing behind Alex, called for backup and the Shore Patrol.

Through the din, the now monotonous *riiip . . . riiip* continued.

After each effort, Alex pressed his hands into his armpits to ease the pain. His shirt was getting stained with streaks of blood.

As the twentieth minute passed, Murray shouted, "Keep going, Alex! You're in the home stretch, there's only thirty-one left."

Riiip!

"Make that thirty!"

The first backup to arrive was a gray U.S. Navy pickup with two Shore Patrolmen in it. They parked about fifty yards from the crowd. One patrolman tried to get through a solid wall of revelers, who quickly overpowered him and took his nightstick. The second returned to the truck and called for more backup.

Alex ignored the disarmed Shore Patrolman's orders to stop. Triumphantly, he yanked the 129th picket off the fence in a little less than twenty-eight minutes, to applause and shouts from the crowd.

By that time, patrol cars blocked all the intersections and officers in riot gear were forming phalanxes to advance on the crowd. The revelers moved away from the police cruiser and handed the Shore Patrolman his nightstick. Two more Navy vehicles, including a black sedan, joined them.

As Alex was being led away in handcuffs, Felicity stuffed two hundred Australian pounds in his pocket and kissed him on the cheek, leaving a bright red lipstick imprint on his sweaty face. She stepped back and said, "Damn, Alex, you're too good to be a Yank! Come on back to The Boar's Keeper . . . anytime."

CHAPTER 12

Eva and Frenchy

Joe was just finishing up a discussion with the warrant machinist about which other pumps needed to be inspected, following the discovery of a badly eroded impeller on one of the centrifugal pumps used on the main evaporators, when he heard himself being paged from above.

They were standing by a workbench on the lower level of the forward engine room when the yeoman from the log room approached and said, "From the Executive Officer, sir. You are not to go on shore leave until you have seen him, and he'll call you when he wants to see you."

The Ensign could feel the blood draining from his head and pooling in his feet. He was sure that the people at the Olympic Village had connected him to Eva's disappearance. Certainly something had happened to Frenchy. It had been foolish to get involved. He followed the yeoman back to the log room.

On entering, he found Chief Engineer Moran sitting at his desk, scowling at a newspaper front page where a picture of Fred Phinney's destroyed fence occupied the top center below the headline, "POLICE AND US NAVY COULDN'T SAVE THE FENCE."

Tossing it at Joe, he growled, "The XO is really steamed about this! Don't tell me, I don't want to know if you were the American naval officer, named Joe, at The Boar's Keeper. You've lived a charmed life up to now, but I knew that sooner or later you'd trip and fall."

Joe picked up the paper and read the article that included interviews of Michael Horan and William Saxon, who said that the idea to pull the pickets from the fence had originated with an American naval officer named "Joe" from the USS *Beaverton*. They went on to say that wagers grew over the evening and that a considerable sum was won, thanks to the detailed instructions the American officer gave them.

Joe put the paper down on the desk. He smiled and ran his hand through his dark hair. "Whew! Is this all there is? I thought it was something serious."

"You don't call this serious? The XO is threatening to curtail liberty for the entire Engineering Department."

"Sir, I don't know what happened out there. There's no way I can be brought into this. It says this happened after eleven o'clock last night, but I was back on board by then. Ask Cy Penelton and Inside White."

"Don't say any more. I have to give you an Article 31 warning. You understand that you do not have to make a statement and that any statement you make can be used as evidence against you . . . et cetera."

" I understand, Commander, but I wasn't involved. I was at The Boar's Keeper only long enough to eat a sandwich and drink two beers before going to the XO's command-performance cocktail party. I left that place close to eight thirty."

"What were you doing on liberty with a couple of enlisted men?"

"They gave me a ride from the Olympic Village. I got separated from Frenchy and was walking to the cab stand when they came by. The Boar's Keeper wouldn't have been my first choice as a place to stop, but I didn't want to go to that party with an empty stomach."

"Did you suggest that they pull the pickets off that old man's fence?"

"No, sir. One of the Aussies asked me what an industrial engineer did and I used the example of likening the picket fence to an assembly line. I can see how the idea was planted, but there's no way I started some plot or conspiracy to tear up this man's property."

Laughing, the Chief Engineer shook his head. "Joe, if this were the first time, I think you'd be on firmer ground. Why is it that the cops come through the door just after you leave?"

Joe shrugged. "Good judgment, I guess. I seem to know when things are going to get out of hand."

"That answer would probably raise the XO's blood pressure by at least twenty points. Let me talk to him. I don't know if I can get you off the hook this time, but I think we have the need for some serious damage control. We should literally be mending fences right now. Making this right for old Fred Phinney is the best kind of an apology we can make. I want you to be prepared to be in charge of the work party."

"I don't object as long as it's understood that I had nothing to do with this thing."

Lieutenant Commander Henry Moran called the XO and very succinctly stated his case to send a work party out to fix the man's fence. Then for almost five minutes he listened to Longstreet's tirade. Joe could hear snatches of the XO's conversation, and it didn't sound good at first. In the end, the XO calmed down and agreed that a work party would be appropriate, but without Joe Xylos. Instead, carpenters from R Division would go do the work with Inside White as the officer in charge, and Joe would remain aboard to stand his duty.

At lunch, Joe felt all eyes follow him as he went to his seat. His roommate Carter Sawyer averted his eyes when they met. He found a copy of the Melbourne paper on his chair.

As Joe was finishing his coffee, Harry Leach bellowed from two tables away, "Mr. Zilch, you would have been better off to have stood the duty yesterday. That was a rotten trick to pull on that old man."

"Lieutenant, you should have been there. I kept thinking that if ever I'd seen a place that was your kind of bar, that was it. The name has such a descriptive ring to it, The Boar's Keeper."

"Mister, you can bluster all you want. I was with the XO when he read the Shore Patrol reports. You've been found out. Nobody in his right mind ought to go on the beach with you. You're the original liberty risk. And if Commander Longstreet follows my advice, he'll recommend to the Captain to make a bloody example of you."

"Thank you, sir, it's so nice to hear the sentence before the trial."

Joe stood the entire duty for his shipmate. He ended the day with the morning watch from four a.m. to eight a.m. as the JOOD. Early in the watch, a car, identical to the one in which the Poles had given Frenchy and Joe a ride to the Olympic Village, cruised slowly up to the foot of the brow, stopped with the window partway rolled down, then continued to a parking lot at the head of the pier. The occupants remained in the darkened car.

The next morning, a hapless Ensign Xylos reported to the XO's cabin. His roommate, Lawyer Sawyer, sat nearby with a clipboard on his lap. He recited to Joe, once more, the Article 31 warning against self-incrimination.

Commander Longstreet took a sip from his coffee cup, then lit a cigarette before beginning. "Mister Xylos, if I had seen you yesterday at this time, I don't think I could have controlled myself. All the time I've been in the Navy, I've never served in such a notorious ship that made the front page with such humiliating regularity. And always, you seem to have just walked out the door before the roof collapses. With the *Beaverton*'s name tied to a stunt like this, I am mortified!"

He struck the folded newspaper that lay on his desk. "In my heart of hearts, I know you set the wheels in motion. But your boss and Mr. Sawyer came to bat for you. Commander Moran says you're doing an excellent job in M Division, and Sawyer has convinced me that the boiler tenders back your story one hundred percent. Again, you're lucky there isn't enough credible evidence to tie you to this most regrettable incident. I've held Executive Officer's mast on those two. Petty Officer Allen seems to have been more of an interested spectator, and I'm recommending restriction for him until after we leave port. The other, Frisch, will lose his stripe and become the charter member of the enlisted men's Sundowner's Club. The next time he sets foot ashore after dark will be after we return to Long Beach. This is strictly an administrative remedy that ought to send a message to all bad actors."

He moved the service record jackets of the two men to the side of his desk, rubbed his red neck, then inhaled from the cigarette dangling from his lips and continued, "Mr. Leach pointed out to me that prior to our leaving Long Beach, a pattern was established. You're full to the brim with seductive ideas, like the snake that whispered to Eve in the garden. Why is it that it's always the man behind you who steps on the mine?"

"I don't believe that's at all fair—"

"I won't waste the time going over these episodes. Again we have a major incident and again, there you are in the shadows. Boy, you were saying you want to go to Submarine School?"

"Yes, sir."

"Well, we don't send dirty linen out to be washed. And I'm not sure what kind of endorsement you'll get from the Captain. I can tell you one thing. He is disturbed . . . extremely disturbed. I wouldn't want to see you louse up a fine opportunity. I'm going to do you a favor, although you may not perceive it as such. I have before me a list of functions, social functions for we are obliged to provide officer attendees. There are more of these than we have officers. For the rest of the time in port, you will take shore leave *only* to attend these functions, starting with the Temperance Society's dinner this evening. I know you will return to the ship immediately afterward."

"Aye, aye, sir."

"I have instructed the Operations Officer, who is the social event co-ordinator, to fill your days and evenings until we get underway. I trust his judgment to select those events that will keep you out of harm's way. I recognize that I'm taking a calculated risk here. I'll trust you not to louse it up."

"I understand, Commander. Is that all, sir?"

"Yes."

Half an hour later, he was given a message to call a local phone number. He made the call from the wardroom.

Frenchy answered, "Joe, thanks for returning the call."

"Where have you been?"

"In the woodwork. I confided in Mrs. CC at the party about Eva's dilemma, and she sent us upstairs. I cleared taking leave with the XO. I need your help. Could you pack my small bag with my shaving gear and a few changes of clothes? And get someone to bring them out to the place where the party was held the first night? It's the Collings-Cartwright place; I'm sure the address is on the master list. Eva is certain that the ship is being watched and that they will tail you; so, whatever you do, don't bring the stuff yourself. I'd rather go without than take a chance. Get one of the others from Boys' Town. The best time to come is just before six. Mrs. CC is entertaining tonight, so the messenger will get a free dinner. And it's a perfectly plausible reason for him to be coming here, in case he's followed."

"Okay, I'll see what I can do. My stock hereabouts is rather low at the moment."

"Oh, I get it, you were the "Joe from the *Beaverton*" in that mess at The Boar's Keeper. Are you in hack?"

"I would say close enough to have one foot on a banana peel. The

XO has directed me to remain aboard except to go to assigned official functions. I'll be going to some Temperance banquet tonight. Frenchy, when I got called in about the fence, I thought it was about you and Eva. I was so relieved when it wasn't. Any more trouble and my goose is cooked."

"I thought you were listening to your old sea father and had stopped pulling all these stunts."

"I have! I didn't set that thing up. They did it hours after I left. Between now and the tenth, all I'm going to worry about is getting to the party on time and getting back aboard before my coach turns into a pumpkin."

"That might work in my favor. Joe, we're getting married Wednesday evening. I'd like for you to be my best man. Let me talk to Mrs. CC, she's calling the plays."

"Getting married! Frenchy, are you sure?"

"Sure enough to know that if I don't marry her, I may never see her again. You quoted Shakespeare about 'taking the tide' to prompt her to make her move. I awoke yesterday morning and decided I'd better set my sail when the tide is running."

"Frenchy, I think there's more to Eva than meets the eye."

"I'm sure you're right, but I've never been with such an exciting and sophisticated woman in my life . . . and she says I turn her on. We fit together as if God made us to be. Please, whatever you do, don't say a word to anyone. Until the games are over and maybe even later, the woman I love isn't safe. I'm sure they want her back . . . bad."

"Frenchy, don't count on me unless it can be worked around one of the official functions."

"Don't worry. I'm sure Mrs. CC will come up with something."

⋅→⊱⋅⊰←⋅

The next two days were far busier than Joe would have liked. He started the day watching a cricket match some ten miles north of Melbourne; had tea with a dozen grandmotherly matrons about five miles west of the city; and spent the evening watching movies of Australia's Outback. The second day was a clone of the first. He spent the better part of his duty day catching up on the work delayed by his social calendar.

In mid-afternoon of his regular duty day, there came a personal invitation to attend a private dinner the following evening at a country home some thirty miles west of Melbourne, followed by a fox hunt the following morning, Thursday morning. The host was a Mr. Gerald Fitzhugh, whose car would pick Joe up close to five in the afternoon. The small note with the invitation indicated that Mrs. Fitzhugh had met him at the reception the first night in port. The Operations Officer penciled him in to attend and dropped him from four other events.

When he called to accept, the hostess asked him to bring Frenchy's dress blue uniform, plus a long list of other items. She cautioned Joe to bring everything in Frenchy's suitcase.

The next day a chauffeur-driven Bentley pulled up at the foot of the forward brow, and a skinny, pimply-faced boy in his late teens walked up to the quarterdeck.

On seeing Harry Leach, he said, "I say, Leftenant, would you please apprise Mr. Xylos that I am here to collect him?"

"Who shall I say is here . . . to collect Mr. Xylos?"

"Whom shall you say? Brian Fitzhugh, sir."

The tubby Lieutenant waved to the Boatswain. "Call the wardroom and tell them that a Mr. Brian Fitzhugh is here to 'collect' Ensign Zilch."

Brian said, "Pardon me, sir. I distinctly told you I am here to collect Mr. Xylos."

"Xylos, Zilch! Same difference! When you said, 'collect Xylos,' I must compliment you on the proper use of the English language. Only thing, that car looks too good to carry garbage in."

"I beg your pardon!"

Leach gave the youngster a satisfied smile and strode to the other side of the quarterdeck.

Moments later, Ensign Xylos stepped onto the quarterdeck in his dress blues with Frenchy's suitcase. After he was ashore with his host, the youngster recounted his conversation with Leach.

As Joe slid into the back seat, he said, "You'll have to forgive Lieutenant Leach. He's a rare North American marsupial. I understand your game department is keeping a close eye on him to make sure he doesn't contaminate the bloodlines of your animal population."

"Oh, that's capital. Now that you mention it, I do see the resemblance to our native koala. I take it that you're not on the best of terms with your senior."

After the car door was closed, Joe lowered his voice. "I haven't been from the minute he laid eyes on me. Let's change the subject. Are Frenchy and Eva out at your place?"

"Yes. They've been staying with us since the weekend. Other than dinner in the evening, I've hardly seen them. They've kept pretty much to themselves. I was quite surprised to find out that he is an American. Most of the time when they are alone, they converse in a foreign tongue. Sometimes it's French, of which I have a small understanding; and most other times, Russian, of which I am totally ignorant. I understand that you're going to be part of their wedding."

"Yes. This may sound a bit strange, but I don't know where or when they're going to hold it."

"I overheard Father talking. The vicar refused to marry them because the Leftenant is a divorced man and she is a, quote, 'Godless communist.' Judge Hopkins will perform the rites. He's an old family friend. The wedding will take place just before dinner. Mr. Villerouge speaks very highly of you, unlike that Leftenant Koala. And my first impressions certainly coincide with Mr. Villerouge's."

"Thanks, Brian."

Joe looked out the back window and felt relieved that the road behind them was empty. Soon the Bentley pulled up in front of a stone house that looked as if it had been transplanted from some English manor.

The short Ensign lugged the suitcase up the stairs to the room where he'd been told Frenchy was staying. He dropped the bag on the floor, knocked a flourish on the door, and called, "Frenchy, it's me, Joe. I've got your blues."

With his hand on the knob, he heard bedsprings straining, followed by bare feet thumping the floor. Mixed with the sounds was a suppressed giggle. Frenchy sang out, "Just a minute. I'll be right there."

Joe placed the bag close to the door and stepped back. Frenchy pulled the door open, wide enough that Joe momentarily saw Eva through the space between the hinges. She was sitting in bed facing away from him. A single thin strand of golden hair curled down an otherwise white, flawless back. Her head was turned so that the rays of the late afternoon sun created an aureole around her silhouette. He focused on her long enough for the vision to imprint on his memory before he shifted his eyes to meet Frenchy's. Her man was standing in the door wearing only a pair of trousers. Joe watched as he zipped his fly and buckled his belt. Once finished, with one hand resting high on the open door, Frenchy broke eye contact with Joe for a moment and looked toward Eva.

"Frank, you can't invite him in now."

Frenchy blushed, and the color extended down to his well-muscled chest. He pushed a finger up his nose in the gesture he used to push up his glasses (apparently forgetting that he wasn't wearing them) and cleared his throat before croaking, "Good to see you, old buddy. You caught us by surprise. We were . . . Yes, we were taking a nap. We'll be up most of the night flying."

From behind the door, Eva laughed and said something in Russian.

Frenchy grunted a reply and then, looking at his shipmate continued, "Joe, give us time to pull ourselves together. Again, thanks for coming! I'll see you downstairs."

While Joe was waiting for them, he met his hosts and learned that Mr. Fitzhugh owned ten sheep stations in the Outback. Over the next half-hour, guests began to arrive. Joe vaguely remembered meeting some of them at the cocktail party that eventful first night in port. Their talk seemed to reflect a feeling of light-hearted conspiracy in the air as they sipped their cocktails.

Almost an hour later, Frenchy motioned for Joe to come to the bedroom door. He handed Joe a small box. "Put this in your pocket. I'm sure glad you didn't show up twenty minutes earlier. I apologize for not inviting you in."

"Don't worry about it. When is the ceremony? What am I supposed to do?"

"Give me the ring when the judge says so. Mr. Fitzhugh is going to play father of the bride. I took your gear out of the bag. They'll let you borrow something to carry your stuff back in."

"What do you need the suitcase for? Your honeymoon?"

"Of sorts. We're flying out tonight. I'll be back in time to get underway next Monday."

"Where are you going?"

Frenchy smiled. "Eva and I don't want to endure a shivaree, especially one by her people. Leaving this way ought to make tailing us nearly impossible. My goal is to get her passage to the States before we get underway. It's going to be tough because she doesn't have a passport. Let's get a drink. We have time before those women will be finished with Eva."

Forty minutes passed before the bride made her entrance. For a fleeting moment, Joe wished that she had looked at him first on that first day in port; then he felt happy for his friend whose love had transformed this ordinary woman into an extraordinary beauty. She glowed through the lace veil, from the sparkle of her eyes to her broad smile. Her light tan suit was cut to accent her long legs and broad shoulders.

The ceremony was brief and to the point. Both answered strongly their "I do's." On its conclusion, the guests, whom Joe estimated numbered just over twenty, applauded as they kissed. The party immediately went to the dining room, where Mr. Fitzhugh reminded Joe to propose the toast.

Joe raised his glass in salutation. "To Mr. and Mrs. Villerouge, Frenchy and Eva! May they find happiness, a long life together, and at least one child for every language spoken in their home."

Next Eva said, "To the many good-hearted, generous friends I have found here. To your hospitality and generosity. And to the man whom I love. I owe my life and my freedom to him."

Frenchy looked into his glass for what seemed like a minute while all eyes focused on him. He adjusted his eyeglasses and raised the fine-stemmed goblet. "To my shipmate, Joe Xylos, who made me realize that you can only take the ring that is in front of you and that it may never come around again. And yes, to you, my Eva, my love, who had the guts to act on impulse and grab the same ring."

Eva, who had been teary eyed as she finished her toast, cried and sniffled through dinner as first Mrs. CC, then others, recounted how Amy from Ames, Iowa, turned out to be Eva from Budapest. The details of the stratagems and precautions, as well as Eva's fears of capture or murder, were hashed and rehashed.

After dessert, Brian whispered to Joe, "The pilot says it's time. The servants have loaded their luggage. Please ask them to come, but do it quietly."

Joe walked with the newlyweds to the door, where Eva kissed him on the cheek. "I remembered more what you said than what you did at the village. Thank you for the pass. We have you to thank for our happiness. I too should have toasted you. Please don't become a stranger. Come see us."

Frenchy and Eva stepped into the darkness of a warm, starlit summer evening. Brian led the way with a flashlight. Eva insisted that they walk behind him in the darkness. Ahead of them, the plane was guarded by two Australians carrying large-bore hunting rifles.

Joe walked back to join the others, who had moved outside to a large veranda.

Mr. Fitzhugh handed Joe a snifter. "What kind of brandy would you like to follow your fine performance? I have a wide selection."

"Do you have Greek brandy, Metaxa?"

Laughing, he said, "Good taste! So you're Greek?"

"Yes."

Just after the plane's two engines sputtered to life, the field below the house lit up with two long rows of dim, parallel green and white lights. The plane started to taxi in darkness, with reflections of the runway lights on the wings as the only mark to fix its location. At last the red flashing lights on the plane were turned on, as well as the landing lights. The engines revved to full throttle. By its sounds, it was obvious the plane was moving and rushing toward the sky. All conversation stopped until the engine sounds diminished in the distance, throttled down for level flight. Joe, like the others, stood transfixed, watching the lights blink into the distance.

Mr. Fitzhugh touched Joe's arm. "Well, young man, you should feel proud of bringing such a fine couple together."

"Yes, sir, I am, for what little I did. The major credit must go to all of you."

"Nonsense. We didn't do it for love. Anything to give those Reds a bruising. The news tonight reported that twelve Hungarian athletes are seeking asylum here in Australia. They're finding out that you can't keep the herd together when you're busy combing the countryside for a stray. It is most interesting that the Hungarians haven't reported to the authorities that Eva is missing. Undoubtedly you'll be questioned. Have you thought of what you are going to say?"

"The truth. That Frenchy and Eva married and she is on her way to the States."

"Good. Did they tell you the destination?"

"No. Frenchy was downright secretive—"

"Splendid, then do me one favor. Not a word to anyone. Be like everyone else here and say that you saw the plane take off and disappear over the western horizon."

"Why?"

"It will buy them a little more time. I don't think Eva is a run-of-the-mill interpreter, and I'm certain Leftenant Villerouge isn't an ordinary naval officer. I've never met an American who had such a facility for language. Don't be surprised if your friend doesn't return to the ship."

"Wait a minute. He said he would."

"Really! And how many Leftenants hobnob with Ensigns?"

"We just happen to bunk in the same stateroom. . . . Well, maybe you're right. I never thought about it that way."

CHAPTER 13

Departing Melbourne

Joe returned to the ship late Thursday afternoon after the fox hunt. His progress up the brow was slow due to saddle sores on his knees and inner thighs, plus the muscles made sore by the ride. In spite of all the riding and the yelping dogs, he never did see a fox.

As he painfully raised his right arm to salute the ensign and turned to ask permission to come aboard, Piotr, the Polish interpreter, came out of the shadows saying, "Joe! Ensign Xylos! I must talk to you."

Joe ambled forward as Piotr came to his side, waving his arms. "Where is Eva? What has been done to her? The Hungarians are fearful that she has been kidnaped. They are about ready to go to the authorities."

The slight young officer shrugged. "What took you so long to get worried?"

Piotr shrugged his shoulders in imitation of Joe. "The Hungarians thought she strayed. Apparently she has habit of that kind of thing. But she has never been away so long before."

"Don't sweat it! She's with Frenchy."

"Are you sure? She's never called or made any contact."

"I think she's afraid of them. She isn't coming back. They're married."

Cracking his knuckles, Piotr said, "I don't believe it. She's too smart."

Joe tried to catch the man's eyes, but he averted them. The interpreter puckered his lips, then twisted his mouth as if he were going to cry. "The Hungarians will be going to the Australian authorities and reporting her disappearance this evening. You will be implicated. We are convinced that she had your pass when she left the village with that smooth-talking seducer. We figure that the riot you instigated at The Boar's Keeper was a botched attempt to divert anyone from following you. The Australians will know you used them."

"You know what I think, Piotr? Both of us are caught in the middle on this. You introduced Eva to the man who spirited her out from under their noses. And now they must be getting suspicious of you. After all, as an interpreter, you're in the ideal position to lead a double life. If you feel you're in danger, I know people who could help you start a new life here in Australia."

"I can't. I love my country. My wife and child, my baby, they are back home. The two of you fooled me. You are *agents provocateurs*. The Hungarians will lodge serious protests. Your country will be made fools. This kind of conduct harms the Olympic spirit."

Joe laid a hand on his shoulder. "Piotr, what happened at that pub had nothing to do with Eva. I wasn't there, and I didn't ask anyone to do it. All I've done since I've been here is go to these damn functions. Today I went on a fox hunt; I have sores on my legs, and every muscle in my body aches. Believe me, Eva and Frenchy want to be together. It's no Cold War plot. It's basic boy-meets-girl chemistry."

"How do you know they have married?"

"I witnessed the ceremony. I was the best man."

"When?"

"Last night. Piotr, they're gone. They left in a plane."

"Where to?"

"I don't know."

Piotr had regained his composure during the exchange. As he studied Joe, he pulled his worn suitcoat by the lapels until the collar pressed against the back of his neck, and left his hands there. After a long pause, he announced, "I know that Lieutenant Villerouge is no ordinary naval officer. And your casual offer of asylum says more than all your posturing. You are very clever actor, comrade. The Hungarian Olympic Committee is responsible for the people on the team. They must know if she is all right and is not being held against her will. Yesterday, two members of their team applied for asylum. They will not be harmed. Eva Atvar must personally contact the Hungarian Committee as soon as possible. She will not be harmed either. If she does not, the chairman will hold a press conference and name you and that Lieutenant as CIA agents who abducted the niece of a principal assistant to a member of the ruling Hungarian Central Committee."

Joe groaned, "Oh, I don't need that! Piotr, with God as my witness, I don't know where they are. Nobody said word one about who she was. There are some Australians who may know. Could you give me until tomorrow at this time to see if I can get through to her? I agree that she should have at least had the courtesy to let you know she's not coming back."

"Who knows where they are?"

"I don't know. I'll have to ask the people they were staying with."

"Who were they?"

"I'll let you know tomorrow. Just give me some more time, please."

"It is not my decision to make. The Hungarian leadership has full responsibility. For your sake, Joe, I hope you are telling the truth. Take my card and call me if you find out anything. I can promise nothing." Piotr thrust his hands into his coat pockets until his balled fists showed through the thin material. He walked slowly to the forward brow and went ashore with Joe following behind him. The Ensign walked as bowlegged as he could, to keep the cloth of his trousers from touching his badly chafed thighs.

Joe paused at the bottom and watched Piotr join Col. Rapishinski. They paused to talk. The two cast a long glance toward Joe before marching off the pier.

After dinner, Joe called Mrs. Collings-Cartwright, who said she would relay the message to the Fitzhughs, but she doubted if they knew where the couple could be located. She urged Joe not to be intimidated by the communists because he had done nothing wrong in helping the young woman escape.

Joe was relieved to see his boss sitting in the wardroom. He painfully eased his aching body down next to him. "Commander Moran, I've got a problem I think you should know about. Could we go to your stateroom to talk?"

Joe retold his story over the next ten minutes while the old mustang listened. He asked only a few questions, and only to clarify what Joe had said.

Moran drew a long puff on his cigarette before saying, "Joe, I wish you would have said something earlier. And yet, why should you? What business is it of yours who your roommate shacks up with? However, I don't know if you'll survive another trip through the headlines of the Melbourne dailies—deserved or undeserved. When the shit hits the fan, the higher-ups are going to say we weren't down here to rescue damsels in distress. And you'll be back in the soup over the picket fence affair. There's nothing that can be done now. The XO won't be back until late Saturday or early Sunday. The Old Man is 'discreetly indisposed,' with instructions not to be called unless it's an emergency. I'd say this qualifies. I'll call him and recommend that we alert the Admiral of a potential public relations problem. The one pair of shoes I wouldn't want to be standing in is those of Lieutenant Villerouge. I don't know what he does for CINCPAC Fleet, but whatever it is, it requires a clearance. He's just fallen on his professional sword."

Joe went to sick bay the next morning and was advised to stay aboard and let the sores heal. He was awakened from his nap about four in the afternoon when Frenchy dropped his suitcase.

"Where the hell you been?" Joe shouted.

"Canberra, Sydney, and back."

"Where's Eva?"

"Somewhere between here and Hickam Field, Hawaii. I got her on the Friday embassy flight as a military dependent and caught the next plane south."

"I didn't know you could do that!"

"I'm not sure how it was done, but I collected all my markers. The naval attache is an old friend. The real test comes when she gets to Immigration."

"Frenchy, the Hungarians are angry—no, mad as hell."

"Yes, 'mad as hell' better describes it. Eva's related to somebody high up in the Hungarian Communist Party."

"They're going to say you kidnaped her. It will be a big international incident."

"No, they're not. I've already talked to them."

"What?"

"They don't want to advertise their failures. I gave them the letter she wrote and a copy of the marriage certificate. They refused to give me any of her things. Unfortunately I don't have an address other than the ship, and for a time they didn't believe she had left the country. In the end they cooled down and called me 'Mr. CIA.' I guess that's because I talked in Russian and German after they began struggling with their English. The guy in charge told me that it really hurt them not to have Eva around because she was their best interpreter."

"Frenchy, I told the Chief Engineer about you and Eva. He thinks you're in deep trouble . . . that you'll lose your security clearance."

"True, I will be drummed out of the agency and banished, if they can, to the American equivalent of Siberia."

"You knew this, and you married Eva anyway?"

"Don't make me sound like a martyr. Joe, I've just been through a divorce that was caused by people who just didn't care when my life was coming apart. I owed them time for education, and they stiffed me."

"Did you want to get out?"

"Not after sixteen years. I have four years until retirement and no mark under three point six on a fitness report. With no wife to complain, I decided to make the best of the international crisis by recommending pre-positioning a group of us on a ship deployed to Melbourne. I've been looking for a graceful way to say I want out of the club. Eva is my ticket. I've just come from an unaccompanied hardship tour that was extended twice, so I can refuse any orders that separate me from my wife."

"How about duty on the *Beaverton*?"

"I'd love it personally. If Eva had a proper passport, she could follow me around from port to port. Ah, my girl in every port!"

"Earlier, you said you'd be drummed out of the agency. Is that the CIA?"

"I let that slip. I shouldn't have. I work for the National Security Agency; assignment to CINCPAC Fleet staff is my cover. I'm not some cloak-and-dagger type, just a technician. You don't have a need to know as much as I told you. Please, not a word to anyone."

"Does Eva know?"

"No. The first night, I told her I didn't want to know what she did or anything about her past and I didn't want to tell her anything about mine. She never probed, and I never asked."

Frenchy looked at his watch. "I've got to hurry. The Fitzhughs are sending the car for me. You and I have been invited to a coming-out party tonight at their beach house. Here's the invitation."

Joe tossed the envelope on the bed. "Not me. I'm so sore I can hardly walk. I'm dreading standing watches tomorrow."

"Well, if you feel up to it, come on Sunday. It's going to last the whole weekend. Give me that envelope, and I'll write the number so you can call."

Joe spent a sleepless night. In addition to his aching body, the worry over what would happen when the Hungarians went to the papers aggravated his restlessness. Sunday morning came without any sign of trouble. The papers were full of news about the end of the Games. Joe almost missed the article about Eva. It simply said that Eva Atvar, who had informed her team that she was defecting, had not contacted the Australian government yet. More on her defection would follow.

Joe was standing watch on the quarterdeck when partygoers returned Saturday morning. He heard tales of a bacchanal at the Fitzhughs' with a band that played until dawn to celebrate the coming-out of a Melissa Peters, whose father owned seven sheep stations in the outback. They forwarded a card from Mrs. Collings-Cartwright, asking him to join the party after he attended the Sunday afternoon tea of the Victoria Garden Club.

◦►─◉ ◉─◄◦

Joe arrived at the house as the last shades of day were turning to darkness. Being cold stone sober at a party where everyone else had a two-day head start didn't make the evening a particularly memorable one. Between drinks, they danced intimately to phonograph records. Joe noted that better than half of the wardroom were there, single and married alike. He managed to dance a few dances, but didn't enjoy it because his partners were so drunk.

Halfway through the evening, a tall, thin brunette with angular features and a pale complexion sat down next to him. "I'm Melissa Peters and this is my party. You must be the American cavalry sent to save me from the savages. My escort passed out. Would you like to dance with me?"

As she leaned heavily against him on the dance floor, he was soon aware that all that protected her dignity was a thin, wispy cotton dress. Joe stuck to drinking Coke, fearful of what awaited him on return to the ship. Melissa matched him drink for drink, but hers were shots of whiskey chased by champagne.

The party continued thus through the night as Joe waited for transportation back to the *Beaverton*. A beach fire was kindled, and he sat by it in the sand, dog tired and vaguely aware of the changes in the sky, the first outriders of the returning day. The circle gradually grew until about half the party were gathered around the blazing logs. Some of the couples were wrapped in blankets in the shadows.

He came back in from the fire to find Melissa asleep on a canvas chair, her legs spread askew like a discarded rag doll. Joe watched the black night sky lighten to purple over the bay. Pale white clouds acquired pink fringes that barely reflected on the water before them. As the day grew closer, Joe wrapped Melissa in a blanket, more to keep the world from seeing the obvious than for her comfort. Frenchy saw Joe cover her, then joined him to watch a breathtaking sunrise unfold. The Lieutenant took a sip from his glass and noisily swallowed it before saying, "I'm scared as hell, Joe."

What has he to be scared about? I'm the one who's gonna be put in hack.

Frenchy's hand trembled as much as his voice. "I mean, I'm scared that once she reaches the States, she'll look around and realize she's tied her wagon to the wrong star. Eva is a quality woman. She could have any man she wants. She has brains, beauty, and on top of it, is a world-class athlete. What am I? . . . A ne'er-do-well naval officer who is about to be passed over for Lieutenant Commander. It's altogether possible that they'll revert me back to Chief or First Class. I keep asking myself, what does she see in me? I feel like the man who walks into a room to find that Marilyn Monroe only has eyes for him. What if this marriage goes the way of the other one? How do you make it last? We should have had more time together before we married. What do I say to her?"

Joe said, "There was a physical change in Eva at the wedding. She was glowing . . . a classic bride. How do you hold that moment? I don't know. It made me feel good to know I had a hand in making it possible. Frenchy, my father and I talked quite a bit before he died. He didn't meet my mother until the day before their wedding, but theirs was a happy marriage. He told me he valued his father's judgment and went into the marriage with the idea that she was the best woman he could marry. You must feel as he did."

"Well, yes . . ."

"He said that love starts like a little sprouting seed, the *eros* love. You see the little green leaves, but they aren't what is important. It's the soil and the water, the nourishment that is unseen. Love grows and changes through commitment. That adds filial love that is crowned by *agape* love. And commitment is something that has to keep coming, like the water that feeds the plant as it grows into a mighty oak. He used to tell me that marriage is like driving a car. You've got to keep your hands on the wheel and your eyes on the road. That's what he called commitment. Maybe you could tell her about the kind of commitment you are willing to make and see what her response is."

"I never thought about it that way. I don't think I had a clear thought in my head from the moment we met. Joe, she is the woman every man dreams of . . . the most exciting woman I have ever touched. Never in all my life have I been so physically excited. She makes me feel like an eighteen-year-old all over again."

"There's more going for you than *eros*. The way you two communicate in different languages . . . the two of you have something special going."

Frenchy took a large swallow from his drink. "Shades of love . . . I've run across them in Russian, but to me, love is love."

"It may be, but there is a difference between the passion of a first night and, say, a sixty-year-old couple holding hands. Yet both are love."

"Yeah, damn, Xylos, why are you so profound? I've never met an Ensign before who quotes Shakespeare and spouts Greek philosophy—"

Just then, Brian Fitzhugh stepped between them and put his arms over their shoulders. "Look! Look, gentlemen, to the east! There it is! Behold, the sun!"

The top arc of the sun had shown itself through a very red sky in the band of blue between the rose-fringed clouds and water that was rapidly turning from black to grays and blues with red hues here and there. The three men stood in silence.

Squeezing their shoulders, Brian continued, "Behold, mates, this is what we call 'Black Monday'—the agonizing day you must get through after a weekend of hard partying. Come now, help me rouse your mates. We have the transport ready to give all a lift back to Melbourne. You're leaving after high noon, I understand."

⋆─◉─⋆

The departure, just after noon, was from a pier filled with well-wishers and girlfriends. On that warm, muggy day, women wore sundresses and wide-brimmed hats to shade their faces. Children in short pants ran among the dignitaries, who wore light-colored suits. Frenchy waved to the crowd from beneath a canvas awning.

After the first rush of steam was sent to the backing turbines, the fire rooms responded by throwing more burners on line. They turned up the speed of the forced-draft blowers, which increased the flow of air to the boilers. Orders that tubes would not be blown in port had been faithfully followed, and as a result cinders had accumulated for ten days on the boiler surfaces and in the uptakes to the stacks. Now, in the rush of air, these were pushed skyward like a minor pyroclastic explosion and rained down. The black debris struck the white awnings and pelted the teak decks.

Everyone on the port bridge wing ran to cover except the Captain and the pilot, who had to remain at their stations. A light wind blowing from the starboard quarter carried the cloud onto the pier, where the remainder of the cinders fell. As on the ship, each nodule of accumulated soot left a black punctuation mark where it struck.

Captain Slaxman stood on the wing of the bridge, black marks spotting his cap and shirt collar, surveying this latest public relations disaster. Below him the crowd on the pier—who were now ex-well-wishers—either fled or shook their fists at him. He forced a smile and waved to them before returning his attention to piloting the ship. Out of the corner of his mouth, he barked, "Lieutenant Leach, tell the Chief Engineer that I want a full explanation as to why he chose to blow tubes as soon as we gave him the first bell."

Straining to hear over the whoosh of rushing air, Leach asked, "Did you say 'blow tubes'?"

"Of course I did! Look at the black mess everywhere!"

Leach relayed what he thought he'd heard. "Main control, bridge. Blow tubes."

"Now?" responded the main control room.

"Main control, bridge, I said blow tubes!" Leach shouted into the microphone.

"Main control, aye."

The tugs were turning the bow just off the end of the pier when the first blast of steam hit the outside of the bank of steam tubes in the boiler uptakes. This time the cloud cleared the ship, but rained soggy black goop on the few brave souls left on the pier.

Frenchy had watched the departure from the main deck just forward of Number One turret. As the crowd melted away, a small group of men stood in the middle of the pier. On one side was Piotr. Next to him were the Hungarians to whom he had delivered the letter, and the others he didn't recognize. Piotr was taking pictures of the masts and radar antenna when the first wave of soot-laden moisture rained down on them. The others retreated. Frenchy waved. Two of the Hungarians shook their fists at him. The Pole took one last picture of him before turning his back and scampering away.

CHAPTER 14

Top of the Mar

The expected message directing Lieutenant Villerouge's relief arrived two days out of Melbourne. He and his team were directed to return to Pearl from Guam aboard the first available aircraft. With approval from the Captain, he had stood JOOD watches for most of the trip to Melbourne and on departure was added to the watch bill as the OOD.

The trip back across the Equator was uneventful. Over coffee and dessert, Joe listened to the tales of exploits ashore. It seemed that almost everyone had found a "friendly native" except a handful of the most devoted married men and Joe. Among those few was his roommate, Carter Sawyer. At Frenchy's request, the Ensign said nothing about Eva; and he didn't feel his hours spent at official functions were worth recalling.

He did manage to share his Australian host's comments about Lieutenant Leach. Leach's reaction to the name "Leftenant Koala" guaranteed that the name stuck. The stewards, whom Leach always treated as if they were idiots or worse, announced at least twice that "Leftenant Leach" was wanted on the phone.

Leach's gaffe at the Melbourne pier had already made him the laughingstock of the wardroom. Thus, when a plate of eucalyptus leaves was mysteriously offered at his table as an additional condiment boat with a curry dinner, he found no humor in it. He seethed and glared at Joe throughout the meal. Afterward he strode to Joe's table and said imperiously, "I made the offer to the XO to take you in when the Chief Engineer fires you."

Joe smiled. "That's kind of you, Lieutenant. Perhaps you could enlighten me, sir. All I've heard from Commander Moran has been compliments. In what way has my performance not been satisfactory?"

"You are a liberty risk, Mr. Zilch." Leach took a step back from the table and did an about-face as if he were in ranks before marching briskly from the wardroom.

⇀⊨◉ ◉⊨↽

On one of the last afternoons before they were to arrive at their next port, Joe and Frenchy stood topside, leaning against the barbette of Number Two turret. Frenchy lit a cigarette and exhaled the smoke in a steady, measured manner. "Joe, I'm full of mixed emotions. I almost dread leaving the *Beaverton* and going back to Pearl."

"Getting cold feet?"

"A little of that. Much more than that . . . thinking about the things I chose not to see when we were together."

"We? What do you mean?"

"Eva . . . Yes, she is a lovely, loving, exciting woman, and yet . . . there was an undercurrent. She never relaxed; and by some of the things she said, I sensed that she could be an entirely different person. I didn't want to talk too much about my past, because it's either classified or not worth mentioning, but she said something that I've played over in my mind more than once."

"What's that?"

"She said that the one thread that has been constant through her life is that she is a betrayer, starting when she was a child when she betrayed her mother . . . and including the times she betrayed her country and the people who trusted her."

"Did she elaborate?"

"A little, but I didn't encourage her and now I wish I had. She said that after she was taken to Russia with her aunt and uncle, her mother was supposed to follow, but she never saw her again. Her mother was arrested by the NKVD on account of her religion. Apparently Eva had told someone that her mother said prayers and taught her about God. The way she found out was that she was given an award for doing her duty. I'm aware that they did this sort of thing, but I never gave any thought to experiencing it on a personal level. I didn't know how to respond to her. What do you say to someone who turned in her own mother?"

"Is this why you were expounding the other day on how Stalin extended the power of the state into the homes by encouraging the kids to rat on their parents?"

"Yes."

"Frenchy, imagine how she feels, knowing to this day that in an effort to please the teacher or whomever, she told them about something she thought was innocent. Then she found out later that her own words condemned her own mother. I'd conclude that beneath the surface there's a lot of hurt and guilt. I think she needs trust and support as much as you. Yes, even forgiveness."

"Joe, I'm going to miss having you to talk to. You said it all."

⋄►═◉ ◉═◄⋄

Four days before Christmas, the *Beaverton* moored at Agana, Guam, in mid-morning. Harry Leach gloated over shifting Joe into the first day's duty section. The Ensign found it easy, however, to arrange a swap for the last day so he could have one last liberty with Frenchy, whose plane was scheduled to leave from Naval Air Station Agana the next day at nine a.m.

By the time all the necessary work had been done after mooring and Joe was ready to go, it was close to four p.m. He found his roommate holding a lavender-colored piece of stationery and grinning as if he'd just won the Irish Sweepstakes.

Frenchy tapped the sheet with his free hand as he announced, "She's okay! She says that all is well and I shouldn't worry. No one will throw her out of the country. A man from the Navy talked to her. She says she never realized what I had given up to rescue her . . . she wants to spend the rest of her life paying me back with her love and devotion. No one will tell her what will happen to me, but they did promise that wherever I went, she would be permitted to follow. I can't wait to step off the plane at Hickam. Let's go over and celebrate!"

Their first stop was the air station, where Frenchy confirmed his crew's departure arrangements. From there they caught a taxi to the hill where the Bachelor Officer's Quarters and Officer's Club were situated. The taxi was a rusty 1950 DeSoto whose interior was blast-furnace hot. The ship's policy of wearing a long-sleeved khaki shirt and necktie in the tropics aggravated their discomfort. The cab driver found little humor in Joe's suggestion that he name his cab company "Purgatory Taxis."

The high humidity gave them little relief as they walked to the O Club, which was called " Top of the Mar." Talk of a tall, cool drink in a cool place dominated their conversation while they wiped away the sweat running down their necks.

Once inside, while their eyes were adjusting to the dimness, a bourbon-slurred female voice called, "Why if it isn't Frenchy Villerouge! Long time no see. Where was it last? Midway?"

"Betty, you've got a good memory," answered Frenchy. "Let's see, you were coming through to start your tour out here. You must be overdue for orders."

"I'm going back to D.C. in January. The orders are for Suitland, Maryland, but they haven't told me what I'll be doing yet."

As Joe's eyes adjusted, he identified the speaker as a woman officer, a Lieutenant Commander, who looked to be in her late thirties if not forties. She was matronly plump, with pillow-sized breasts. When Frenchy introduced her as Betty Gates, she shook his hand hard, crushing his fingers between sharp-edged rings. She bought the first round. Joe surveyed the room, and his eyes focused on a silk painting of a bare-breasted South Seas woman that hung behind the bar. That was something he had never seen at any other O Club. *That's more like the women I wanted to see ashore*, thought Joe, *not an overstuffed WAVE officer.*

Betty patted and shaped her faded brown hair as the two men reached for their glasses. As they took the first sips from their first round, she asked Frenchy, "The last I heard about you was that you were on the outs with Sandra. Did you get that patched up?"

"No. She wouldn't wait for me. I'm divorced and she's remarried."

The woman visibly relaxed in her seat. "I'm sorry to hear that. I think she had rocks for brains."

"A month ago, I wouldn't have said it, but that was the best thing that ever happened to me."

"That's not what I heard. You were way down, I understand."

"That I was. But if she hadn't forced the divorce, I would never have known what it's like to find the ideal woman. Eva is what dreams are made of."

"Eva? Do I know her?"

"No. She was an interpreter for the Hungarian Olympic team."

"Aha, the girl in the last port! So you're from that crowd that pulled in today. Now how did you hornswoggle a trip to Melbourne? Or are you ship's company?"

"No, my crew and I are CINCPAC Fleet staff. We were pre-positioned due to the dustup along the Suez Canal. I was in my usual role as a rider."

"So you left your heartthrob Down Under?"

"Not quite. We married just before I sent her back to the States. I had to make sure she wouldn't be shipped back to Hungary. I got a letter from her today. Apparently everything is fine."

"She's a Hungarian? A foreign national from behind the Iron Curtain! And you married her?"

"I did."

"Frenchy, do they know this?"

"Yeah. I've been thrown out of the club and my clearances revoked. I'm not sure I'm even cleared to read weather reports."

"What are you going to do now?"

"Accept orders to wherever they send me as long as Eva can accompany me."

"She must be some honey. You must have known her from before?"

"No. I proposed to her on the morning of the second day I knew her."

"That must have been one hell of a first impression!"

"I don't know how to put it in words. From almost the moment our eyes met, I had this feeling that she and I would get on well. By the next morning, I knew she was the woman who would pass through my world once in a lifetime."

"How much do you know about her past?"

"Very little other than she was orphaned early in World War II and raised by her uncle. She wanted out . . . to defect. After we married, I found out her uncle has some sort of job with the Hungarian Central Committee."

"Frenchy, I can't believe it. You were true blue, Mr. Regular Navy, the original Cold War warrior. You surprise me. I never visualized you as the impetuous Latin lover. Babe, you've committed professional suicide. Surely you understood the consequences?"

"Yeah. I gave it about thirty seconds thought."

"What if she's an agent? What if she's just using you to get into the country? Did you ask her? . . . Question her?"

"I didn't want to, Betty. She is the most fascinating, most wonderful woman I've ever met." Frenchy's voice choked up, so he took a sip from his drink. "From the first day, I felt like I'd always known her. You're right, I don't know much about her past. My only concern is our future. I'll know soon if I've been a fool in love for the second time. The letter she sent from Pearl sounds encouraging. I want to make this marriage take."

"Frenchy, she must be one fine woman."

"She is that and more. The thought did occur to me that she was some sort of agent. I didn't want to give her the opening to question me about what I do, so I made an offer not to query her about her work or past if she wouldn't ask me about mine. She acted as if I'd lifted a burden from her back. She relaxed and lost any reserve she may have had. It became an unspoken condition of our relationship. Before I put her on the plane, I told her she would be questioned on arrival in the States and shouldn't say anything until they agreed in writing that she could stay with me. I tried to prepare her . . . warn her that things could get sticky or even rough. She gently patted my arm and simply said, 'Don't worry. I'm fully trained on interrogation techniques. I won't let you down.' I didn't know about her uncle until after I delivered her letter to the Hungarians at the Olympic Village. I waited until I was pretty sure she would be clear of Immigration to send an encrypted message breaking the news to my boss."

"Frenchy, they're going to make an example of you. You're dead meat."

The Lieutenant nodded and emptied his glass. "I made a judgment that she is far more important to me than anything the Navy has left to offer. It would have happened if I'd married any foreign national. I'm praying they don't get to her."

He raised his empty glass, and the waitress acknowledged. The trio sat in silence. Joe had heard all of this before.

After the Ensign drained the last dregs from between the ice cubes, he asked, "Betty, how did you come to know Frenchy? Did you serve together?"

She laid her head back and laughed. "I'll never forget that day if I live to be a hundred. I was a Jay Gee in San Diego and working for the custodian of registered publications, the manuals that the Navy doesn't want the bad guys to have access to. Frenchy came in, and was he ever handsome . . . a newly commissioned Ensign on his first assignment. He needed glasses but wouldn't admit it, so it took forever to go through the inventory of pubs and get everything signed off. I was a little exasperated with him because I had to spell out about half the numbers on the list. I thought it was a stall to make time with me. The last thing he did before he left was to take out his pistol and cycle the receiver. He pointed it up toward the ceiling and . . . bang! It went off. It was a poured concrete building, built like a fortress, and the bullet must have zinged around the room a dozen times. He hit the floor in front of the counter, as pale as this tablecloth. I thought he'd been shot, but he was lucky, the bullet missed him. He was shaking like a runny bowl of jello; I had to practically carry him and his bag of pubs to his car."

Frenchy snapped, "I knew when I saw you that you were going to tell that story. And it gets worse every time. Runny bowl of jello! Anyway, I learned very important lessons that day. Never, no never, pull the trigger without visually inspecting the bore. Never put a round in the chamber unless you are going to shoot the gun. There, Joe, you've heard a genuine piece of wisdom that wasn't found in one of your books."

They all laughed and ordered another round. When the dining room opened up, they had dinner. Afterward they returned to a table in the bar where a Guam native, or Chamorro, in light-colored matching trousers and open-collared shirt was playing the Steinway. Night had fallen, and the popular favorites he played had a rich tone that blended nicely with the conversation. As the bar filled up with officers from the fleet, the music faded beneath the vocal din. After a while, there was only standing room at the bar.

Through the evening, shipmates joined them briefly and left. By ten thirty, the numbers had dropped to the point that the piano's melodies could be heard again, mingling lightly with the chatter that filled the large room.

By the time it was Frenchy's turn to buy the drinks, service at the crowded bar had deteriorated from poor to nonexistent. While he stood watching the bartender fill his order, the house lights flickered out. In the shadows, Frenchy made out the dim figure of a two-hundred-pound man in a sports shirt running toward the open end of the bar. The lights blinked back on as the big man threw a block on the small Oriental bartender, who tumbled the length of the bar, taking glasses and bottles with him to the floor.

Just behind the hulk, a smaller man grabbed the frame of the painting of the nude. He grunted and pulled, but it would not come off the wall and his hands quickly slipped off the frame. Clearly, it was securely bolted to the wall. He swore, "Damn! It won't come!"

The big man had his back to the room, watching his accomplice, when Frenchy leaned over the bar and caught the man's armpits from behind. He slung him upward, then backward onto the bar. More glasses and bottles broke as the man rolled back and forth on the bar, arms and legs flailing the air like a crab on its back. As he rolled away from Frenchy, he bellowed, "I'm gonna kick your ass!" At that point the Lieutenant's fist caught him under the chin, driving him into a crouch before he sank limply into the well behind the bar with more crunches of broken glass.

There was a third intruder, who started to move toward Frenchy but stopped cold when their eyes met. Pointing at him, Frenchy barked, "Stay right where you are, mister!"

The man who had tried to snatch the painting hesitated only a moment before fading toward the open end of the bar in spite of Frenchy's order to stop.

Joe was out of his seat at the breaking of the first glass. He collided with a table, spilling drinks and bringing curses. A well-placed foot between his legs sent him sprawling amid guffaws and more profanity.

He picked himself up off the floor and was heading toward the bar when he saw the second man fleeing from Frenchy. The chase was brief. He dragged the man to the ground with a very amateur but effective open-field tackle. While the man struggled, two or three more piled on to help Joe. The melee rolled into a bystander and spilled his drink. As the heavy scent of the thick, dark Jamaica rum and fruit drink leavened Joe's senses, the added weight pressing on his already distressed stomach brought quick results. He threw up.

At this, the pile of bodies quickly broke up. The tackled man on the bottom, who had received most of the contents of Joe's stomach, swore and squirted free. He had barely gained his feet when Frenchy ordered, "You there! Get over to the bar before you give me the pleasure of splitting your head open!"

The man eyed the others blocking his exit, then walked slowly to the bar, trying to wipe the vomit off his face and out of his hair. No one blocked Joe's hurried departure to the men's room.

Joe surveyed his personal damage in the restroom mirror. His shirt collar was torn. One button was missing, and two more were smashed. The right shoulder and sleeve were soaked with a cloying-sweet, syrupy mixture. The left cuff was caked with part of his stomach contents. His left shin was bruised, and his right had a wood burn from the fall. He painfully removed his shirt to see if there were any marks on his ribs because they hurt so much. There was nothing.

The mixture of the sweet fragrance and stench didn't help him keep down the rest of his dinner. After two more bouts over the toilet, he washed up and rinsed his shirt. His initial effort concentrated on the soiled parts so that the contrast of wet and dry areas made it look like a camouflage outfit. He filled the sink and soaked the shirt before wringing it out and putting it on. It looked bad, but at least it was uniformly bad.

Joe came out of the restroom, trying to look invisible. The club was now full of uniforms and raised voices, and the lights were turned up to their brightest. He walked as quietly as he could toward the front door, stopping when he saw a Shore Patrolman standing outside. He eased his way back toward the bar, trying the doors along the way, but all were locked. He found a water fountain and sipped the tepid water to take the bitter taste out of his mouth.

On reentering, he saw that everyone was gathered near the bar. A Medical Corpsman was wrapping a bandage around the bartender's arm. Joe slowly returned to his table, eased himself into his chair, and took a sip from his glass. He watched in silence, shivering slightly from the dampness of his shirt.

Commander Longstreet marched into the bar and halted where he could survey the damage. There before his eyes, soaked and disheveled, sat Joe.

"I knew it! I knew it!" he bellowed, throwing his khaki cap to the floor. "Boy, you are like a Tasmanian devil! Wherever we let you loose, it's like a cyclone hits. I guess the words we had in Melbourne were a waste of air. Well, it looks like you got the worst of this one. I won't have my officers brawling at the O Club . . . Get your skinny butt back to the ship!"

From across the room, Betty interrupted. "I beg your pardon. Commander, Mr. Xylos wasn't brawling. I saw the whole thing. He was the only officer here with the presence of mind to stop the man who tried to steal the picture from behind the bar."

Other voices joined. "The guy would have gotten away if he hadn't stopped him. . . . He's okay! . . . Chew on these guys, they're the ones!"

Commander Longstreet pointed at the picture. "What do you mean? The picture's hanging straight on the wall."

An angry bartender held up his bleeding arm as he stood up. "Of course it is! It's bolted to the wall. They had to do that to keep it from being stolen again. Obviously these assholes didn't know that. The big guy hit me so hard, I fell down and cut my arm on the broken glass. They made one hell of a mess! Talk about stupid, they could have gotten away in the dark if the one who turned out the lights knew what he was doing. As it was, he turned them off and then on here. Finally he turned off the lights out in the parking lot."

Now adjusting his tie, the tall, red-necked *Beaverton* XO walked slowly to the biggest of the three offenders, who had a large lump on his jaw. Looking first at the man's soiled attire and finally upward, he locked a steely gaze on the other's eyes from six inches away. Lowering his voice to almost a whisper and pointing toward Joe, Longstreet said, "You mean to tell me that you assaulted my officer in the course of this outrage?"

Coughing, Joe answered from across the room, "I tripped, sir, when I was going after the little guy. Everybody piled on because they thought he was going to get away. It just happened."

The man Joe had tackled volunteered, "That little runt barfed all over me. These two guys way overreacted. The Lieutenant could have broken Wally's jaw. Like I told Shore Patrol, we were just taking the picture to hang in our wardroom. What I'd like to know is, why did you two feel compelled to play hero?"

A voice in the crowd said, "Don't screw around with cruiser sailors!"

Joe walked slowly across the room and picked up the Commander's hat. He gently held it in both hands and blew imaginary dust off the scrambled eggs on the visor. He managed a weak smile as he handed it to Longstreet.

Pulling himself up on a barstool, Joe then addressed the man he had tackled. "Buddy, I've been working in night clubs since I was twenty. After a while, you learn to react almost by reflex to clowns like you. Taking the picture off the wall is one thing, but injuring the bartender and breaking the place up are something else. Anyplace Stateside, you'd be on your way to the county lockup. Count on it!"

The third man, the one Frenchy had stared down, said, "Don't worry. We'll pay the damages."

The big man, who had tangled with Frenchy, bristled at this and yelled at the third man, "You're the one who screwed this up. You turned off the wrong fucking lights! "

Longstreet asked, "Where are you people from?"

A Lieutenant wearing a black armband with the yellow letters `OOD' on it replied, "These are our resident pranksters from Guam's own LST 996, the terrors of the Trust Territories. We will take them back to their ship. I'll need statements from your Ensign and the Lieutenant."

The XO nodded and put an arm on Joe's shoulder to guide him toward the door. In a low voice, he said, "Son, you've got more balls than a brass monkey. You draw trouble like open food on the mess decks draws rats. I'm not sure how you pull all this off. Or am I going to find out tomorrow that you visited the LST and laid out the plan?"

"Commander, Frenchy and I were up here minding our own business. I never saw these people before, and the first time I laid eyes on that painting was tonight. I may yet pull a practical joke or two, but give me a little credit. It won't involve injury to an innocent party or tearing up property like they did. You should have seen the way that guy knocked the bartender down. Those guys deserve to hang.”

“Son, you look a mess. I don’t like to have my officers seen looking so bad. As soon as you and Villerouge finish those statements, I’ll give you a ride back to the ship. If you start feeling worse, say something right away. Getting hit hard enough to lose your dinner could be a sign of serious injury.”

“Commander, I wasn’t feeling all that good when this started. I made the mistake of trying to keep up with Frenchy. I’m good for a couple glasses of wine and a brandy perhaps, but not steady drinking like he does. I don’t know how he can function while carrying such a load.”

⟡

Before quarters the next morning, Joe accompanied his friend to the pier where the detachment had gathered with their luggage and equipment to await transportation to the air station. Bleary-eyed and grumbling, the group, to a man, were grousing over the change in plans that cut them out of a trip to Yokosuka, Japan. Frenchy stood by himself, looking across the turquoise-colored water.

Kicking the ground lightly with his toe, he said to Joe, “The crew is right to blame me. I’m sorry I screwed up their plans, but I still think that a lifetime of freedom for one person is far more important than two weeks of good times for a dozen sailors.”

He pulled his wallet out of his pocket and fanned out a small stack of calling cards. He pulled one from the stack, studying first the side that had Japanese script, then flipping it over to the reverse printed in English. Extending it to Joe, he said, “And speaking of good times, take this.”

“Sunshine Suzuki?”

“An old friend. I’ve always stopped by her place. She’s Mama-san at the Suenohjo. Just tell a cabbie to take you to the Sewer Club.”

Joe studied the card. “Sewer Club?”

“She has the best-looking string of lovelies in town. Stop wrinkling up your nose, Joe. It’s different out here. They’re the real McCoy. Two weeks in Yokosuka and you’ll forget that round-eyes ever existed. It’s sure a hell of a lot better than what happened to you last night. Do me a favor, please. Stop by and tell her I sent you. Say hello for me. Tell her

163

I got married."

"Anybody else?"

"No, it's been a long time. Besides, the girls come and go. Joe, you're one hell of a fine shipmate. I'll miss you, buddy."

Frenchy drew another card from his hand and said, "Without fail, go see this man and either have him alter your uniforms or make you new ones."

"Toshiro Ito, Custom Tailor?"

"He is the best. You'll get better prices in Hong Kong, but nowhere in the world better workmanship. He's even been approved to make uniforms for the Marines."

"Frenchy, I just got these uniforms."

"And they fit you like you're a Reserve too. Do it. Don't argue. Remember the cliche that you never get a second chance to make a first impression. Joe, I'll let you know where they're going to send me. With any luck, it will be right there at Pearl. Wherever it is, you're always welcome at my house. Eva feels the same way."

They shook hands. Frenchy picked up his suitcase and walked to the bus that had just driven up. Joe thought, *I'm gonna miss you, old man. You've been a good friend.*

CHAPTER 15

Harry's Christmas Tree

Lieutenant Milt Kane's transfer to inactive status resulted in Joe's promotion to Main Engines Division Officer, and with it the problems accompanying the position. Thus it was that on the second morning in Guam, Joe sought out the ship's Personnel Officer, Barry Tumwater, to learn what he could about personnel management. They conferred after breakfast at the central mess table, which was decorated for the holiday with a sad little pine tree, barely two feet tall. When Harry Leach waddled across the wardroom, Tumwater enlivened the morning with a challenge to him. "Harry, you're the Mess Caterer, please don't tell me that you're charging the members for that poor excuse for a Christmas tree; it may have limbs, but it hardly has any needles, and it smells like dog urine."

Leach shook his head. "Patience, Barry, patience, please. What survived the flight from Alaska is the best we can offer. Sir, you elected me Mess Caterer and I take my duties seriously. Rest easy, sir, with Outside White's able hand, I am working on a solution."

Joe said, "Barry, tomorrow's Christmas Eve. I say, leave it up until we're alongside in Japan. Then we should be able to finagle something better."

Leach snarled, "Mr. Zilch, don't even think about any more finagling! Mister White and I are working on the transfer of a handsome tree from Andersen Field. You have the duty tomorrow, don't you? Our operation will be safe with you on board standing the watches. Isn't that right, Wayne?"

Outside White grinned. "Yes, sir. Say, Mr. Xylos, I thought you had the duty on arrival too. How did you get off the ship to create all that trouble at the Top of the Mar last night?"

"I swapped."

Leach snapped, "You swapped? I understand, then we can count you out tomorrow? You won't be attending the Christmas party at Andersen Field?"

"That's right, sir."

"Is your commie-loving bunkmate on his way to Pearl?"

"Lieutenant, I don't think you'd have the courage to say that to his face. Yes, Frenchy's plane took off yesterday morning."

Harry gave him a thumbs-down. "Good, the two of you must be popular aboard LST 996. They've been directed to remain underway until the day after Christmas. Had you not been so drunk, you would have recognized that snatching a painting from the club was good clean fun. But no! You and Golden Boy had to play hero."

Joe assumed a stance with his arms out from his sides and his thumbs pointing downward. "Sir, perhaps you're unaware that their 'good clean fun' left the bartender with an arm cut so badly that it required stitches, and half the bottles behind the bar broken. Is that what you call good clean fun?"

Outside White replied, "Well, we'll be in full dress tomorrow and on our best behavior--certainly there for good clean fun."

As Leach and White ambled out, Joe scratched his head. *Hmm. Are they planning to put something over on the Air Force? Is that why they don't want me there?*

⊷━●◉━◦

After lunch, Joe climbed down the ladder into the forward engine room. At the bottom, he inspected the paint job he had requested during this stay in port, and thought it looked worse than it did before. It epitomized what his boss, Chief Engineer Moran, called "polka-dot white." He called his leading Chief Petty Officer over. "Chief, I would appreciate it if you would go down to the paint locker and request another draw. This isn't such a large area that it can't be done by the time we set the sea and anchor detail."

"Aye, aye, sir. Sorry, Mr. Xylos, but they aren't going to give us even another Dixie Cup full. They say they're down to the dregs."

Joe shook his head. "Don't let them feed you that cock-and-bull story.

There's a lowboy loaded with five-gallon cans sitting on the pier back by the stern. One way or the other, we ought to get a fresh coat on. I want to give my boss a good impression."

"I understand, Mr. Xylos. If the First Lieutenant doesn't call out a work party, I'll have that paint on board before we sail."

That evening, during the first watch (eight p.m. to midnight), the after brow was manned by the leading Chief from B Division. Right after the movie was over, he called for a large work party to form on the main deck aft. They filed over to the lowboy and in less than ten minutes stripped it clean of the last can of paint. Interestingly enough, not a single can rested topside; they were all carried directly below. If an astute observer were present, he would have seen small pyramids of cans piled here and there by the covers of some of the ship's voids (empty spaces along the hull), but he would have to be quick before they disappeared.

⋆⊷◉⊶⋆

Joe stood the first watch on the quarterdeck with an eye on the after brow. He was surprised to see Leach and Outside White go ashore shortly after nine p.m., both wearing their dress blues. What surprised him was that they drove away in the First Lieutenant's pickup truck. *What do they need that for?* he wondered. Since the XO was at Andersen Field, he notified First Lieutenant Speed. He told him about the conversation in the wardroom earlier that day.

Some minutes later, Father Finn called Joe aside on the quarterdeck. "Mr. Xylos, you were correct to make an issue of this. I'm terribly alarmed about the damage Leach and White could do. COMNAVMARIANIS could order us underway immediately. I also warned Leach not to go forward with this. They are intent on stealing a tree from the Officers' Club at the air base."

Joe grinned. "So that's why they took the First Lieutenant's pickup."

"This is no laughing matter. If you had stopped them, you would have saved this command a tremendous embarrassment."

"Leave it to Harry. He must want to outdo the crew of the LST."

"Yes, the entire flotilla has been invited to Andersen Field on the far end of the island for a Christmas party. It's a Strategic Air Command base, so the security is extremely high. The XO's got to brief the Old

Man. What do you think? You came through for me on the used cars. Have you any wild ideas? This is no college prank or some political stunt. They could get their brains blown out."

Joe had no ready answer. But minutes later, after the Chaplain left, Joe rang him up on the phone with an idea. "Father, this is all I can think of. Recall that Captain Slaxman was decorated for his rescue of B 29 crews off the Japanese coast in the last days of the war. Might you suggest that the Andersen Base Commander offer a Christmas tree, explaining that our Captain has two loose cannons? We offer to run it as a drill: if we win, we get a healthy tree. If not, we don't get a tree, we buy champagne."

Father Finn began laughing. "Splendid idea, Joe! That will save all our behinds if the brass buys into your idea. I'll fly it by the Old Man."

On arriving at the O Club at Andersen, Harry Leach looked into the still-empty ballroom to double check what he'd done to the base's Christmas tree on the afternoon of the day before. It was a tall, nicely shaped tree without many bare spaces, and, unobserved, he had plugged a short string of lights onto it. Close inspection of the string would have revealed that the wires passed through a dark green metallic cylinder clipped to the trunk. An innocent-looking candy-striped cord led from the cylinder and ended in a brass ring. Leach was elated when he learned that the club manager had invited the wardroom into a separate room to engage in a game of poker dice and then celebrate in the bar.

The fist sign the Air Force had that this would be a Christmas Ball to remember was when the officers in their full dress and their wives in formal gowns arrived to find a corner of the dance floor occupied by a crowd of Navy officers. The Destroyer Squadron Commodore apologized to the Air Force General for attending their obviously formal affair. The General laughed when he was warned of the *Beaverton*'s two Lieutenants; he looked forward to the challenge. In spite of the informal dress of most of the Navy officers and their low-level rowdiness, the General was pleased by the gesture of the Commodore, who left a bottle of champagne with a card on his table.

While they were toasting one another, Leach went into action. The band returned to the stand. The floor filled with couples dancing to "White Christmas." Later, one of the wives recalled seeing a chubby man wearing a Navy dress uniform pull an ornament off the tree. It was a brass ring. Then she saw him walk away from the tree.

Five minutes later, while the band played "Tenderly" with the lights dimmed, the happy event ended with a flash next to the trunk of the tree, followed by the sound of Christmas tree light bulbs popping. Some recalled a fireball rolling across the floor from the tree. Lights in the room flickered, then some of the lights behind the tree went dark. The tree was immediately engulfed in smoke.

Panic filled the room. There were a few screams, and loud-talking people crowded the exits. The same chubby man calmly unplugged the tree and carried it, still trailing smoke, out the patio doors. The sounds of shattering ornaments were almost lost in the cheers and applause of a very tense audience. A finger of smoke hung in the air just inside the door, twisting and withering in the moment of silence as people drew a sigh of relief. The sequence of events happened so quickly that the bartender was still waiting for the base fire department to answer when the tree was carried from the room. By the time the first engine arrived, most of the club patrons were in their cars, starting to leave.

The fire chief asked the club manager, "Where is this flaming tree you called us about?"

The manager went out the same patio door the chubby man had taken. It took no Indian tracker to follow this trail. Sparkling shards of ornaments marked the path, which ended abruptly at the corner of the building. He stood at the curb dumbfounded for almost half a minute; perhaps his mind initially refused to accept the evidence. A waiter joined him, and the two peered into the darkened lot. Other than the whine of a jet on the runway, all was quiet. They continued around to the front door. The manager paused one more time, looking into the night, as if the tree would somehow materialize. "Say, who pulled off this stunt?" he asked.

"I haven't the faintest idea," answered the waiter, "except he was fat and wore a Navy dress uniform. One of the firemen said the smoke was from a smoke bomb used for training."

As word spread from table to table, the remaining Air Force officers rushed en masse to the hat check room. The first man to try on what he thought was his hat, found it to be two or three sizes too small. Another found that his fit over his ears. The confusion lasted from a few seconds to three or four minutes, depending on how highly an individual valued his own hat.

As they milled about in confusion, the General's aide explained what had happened. "The *Beaverton's* Captain told the General he had some jokers in his wardroom who didn't like the quality of tree left for the *Beaverton*, and made a bet that his miscreants could steal our Christmas tree. The General took him up on it because the Air Force owed him one: he rescued some ditched B-29 crews in World War II."

"How do you know they got away?" asked the manger.

"The sentry, along with the Commodore and the General, waved them through the gate just before the alert sounded. It was two guys in a Navy pickup."

⋅⊱━⊱⊰━⊰⋅

The last vehicle loaded aboard the *Beaverton* that night was the pickup, which was swung into the hangar bay just below the crane. Harry Leach had two men from First Division awakened and instructed them to clean the truck bed so that not a single pine needle or shard of glass remained. He checked the shrouded tree, secured to a stanchion in a far corner of the large hangar bay, before he retired for the night.

The *Beaverton* was the first ship to sortie from Guam on 24 December. A Chamorro truck driver stood by the empty lowboy holding a work order in his hand. The order plainly said he was to pick up a trailerload of white latex house paint. This lowboy had the right serial number, but it was empty. He pulled his hard hat back and scratched his thick black hair as he watched the majestic cruiser slowly back away from the pier. Well after the *Beaverton* turned and headed out to sea, he backed his tractor up to the empty lowboy and pulled it away.

As for the Christmas tree, Stan Longstreet grinned from ear to ear when he came into the wardroom at the end of the sea and anchor detail. He hummed as he stood on a chair and placed decorations at the top as the short Filipino stewards handed them up. He noticed that the tree had a strange, smoky smell to it, along with some ornaments he had never seen before. He decided he didn't want to ask Harry Leach any questions until after Christmas.

He returned to his office and sat back in his chair. He blew smoke rings in the air as he thought about this in-port stay. *It's time to count blessings: a few fights ashore, but nothing major. No one missed movement. Ensign Joe Xylos, whom Harry Leach never has a kind word for, through some quirk of luck, for the first time has done something that places the* Beaverton *in a good light. I have come around to share the faith the Old Man has in him.*

CHAPTER 16

Boy-san Meets Girl-san

The passage from Guam to Yokosuka was uneventful. The item most on Joe's mind was submission of his request for Submarine School, which he turned in just before he was relieved as Engineering watch officer for the special sea and anchor detail.

Joe now learned fully the meaning of the word "snipe" (generally used for the Engineering crew, whose duties placed them below decks and out of sight) because he was splitting all his time between Engineering spaces and the wardroom. He didn't go topside until the power plant was wrapped up following the sea and anchor detail.

He finally emerged on deck in Yokosuka harbor to find it was late afternoon on a winter day. It was so overcast that he didn't need to squint, but he was quickly chilled to the bone. His bodily thermostat was still set for the Southern Hemisphere summer, and it was a raw, cold, late December day in the Northern Hemisphere.

With others from the wardroom, he trooped to the O Club for the Friday happy hour. The Captain and XO joined them for a round. Even his roommate Carter Sawyer came along, but soon excused himself to call his wife. The drinks were the cheapest the Ensign had ever seen. He decided that he needed this antifreeze to stay alive.

Joe proposed a tongue-in-cheek toast to Harry Leach, who stood duty that night, and all joined in. Leach had earned their ridicule by attempting to slip his section out of rotation on a flimsy basis, namely the fact that one of them had relieved the quarterdeck for all of half an hour on the day they left Guam.

Inside White, an "old WESTPAC (Western Pacific) hand," had for weeks promised that he would give Joe the grand tour on their first night in port at Yokosuka. By the time happy hour was drawing to a close, the proposed tour had turned into an expedition, with most of the off-duty wardroom members joining them.

They piled into small Toyota cabs and headed into town. The hard-sprung sedans transmitted every uneven paving stone to the passengers, while they swayed from side to side as the drivers cut in and out of traffic, until they arrived at a white-walled compound.

Once inside the gate, they walked through a small but elegantly landscaped garden to a small wooden porch, where a pair of stern-faced middle-aged women in ornate kimonos very politely asked them to exchange their street shoes for slippers.

Soon they were seated on small cushions around a series of low black lacquered tables on a floor covered by very finely woven rice mats. Much to Joe's surprise, Larry White spoke quite a bit of Japanese. Or at least, it seemed that he did. He handled his chopsticks as if he had eaten with them all his life.

The bare rice-paper walls, coupled with strange smells and sounds that drifted in from other rooms and the kitchen, made Joe uneasy in one sense. In another sense, the smells, though unfamiliar, were for the most part intriguing. He cradled a small cup of hot tea in his cold hands, wishing he had long johns. Soon it was replaced by a small cup of hot sake.

The same pudgy middle-aged women who had greeted them were now the waitresses. *I wonder*, Joe thought as he watched them, *where all these exotic Japanese women are that I've been hearing about?* With a flair of showmanship, one of the women cooked his dinner in front of him. He recognized the beef strips and onions, but most of the other items were a mystery.

In time, the feast was over. More little porcelain bottles of hot sake were served. Joe indulged himself because he was still a bit chilled.

At last they decided to move on. Joe hated to leave because, for the first time since leaving the ship, he felt warm.

Larry said, "I think it's time to introduce our friend to what has made this country special . . . the friendly natives. What say we visit the Clover Club?"

Joe groaned, "Not another night club. After a while, I feel like I'm on a busman's holiday."

Larry wrapped an arm around his shoulder. "It's not just *any* night club. It's an official 'ladies of the night' club."

"Thanks, but no thanks. I've traveled this far without paying for it, and I'd like to keep it that way."

"Joe, old buddy, this isn't Stateside. This is a whole new culture. This is the only way boy meets girl over here."

Joe pulled his wallet from his pocket and laid it on the table. Then, with fingers that seemed all thumbs, he pulled out a small stack of calling cards. He spread them in a fan, picked one, and held it up. It was the dog-eared card Frenchy had given him. "Frenchy asked me to look up an old friend, Sunshine Suzuki."

Amid laughter all around, Larry said, "You mean, 'Hello Sunshine – Goodbye Rain' Suzuki?"

"Well, I don't know about that. She's at the S-U-E-N-O-H-J-O."

More laughter. "The Sewer Club! Come on, let's go. We'll hit the Clover Club tomorrow night."

As Joe tucked the card in his pocket, he mumbled, "I don't see what's so damn funny."

Soon the caravan of cabs careened back up the road toward the base. As they approached a traffic circle filled with hordes of other taxis, the drivers accelerated and laid on their horns. They spurted untouched onto a nearly deserted street past shuttered shops. One after the other, the boxy Toyotas screamed under a rail overpass, up a hill, and onto a narrow, twisting street. The cab drivers made quick, short adjustments to dodge the worst of the chuckholes, only to hit another squarely, bottoming out and sending the occupants bouncing almost to the roof.

Following a sharp turn down an alley-wide street, they shot by pale shoji-paneled doors, forcing the few pedestrians to hug the sides of the buildings. The cabs snapped to a halt in a small deserted plaza. The trip cost all of one hundred yen per cab, or about thirty cents American.

Joe gained his feet, feeling more like he'd had a plane ride in unstable air than ridden a few miles in a taxi. The others headed to the far side of the little plaza, onto a narrow, gracefully arched oriental wooden bridge. The clump of their feet, mixed with their drunken voices, marked their progress. Beyond the bridge stood a white, stuccoed three-story building on whose sides an apparently abstract tangle of neon tubes flashed on and off. Cy rested a hand on his roommate's shoulder and, pointing with the other, said, "Each one of those patterns depicts a couple making love in a different position."

"Good grief! What is this place?"

"Your choice. Somebody told me it was once an Imperial Navy officers' whorehouse. Notice that they don't even have a sign in English on the outside."

Joe stood transfixed for a moment until Rufus shoved him gently forward. "Come on, Señor Taco, it's an okay place."

He followed the crowd across the bridge and into the steamy, smoke-filled entryway. A bank of infrared lights buzzed over their heads, radiating a curtain of warmth between the outside and the entry area. Crowded along both sides of the hall were the girls. Black highlights gave the makeup around their dark eyes an unearthly air. They seemed to be all sizes and ages. Sparkling sequins on their dresses and jewelry reflected the purple light. The first women to catch Joe's eye were a pair standing well back into the entryway. Both were barely dressed, wearing shorty see-through negligees with bikini bottoms. The others were fully dressed, with coats and scarves over their heads. Steam blew from their mouths and onto the men running the gauntlet.

A firm pair of hands grabbed his legs as their owner said, "I herp you wit you shoes. You want hot time, boy-san?"

He looked down to see a young girl whose partly opened coat revealed a pair of small, pointed breasts beneath a low-cut peasant blouse. Her very bright smile showed yellowed, crooked teeth. Her eyes extended an invitation.

Joe surrendered his shoes. "Not really. I've come to see Sunshine Suzuki."

Making no attempt to cover herself, the girl pouted. "Why you want see Mama-san?"

"Is she here?"

As he shuffled forward in the slippers, other hands reached out to touch him, and he responded the same way. Then a heavyset, muscular man, wearing a white sweatband tied around his head, stepped into his path.

In a bass voice, more grumbled than spoken, the man said, "Who you? Why you want see Mama-san?"

Pulling the card from his pocket, Joe said, "My friend Frenchy asked me to say hello to Madam Suzuki."

The man pulled the card from Joe's hand. He held it in his large, beefy hands a scant inch from his eye and studied it for what seemed an eternity. Then he handed it back to Joe and bowed from the waist while keeping eye contact. "You far-row me. Bring you friends."

He led the group through a dimly lit bar and around a postage stamp-sized dance floor, where couples moved slowly to the rhythm of a scratchy phonograph record of an equally slow big-band number. They went up a narrow flight of stairs to a narrower landing.

As he looked down on the room below, Joe thought that even the oldest and fattest of the whores looked good at that distance and in that light. The smells of spilled beer and stale tobacco smoke were now replaced with a fresh, almost antiseptic soap smell.

The big man knelt by a rice-paper-paneled door and pulled it open. He motioned with his hands for Joe to enter. A welcome warmth greeted the still-chilled Ensign. In contrast to the other rooms, this one was well lit. It was rather long and narrow, with a single long, low table down its center. Arrayed every three feet down the table were cast-iron teapots surrounded by artfully decorated ceramic tea mugs.

Seated at the far end of the table were two women. The one on the end wore a high-collared black dress elegantly arrayed with a single string of large pearls. As Joe approached, he figured she must be somewhere between fifty and sixty years old. She held a long cigarette holder with a filter-tip burning in the end, in a manner he had seen in the movies.

The woman to her right wore a dark brown kimono. Beneath it were layers of other kimonos in a rainbow variety of colors and patterns. Her hair was piled high and held in place by a series of long hairpins decorated with mother-of-pearl. Her face was painted thickly white with darts of red, framed by purple and yellow, radiating from her eyes. A downcast, red-hued mouth had been painted around her own. She wore fingerless gloves like those he had seen on hoboes. Her fingers, coated with the same white makeup, were long and slender, and the nails were long and very neatly manicured.

The elegantly dressed woman pointed the cigarette holder to the seat opposite her painted companion and said, "Please do sit down. My name Sunshine. This my friend and busy-ness associate, Fumiko."

Joe half-bowed, doing his best to imitate the Japanese bouncer. "I'm Joe, Joe Xylos. My friend Frenchy Villerouge asked me to look you up."

Sunshine smiled, revealing a mouthful of gold-capped teeth. "Ah, Frenchy-san. Now that a real man! So handsome! Umm!"

Behind him, the others from the *Beaverton* dropped to places alongside the table, interspersed with girls.

Sunshine raised her voice and spoke a sentence or two in Japanese in which the only word Joe recognized was "Frenchy-san." There was a ripple of giggles from the women and then a pause that ended when a large-breasted girl, whose gown barely covered enough of her chest to make her presentable, said, "Sarah not wit us no more. She marry a say-ro, I tink."

Sunshine smiled. "Most of my girls leave here to be married. And now they say we must close. But sailors, they come back, cruise after cruise. We have happy home. It is maybe two, three years since I talk Frenchy. Why he ask you come see me?"

Joe felt a hand touching his thigh and looked over to see the same face that had met him at the door, smiling brightly. He brushed the hand away, cleared his throat, and began, "Frenchy and I were shipmates on the *Beaverton*. He talked about this place and wanted to show it to me, but he couldn't make it."

"Ah, so. What happen?"

"He was detached and sent back to Pearl from Guam. He was on board on temporary duty."

"He always pull TAD. How come, he no come Yokosuka?"

"It was because he got married."

"Frenchy, married? Look, most of men at this table, they married, no? Why that a problem?"

There was a nervous undercurrent of laughter. Joe looked at the young woman at his side out of the corner of his eye and decided that she was one of the more homely dogs he had ever seen. Her brother was probably the model for the wartime caricature of the enemy fighting man. Sunshine seemed amused when Joe again placed the girl's roaming hand back in her lap.

The painted woman across from him was a contrast to the eager young girl. Fumiko had high, round cheeks that curved to a very delicate chin. Her dark eyes seemed almost round compared to Sunshine's. Although her lips were well camouflaged by the makeup, they were full, and her mouth was sensuously wide. Her slight smile revealed long, straight, white teeth. Although once or twice her eyes caught his, her face was an emotionless mask.

While Joe poured himself a cup of tea, he began telling about Frenchy and Eva. Just after he started, Fumiko pulled a small, brightly patterned cloth pouch from her sleeve and poured little, hard, dried peppers and garlic bulbs onto a small plate in the middle of the table. She picked up a pair of chopsticks and, lifting a garlic bulb to her mouth, bit it with a less-than-delicate crunch. Then she lifted a bowl of an unidentified dish and sluiced most of its contents into her mouth. Behind him, the couples were pairing off and leaving the room. As Joe finished the story, he casually lifted a garlic bulb from the plate and popped it into his mouth.

He turned to the young girl at his side and, breathing garlic into her face, said, "It's nothing against you personally, but I came here to meet Sunshine. I'm not interested."

She screwed up her face in a scowl and waved a hand before her nose. "You nutting but bad news, boy-san. Gar-ric too strong, *ne*?"

Strong, hell yes! Whew! thought Joe, feeling tears welling in the corner of his eyes as she walked down the length of an empty table toward the door.

After the girl closed the shoji screen with a slam, Fumiko said, "Why didn't you like Tanako? After all, your friends left with Japanese girls." Her voice had a husky quality and her accent, although strongly Japanese, had a British tinge to it.

Joe cast his eyes down the empty table and returned them to meet hers. "I suppose I could come up with a number of excuses, but I guess it all boils down to how my approach to happiness contrasts with theirs."

"Happiness?"

"Yes, happiness. My shipmates are happy with what they get. I get what makes me happy."

Sunshine grunted and slapped her thigh. "That I like! That kind of thing Frenchy say. Joe-san, you come Japan before?"

"No. This is my first cruise."

"Ah, you must be Ensign, *ne*?

"Well, yes. I reported aboard the *Beaverton* this summer."

Joe's and Fumiko's eyes met again. She smiled. "I don't work here. You should ask Sunshine to pick a special girl for you."

"I don't think I'm ready for that."

"Then this is your first time in a place like this?"

Joe rubbed the back of his head. "In a place exactly like this, yes. This is illegal in the States."

From the distance, there was a high-pitched scream followed by breaking glass and splintering wood. Sunshine leaped to her feet and ran from the room as a loud, drunken American voice rose above the din. More voices, both American and Japanese, joined in a disjointed chorus.

Fumiko lit a cigarette and drew a deep breath before letting the smoke out in a slow, even manner, "It's funny you should mention this. Sunshine and I were just talking about what will become of the girls after the new law goes into effect."

"What new law?"

"The government has outlawed prostitution starting in the new year. Undoubtedly it is because of pressure from the Occupation authorities. This is a time-honored profession. Men have always sought personal entertainment. It is wrong to single out one form like this. It won't stop it, because men want women. It will bring it under the control of the Yakuza."

"Yakuza, what's that?"

"The gangsters. Even with them, I believe it will be an opportunity because girls can make far more money with Tokyo businessmen than with American sailors. In Tokyo, the interests are deeply vested and the authorities will be slow to act."

"It sounds like you know something about this."

"Yes. I was discussing the idea of Sunshine moving to Tokyo with her best girls. I have friends there. There is big money to be made."

"How do you fit in?"

Fumiko smiled ever so slightly. "I make things happen. . . . How do you like Japan, Joe?"

"It's all so different. I think I could like it here if I could only get warm. My body has been in summer weather up until I came ashore today. It's the price you pay for being a snipe. Winters back home are far colder. It's just that there I had over six months to adjust to the change from the Fourth of July to New Year's, instead of six hours."

With a flowing move of her chopsticks, Fumiko snared a pair of small peppers from the little plate and held them before Joe's mouth. He opened wide and, as he bit down on them, tears came to his eyes again. He chewed them, trying not to show the agonizing heat burning his tongue and throat. Casually, he took a small sip of tea, but that only heightened his discomfort.

"Now, Joe, do you feel warmer?"

"A little, but my feet are still cold," he croaked.

She laid the cigarette on an ashtray and studied him for a long minute before leaning across the table and gently touching his arm. "Perhaps I can take you to a hot bath. Would you like that?"

"Here?"

"Not here! It would not be good form. Sunshine and I are good friends. I'll show you a very good place."

"I'm not—"

"I know. Let's say I need a young man as a companion for a time. You can be a companion, can't you?"

"Sure."

"Like you, I get what makes me happy. Come, let's leave before Sunshine returns and we have embarrassment. Maybe later you'll come back and give her business, okay?"

"I suppose."

When they stood, Joe found that his companion was perhaps an inch shorter than he was. She was very fine boned, with small feet clad in white leather mitten-like coverings that had a separation next to the big toe. At the door to the room, she pushed him ahead of her and by pulls on his sleeves guided him down a back stairway to a narrow hall that led to the bar and the front entrance. He put on his black leather shoes, and she stepped into a pair of wooden platform clogs that elevated her another inch and a half.

They walked out into the cold night with Joe in the lead. Fumiko stayed right behind him as they crossed the arched bridge at the entrance. Her kimonos made a swishing sound in rhythm to the tap of her clogs on the planks. Once on the street, Joe tried to fall back to walk alongside her.

She pushed him ahead, saying, "In Japan, the custom is for the man to lead and the woman to follow. Please go. I'll give you directions."

She directed him back up the narrow street the cabs had come down. Now, as a pedestrian, he found the barreling taxis to be a hair-raising menace. Each time one approached, Fumiko wrapped an arm around Joe with her hand in the center of his chest and pulled him firmly against her as she pressed her back against the nearby fence or wall. She was slow to release him once the peril passed.

Leaving that lane, they crossed the street that went toward the base and turned onto another street that led into a residential neighborhood. The air was heavy with charcoal smoke. Dogs barked as they passed some houses, while sounds of television or radio drifted through rice-paper walls.

They had walked for close to half a mile when she leaned forward and pulled on his sleeve. "Turn right here and cross the bridge."

"Where are we going?"

"Special place. You are not turning chicken, are you?"

"No, but it looks awfully dark up there."

"Please go. We are almost there."

He stepped onto the convex surface of a little bridge, grabbing the handrail to keep his feet on the smooth planks. Once on the other side, the only place to go was a narrow trail between two houses. Bamboo framed the fences along the way and tickled his face as they went. He felt his way in the very faint light until a large dog leaped against a fence next to him and began barking. He jumped back and came close to knocking Fumiko over backwards.

Again she gently put her hand in the small of his back. "Togo can't hurt you. He's on the other side of the fence. He is a very good watchdog."

At the sound of her voice, the dog whined and retreated into the darkness. The trail led upward over worn stone steps that were dimly lighted by a single bulb in a frosted, weatherproof fixture that looked like it came off a Navy ship.

She stepped to his side and hooked her arm around his elbow, saying, "We are almost there . . . the gate on the left."

After Fumiko unlocked the gate, she flipped a switch that brought a small winter-dead garden into view and lifted the shadows from a small house with white rice-paper walls framed between weathered wooden frames. She led him to a small entryway. Remembering the custom, Joe leaned against the wall and removed his shoes.

He placed his stocking feet on frigid wood, polished satin smooth. "Is this your place?"

"Yes."

As he stepped through the door and onto the rice-straw tatami mats within, she turned on the lights. As his eyes adjusted, he became aware that, although the room was almost bare, everything about it exuded quality and craftsmanship. In its center stood a single low table with a lacquered finish and mother-of-pearl inlay, surrounded by four well-padded raw silk cushions that had golden tassels stretching from the corners.

Joe exclaimed, "This place is beautiful! It's like a museum. Everything is so perfect."

"Thank you. My house means very much to me. Your words are very kind. Let me heat up the bath. Would you like tea while we wait?"

She motioned for Joe to sit down at the table. Moments later, she returned with a coffeepot that she plugged into a wall socket. Both still had their coats on.

Joe asked, "Fumiko, what are you, an actress?"

She laughed. "No, no. I dressed up for the New Year. Today I had my hairdresser paint me up like a Kabuki player so I could go visiting. I enjoy dressing well, but I don't like to be bothered on the street by the sailors."

"Fumiko, you speak beautiful English. After being around Frenchy and Eva and now you, I feel handicapped only speaking one language. How did you learn to speak it so well?"

"I studied English as a girl. Later I went to college in America for two years before the war."

"Where did you go to college?"

"Connecticut College for Women in New London. Please excuse me while I take off this headpiece. It is beginning to give me a headache."

Once she had left the room, the Ensign continued his visual exploration of the house. The focus of the room was a recess on the back wall. Sitting low in the niche were a breastpiece and helmet of medieval Japanese armor, along with an ornately hilted samurai sword resting in its well-polished scabbard on a wooden stand. On a shelf to one side was a yellowed photograph of a Japanese Army officer. Even the uniform couldn't disguise his girth; he looked like an old man. On the other side were color pictures of two teenage boys posing with diplomas in their hands. Both looked Japanese, but the older boy had a lighter complexion and wider eyes that weren't quite dark brown. Joe thought the face looked familiar. He stared at it, trying to place where he'd seen it before. The other had Fumiko's nose and mouth, and his eyes were narrow slits much like those of the older man.

Joe was studying the older man's picture when Fumiko returned wearing a quilted kimono. The makeup and the heavy hairpiece had been removed. She wore her hair in bangs that just covered her neck and were cut evenly above her eyes. Her complexion was smooth and so youthful that she had the fresh look of a college coed. The warmth of the smile from her wide, sensuous mouth quickly drew his attention away from the steely hardness of her eyes.

He pointed to the picture. "Is this your father?"

"No. That was my husband. Those are my two sons."

"Your sons? Oh, come on, you're not old enough to have teenagers. Do they still live at home?"

"You say such nice foolishness. My sons are grown, in their twenties. Shige, on the left, is twenty-four and a chemical engineer with Mitsubishi. Hige is twenty-two and was just hired by Matsushita. Come, the water is hot."

Once in the small bathroom, Fumiko peeled Joe's clothes off him faster than he could have done it himself. She sat him on a small wooden stool next to a sunken white ceramic tile bath, where she scrubbed him down. She then removed the kimono to reveal a one-piece white swimsuit whose top was cut low enough to highlight rather small but well-proportioned breasts. Unlike the American girls he knew, she had a straight waist, wide hips, and a well-developed paunch. Her legs were short and shapely.

She rinsed him before directing him into the tub. When he sank down into the hot water, Fumiko sat on the little stool and started to wash herself.

"Why don't you let me do that?"

"It's okay."

He stood up in the tub, took the soapy cloth from her hand, and began scrubbing her back and neck. When he worked his way down to top of the suit, he made a tentative move to pull down the zipper. She rounded her shoulders. He pulled it all the way down and began soaping her smooth skin.

"Joe-san, I am an old woman. Are you sure?"

"You're not too old for me."

◦◦◦

The following dawn, he was awakened to the smell of hot tea and a gentle touch. "Joe . . . Joe, it's time to get up and get back to your ship."

Slowly he pried himself from between the quilted comforters and sat up, taking the tea from her. She knelt on the tatami mat beside him, wearing the same quilted kimono she had worn the night before. "Hurry, you're late."

As he pulled himself to his feet, Fumiko asked, "Will I see you tonight?"

"I wish I could, but I've got the duty. I'll be off Sunday until late afternoon."

"How can you have duty the next two days?"

"I'm in the duty section today and Shore Patrol officer for a division party tomorrow night. The Chief Engineer said I could have time off from after the party until the morning after New Year's."

"Then come here until you have to go. I'll fix you a very good Japanese dinner. Please say yes. You made me very happy . . . a very good lover . . . maybe one in a hundred . . . no, one in ten thousand."

"Fumiko, I enjoyed it too. I'll be here if it's humanly possible."

"Don't worry, it'll be okay. Now, you don't forget. Okay?"

"Okay. But how will I get in touch with you? Do you have a phone? I'll do my best to make it late tomorrow night, but if I don't, I'm sure I'll get off early the next morning because I worked the night before."

She pulled a piece of paper out of her kimono sleeve and handed it to him. "Show this to the taxi driver."

He studied the oriental script before putting it into his pocket. "How do I get back to my ship?"

"If you want, I'll walk with you to the main highway. There are plenty of taxis there. It's really easy. Once you get to the road, you turn left and follow it straight down to Honcho Yokosuka."

"I think I can find my way okay, thanks. There's no reason for you to go out in the cold."

After he put his coat and shoes on, Fumiko pulled herself into Joe's arms, held him close, and kissed him deeply before cooing, "You are one fine lover, Joe. Please don't forget me."

CHAPTER 17

Yokosuka

Joe's duty day on Saturday was very quiet, followed by a Sunday that began with Carter Sawyer grousing about being awakened early. Joe made ready to leave the ship right after breakfast.

That Sunday he spent with Fumiko was among the most pleasant he could remember. Leaving her house near sunset, he found the late afternoon warm enough to walk back to the ship. He was constantly craning his neck to look at the many small houses with lush gardens and weathered stone retaining walls that were stacked up the heights along the way. Soon he was at the bottom of the hill and dodging the crowds of shoppers. *I could enjoy living in this culture*, he thought.

Early evening found him with his backup crew, three of the biggest men in his division, riding out to the Kanko Hotel to watch over the B Division party. The men were hand picked by the Chief Engineer, who told Joe that having credible people backing him up was the best deterrent to trouble. The most senior of the three was a black First Class Machinist, Richard R. Richards, whom everyone called "Rich." Joe had seen Rich lift machinery by hand that other men used chain falls to move. He was about six foot one and weighed close to two hundred twenty pounds. Everything about him was big, from his head to his feet. Like many big men, he was very quiet and seldom found a need to raise his voice. The other two were Second Class Machinists. One was a farm boy from Wisconsin, Todd Ohnhaus, whose great love was football. Todd had played defensive back in high school and lived for the day he could leave the Navy and play college ball. The third was a six-footer, Karl Pickel, an immigrant from East Germany, who was a good man in a fight despite an unassuming appearance. Karl had boxed in two smokers and knocked out both opponents.

At the Kanko, they were led to the party room, which had Western-style tables spread around a carpeted area and a small, raised hardwood dance floor with a small bandstand behind it. There were two portable bars in opposite corners at the back of the room. The place looked much like a number of clubs where Joe had worked.

Shortly after the first partygoers began to arrive, a Lieutenant wearing a Shore Patrol brassard stepped into the room and beckoned for Joe to follow him. Once outside, he said, "I want a quiet and peaceful evening here. At the first sign of trouble, I want you to get on it. If it gets out of hand, we'll run the whole lot of you back to your ship."

"Sir, I don't believe that will be necessary. I have three good men for backup. The Chief Engineer plus the Division Officer will be here."

"How many times have you had Shore Patrol, mister?"

"This is my first time, sir. But you don't have to worry, I've had a lot of experience working in clubs."

The Lieutenant looked Joe up and down, then said in a flat monotone, "Sure. Sure. Like I'm warning ya. One time, one complaint, and out ya go."

About an hour after the party started, the combo began to play. It consisted of a drummer, saxophone, steel guitar, plus a fourth who shifted between trumpet and trombone. Soon the floor was full of couples. Small groups of young sailors gathered around the tables drinking beer. The room filled quickly because Joe's M Division had taken the watches for the night in exchange for B Division's promise to return the favor when M Division held its own party.

Close to ten, a pimply-faced young Japanese stepped to the microphone. After he blew into it loudly with a sound like blowing his nose, he cleared his throat. "Wercome to Hotear Kanko. We prease to begin whore show." The audience laughed.

The drummer began a slow throbbing beat while the emcee briskly walked to the back of the room. There he manned the single spotlight, which he focused on the door.

The trumpeter played a weak flourish and a dancer stepped through the door. Joe could only remember having seen maybe one or two dancers who were homelier. The woman was around five feet tall and weighed, he judged, just under two hundred pounds. She was dressed in a sarong that stretched and distorted the flowered pattern to accommodate her girth.

She stood stage center on the dance floor, making bump-and-grind motions while maintaining a face that was better suited to a game of poker. Once or twice she moved to the right or left, but for the most part her feet remained motionless while the rest of her shook like jello. The hum of conversation began to rise. Some sailors went to the bar for another drink. In the far back of the room, one sailor did his own dance to the music, getting more attention from those near him than the performer in front.

The stolid stripper dropped her vacant gaze from a point on the back wall to a knot on her hip, which she tugged on while the band played "The Stripper." With the knot undone, the sarong came free. The sailors down front cheered. Much to Joe's surprise, there were no pasties or G-string, just one overweight, bored, but stark naked woman going through the motions of a dance.

As the stripper's dance progressed, the young sailors, one after another, moved closer and closer to the front. The band shifted to a very rapid jazz beat, which quickened the jiggling of the many folds of flesh but did not change the dancer's expression. Meanwhile, her young audience inched forward until she stood in a U-shaped pocket of blue.

Joe stood by the door. Outside, he could see two other female entertainers waiting their turn. Both were taller than the first dancer and far prettier. The one closest to the door looked more like a junior high schooler, she was so thin. She wore a red formal that was too big, as if she'd borrowed it from a big sister. She teetered on high heels, shifting her weight from one foot to the other while nervously pulling the ends of long gloves up her arms and working a wad of gum from cheek to cheek.

The other wore a tuxedo jacket, formal shirt, black shorts, black net stockings, and heels; a black satin top hat rested on her head. She leaned back against a waist-high pushcart that had a number of magic symbols painted on it. Of the three, Joe decided that she had the prettiest face. When she saw Joe looking at her, she pushed the hat brim down her forehead, tilted her head back, and gave him an inviting smile. He returned the smile but said nothing.

Behind him, the band wound up to a Tahitian beat with the stripper quivering in tune to the number. The number ended with a final resounding thump, and the fat woman bent over. She picked up the sarong off the floor, wiped the sweat off her face with it, and walked off the stage, pulling it around her ample midsection.

Joe walked to the microphone and pointed at the many young men who had encroached on the dance floor. "Gentlemen, as much as I know that you down in front have nothing more than healthy curiosity to find out if it's really true what they say about Japanese women, you'll have to move back clear of the dance floor before the entertainment can continue."

Following the laughter, there were some groans and barely audible protests, but the men pushed back into the carpeted area beyond the dance floor.

Meanwhile the dancer in the red formal clopped into the room. She bowed to the bandleader and handed him a small sheaf of music before walking somewhat clumsily around the edge of the dance floor. She made pushing motions with her arms toward the few laggards who had not moved all the way off the floor.

Standing in the center of the floor facing the audience, she swallowed hard and managed a brave smile as she raised her arms. The drummer began with a slow single beat on his tenor drum, which after twenty beats was followed by sad, soulful, slow oriental music. The dancer swayed slowly, moving her arms and body gracefully to the music.

The conversational hum, which had been interrupted by the change of musical pace, picked up. Lines were forming at the bars. Here and there, snide comments were being made. The crescendo of discontent was building. The bell cow of the group was a thin, intense dark-haired fireman whose profanity-laced commentary had people around him laughing loudly. On a hand signal from Joe, Rich worked his way to the man and whispered in his ear. The sailor gave the black man a dirty look, but immediately became quiet.

Although the skinny girl's body was making all the motions a dancer should make, Joe thought he saw terror in her eyes. When she wasn't smiling, she was biting her lower lip. *I've seen more confidence on amateur night*, he thought.

She made several feints toward the buttons on her left glove before popping them open and beginning to pull it down her slim arm. Joe cheered, whistled, and applauded. Others joined in.

The red-clad dancer wiped a tear from her eye, then smiled. The band was playing the second repass of her music by the time she had taken both gloves off. She grunted something in Japanese, and the music stopped.

The dancer turned her back to the audience and looked back over her shoulder at them while pulling the zipper of her gown down ever so slowly. By the time she had it halfway down, the noise level had dropped to where those in front could hear its progress.

The combo then began a fast-tempo Japanese number. The dancer swept around the floor, playing with the audience, bending over so her top fell away for a moment to show her breasts, then back up to dance some more. The young sailors in front seemed to be enjoying it all, but the older hands showed little interest.

While the drum beat a steady thum, thum, thum, the lithe young dancer again turned her back to the audience. She blushed and bit her lower lip again, then looked toward the door before letting the gown fall to the floor around her ankles. Wearing only a red garter belt, black net stockings, and heels, she made small bumps and grinds before stepping away from the fallen formal.

Joe thought, *From her narrow, bony hips to her budding breasts, she looks too young and too undernourished to be a stripper.*

Throughout her act, there had been some cruel comments from the audience. The stripper had not shown that she understood them. It wasn't until she turned to face the audience that the same group of young sailors pointed at her and began laughing loudly. She stopped while the band was still playing, picked up her clothes, and ran from the room. Although there was scattered applause, there was far more laughter.

Joe felt bad for the girl. He followed her out the door into the hallway. She was in the process of stepping back into the formal while an extremely angry young Japanese man, whom he took to be her manager, shouted at her.

The third performer, the magician, was busy making some last-minute adjustments to the equipment in her six-foot-long cart.

Joe asked, "Do you need some more time?"

"Maybe yes. But I have to start."

"Take your time, I have a word or two to say. If you'd like, I'll announce you. What's your name?"

"My name Mieko."

"Don't you have a stage name?"

"Stage name? What mean stage name?"

"How about Mimi the Magician?"

"Whatever you say, okay."

He walked over to the girl in red and asked, "Was this your first show?"

Both she and the manager looked at him uncomprehendingly.

With much body English, Joe asked again, "Was this your first time to dance?"

Mieko/Mimi answered, "I don't know if first, but Toshiko very new."

Joe took Toshiko by the hand and led her back into the party room. He walked to the microphone and announced, "Ladies and gentlemen, may I have your attention. We had a privilege tonight of seeing a brand-new act from a brand-new performer. Some of us were rather critical. Before we pass judgment, how many of you have done something for the first time and done it right? Let's give our second dancer a big hand for having the guts to stand up in a room full of strangers and take off her clothes for the first time. How about it?"

The applause wasn't deafening, but it was genuine. Toshiko bowed to Joe two or three times. Each time, the top of her dress flopped down, revealing her not-too-ample bosom.

As she backed out of the room, Joe lifted the microphone from its stand and thought it felt good in his hand. He surveyed the crowd, which didn't show a lot of interest in the floor show. He knew from experience that an entertained crowd is generally a peaceful crowd, whereas heckling from the audience, if it got out of hand, could spark fights and create problems for him. He looked across the room to the B Division Officer, who was French-kissing his girlfriend. The Chief Engineer's eyes were rolled halfway up so they showed more white than iris. Joe decided that if there was going to be any leadership tonight, it was up to him.

He noted that, other than one or two exceptions, the sailors had been keeping their distance from the floor. He continued, "I want to thank the vast majority of you in front for being considerate of your shipmates and the floor show. As for the few who prefer hardwood to a carpeted floor, please take this one last warning . . . Move back!"

While two or three young firemen wormed their way backward into the rather dense ring along the edge of the dance floor, Joe said, "There's a saying that the show's not over until the fat lady sings. We have more surprises for you tonight in a variety show featuring some unique local talent. About the fat lady, maybe she can sing too. Who knows, that may come later. Coming up is more *Beaver . . . ton* entertainment. Stick around. The best is being saved for last. That's 'best' as in 'B Division.' There are so many familiar faces out there . . . Hudson . . . Burley. I can't thank you all for the excellent start you gave me on the *Beaverton*. Just think, five months ago, if you asked me where the feed water was, I would have told you to go out to the barn because that's the water next to the feedbag.

"And being a country boy, I've been to my share of rodeos. After riding the taxicabs here in Yokosuka, I've come to envy those bronco riders. At least after things get rough, they get thrown off. Here, you just get thrown around . . . from the floor to the ceiling and back again."

The laugher wasn't so strong, but the people were beginning to face the stage.

"Boy, am I having a time with the language. Yesterday morning, my friend awoke me and said, 'Ohio'. . . and I said, 'No, I'm from Missouri.' Then when I was on watch, a Japanese man came aboard and said he wanted to see 'Sam-san.' Well, I knew about these here Japanese banjos and I told him we didn't have any. He then told me he was the 'shop pranner' and wanted to see 'Craptan Sam-san.' When he tried to pronounce the CO's name without sounding the 'l,' I knew why he had called him Sam-san. Now isn't this a good liberty port?"

There were some "ayes" and some applause.

"This is the kind of place a sailor can identify with. It's a town where the working stiff gets together with the working girl on a regular basis.

It's a place where you get to see two different cultures meet . . . intimately."

Behind him, he heard Mieko/Mimi making a hissing sound. She was standing just inside the door. Joe turned to the band and made motions for them to start playing. It wasn't until he pointed at the drummer and made a rolling motion with his hands, that the latter caught the hint and began a roll of his drums.

"The Hotel Kanko and B Division are proud to present an act that is different from what you would expect at a ship's party. You have come to the right place, the mysterious Orient, to see an act that is unique in the field of magic. Remember that the hand is quicker than the eye. Of course, if you can, keep your eye on the hand. Here she is, ladies and gentlemen . . . for your entertainment . . . Yokosuka's own . . . Mimi the Magician. Give her a real *Beaver . . . ton* wel . . . come!"

The single spotlight shifted to the door and illuminated the black cart that the magician pushed. By the time she had taken another two steps, it was focused on her. The sailors cheered and applauded as Mimi gained stage center.

She parked the cart and walked over to the edge of the dance floor. With a flourish, she reached behind a sailor's ear and pulled out a silver coin, which she flipped onto the top of the cart. From another sailor's ear, she pulled out an egg. After pulling two more coins, she stopped, bent over, and straightened the seam on her net hose.

As she stood up, she reached into the coat of one of the Chief Petty Officers and pulled out a flimsy bra, which brought howls from the audience. Out of the Chief Engineer's pocket she brought forth two pairs of women's panties.

On returning to the cart, Mimi removed her hat and tossed it effortlessly on top of the cart. She faced the audience and unbuttoned one button on her shirt. She lifted up the hat and two pigeons flew out. They circled around the room until she clapped her hands twice. They flew back to the cart and disappeared into an opening in its rear.

While the birds were circling the room, she removed the tuxedo jacket and stuffed it into the hat. There were more eggs and coins produced, along with a cane that, after she twirled it, mysteriously became a parasol.

The magic tricks followed one another with a professional flair. Mimi marked the end of each by some simple act of getting undressed. She would undo a button at a time and then, when they were all undone, remove the garment and stuff it in her hat on top of the cart.

Finally Mimi dropped the net stockings into the hat and faced the audience wearing only a wisp of a black G-string. If the first dancer was too fat and the second too skinny, the third was just right.

A tab of red cloth peeked over the top of her G-string. As Mimi touched the cloth, the drummer began a roll. She set her legs wide and made a bumping and grinding motion as she began to pull out a wide silken streamer. Out it came, yard after yard, until there was a pile of reds, yellows, greens, and purples.

When the last bit of material fell free, the band began playing a fast jazz beat. Mimi picked up the streamers and began twisting and dancing around the stage. Soon the streamers were wrapped around her ample breasts and hiding most of what she had revealed. She continued her dance number for perhaps another three minutes. When the music stopped, she stood tall on her toes with her arms above her head, and the multicolored bands slowly settled to the ground around her ankles. Mimi was now totally naked. The audience burst into cheers and loud applause.

As she bowed the third time, there was a pop followed by jets of smoke swirling upward around her and rising to the ceiling. From Joe's vantage point behind her, he watched her spring upward, do a backflip, and land on her feet behind the cart. She reached through a door in the back of the cart and retrieved the tuxedo jacket. After she donned it, she pulled the tails between her legs and snapped the ends onto the front of the garment.

The applause drifted away as the smoke thinned. There were some voices starting to ask, "Where is she?" and "What happened?" As the first of the audience began to stand up and approach the stage, the magician stepped from behind the cart and bowed.

Joe shouted through the microphone, "That is one of the best acts I have ever seen! Give Mimi a big hand!"

She pushed the cart toward the door again and, with a broad smile and a wink at Joe, said, "Thank you very much for announcement. You very good."

As he fell in beside her, he said, "Mimi, you have a great talent. I'm sure you could take your act to the States. It was terrific!"

"You tink so, *ne*?"

He pulled a card from his pocket. "Let me give you the name of an agent friend. If you're interested, write Herman Gunderson. He's a straight shooter. Get some high-quality glossies of yourself. And don't send any nude photos. I'll write him a letter and tell him what I saw, if you'd like an introduction. Would you like that?"

She laid the card on top of the cart and then asked, half-smiling, "Dis big snow job, *ne*? You want me be you girlfriend, *ne*?"

"Mimi, I already have a girlfriend. I worked as a master of ceremonies for four years. The compliments were sincere. You have a real talent, and you should make the most of it. I think that with very little effort you could be billed into the top clubs in the States."

"Tank you very much. I never tink about go United States. You tink I make big money?"

"I think you'd have a good chance."

"Okay. You tell you friend."

She stopped pulling the cart and waited while he finished writing the address.

Toshiko, the young undernourished stripper, now stood by the door wearing her red formal. Her narrow eyes were red, and her cheeks looked red as if they'd been slapped. She pressed herself against the wall to let the cart go by, then followed it out.

Joe looked back across the room to the buffet table and saw that it was still loaded with food. He checked his watch and saw that it was ten thirty, just thirty minutes before the party would be over.

He caught up with Mimi and Toshiko just outside the door, where the young Japanese manager was barking orders.

Joe put a hand on the young girl's shoulder. "Won't you take a moment to have a bite to eat before you go?" The magician translated his offer.

Toshiko immediately turned around and melted into Joe's arms. He steered her back into the room while the manager shouted commands. Mimi parked the cart by the wall and followed them back into the room. The manager followed, waving his arms and pointing at his watch, but they ignored him. He knitted his eyebrows and scowled at Joe while muttering in Japanese. Once at the buffet table, however, he ladled large portions onto his plate. The women weren't bashful either.

Joe made a tour of the room to find that some of the people had left as soon as the floor show was over. The combo were packing up their instruments except for the drums. A few couples were dancing to slow big-band numbers coming from a central sound system. Standing near the door, he heard a shrill Japanese voice coming from the back corner, where he had left the entertainers.

As he approached the corner, he could see Toshiko nose to nose with the Japanese manager. Joe's Shore Patrol helpers arrived just as the man shoved the slim girl. Joe asked, "What's going on here?"

Mimi said, "Toshiko mad because he no pay for work tonight because she walk off floor."

The manager jabbed an angry finger at the skinny young dancer. "Dat right. She quit. No pay nutting."

The girl kicked off her heels, crouched in a karate stance, and circled the manager while glaring at him.

Joe surveyed the room. The crowds were back at the bars. All seemed quiet other than the entertainers.

Joe pointed to Toshiko while asking Mimi, "Would you ask her if she would like a dance lesson? Like I said, I've worked in supper clubs for years. Maybe I could help her."

After a brief translation, the girl said no with a shake of her head.

The manager made some whining comments in Japanese.

Joe asked, "Would she like to dance again if we pass the hat for people to put money in?"

The translation was a bit longer this time. The girl at first was saying no, but finally and very reluctantly agreed after Joe added that the collection all ought to be hers. Her manager grumbled, but nodded his approval.

Over the next ten minutes, Joe taught a quick course in exotic dancing to the young girl, using her glove and napkins from the table as props. By the time he was done, he had gathered a small crowd who were becoming noisier and calling for others to join them.

Toshiko seemed far more relaxed and was laughing as he led her to the dance floor and took the microphone. "May I have your attention, please. The second young lady, who danced earlier this evening, has agreed to an encore performance if we'll pass the hat. Is that agreeable?"

The yeas poured from the group who had been watching the impromptu dance class.

Joe placed a pair of chairs in the center of the dance floor and asked the few couples who were dancing to clear the floor. After a few jokes, he announced, "The Lady in Red." He dropped a five-hundred-yen note into the hat and placed in at the floor's edge.

The girl again went through her routine, with Joe's coaching being translated by Mimi and the manager. The sailors were laughing and enjoying Joe's pantomime on the side as much as they were her act. With every garment she took off, more coins and yen notes were tossed into the hat.

With his encouragement, the audience began clapping to a steady beat, which the youngster followed. Even after she had peeled off her last stocking and was dancing in her altogether, Joe had her first twisting around one of the chairs and finally playing with one of the red gloves in imitation of what he was doing.

The Shore Patrol Lieutenant who had talked to Joe earlier entered the room as they were pulling the gloves between their legs while bumping and grinding. On seeing the officer, the Ensign signaled an end to the dance and bowed. Coins and notes showered the floor around the hat as the audience applauded loudly.

Joe checked his watch and saw that the witching hour of eleven p.m. was less than five minutes away. He went back to the microphone and announced, "The party will be over in less than five minutes. I want to thank all hands here for your excellent behavior. The rules are that we must be out of here by eleven. Please gather up your gear and your friends. We have base taxis standing by at the front entrance to take you either back to the ship or into the center of Yokosuka. *Beaverton* Shore Patrol will be secured when the last of B Division people are cleared out."

The Lieutenant shouted, "Not so fast, Mister!"

He stomped across the hardwood floor to where Joe was standing, waiving a nightstick. "What the hell were you doing with that stripper?"

"Giving her dance lessons."

"Mister, you were assigned out here to keep this party under control and not to play games with the local whores."

"I beg your pardon, sir, this party was at all times under control. There were no fights, and the one or two who drank too much were given taxis back to the ship."

Henry Moran walked up behind the Shore Patrol officer. "Lieutenant, Mr. Xylos exerted more control over this division party than I've seen in the past. We had a good party and no one caused any trouble. You're right. It isn't becoming to the uniform to play games with the dancers. But as for teaching that kid how to strip, it didn't cause any harm."

The Lieutenant shifted from one foot to the other. "I'm sorry to cut you short, sir, but we've got a real problem downtown. There's a full-scale riot going on at the Yellow Dragon. I've been directed to get every available man on Shore Patrol down there right away." The Lieutenant tilted his head back and stared down his nose at Joe. "Although in this case, I'm not sure what contribution you can make."

CHAPTER 18

Yellow Dragon

At Richards's urging, Joe joined his three enlisted Shore Patrolmen in the back of the paddy wagon. They raced toward the disturbance with siren screaming.

Richards shouted over the din, "Sir, I've been through this before. You'll notice when we get there that everyone will be standing outside watching, safe from it all, and arresting the busted and broken when they stagger out. If we're lucky, somebody may tell us to go into the bar and break up the fight because the sailors are from the *Beaverton*. If they don't, we have to wait around until either they get so tired of fighting that they quit or until the few who are left are totally outnumbered. After that we have to herd them around until they're loaded in these wagons. I got a date with a hot number, and she gets off at eleven thirty. If I don't take her home, somebody else will. I'm sure I can get this settled in a few minutes if you'll just order us to go inside."

Joe said, "Richards, I'm not anxious to spend the night here either. What do have you in mind?"

"I'll grab 'em and sling 'em out the door. All you have to do is tell the guys standing around to push 'em into the paddy wagons. Most of them will have their ship's names sewn on their jumpers. You'll have to handle the matter of sorting them out. Sir, the critical part is getting them into the correct wagons quickly." Richards smiled while he tapped his nightstick against his palm. "I do love to break up fights . . ."

The driver had to stop a few doors short of the Yellow Dragon because the narrow alley was jammed with crowds of gawkers, local police, and Shore Patrol.

As Joe stepped onto the pavement, he heard sounds of combat . . .

breaking glass . . . screams . . . punches . . . more breaking glass . . . shattering wood. The four men pushed through a half-circle of onlookers who were peering into a darkened room where full-scale combat was underway. Through the broken front window they could see a sea of flying fists, ducking sailors, and Marines, that blended into moving shadows far in the back.

Joe saw a tubby Lieutenant Commander, in a uniform that fit him perfectly when he was thirty pounds lighter, wearing a Shore Patrol brassard tightly tied around a fleshy arm. He was talking to a muscular Chief Boatswain's Mate. "I don't know if we have enough people out here to control them."

Joe said, "Commander, they sent us here to break up the fight."

The Commander eyed the slight, short, stoop-shouldered Ensign with a look of disbelief. "You?"

"Yes, sir! They brought us in from the Kanko."

One unfortunate sailor was backed out the door by his opponent, only to be grabbed by two Shore Patrolmen. While they had him pinned and helpless, his attacker stepped through the door and delivered a solid punch to his head. The attacker danced back into the bar, but a hard hit pushed him back out. He put his head down and rushed one of the Shore Patrolmen, who fended him off with a club.

The Lieutenant Commander growled, "Well, mister, get your men deployed and contain this outbreak."

Joe turned to Richards. "As you suggested on the way down, do it. Work your way in carefully. Grab the ones closest to the door and send them out. Be careful. I don't want to see you hurt."

"Aye, aye, sir!"

Richards dashed the ten feet to where the belligerent sailor was bobbing and weaving. He hit the man once soundly on the head and grabbed him by the arm before he hit the ground. Swinging the man in an arc, he threw him in the direction of the closest paddy wagon.

Joe noted the shoulder patch. He called out, "USS *St. Paul* . . . Designate this wagon for the *St. Paul.*"

Next, as the man the *St. Paul* sailor had hit was being led away, Joe pointed to the next wagon and said, "*Beaverton.* . . He goes to the *Beaverton* wagon."

The other two *Beaverton* men, Ohnhaus and Pickel, fell in behind Richards, who led a wedge in through the door of the bar.

The Commander said, "Just a minute, I want to make sure we're organized and don't have this spreading up and down the street. I have backup on the way."

"Sir, I understand we are the backup. There's enough Shore Patrol here to put them in the paddy wagons as soon as they come out."

"Mister, this isn't what I have in mind—"

The first dull thump of nightstick on bone punctuated the din of the fight. As the second thump echoed, sounding like a bat driving a ball into the outfield, a sailor flew out the door and landed on his knees on the pavement. Before they had a chance to pick him up, a second was pushed through the door with a big red knot on his forehead. He fell on the back of the first.

After seven more flew through the door, the message got across: a sailor ran out on his own, yelling, "Don't hit me! Don't hit me! I quit!"

Other Shore Patrol, emboldened by Richards's success, ran into the bar and formed a chain passing the rowdies out. The street quickly filled with them. Some were on their knees holding their heads. Others lay on the wet, cold cobblestones, unable to get up. The other officers and Chiefs quickly pushed Joe aside and took charge of handling the arrested sailors. The crews loading them into paddy wagons no longer attempted to seat them inside; they just tossed them in like cordwood. Just when Joe thought there couldn't be another man inside the club, one more would squirt out the door into the waiting arms of their captors.

A squad of Marine Military Police and another half-dozen Shore Patrol pushed through the crowd. The Commander directed them to go inside and back up Richards. The first Marine through the door collided with a semiconscious sailor being ejected. The din of combat was now reduced to groans and slurred profanity, punctuated by an infrequent thump of the nightstick. The Marines found the remnants of a very cowed bunch of drunks amid the thoroughly trashed bar. Those who could stand had fallen into line against the bar.

With the battle over, Joe went in. Each step was heralded by the crunch of broken glass under his soles. Looking about the place led him to the conclusion that everything breakable had been broken and everything movable had been turned over.

One of the sailors next to the bar shouted, "You mothers ain't gonna run me in." He broke from his place running.

Richards caught the man with one solid hit behind the knee. He screamed painfully as he collapsed on the floor. Two Marines pounced on him and swiftly cuffed his arms behind his back. He was lifted to his feet with cuts from the glass on the side of his face and neck.

Joe first noticed how white Richards's eyes and teeth were when he grinned in the semi-darkened room as he shouted, "Well, Mr. Zee, we cleaned this place up damn quick, sir. There ain't no more heads to knock. We've done all the dirty work. Sir, why don't you ask if we can be secured so we can get on with our liberty before curfew?"

Taking his three men to the senior Shore Patrol Officer, Joe said, "Commander, request permission to secure. We were the Shore Patrol at a ship's party and we were supposed to be off as soon as it was over."

Adjusting his hat on his head, the Lieutenant Commander said, "Certainly. Mister, you surprised the hell out of me. I didn't tell you to send your people into that brawl. It's far too dangerous . . . But what the hell, your people got the job done."

Richards waved his big hand. "Sir, it was easy. Those boys—other than one or two—didn't resist at all, once I got their attention. As for danger, that was just enough exercise to get my juices flowing. Other than somebody ruining my shoeshine, it was a piece of cake."

"Who are you people, and where are you from?"

Joe pointed to Richards's shoulder patch. "We're from the *Beaverton*, M Division. I'm Ensign Joe Xylos and this is Petty Officer Richards."

"I'm not sure whether I should commend you or chew you out. Based on results, I have to say 'well done' to you and your men. Richards, you've got more guts than common sense. If you want foreign shore duty, I'd be pleased to have you."

"Thank you, Commander. I'd just as soon pass on that. It's best if I keep my social life and my married life on different sides of the Date Line, if you know what I mean."

Laughing, the Commander clapped him on the back. "Certainly, certainly. Have a good night. We've got this well in hand."

Half an hour later, a taxi ride landed Joe by the wooden bridge leading to Fumiko's house. He threaded his way up the twisting, darkened path with less confidence than the night before. The bamboo leaves brushing against his face made him twist and turn as he climbed the path. The dog near the end almost leaped over the fence, sounding more like a hungry wolf than a pet. Fumiko turned her outside lights on at the sound of the barking. Walking as quickly as he could, Joe hugged the far side of the path until he was well clear of the property where the dog roamed. As he kicked off his shoes, Fumiko slid the rice-paper door open just enough to show her eye. She asked, "Was there trouble at your party?"

"No. There was a riot in one of the bars downtown, the Yellow Dragon. They sent us down to break it up."

"They're always having fights there. But why you, when they had the regular Shore Patrol?"

"It was too big. I've never seen so many people in a free-for-all in my life. I hope I'm never in a place when that kind of fight breaks out."

Fumiko pushed the door open all the way. He gathered her in his arms and pressed her close against him. She was wearing a quilted kimono and heavy sheepskin-lined slippers.

After he kissed her, she said in a small voice, "I was thinking that you weren't going to come. I was just about to take a hot bath and go to bed. Come, join me."

Later, as they curled in the tub with only their heads above the steaming water, Joe shared his impressions of the evening. "Fumiko, I had a chance today to meet other Japanese for the first time. You're different, like night versus day. In the taxi tonight, I thought about the night we met. All my friends went with women who were trying to look as Western as possible, but they've ended up with Japanese girlfriends. I picked the one who looked the most Japanese, and it turns out you're the most Western. You don't mispronounce your letter 'l,' and you use far better grammar than most Americans. I almost feel you *think* in English. Who taught you so well?"

"I was born in London, England, and stayed there until I was twelve. We moved back to Japan for two years before my father was transferred to New York. I graduated from an American high school and went to college there too. You're very perceptive, Joe. When I came home to marry, I used to think as much in English as much I did in Japanese."

"That's right, you told me you went to college in New London. If they select me for Submarine School, I suppose I'll get to know it well. I turned in my request just before we tied up."

She wiped a hair away from her eye. "Yes. It's right across the river."

"What was your major?"

"Freshman courses. I—I quit after the first term and came home. I asked my father to arrange a marriage for me."

"Why?"

"It was a very unhappy time in my life. People were unkind to me because I was Japanese."

"And you married a Japanese Army officer?"

"Yes, a career soldier, a major. He was a very good man. Joe, I know you mean no harm, but I don't like to talk about the past. It brings back so many painful memories. Joe, tell me, what attracts you to an older woman like me?"

"Fumiko, first of all, you're not an older woman to me."

"Ah, you make me feel so good."

"And second, why shouldn't an older woman enjoy the company of a younger man? I remember reading 'The Assembly of Women' to my father, in which there was a law that young men were required to give sexual satisfaction to older women before they could enjoy women of their own age."

Slapping the water at him, she exclaimed, "Now that's my kind of place! Where is this country?"

"Ancient Greece. Aristophanes was the author."

"Joe, in all the years I've known Americans, you're the first to talk about Greek literature."

"Well, I am Greek. Actually I didn't know anything about it until after my mother died and I had to take care of my father. He lost both legs when the Germans bombed his ship on the way to Murmansk. When I was a freshman in college, he lost his sight because he was diabetic. For the last two years before he died, I was his eyes. Every day I read to him. We read Plato, Socrates, Aristophanes, and so many more. We spent hours discussing what they wrote. It wasn't until the final days that I realized he had given me a classical education and an appreciation for my Greek culture. I loved that cranky old man. I still miss having him to come home to at the end of the day. He had more wisdom in the tip of his little finger than I'll ever have. Fumiko, I think he'd approve of you."

She floated into his arms and lightly kissed him. "You are a very strange boy who would love a woman with children older than he is."

"Not quite, darling. I'm twenty-five."

"Ah, such a big difference. Come, let's go to bed before this water gets too cold."

⊷⊶

Joe stood another duty day, then took a week's leave. Over the next few days, Fumiko introduced him to a side of Japan that his shipmates were missing. They spent nights in quaint inns, from the foot of Mount Fuji to the shores of nearby Sagami-wan. They enjoyed the theater in the form of Kabuki and Noh plays. They visited Tokyo, where Fumiko pointed out four buildings she owned. Afterward, they toured the central part of the city near the Imperial Palace. They visited intimate little restaurants and bars in both Tokyo and Yokohama. Although Joe paid for train tickets and taxis, Fumiko gave him the tickets to the shows and paid for most of the meals.

As they rode the train back to Yokosuka on Thursday evening, Joe suggested that he would like to take Fumiko to the Officer's Club for dinner.

She replied, "I will go if you want to. There are many people who know me. They could cause trouble."

"What kind of trouble?"

"Maybe they would want to steal me."

"Do you want to be stolen?"

"Of course not!"

"Then I don't see any problem. We'll go to dinner and dance afterward. We don't need to stay too late because I have the duty tomorrow."

Once they were at the house, she produced a $10 Military Payment Certificate or MPC, the funny-money currency used by the U.S. military in Japan. "Here, take this."

"I have enough for dinner. You don't have to cover this. Besides, isn't it against the law for you to have this kind of money?"

"Well, I have it; and they change the money every so often so it becomes worthless eventually. Take it. It will just go to waste otherwise."

"Where did you get it?"

"It doesn't matter. I won't be needing it. Please take it." She stuffed the bill into his breast pocket.

He leaned back on a Japanese pillow called a *zabuton* and watched his mistress squeeze herself into a girdle. She knelt next to him, and he zipped it up her back. His gaze focused on the one blemish on her body that he had found. It was an ugly, though faded, scar, three inches long by nearly one inch wide, just below her right shoulder blade. It was a place his fingers often touched, but one that Fumiko would not talk about.

She slipped on an expensive silk dress with a delicate black-and-white flowery print. The spreading of her skirts wafted a light musk perfume that teased his nose. While she combed her thick, shoulder-length black hair and applied her makeup, Joe decided that she looked ageless, perhaps as young as the late twenties but not older than the mid-thirties. The dress with its high collar and long sleeves certainly wasn't the kind that would attract attention. She brought him a coat with a fur collar, which he held for her.

As always, they walked down the hill in single file. He would have preferred to have her at his side, but after two weeks he was becoming accustomed to the dominant role she required of him.

CHAPTER 19

Sayonara, Sam

Joe was hungry by the time the maitre d' at the Officer's Club signaled that their table was ready. He was surprised and a bit annoyed when he felt Fumiko's grip tighten on his arm and heard her sucking in her breath. She had slowed to a crawl and was leading him to the right toward his commanding officer, Captain Sam Slaxman, who was seated with two other older men he had never seen before. Both men smiled at Fumiko while Sam looked at him with a puzzled expression. Both rose to their feet, and Sam belatedly followed.

He wiped the corners of his mouth with his napkin after the closest man exclaimed, "Fuji! The Original Fuji-san! They told me you'd retired. What are you doing here?"

"'Original Fuji-san,' not many around to remember those good old days," Fumiko said, ever so briefly cupping her breasts and turning to the right and then the left. "Ole, I am flattered that you remember. Robert and especially Sam, hello. It has been a long time. Yes, I've retired. I'd like for you to meet my companion, Joe Xylos."

" Pleased to meet you, young man. I'm Captain Ole Nuslund. That name sounds familiar. What ship are you on?"

Joe stiffened for an instant, then cleared his throat. "I'm on the *Beaverton* with Captain Slaxman, sir."

"Then I need only to introduce you to Captain Price."

Fumiko asked, "May we join you?"

Captain Nuslund motioned to two empty chairs by the aisle. "Certainly." As they all sat down, he jabbed Captain Sam in the ribs. "Sam, I thought you told me this was the first time you've ever set foot ashore in Japan?"

"Well, it is."

"Then how come Fuji-san knows your name?"

Captain Sam looked blankly at Fumiko for perhaps thirty seconds before saying, "I don't know. Maybe I'm losing my edge."

"Well, this is a day to remember! Sam Slaxman can't place a name with a face. Fuji-san, would you care to help him?"

Fumiko smiled slightly while playing with a corner of her napkin, then forced a pout. "Any man who would forget spending over a week with Fuji doesn't deserve help."

Captain Sam tossed down a swallow from his drink and pointed toward Joe. "Ole, I think Joe here knows your daughter."

Captain Nuslund scowled. "That's it! You're Joe Taco. You're the one! Tammy will never forget that you left her in the Tijuana jail. What have you to say about that, Mr. Xylos? You know she lost her job because of you?"

Joe shifted uncomfortably in his chair and whispered to Fumiko out of the corner of his mouth, "So you think you've got skeletons in your closet? I'm going to be lucky if I get out of here alive."

Captain Nuslund overheard him, and his face reddened back past his thin forelock of light brown hair. "Skeletons, indeed. Well?"

Joe leaned back in his seat and toyed with his soup spoon before looking up. "What do I have to say? Yes, sir, I'm the one who made the decision. I found four people in jail and had enough money to spring three of them. Two shipmates, who would have missed movement. No question there. That left two girls rolling the dice for one seat. Your daughter is lost. I thought that the other girl, Lyla, would have done something to bail Tammy out. It wasn't until we cleared the border that I found out she was a stewardess with a plane to catch."

Nuslund glared at Joe. "Mister, I don't think you could imagine the distress my wife and I experienced. We received notice of her termination from the school district before we heard from Tammy. Some one of you could have called."

I'm sorry Tammy had a tough time; and if I were her father, I would have been mad as hell. About Tammy, did she get a better paying job?"

Captain Nuslund sat tall in his seat and continued to glare.

"I used to have a line in my routine," Joe went on, "whenever I knew a bunch of people had been laid off . . . 'Two-thirds of the people who get fired get a better paying job.' How did she do?"

"That's beside the point. What gentleman would abandon an innocent young woman in a foreign jail?"

"My responsibilities were to my shipmates. Sir, every cent I made selling tacos that weekend went to get three people out of jail."

Nuslund looked at Captain Sam with palms upward. He shrugged his shoulders. "This Ensign isn't like any I've met before!"

Sam swallowed a swig from his glass, then smiled. "Before you invited my Mr. Xylos and your Miss Fuji to join us, Ole, recall we lamented how the peacetime Navy promotes a class of risk avoiders, time servers. About Tammy, I understand you have every right to be sore about her treatment. However, if we went to war tomorrow, I'd love to have a whole wardroom full of officers like Joe Xylos. The sad truth is I have more officers aboard who would have left all four behind rather than get involved. Here is a young officer who reported aboard in August, and the Chief Engineer has already begged me to assign him to be his Main Engines Officer. This is a Reserve officer, mind you . . . who didn't have steam courses at the Academy as a foundation. He makes things happen aboard and ashore. Although the things that happen around him in port give me gray hair, he's had good judgment. The latest event happened when he was assigned as Shore Patrol for a division party. They called him and three of my sailors down to Honcho Yokosuka to shut down a riot in one of the bars. Peace was restored in short order."

While the Captain was talking, Joe suddenly realized why Fumiko's oldest son Shige looked so familiar in the photo. He looked like a young Sam Slaxman.

In the lull as the waitress left, Joe asked, "Captain Slaxman, when did you go to Sub School?"

"1930."

"And were you in New London in the fall of 1931 and early 1932?"

Joe felt a sharp pain in his calf from Fumiko's kick.

Captain Sam looked first at Joe and then at Fumiko. He pointed at her and said, "Fumiko . . . Tann . . . Conn College."

She reached a hand across the table and touched his. "Fumiko Tanaka. It has been a long time, Sam. Indeed, I'm glad you remembered."

"You left suddenly."

"Yes. I came home and married. My husband died in the war in China."

"I'm sorry to hear that. The war must have been hard on you."

"The war was hard on us all. I was fortunate compared to many others. Let's talk of the good times. Robert, you haven't said a word. Do you remember Kyoto and Nara? That was the spring of 1950 right before Korea blew up, wasn't it?"

"That's right, Fuji. What a memory!"

Following dinner, Joe asked Fumiko to dance. Once they were out of earshot of the table, he whispered, "Fumiko, I don't know about you, but I feel like I've just jumped from the frying pan into the fire. That Captain Nuslund is still burned about Tijuana. You've been wonderful about changing the subject. My skipper has been sitting over there staring at you and slugging down one drink after another. Every time one of your old boyfriends stops by the table, I can see the sinews in his neck stand out. The third guy's attempts at double entendre are as subtle as a piledriver. Honey, I'd like to get out of here. There isn't a hand they can deal me that can be a winner."

"I understand, Joe. Yes, we should go, but before we do, I would like to have one dance with Sam. I've waited twenty-five years to see him again. There is something I must tell him."

"About Shige?"

"Yes. I sensed you had guessed when you asked him where he was in 1931. There is no need for you to worry. He burned his own bridges."

When they returned to the table, Joe said, "Captain, Fumiko would like to have one dance with you for old time's sake."

Joe turned in his seat to watch his CO dancing with Fumiko. He was holding her away as if dancing with his mother-in-law. Fumiko was doing all the talking.

Behind him, Captain Nuslund laid a hand on Joe's shoulder. "Mr. Xylos, you pass muster with Sam, and that's good enough for me. You hit the nail on the head about Tammy. She got a job selling books for Holt Rinehart. Her salary before bonus is almost twice what she made teaching school. Sam says you have a way of making things happen.

Your XO put it a different way . . . that lighting strikes just after you leave the room. I don't need any lightning strikes in my life."

Knitting his eyebrows, Joe asked, "Sir?"

"This is a small world. If you're around my family after this deployment, I would hope you have the sense not to mention this evening or Fuji-san. I'd like to keep things on an even keel, if you know what I mean."

"Aye, aye, sir. I understand."

"Is she telling it straight? Have you been with her for two weeks for free?"

"I don't make a practice of saying much about my private life, sir, other than to say I never could enjoy commercial sex."

"I don't know how you do it, son. But more power to you. You aren't engaged or something stupid like that?"

"No, sir. We're good friends. That's all."

The band stopped playing. When Joe saw them approaching, he stood and held Fumiko's chair. He caught her eyes and saw tears filling the corners.

Her response was in a barely audible voice. "We must go. I can't stay here another minute. Please don't say anything. He did nothing. It was all me."

Joe looked at Slaxman and could see the whites all the way around his eyes. The Old Man looked at him but didn't seem to be focusing. He picked up his drink and poured it down his throat; some of the ice cubes struck his cheek and tumbled to the floor. He sat down and stared at his empty glass, obviously lost in thought.

The Ensign said, "Captain, gentlemen, please excuse us. We need to be leaving. Thank you for sharing your table with us. Captain Nuslund, Captain Price, I enjoyed meeting you both."

The two men stood and shook Joe's hand. Captain Sam belatedly stood and did the same. Fumiko kissed Nuslund on the cheek. She gently removed Robert's hand from her breast after they hugged. Lastly she touched Slaxman's cheek. "I'm glad we met again after all these years. I feel I can close that chapter to my life now. Sayonara, Sam."

Nuslund said, "Fuji, is there something wrong?"

"No, nothing's wrong. There's too much smoke. My eyes burn."

Fumiko said nothing all the way back to her house. She sat on the far side of the cab and stared out the window. Once or twice she sniffled, but she ignored her lover's attempts to make small talk.

After the hot bath, which had become a ritual with them, Joe unrolled the futon and crawled in.

Fumiko got down next to him, sitting on her heels. Her eyes were red but dry. After looking at him for what seemed an eternity, she said, "When we returned today, I knew that this would be our last night together. I had hoped to stay another week, but the reservations can't be changed."

"Wait a minute! If you're changing horses in midstream, I understand. But I don't like it. Like they say, rank hath its privileges. Why didn't you just say so at the club?"

She put one hand on him as he sat up. "It's true I haven't been straight with you, but it's not like that. Please understand."

She pulled a business-size envelope out of her kimono sleeve. It had U.S. government franking and was addressed to Mrs. Fumiko Sullivan. She pulled a letter from the envelope.

Joe scanned the contents almost in disbelief. "Fumiko Sullivan . . . dependent spouse of COL Delbert C. Sullivan, USAF . . . will board MATS flight . . . at Yokota Air Force Base on Saturday 11 January 1957 at 0900 hours . . ."

He dropped the notice on the comforter. "I had no idea. You're married! It does explain a lot of things. It's a good thing you never told me, because I've never fooled around with married women."

Tears were running down both of her cheeks as she pleaded, "Please don't leave me tonight! I need you to hold me. I hurt so much. Please stay."

Fumiko pressed herself against him, wrapping her arms around his back. Seismic sobs shook her frame as she burrowed her face into his chest. "I have always made one big mistake after another."

"I don't know if I'm in much of a mood for anything."

"It doesn't matter. I just can't bear to be alone tonight."

He sat her upright and, looking her in the eye, asked, "Who is Colonel Delbert Sullivan? Do you love him?"

Fumiko wiped the tears from her right eye with the back of her hand, much the way a little girl would. She looked down at the pattern on the futon before she said very slowly, "Yes, he is a very good man and a very tender man. I love him very much."

Joe let the words sink in before he said, "Why in the world did you pick me up and why are we having this affair?"

She turned her head away, then, looking at him out of the corner of her eye, said, "I am a bad butterfly. I—I was visiting my friend Saeko—Sunshine—and she had a list of ships and commanding officers that I happened to see. And there was Sam's name. I was just visiting, so I stayed, thinking I would see him there or do something with one of the *Beaverton* officers . . . You came in. Saeko said you acted like a pimp, so cocksure. I didn't know why you would have nothing to do with the girls and looked only at me. I told myself I would only stay with you long enough to find out about Sam. I remember I did ask you about your Captain and you said you hardly knew him . . . that you were a snipe. By then I was hooked. Then I thought that this would be the last fling. Del just retired, and he will be working for Honeywell Corporation . . . maybe in Minnesota or maybe California. I will never come back."

"You're leaving? This house doesn't look like you're packing out, never to return. What will happen to this place? Are you selling it?"

"Next month, my oldest boy, Shige, and his bride are going to move in."

"What about all that real estate in Tokyo?"

"It is my family's. My children will take care of it."

He brushed another tear from her cheek and whispered, "Fumiko, what did the Old Man say that upset you so badly?"

She ran her hand along the edge of her kimono and stuck a thumb under the obi around her waist. "When he asked how I could remember his face over these twenty-five years, I told him I had every reason to: I had been looking at his son since he was born. And that I never forgot the week we spent together. He said that if he had known, he would have married me."

"Why didn't you tell him?"

"I—I pretended he didn't care because he had hurt my pride. He was my very first love. I loved him more than any man I have ever known. I went back to school and I was in the clouds. Then one of my friends told me that my panties were hanging in his room with a note saying, 'I got the Jap.' I was so angry . . . humiliated. I thought of committing suicide. I returned to Japan. By the time I boarded the ship, I was sick all the time. Right before we arrived in Yokohama, the doctor told me I was pregnant. I told my father and asked if he could arrange a very quick marriage. He wanted to send me back to America and confront Sam. He wanted to make sure that Sam's career was ruined."

"Shotgun marriage, eh?"

"I begged him not to send me because I didn't like the prejudice. Instead Father married me to a friend, an army officer, who had been injured fighting the Russians in Siberia. He was thirty-five and I was eighteen. He didn't think he could father a child. He was pleased I was with child. He died in the war."

"Yes. You told me before."

Joe snuggled himself inside the futon, turning his back on her. She turned out the light and slid in beside him.

Some hours later, Joe was awakened by a low, steady moan. "Ohh-hhhhh."

He reached over to the other side of the bed and it was almost cold. Through the half- light of dawn, he made out Fumiko's silhouette kneeling before the alcove with the military relics. Her back was to him. He realized that she was the one moaning.

"Fumiko, what's wrong?"

She continued to moan. He asked two or three more times. She continued. Then he heard the dry metallic grind of the steel blade on the scabbard. It wasn't until the steel flashed in the dim light that he realized what she was about to do.

Joe leaped from the bed and bounded to where she knelt. The blade lay across her knees. She was in the process of opening her kimono. He brushed the sword from her lap. Steel clattered on hardwood.

He pushed it farther from her grasp, saying, "Why, Fumiko? This won't solve anything."

"I'm very bad . . . very bad. I'm bad for everyone. I must end this badness."

"I don't understand. After all you've been through!"

In a very little voice, she said, "I have never been able to keep a relationship. I am growing old. I am alone. I am very bad. I disgraced my father . . . my children. Even last night, you didn't want me."

He pushed the sword, and it slid across the smooth floor to rest against the shoji. He pulled her into his arms. "Fumiko, I was probably the wrong guy for you to pick up. All my life has been one-night stands with some honey in the floor show or girl at the bar. I'm always on my way to another town. What's happened to me over these past two weeks is that I realized I've been living in a world that has been for me, and never in a world for us. I'll never forget these past two weeks. I know that we are two people who could never make a life together. There are too many years between us. I envy your Colonel Sullivan. I think you can be happy with him and he with you. You have to make the commitment to do it."

"Then you're not angry with me?"

"I was mad last night. Damn right! My pride was hurt. After a night's sleep, I can't say I'm angry with you. Confused, yes. I don't understand why you took this so hard after all this time."

"When I told my husband I was pregnant with Hige, he didn't believe the baby was his. In Seoul in 1939, he came home drunk and accused me again. He wanted me to commit seppuku, saying I was an unfaithful liar. I was very hurt and angry. I had been faithful. I had heard about Japanese atrocities on BBC News, so I said, 'You've been so used to killing Chinese women and children that you want to kill your own wife. You would leave your own two children to grow up as orphans.'

"I was kneeling with my head down. He could have easily cut off my head. I said, 'Go ahead. Kill me. Be a murderer.' I saw him spread his legs and heard the sword cut the air. He hit me very hard across the back . . . so hard that it split my kimono."

"Then that's the scar below your shoulder blade."

"Yes. I didn't go to a doctor. I was so ashamed. He left the house, and I packed up the babies and came here to live with my sister. I saw him once in 1942 when he came home for a month. He was very tender with the children. In the beginning, it was like our honeymoon, but then he accused me again of being unfaithful. And this time . . . he was right. I was desolate because I had learned that my lover died when the *Akagi* was lost at Midway.

"My husband left early for the front. I never saw him again because he committed suicide after his regiment had very heavy losses in 1945. One of his officers brought me his sword with his blood still on it. I never felt anything when I washed the blood off, but I made this shrine for my sons."

"After all you've been through, why would seeing Sam Slaxman after twenty-five years bring you to do this?"

"In the time after the war, I found I could make the most money working as a whore . . . and money was what I needed most. When I was with those men, I used to imagine I was with Sam and I loved him very much. Then I got sick and couldn't work. But I had something the other girls wanted. I could speak good English. I taught them English and about Americans in exchange for a quarter of their income for the first six months after I taught them. They made money, and so did I . . . far more than I made working. I became very selective. The men were always very special. I am amazed at the number who went on to become Admirals."

"All those fantasies for all those years came to life right before your eyes."

She nodded. "I didn't like what I saw. Over the years there have been maybe two, three, five men like you that I could really love . . . but now it's too late."

"What about Delbert?"

"He's a nice enough guy, good company. But he doesn't make me laugh like you do. He doesn't make me feel good to be alive." She looked down at her watch. "You've got to get dressed or you'll be late getting back to your ship."

When Joe was leaving, suitcase in hand, Fumiko handed him the samurai sword, now in its scabbard. "Take this."

"Why?"

"I think you should have it. I'm afraid for it to be around here."

"Shouldn't this sword go to your children?"

"They have so much else. For me, please, take it."

"I don't feel right about taking it. I'll keep it for the time being."

Joe stepped aboard, the suitcase in one hand and the sword in the other. "Permission to come aboard, sir?"

His roommate Cy Penelton, who was OOD of the day, saluted. "Permission granted. Looks like you've been over to Kamakura and bought a sword. Couldn't resist a good deal, eh? I thought you said you were going to save some money."

"Well, I am . . ."

Taking the sword from his hand, Cy pulled the blade halfway out. He studied it carefully. "This is a beautiful weapon. It looks like an antique. How much did it set you back?"

Joe, in the meantime, focused his gaze on a bronze casting of the new ship's insignia, which hung on the bulkhead facing the brow. The body of the insignia was a shield whose surface was burnished except for a pair of diagonal lines coursing from upper left to lower right. Evenly spaced between them were three highly polished projectiles. At the top was a single hand rising above the center with two fingers held out in a "V" for victory. On a streamer across the bottom were the words "Always Prepared" and below that, "USS *Beaverton*."

He recognized the design immediately as a close imitation of the Shield Rubber Company logo right down to the motto "Always Prepared."

Joe smiled and jerked his thumb toward the insignia. "Where did that come from?"

Cy handed back the sword. "Ensign, don't you ever read the plan of the day? This is the new ship's insignia. Oh, that's right, you were on leave when they held the dedication ceremony. Frankly, I think it's got class . . . simple . . . uncluttered."

The OOD pulled a chromed lighter from his pocket. "Look here, they're already sold out of these Zippos. I was lucky to get one. It's a good souvenir to take with me when I get detached."

"That's right, Cy, you're real short. This must be your last duty day. No more Sundowners Club!"

"That's right. L.A., here I come!"

Joe took the sword back and studied each segment of the brass insignia before he left the quarterdeck. He paused in the light by the ladder down to the forward officers' quarters. There he pulled a condom box from his pants pocket and chuckled to himself as he opened the door to Boys' Town. *The best thing I can do is toss the whole bunch of these rubbers over the side. If I'm connected with these little jewels, I'll be in the Sundowners Club and miss seeing Frenchy when we go to Okinawa.*

CHAPTER 20

Okinawa

Joe arrived on the quarterdeck with his roommates just in time to board the officer's motorboat for the beach. The black of a winter's night mixed with the fog made him appreciate that he wasn't in the duty section and assigned as a boat officer. He clutched in his hand a copy of the flashing light message he'd received from Frenchy.

For a time he was lost in thought, reliving the recent stay in Melbourne and speculating about how his former shipmate and Eva wound up here in Okinawa.

His reverie was broken by Harry Leach's gruff voice. "Well, mister, the gun boss says you'll be working for me when we get underway. I understand they can't stand you down in the hole anymore and are foisting you off on me."

"Lieutenant, let's not start off absolute enemies. The truth of the matter is that Commander Moran is quite upset that I'm being moved. Give me half a chance, I'll serve you equally well. The word I got today was that the Old Man wants me where I can stand bridge watches because of the endorsement he made on my request for Sub School."

"Bridge watches? You won't get out of Combat before next Christmas, the way watch qualifications progress on this ship."

Joe, like the others, crowded close to the man next to him, seeking warmth from the raw winter dampness. It wasn't until they were approaching the fleet landing at White Beach that the impact of having most of the Seventh Fleet in Buckner Bay at one time hit home. The boat traffic off the landing was a waterborne version of rush hour on the Hollywood Freeway. Soon the sonorous rumble of the numerous ship's boats raised the noise level to where conversations had to be shouted. The combination of the many wakes, as well as the stale boat exhausts, made the ride's end a queasy one. At last the boat was alongside the landing, and the group stepped onto the float. The steel surface was slick with dew and oil, and tainted by salt spray. Just ahead of him, Harry Leach paused and looked back at the boat. When Joe was almost abreast of him, Leach stepped forward half a step.

"A-a-a-w-w-w!" Joe was so concentrated on his rotund adversary that he failed to see a leg-size hole in the deck of the float where the irregularly shaped plates gaped around the framing. He stepped through the hole and sank down to a sitting position before Leach latched onto his arms and swiftly pulled him to his feet. The ankle of Joe's left foot, which remained on deck, was sharply twisted, causing him to walk off painfully with a slight limp. He thanked Leach for saving him, but mentally he burned as the cold, wet trouser leg chilled his shin and water squished in his shoe.

Leach half-whispered, "It may be wet and cold, Ensign, but it's better than what you usually step in."

Joe tensed for a moment as Larry White pulled him shoreward. Leach smiled smugly while thrusting his hands so deeply into his coat pockets that he was almost hugging himself.

Stamping his soaked foot on the deck, Joe felt the need to make a retort to the Lieutenant's nasty remark. He spat at Leach through clenched teeth, "Yes, sir. I'll have to get used to the squishy feeling between the toes, following in your footsteps."

Leach raised his beefy arm as if he were going to backhand the smaller man, then turned quickly and walked off at a brisk pace. All the way up the wide gangplank from the float, Leach snapped and snarled at Joe.

Joe kept silent, but thought, *The prospect of working for this asshole on leaving port can only be a test to find out how much I want duty on a submarine.*

Once at the White Beach Officer's Club, Joe searched for a phone to call Frenchy while the others ordered the first round. He returned to the bar where perhaps twenty of the *Beaverton* wardroom congregated and were growing noisier with each round.

Forty-five minutes later, Frenchy and Eva stepped into the very crowded room. Other than the local waitresses, she was one of maybe three women in the packed O Club. A path opened for her like Moses crossing the Red Sea. The noise level appreciably dropped as many eyes hungrily followed them toward the one reserved table in the club. Frenchy waved for Joe to come along, and a crowd of *Beaverton* officers followed.

Eva flashed her smile every inch of the way while holding tightly to her husband's arm. Her long blonde locks curled down to her shoulders, making her look like a schoolgirl.

Behind him, Joe heard, "That's the White Beach Officer in Charge and his wife. Can you imagine being stranded on an island with her? I think the detailer makes sure there is at least one woman like her out here so we don't forget what it's like on the other side of the Date Line."

Once the couple were seated, the din quickly built up to its level of moments before. Eva's mellow voice was music to Joe's ears as she was introduced to the others at the table. When the drinks were ordered, she asked for soda water with a twist of lime, while Frenchy had a scotch neat.

Over the next two hours they drank, reminisced, and finally ate dinner. Although a few questions were posed to the couple, most of the evening was spent retelling adventures in Australia, Guam, and Japan, with Joe's vignettes the catalyst for most of the sea stories. They laughed about Harry Leach's predicaments.

The others at the table excused themselves after dessert, leaving Joe, Frenchy, and Eva alone. The crowd had thinned out somewhat, but was noisier and drunker than before.

After the third stranger had approached the table feigning previous acquaintance with either Joe or Frenchy, a very tall and quite handsome man with a light brown crewcut arrived. He leaned across table and took Eva's hand.

A cloud of stale bourbon preceded his words. "Do you remember me? I'm Commander Howard Cannon. It's been such a long time since we met in Berlin. I've been trying all night to remember your name."

She pulled back her hand and thinned her lips. "Commander Cannon, you must be mistaken. I have never met you before."

"Oh, yes. I never forget a pretty face like yours. You were in Berlin two years ago . . . an exiled Hungarian."

Her Hungarian accent becoming more pronounced with each word, Eva said, "Please leave us alone. I don't know you and I don't want to know you. You're drunk!"

Frenchy stood and rested his hand on the man's elbow. "Commander, the game's over. This is my wife, and we'd both like to be left alone."

The stranger stared at Frenchy as if having trouble focusing his eyes. His gaze returned to Eva in a like manner before he turned unsteadily on his feet. As he walked away, he said, "Maybe it was Paris or London. Or maybe it was Jacksonville."

Eva swallowed the last dregs of her soda as her eyes followed the retreating stranger. The ice cubes in the glass rattled, betraying her shaking hand as she placed it on the table.

Her voice betraying her unease, she said to Frenchy, "Darling, let's show Joe our wonderful big house."

When Joe stood up after polishing off his drink, the effect of the hours of celebrating on this first night in port hit him hard. Although his head was reeling somewhat, the drinks anesthetized any pain from his twisted ankle.

Frenchy drove them back to his quarters in his red-and-white 1955 Chevy. On the way, Eva rhapsodized about their house as if it were a palace. Joe was surprised to see that it was a small, two-bedroom Quonset hut.

Directing him to a well-worn upholstered chair, she bubbled, "All my life I have lived in apartments. And now, for the first time I live in such a wonderful big house."

Frenchy eased himself onto a vintage sofa, muttering, "It's okay except when it rains hard. Then it's like living inside a snare drum. Thank goodness for surplus BOQ furniture or we'd be sitting on the floor."

Joe bounced up and down lightly on his worn leather chair. "It isn't so bad," he said. "At least I don't feel the springs."

"The quarters were unfurnished, and I had nothing when we arrived here," said Frenchy. "Fortunately, Housing had this supply of vintage castaways."

Eva entered the room carrying a pair of cocktail glasses. "Darling, we are so very fortunate. We have chairs. We have beds. And a good stove and refrigerator. And most important, we have each other."

She handed her guest a fresh scotch and soda before joining her husband on the sofa.

Joe felt a sense of satisfaction as he watched Eva snuggle against Frenchy's side and rest her head on his shoulder. In the dim light, her eyes were like vibrant black coals. Frenchy's lips touched her hair in a very light kiss, and she flashed a beautiful smile.

Raising his glass slightly, Joe asked, "Eva, aren't you going to join us?"

"No, I shouldn't. It's not good for my . . . condition."

"Condition? That's quite a change from Melbourne. What condition?"

She poked her husband gently in the ribs and looked him in the eye. He smiled ever so slightly as he nodded.

"Joe, I am with child . . . pregnant. I do not wish to harm my baby."

Joe raised his glass in a toast. "Congratulations! You certainly don't let moss grow under—No, that wouldn't be appropriate. Let me propose a proper toast. To the couple whose happiness makes me aspire to find as wonderful a wife. To this very love-filled house. To many, many healthy babies!"

Frenchy laughed. "Not on a Lieutenant's pay!"

"When is it due?"

Eva replied, "The doctor said it would be the twenty-fifth of September. I found out just two days ago. You are the first to know."

"Eva, Frenchy, I'm so happy for you. Now that we're away from the crowd, my curiosity has gotten the best of me. Tell me . . . How did you get orders here?"

His friend stared at the glass he rolled between his hands. "Eva beat that low-priority message I sent, confessing all. Following my instructions, she broke the news to them and asked for a debriefing by the CIA. She had just finished with them by the time I arrived."

He took a deep drink from the glass. "My boss told me he wanted me hung out to dry in some zero job as far away from civilization as possible. The terms of her deal were that we wouldn't be separated. They gave me the choice of here or Johnston Island. I've been promised twenty-four months here followed by three years of shore duty. This has been like a rest home until the fleet came in yesterday."

"Frenchy, I still can't understand. How can they fire you from a job just because you got married?"

"Believe me, it's reasonable. I don't argue with the requirement. I knew it was going to happen. I even knew they'd give me orders to the equivalent of Siberia."

Eva rested her hand on his thigh. "This man of mine! I had no idea what he was giving up to save me. He never said a word about how our being married would affect him. That Captain from the National Security Agency, who interrogated me, made me feel like I had picked him on purpose."

"The NSA? I thought it was the CIA who interrogated you."

Eva said, "They were next in line. Now I'm on their watch list."

Joe asked Frenchy, "Did you tell her what you told me on the way to Guam?"

Frenchy took another swallow. "Sure, but she doesn't believe me. They've taken enough pounds of flesh from this old body. I've got less than four years to go before twenty. Besides, I'm not destined to be Chief of Naval Operations . . . or Lieutenant Commander, for that matter."

"I can't believe that."

"Realistically, the game is over. They make selections for promotion based on your performance and the availability of billets. I'm starting at ground zero in a backwater, competing against people who have spent a whole career in the fleet honorably making a fine reputation."

"Frenchy, you're one hell of a fine officer. They won't throw your kind of talent away."

"Joe, I'm not going to worry about it. The most important side of my life is Eva. I don't want a job that keeps me away from home nights."

"And how do you find life on the free side of the Iron Curtain, Eva?"

"There is so much of everything. When I shop at the commissary, I hear women complain about choices being so limited. My difficulty is making up my mind. And there is so much more time when you don't have to stand in line for everything. For me, there are too many things. I am always surprised that there is so little security . . . no passports . . . so few police. Life for me is so happy. Frenchy is very good to me.

Heaven could not be as good as here."

The phone began ringing. Frenchy excused himself to answer it.

The first words he said after the greeting were, "Scoggins! You've got to be kidding! Where in the name of Sam Hill did that clown get a gun? . . . There are five of you there? You say he wants to trade all of you for me? . . . It sounds to me like he's working his way up to a dishonorable discharge. . . . Yes, put him on the phone. . . ."

Putting his hand over the mouthpiece, Frenchy said, "One of my black sheep, Seaman Apprentice Tom Brown, is holding the Duty Section at gunpoint. He's threatened to kill them one by one unless I show up."

Frenchy continued, "Brown, what the hell are you trying to do? . . . As I told you yesterday, in another ten days you'll be on your way Stateside. . . . Come on. Calm down. Give Lieutenant Scoggins the gun. . . . I can't promise you anything, but I'll try to ease you out of here. I'll try to convince the Old Man to handle this at mast. . . . Brown, please don't dig yourself a hole. . . . Of course I know you're under pressure. . . . Nobody ever died from scraping and painting a hull. You're what? Brown, why? . . . Come off it! . . . There's no way on earth you'd ever get away with it! . . . Yes, I heard him! Brown, for God's sake, please don't pull that trigger! . . . Yes, you have my attention. . . . Don't!"

Frenchy pulled the receiver from his head and looked into the mouthpiece. "He hung up."

Both Eva and Joe chorused, "What's happening?"

As he dialed the duty office, Frenchy said, "I have a serious problem child. They were in the process of surveying him off one of the fleet oilers when he went over the hill. Shore Patrol picked him up in Naha City after the ship left. He convinced the Old Man at mast that they were picking on him on his last ship and begged for one last chance to redeem himself. They gave him to me. I put him to work scraping paint. He requested a transfer to the Personnel Office on the grounds that the lead in the red lead paint is poisoning him. He requires one hundred and ten percent supervision. The Old Man's response to the request was to restart the wheels turning to survey him. Until tonight he was on his way to an easy out. I've got to get dressed. It's going to be a long night. Joe, I'll give you a ride on down. You'll be in walking distance of fleet landing from there. Darling, would you please fix me a thermos of hot coffee?"

Frenchy placed the phone back in the cradle. "No answer. That's funny. He must have disconnected the phone."

After changing into uniform, Frenchy called his superiors, but none were home. He finally located the XO, Commander Bob Munday, who was at the Army Officer's Club on the other side of the island. On Munday's advice, he made more calls to line up help and alert others to the situation at the Duty Office.

Later, as a grim-faced Lieutenant Villerouge walked toward the door, Eva held his arm tightly. "Please, darling, be careful. Don't go near that man. They could be setting a trap. You're all I have! Please be careful!"

Her lips trembled and her eyes looked a little watery following his goodbye kiss.

Joe said, "He'll be okay, Eva. Don't worry. I'll keep an eye on him."

They sped over the twisting, rain-slick roads with the headlights cutting tunnels in the foggy mist until they reached the cinder block building of the Duty Office. The parking lot was empty except for a pair of Navy pickup trucks. The building appeared deserted, but cracks of light peeped around the edges of shutters and under the front door.

A lone enlisted man appeared out of the mist. On recognizing Frenchy, he picked up his pace to a fast trot. "Sir! Sir, I'm glad you came. That nut Brown has the whole Duty Section lined up against the wall. He's got a forty-five. I started to go in, but he told me to leave or he was going to kill me too."

"Did he? Have you heard him shoot anyone?"

"No, sir."

"How long have you been here?"

"About ten minutes, sir. The guy is crazy as a loon! I heard him screaming in there. You've got to do something!"

Frenchy said, "Maybe I could go over next to the building and talk him out into the open."

Joe exclaimed, "What am I supposed to cover you with, a coffee cup? Let's wait for help to arrive. I like the idea of Marine sharpshooters and plenty of people with guns to back us up."

"The way he talked, I'm not sure we have the time to wait for help to arrive," replied Frenchy.

"Frenchy, that man wants you because he wants to kill you! If he does show himself, he'll probably use a hostage as a shield. Let him stew in there. He hasn't shot anyone yet."

"Joe, I've got to do something to save those people. I just can't stand out here by myself and do nothing."

"Wait! Time is the one thing we have more of than he has. Think about the people he has inside. It's time to play the joker in the deck. He doesn't know me from Adam. I'll go in and talk him out."

"Come off it! You?"

"Yeah, me! If there's one thing I can do, it's talk people into doing the right thing. I've had to deal with people like him before. Last year in East St. Louis I had to sweet-talk a black who cold-cocked the bouncer. I kept him thinking and talking until the cops arrived. Frenchy, going in there shooting is the best way to guarantee someone gets killed. He needs to be persuaded to give up."

"You'll need a weapon."

"No! I'll go in unarmed."

"Joe Xylos, you're nuts. There's no way I'm going to tell you to go in there!"

"Thanks for your concern. You're not telling me. I'm volunteering. Frenchy, my friend, you keep your head down. Remember what Eva said. One last favor . . . give me that thermos and cup. I'm going to need to sober up and stay awake far more than you."

Come on! Unarmed! What can you do?"

"Talk. That's more than you're doing here. He hung up on you."

Frenchy waved his arm in the direction of the building. "And you think he'll listen to you?"

"They pulled all the pickets off the fence, didn't they? You married Eva, didn't you? Maybe not at first, but he will in time. He hasn't killed anybody yet. And the odds are, he won't. Let's look at the downside risk. How many people does he have in there? Five? Six?" Joe asked.

"Duty Officer, Chief, a First Class, and probably two drivers."

"And he has one forty-five with one clip, most likely?

"We don't know what all he's armed with," Frenchy said.

"Odds are, he has no more than one bullet per man. He can't afford to shoot even one man if I can plant the right seed in the others' heads"

"What if he shoots you first?"

"He won't. I'll be his friend."

"Joe, what makes you think you can perform this miracle?"

"Who else have you got? He's threatened to kill you and probably would feel like a hero to bag his boss. I'm a Reserve Ensign . . . barely able to pass as an officer. If I can't convince him, I can at least act as an intermediary, giving you information you don't have. At worst he'll have one more hostage. What have you got to lose?"

Frenchy laid his hands on his friend's shoulders. "A true friend, a damn fine shipmate. Stay here. Let the experts handle it. This guy is unglued."

Joe poured a cup of coffee from the thermos. "Then it's settled, you're the outside man. I'm the inside man. If that guy starts shooting, get me help as quickly as you can. I don't want to bleed to death." He began walking toward the building, slightly favoring his left leg. When he was halfway to the door, he turned toward Frenchy and shouted, "Announcing the next act! Joe Xylos, fresh from successful appearances in the best bistros in Yokosuka and points East. Give the man a hand!"

Frenchy shouted, "Damn it, Joe! Get back here! I don't want you to go in there. Joe! You heard me!"

"Your job, my friend, is to love and care for your wonderful woman. Don't you forget it."

CHAPTER 21

Duty Section Held Hostage

At the entrance, Joe stood to one side of the door and knocked.

"Is that you, Lieutenant Villerouge?" came a voice that sounded high and strained.

"No. My name is Joe."

"Joe? Joe who?"

"That's not important. Brown, I'm going to open the door slowly."

"I didn't say you could come in!"

Joe turned the latch and eased the door ajar, still standing to one side.

"I didn't say you could come in!"

Joe pushed the door open. He stuck out the arm that held the thermos. He counted at least two slow breaths before he slowly stepped into the room.

Brown screamed, "You don't listen. I didn't say you could come in, shorty. You're in trouble! Damn you! What sort of trick is this?"

Joe lightly kicked the door shut behind him. Standing on either side of the door were the five hostages. All faced the wall in a parade rest position with their feet about two feet out, their foreheads against the wall. Joe turned slowly to face Seaman Tom Brown, who was crouching behind a desk in the far corner so that only the top of his head and the muzzle of a .45-caliber pistol were in view. The man's short dark hair sprouted like stalks of untended grass. His eyes bulged, exposing white around their entire rims.

"Didn't your mom ever tell you it's impolite to point?" said Joe.

"Turn around and assume the position, shorty. Lean against the door just like the others."

Joe made an effort to look at the five captives. Two of the enlisted men were shaking. The officer standing closest to him smelled like an overflowing toilet. His shirt collar was soaked with sweat.

Before walking across the room, Joe casually took a sip from the coffee cup. "You must be planning to get this over real quick, from the way you're treating these men."

Brown stood and pointed the gun directly at Joe's head. He snarled, "I said assume the position!"

Joe met the man's gaze, doing his best to focus his eyes on his face and not the gun muzzle. Brown was just short of six feet tall and chubby. The two fatty jowls on either side of his large square jaw began to twitch. He raised his left hand to support the right, which had begun to weave. His fingertips were turning pale.

The Ensign slowly placed the thermos on a nearby desk and looked his adversary in the eye. "Brown, you don't have a beef with me, so why don't you save your strength and relax?"

"Look, you little shit! If you're stupid enough to come in here, you're going to do what I say or it's gonna be bye-bye. Now face that wall!"

"Are you sure that gun is loaded?"

"Damn right!"

"You're absolutely positive that there's a round in the chamber?"

Brown curled a lip to show nicotine-stained teeth. "Do you think I'm stupid?"

"No, after looking down that hole since I met you and in light of these threats, I'm just curious. You could be bluffing."

The big seaman bent his arms to a forty-five-degree angle and pulled the receiver back. A single round tumbled out. It made a single tap on the oak desktop and rolled to a stop next to a china coffee mug. He slowly lowered the gun, still aiming it at Joe's head.

Joe slowly leaned back, putting a finger against his cheek. "Where did you get it? . . . The gun?"

"I took it from a security guard. He'll have a headache tomorrow. Look, shorty, I don't have to answer your questions."

Joe pointed to the man's dungarees, which were paint stained where they weren't dirty, and calmly observed, "Brown, you must have come here straight from work. You must be tired after a full day's work."

"Tired! Tired!! You sonofabitch, I'm dying, and I'm gonna get that bastard that made me eat and breathe all that red lead . . . or I'm gonna—You're baiting me! Get over against that wall or I'll shove this gun down your throat and make you shit your pants just like that slob of a Lieutenant."

"All that will get you is more shit to smell. Look, I'm tired. I had the mid-watch last night. Do me a favor and give me the gun so you won't get blown away."

"Do as I say."

Joe removed the cap from the thermos and refilled his mug. He took a sip and stared at Brown, then replied, "I've been running hard and drinking hard since I came ashore. I turned my ankle on the float at fleet landing. It's sore as hell. There is no way I'm going to play your silly game. I wouldn't do it for the Chief of Naval Operations, and I sure as hell won't do it for you. Do what you want, but don't do something you'll regret tomorrow. Brown, I'm not here to be your enemy. I'm here to help you."

Joe eased himself into a sitting position on the corner of the desk and sipped his coffee very slowly. The room was so still that it echoed the sound of each man's breathing like the inside of a cave.

After almost five minutes of silence, Brown more calmly asked, "Why did they send you here, anyway?"

"They said something about the phone not working."

"Damn right! I yanked it out of the wall. Now are you going to assume the position?"

"No, I'm assuming any position. Brown, I'm all you've got between seeing the sun rising tomorrow and a round through your head."

"Do it now."

"You look like a pretty sensible fellow. Fire that gun once, the Marines out there are going to shoot first and identify your corpse later. Right now, there are six people in here with you. If you shoot me, the others here would be fools to stand idly by and let you shoot them. How many times can you shoot before you have to reload?"

"Look, shorty, you don't have to worry about how many shots I fire before I run out of bullets, because your name is on the first one. Now get off your ass and stand facing the wall just like all the others!"

The veins on Brown's neck stood out as he motioned with the gun.

Joe remained motionless, looking him squarely in the eye. After almost a minute, the harried seaman broke off his stare, went to a window, and lifted a shutter enough to peek out. "I don't see anyone out there."

"For God's sake, get away from that window! There's a dozen Marine sharpshooters out there. They'll put a bullet through your head in an instant."

Brown jumped back; his eyes bulged, revealing red veins, and his lips peaked in a pucker. He turned the gun toward Joe and sighted down the barrel. Almost mumbling, he said, "Marines? I didn't see any Marines out there."

"Of course not. They are professionals, believe me. They're not going to give you a target. They're hiding back in the shadows. As long as you don't start shooting, they're going to wait. They expect me to bring you out."

The seaman tilted his head and closed one eye, aiming carefully down the barrel. His mouth twisted in a grimace, and his hands began to shake.

Softly Joe said, "Brown, you don't strike me as one who would needlessly kill an unarmed man."

"Watch it! I could still pull this trigger."

"I know. Suppose you did. And suppose the red lead paint didn't kill you. There are sixteen-year seamen on the *Beaverton* who've made a career of scraping and painting. They're some of the healthiest men on board. Can you imagine spending the rest of your life in a place like Portsmouth or Leavenworth, Kansas? You could live to be one hundred. And it's confinement at hard labor. You know what they'll have you do? Scrape and paint the cell bars. For a few seconds satisfaction that you killed the one man who tried to save your life, followed by these other innocent men . . . you'd have the pain of knowing the loss, the hurt that their parents . . . their wives . . . their children would carry with them the rest of their lives. Is that what you want?"

"Hell no! If I did, I would have shot them long ago. I want that Lieutenant! I want to watch him squirm, and then I want the pleasure of seeing him die. I want to see him crap his pants just like Mr. Scoggins over there. Yeah, I could live to be a hundred just remembering over and over the look on his face when I pull the trigger—What's all that noise?"

"They're probably setting up a command post and bringing in more people. They mean business. Please! Hand me the gun and let's go outside together."

"Bullshit! You set me up! You tricked me! There was nobody out there before. Why should I listen to you?"

◈

After Joe Xylos disappeared through the door, Frenchy stayed in the shadows, feeling very much a coward. Time and again, he stared at the closed door and asked himself how he could ever allow his friend to go into that room with that full-blown psycho who was liable to do anything.

Soon after Joe entered the building, the first help to arrive was two vans filled with Shore Patrol. All of them had nightsticks; none were armed with guns. They huddled in tight knots behind their vehicles.

Next to arrive was Commander Munday, the White Beach XO. As was customary with him, he was dressed in a dull plaid sports jacket and bow tie, looking more like a college professor than a naval officer. He smoothed his silver sideburns and pushed a cigarette into the corner of his mouth.

After lighting it, he said, "Lieutenant, the Gunner's Mate is on his way over with small arms. I've talked to both the Marines and the Army. The Marine Colonel is sending his special response team. Three of them are sharpshooters. The Army will be here later with an MP detachment. I'd like to have this wrapped up before it becomes a full-blown joint operation. The first priority is to establish communications with the seaman. Is there a way we can patch a phone into the office? Maybe we can talk him out."

"I'll find out. I tried to call after he hung up, but I got no answer."

"I tried calling just after you reported to me. I had the same luck. By the way, besides Bill Scoggins, who else is in there?

"I don't know who the four enlisted men are. There is one other officer in there now, Ensign Joe Xylos."

"Ensign who?"

"Ensign Joe Xylos of the *Beaverton*. He was visiting at my quarters when Brown called."

"How in the name of heaven did he get in there?"

"He walked in. He volunteered. He thinks he can talk Brown into surrendering."

"How could you let him go in there? Giving that man more hostages is not the way to solve this problem."

"He insisted."

"Damn! I thought Lieutenants told Ensigns what to do! Well, he's in there, and there is nothing we can do to change it. I thought you had more smarts than to let some Ensign get his head blown off."

Munday stomped his feet to stay warm. He smoked one cigarette after another, lighting the next off the last butt. A light misting rain wafted drops that created abstract patterns in the cones of the lights illuminating the night. Visibility steadily dropped until the far corners of the building were indistinct shadows.

Beyond the shore, the ethereal sounds of the many boats ferrying liberty parties home grew louder, then faded, with the shifting intensity of the wind and the rainfall.

Half an hour passed before the Gunnery Mate arrived with foul-weather parkas, an urn of hot coffee, weapons, and ammunition. Commander Munday ordered, "Prior to issuance of guns and ammunition, instruct those armed that no one will load their weapon unless Brown starts shooting. There is a greater risk of killing each other than killing Brown. I don't want this to get out of control."

"Aye, aye, sir," said Frenchy. He was shivering, even with a parka on. *Damn Xylos, why wouldn't he obey me? Now I'm to blame because he went in. What was I supposed do, anyway? Shoot him? In the end, I'll be the one to go into that building and bring Brown out.*

Once Commander Bob Munday was satisfied, he tested a loud hailer and stepped onto the walk leading to the front door of the building. His blows into the mouthpiece came out of the speakers as bursts of static that echoed around the building.

Satisfied with the adjusted volume, he raised the horn, pressed the switch, and said, "Seaman Brown, the building is surrounded. We have a fully armed party deployed. Come out of the building with your hands up. We don't mean you any harm."

There was no reply.

"Brown, what do you say?"

After what seemed an eternity, a breaking voice squeaked with fear, "He says he'll let us all go in exchange for Lieutenant Villerouge. He says that otherwise he's going to kill all of us."

"That's Scoggins," said Frenchy.

Commander Munday repeated his demands, but there were no more replies from the building.

Outside help soon arrived in the form of a Jeep loaded with four Marines in full combat gear. Three had sniper rifles, and the officer carried a .45-caliber machine pistol with two bandoliers of ammunition crossed over his chest.

⋅⊷▄◉ ◉▄⊶⋅

Seaman Tom Brown tensed with the arrival of every vehicle. With the storm shutters closed, he felt safe from observation or being shot, but it left him blind.

Each of the messages by loud hailer brought from him a stream of profanity coupled with the universal middle finger salute directed toward Joe, who remained on the corner of the desk, coffee cup in hand. After the crowd of SPs and Marines surrounded the building and the barrage of messages, warnings, and threats intensified, they ended mysteriously.

Lieutenant Scoggins, who had talked for Brown earlier, peeked out through a cracked door to report that, other than two shadowy occupants of a lone Navy truck parked in front, no one was in sight. Brown again peeked out the shuttered windows. He laughed and then sat down in the chair behind the desk he had commandeered.

Joe shifted to a chair behind the desk, took off his left shoe and sock, and rested his swollen ankle on the desk. Brown had given up on making him stand with the others. Feeling relaxed, he ordered the other hostages to sit facing the wall. Soon one of the young seamen, a duty driver, was sprawled on his side and snoring loudly.

When the room was quiet, the deranged seaman's head bobbed like a bee settling in for a landing on a blossom. For an instant, only the whites of his eyes showed. Just as the muzzle of his gun began plowing papers across the desktop, his head snapped upward. He half-yawned as his eyes darted from hostage to hostage and then settled on Joe. This cycle repeated again and again as he fought sleep.

Joe asked, "Tom, have you ever tried to make a teacher think you were really awake when you were actually more intent on sleeping in class?"

"I hated school."

"I did too. And looking back on it, I don't think I fooled anyone but myself. Watching you reminded me of the times I used to struggle to stay awake. I worked every night until two a.m. Early morning classes were pure torture."

"Worked? What did you do?"

"I was the emcee at some night spots . . . strip joints, actually."

"Strip joints! An officer? Come on, they wouldn't let you do that."

"I wasn't in the Navy then, and I needed a job."

"You must have gotten a whole bunch of poontang, huh?"

"I had plenty of opportunity to meet the girls, but it wasn't like that. Maybe over here it would be that way. Frankly, I used to sweat falling asleep at the wheel on the way home. Tom, what are you going to do about sleep?"

"I can outlast you."

"Maybe you can outlast each of us. The proper question is, can you outlast *all* of us? Remember, those other guys can catch their Zs while you struggle to prop your eyes open. How about the people outside? I think the reason they left is that they've gone home for a good night's sleep while we have to stay awake. They have so many people that they're standing watches. After four hours on, they'll be sleeping. How long—"

"I'm going to give that coward Villerouge until morning and then I'll put you in the doorway and drill you! Then one by one until the last of you are laying out there. It really doesn't matter if they kill me because I'm dying anyway."

"What did Mr. Villerouge do to make you want to kill him?"

"When I asked to be switched to office work, he said I should be 'surveyed.' That means 'discharged for unfitness,' doesn't it? He assigned a man to watch me to make sure I worked all the time. All the time I had to breathe first the dust and then the fumes. The lead is killing me. It's all his fault!"

"You jumped ship when they tried to survey you, didn't you? It sounds like you want to stay in the Navy. Am I right?"

"I don't want to talk about it." The young man's jowls were trembling. He sniffled loudly.

"Tom, did you join the Navy to avoid some trouble with the law?"

Brown looked first at the ceiling and then the floor before beginning, "Well . . . kind of. My friend and I kind of borrowed a car. My Dad is a cop . . . a detective. And when we were arrested, I figured he'd fix it for me. Only they really came down hard on me . . . said that because my Dad was an officer, I should know better. In the end, my Dad talked to the prosecutor and the judge. He talked to the man at the dealership. The dealer agreed to drop the charges if my Dad bought the car and I joined the Navy. I promised my Dad that I wouldn't get in any more trouble. And I meant it. On that oiler, they picked on me . . . gave me every shitty job, starting out with being mess cook. If the Master at Arms called for a one-man working party, I was it. They picked on me all the time. I knew that if I got a fair chance, I'd make good, but that Villerouge had it in for me from the start."

"Tom, it sounds to me that you'd go an extra mile to please your father. Am I right?"

Joe watched Brown's eyes flit about until they met Joe's for an instant. His eyelids fluttered, and tears welled up in the corner of his eyes before he looked down.

Joe continued, "I felt that way about my Dad. I loved him. Do you feel that way too?"

"Oh, I don't know about that. He's the one who got me stuck in the Navy for four years."

"Think how much it took out of him, a cop, to ask . . . no, *beg* them to not throw you in jail. Humbling himself for you . . . Isn't that love?"

"I never thought of it that way."

"Tom, how do you think your father will feel when they tell him you were wounded and then arrested while you were murdering six unarmed men?"

"I'll be dead anyway."

"If you're dead, he'll carry a hurt with him the rest of his life. It will especially bad if it was because you were a murderer. Tom, what you've done so far can't be undone, but I'm sure your Dad won't desert you if you do what a man does . . . admit you made a mistake and take your due like a man. If you are dying of lead poisoning, wouldn't you rather have your mother and father at your side than die alone out here? Tom, this is your time to stand tall."

Seaman Brown still held the forty-five in his right hand as he rubbed his tear-filled eyes with his hands. His lips twisted like those on a Greek tragedy mask. Slowly, ever so slowly, his arms relaxed until the weapon was lying on the desk, barely in his grasp.

Joe said, "Tom, you're doing the right thing by putting the gun down. You're making a man's tough decision."

Brown tentatively released the pistol grip and slowly stepped back about half a step.

"Tom, you're doing the right thing. Putting the gun down took guts. I'm going to come over and pick it up."

Joe was at most two steps from Brown when the front door slammed open. Frenchy stood in a crouch with his gun pointed at Brown as he shouted, "Freeze! Don't make a move or I'll shoot!"

Instinctively the Ensign stood immobile facing Brown, who scooped the gun up from the table.

Click! went Frenchy's gun as he pulled the trigger. From that instant, events unfolded in slow motion for Joe.

"Damn!" said Frenchy as he realized there was no round in the chamber. He was pulling the receiver back when the seaman's bullet caught him in the forehead. The impact threw his head back and tipped him backward into a sitting position. There he remained for silent seconds until his momentum carried him all the way back, to lie face up in the entryway.

CHAPTER 22

Brown Pulls the Trigger

Joe regained his senses as Brown's gun recoiled and the seaman's wild eyes focused on him. He threw the better part of the cup of coffee in his hand at the gunman. The fluid hit the seaman's face, making a wet slapping sound, just before Brown pulled the trigger again.

Joe had no idea where the bullet went, except that it missed him. The shot passed well above Joe's head and burrowed into the wall high up. As the gun recoiled, Joe dove between Brown's arms, throwing him off balance. Toppling onto his back, Brown pulled the trigger with the muzzle just above his eye level. The slug slammed into the acoustic tile above them, breaking loose a cloud of dust particles from the many holes in the board.

Brown, who was blinded temporarily by the flash, loosened his grip on the gun. He put his hand to his eyes long enough for Joe, who was on top of him, to drive a shoulder into his elbow. When Brown fired this time, he lost control of the weapon. The pistol hit the lower front of the desk and fell next to it. The big seaman reached out for it, but his fingertips only touched the weapon just enough to push it away. It hit the far side of the desk and clattered to the floor as the dust particles snowed around them.

The small Ensign threw his body fully against Brown and they fell in a heap between the chair and the wall. Thanks to his greater size, the seaman easily began to lift Joe, who shouted, "Brown, lay still! Stay under me or they'll shoot you! Stop struggling!"

As the bigger man rolled on top of Joe, the Marine First Lieutenant raced in and laid the butt of his weapon hard alongside Brown's head. The crazed man went limp, and the Marine boomed, "Damn, Ensign, you got enough fight in you to be a Marine. You done good!"

Joe was lifted to his feet by his fellow hostages amid cheers and shouts. Hands slapped him on the back and others tried to shake his hand, but he paid no attention as he ran to the door where Frenchy lay sprawled. A fan of blood and brains spattered the pavement behind his fallen friend.

As he looked down, Lieutenant Scoggins slapped him on the back. "Joe, you did exactly what I was planning to do. I didn't think he was ready when you came in. You've got more guts than sense. Well done! Well done!"

Scoggins handed Joe his shoe and sock. Joe turned pale and began to tremble as he looked down. He could feel his blood settling as the adrenaline subsided, and the onset of the worst hangover of his life. He cried, "Dear God! He's dead! Why? Why? Frenchy, why didn't you wait just another half a minute to come through that door? Frenchy is dead! How am I going to tell Eva?"

Sinking to his knees, he knelt and touched the rapidly cooling body. Behind him, the killer regained enough of his senses to begin fighting with his captors. The others rushed to be part of the action. Amid screams and curses, a Medical Corpsman, who had been in the truck, paused to check Frenchy for a pulse before stepping around Joe and into the confusion.

Alone with the body for a moment, Joe saw Frenchy's red plastic key fob hanging out of his jacket pocket. He took it and limped out the front walk, past the now-deserted vehicle that had been the command post.

As he passed it, the radio blared, "White Beach Four! This is White Beach One! White Beach Four! Come in, White Beach Four! Report status! I want to know what the hell is going on! Over."

Joe reached for the microphone lying on the seat, then thought better of it. He leaned against the truck and rubbed his aching leg before stumbling through the swirling mists to his friend's car. Once inside, he sat behind the wheel and buried his head in his hands. He felt the physical pain from his struggle and the fatigue of his ordeal, but these were minor compared to the hurt of his friend's death.

When Joe raised his head, the area in front of the building was filling with emergency vehicles whose rotating lights cast abstract red and white patterns on the descending clouds of mist. There was a knot of people around where the dead Lieutenant lay.

Emerging from the crowd, Brown struggled like a freshly landed shark as they dragged him outside. Joe watched them roughly shove him into the back of a paddy wagon. Joe managed to get the car started before the back doors of the wagon were shut. He turned the car around and headed in the general direction of the Villerouges' quarters.

A block away from the building, there was a sentry standing in the road. Joe stopped the car with the paddy wagon right behind him. The man asked, "What happened? I heard shots. Is everybody okay?"

"No. Frenchy . . . er . . . Mr. Villerouge is dead and Brown has been captured. Everybody else is okay. I'm taking his car back to his quarters, but I've only been there once. Can you tell me how to get there?"

Joe appreciated the directions because they got him directly to the only Quonset hut whose outside light was on. He decided he would wait for someone else to break the news to Eva. That hope was dashed when she opened the door and stood there looking at him. Slowly he gained his feet and limped to the front door.

Eva was wearing a light blue robe. The room lights outlined her beautiful figure. The lace of her nightgown showed around the collar. Joe watched as the corners of her mouth, which had turned up in a bright smile, turned down and fear filled her eyes. She stepped back from the door. "Joe, where is Frenchy? What are you doing here?"

"I . . . I . . . I brought his car home. May I come in for a moment?"

"You? You look terrible! Have you been in a fight?"

"Yes. It was the fight of my life. Brown was captured. Please sit down."

She stood just inside the door with her fists clenched. "Why should I sit down? What happened to my husband?"

"If you don't want to sit down, I have to. I feel sick." He dropped into the first chair and looked up at her with tears streaming down his cheeks. "Brown shot him. Frenchy is dead."

She shut the door hard and stood with her back against it. "I knew it! I knew it! They had to protect their precious secrets! They sent him here so it would be out of the way. That means I'm next!"

"No, Eva! It didn't happen that way! Nobody set Frenchy up. He didn't put a round in the chamber, and Brown shot him while he was loading the gun."

"Joe, you don't know about me . . . about who I was and what I did. I'm not the girl you think I am."

"I don't understand. What does this have to do with Frenchy?"

"I was in the AVH in Hungary."

"AVH?"

"Allamvedelmi Hatosag. State Security, the secret police, like the Russian KGB."

"What's this got to do with what happened tonight? Wait, you think somebody had him killed because the two of you got married?"

"He knew many secrets. He never told me any of them . . . but he knew. They had to solve the problem one way or the other. I would have done no less."

"Eva! We are not that kind of people!"

"Oh, no? I could tell you a few things about your CIA . . ."

"Please wait. Don't jump to any conclusions. I was there. I was two, maybe three steps from the desk where Brown had just laid the gun down when Frenchy burst through the door with his forty-five drawn. The guy went for the gun. Frenchy tried to shoot, then realized he hadn't put a round in the chamber. He was pulling the receiver back as he was shot. Why he chose that moment to come in, I'll never know. I had just convinced Brown to surrender. It was a terribly tragic accident. The kid is no trained killer. He's a scared kid, a misfit. If Frenchy had just let me wrap it up . . . I'm sorry!"

She walked across the room to the far wall, turned, then retraced her steps to the door. She moved with the grace of a cat stalking prey. Her eyes darted to explore the shadows. The nylon robe whispered with each step.

She shook her head, throwing the long blonde curls back, before taking a deep breath. "Joe, I'm scared. I can't go home. I can't stay here. I'm going to have a baby. What will happen to me?"

Joe rose from the seat. He limped over to her and took her in his arms. "Eva, you are perfectly safe. No one is going to harm you. The Navy takes care of its own."

"I knew I should have gotten more birth control pills after I left the

Olympic Village, but we were married. He wanted children. Joe, I loved him!"

"That you did. You still do. No one can ever take that away from you. Eva, he was my friend too. I'll take care of you."

She pushed herself away to arm's length and smiled ever so slightly, the corners of her mouth barely turning upward. She looked him up and down and finally looked him in the eye for a long moment before going limp in his arms.

He guided her to the couch. She leaned against him for a time, then began talking in a low little girl's voice. "Everyone I've ever loved has been killed. First my parents . . . and now my husband. It's always because of me. I did it to others. I helped the Russians conquer my country. After what happened last fall, I am so ashamed . . ."

She remained silent for some time before clearing her throat and continuing, "Frank was such a good man. He was gentle and very considerate. The longer we were married, the more I knew about him, the luckier I felt. I kept pinching myself just to be sure it wasn't a dream. My darling, my lover . . . I'll never have another."

Joe said, "I wish a pinch would end this nightmare for both of us, Eva. It will take time to heal, but you'll put it behind you. You'll be okay. You're doing far better now than I am. Look, I'm the one who's crying. Damn! I feel so helpless knowing I'll be sailing on the *Beaverton* the day after tomorrow."

"How do you know he's dead?"

"It wasn't a pretty sight. He was shot in the head."

"Joe, I want to see him. Where have they taken him?"

"I don't know."

"Please come with me. Help me find him."

Joe's agreed to help, and she left the room, returning shortly wearing slacks that highlighted her trim figure. Her hair was pulled back into a ponytail whose curling ends hung down her back. At first glance, she looked younger. However, the set of her jaw, her muscular neck, and the cold and determined look in her eye gave her almost a masculine air.

While she was putting on her coat, headlights flashed across the windows. They opened the door to face a short, dark, wiry officer whose golden oak leaves on the epaulets of his bridge coat were barely discernible in the shadows. He extended a hand. "Mrs. Villerouge, may I talk with you privately inside? I'm Chaplain Colson."

Her shoulders slumped. "Did you come to tell me about my husband's murder?"

"Yes. How did you find out?"

She pointed at Joe. "He came here right away and broke the news. I want to see my husband."

"Why, yes, that can be arranged. But it's awfully late now. You ought to get some rest. Tomorrow will be soon enough."

"No! Tomorrow will be too late. I demand to see him now!"

"Well, I'm not sure they are done at the crime scene. Who are you, mister?"

She pushed the Chaplain aside. "We must hurry. Come on, Joe."

"Joe? Ensign Joe Xylos? Are you the one who was in there when it happened?"

"Yes, it's important to her."

"They're looking all over for you. Who said you could leave? You had no authority coming out here and getting Mrs. Villerouge upset."

She snapped, "Upset? You're the one who's trying to stall me. I trust him far more than you. Joe, are you coming, or must I go alone?"

Joe stepped up behind her and placed a hand in the center of her back. "It's okay. For as long as I can, I'll do my best to cover you."

⊹⊱◈⊰⊹

They arrived at the Duty Office, with the Chaplain following, to find the outside deserted. The pickup that had been the command post was still there, unmoved. There was a lone Navy sedan on whose black surface moisture beaded, turning it to a wet silver in the lamplight. On the threshold, someone had chalked the outline of Frenchy's body. The fan pattern of bone, flesh, and blood remained untouched. They stepped around the marking, and Joe pushed the door open.

As the door swung open, a stern voice called, "This area is secured. Stay clear."

Joe peered into a room that looked on the surface like nothing had happened. All the faces inside were new.

Commander Bob Munday rose from behind the desk Brown had occupied and rushed toward them. "Eva! I'm so terribly sorry about

Frank. If we hadn't had the problems at the fleet landing, he wouldn't have had to expose himself. We were just spread too thin. My heart goes out to you. What can I do?"

"I want to see my husband."

"They took him to the morgue over at the air base. It's not a pleasant sight for a woman. Are you sure you want to?"

"I've seen more dead men than I care to remember. Why don't you want me to see him? Do you have something to hide?"

"No. It's not that. We're concerned about the shock . . . about you."

Joe said, "Eva and I talked about this, sir. She needs to know. It's important to her."

"Who are you?"

"Ensign Xylos."

"Why the devil did you disappear?"

"I didn't disappear. I'm here! I went to Eva . . . to tell her . . . to comfort her."

Munday's eyebrows arched as his eyes went from one to the other. "What's going on? How do you know her?"

Eva narrowed her lips. "What are you trying to insinuate? Bob, Joe was with Frank when we met. They lived in the same room on the ship. Joe helped me defect and was best man at our wedding."

Munday waved his hand in an arc. "Eva, forgive me. It's been a long, terrible day . . . riots . . . murder. I'm sure you can see his remains. Mr. Xylos, I can't comprehend why you stepped into harm's way as you did. In spite of the outcome, I agree with Mr. Scoggins. You ought to get a medal. To a man, they say he was handing you the weapon when it happened."

"Yes, sir. If Frenchy had waited maybe ten seconds, I would have had the gun in my hand. I don't deserve a medal."

Joe retold the story of the shooting. Eva walked from place to place, visually surveying the room. She stood behind the desk where Brown had been. She held her hands together as if pointing a pistol. She studied the bullet holes in the wall and ceiling.

When Joe was finished, Munday said, "You're going to get tired of telling that story, Ensign. The Office of Naval Intelligence will want to talk to you tomorrow. I don't know if you'll have much luck getting a boat back to your ship tonight; the SOPA has shut down all boating until dawn. We have an extra bunk here."

Eva asked, "What is a zopa?"

Joe said, "The man in charge of it all, the senior officer present afloat, S.O.P.A. I'm too wound up to sleep. I'd like to help Eva. Thank you, sir."

About half an hour later, Joe, Eva, and Chaplain Colson were standing beside the white-draped figure of her husband.

"I'm warning you, it's no pretty sight," the medic said before he pulled the sheet back.

Eva gasped, then bent over and examined the wound. The medic's hand pushed hers away when she attempted to lift Frenchy's head. He said, "Please don't! The bullet exited the back of the head, severing the cortex. My guess is that he was dead when he hit the ground; it was that quick. They'll perform an autopsy this morning to determine the exact cause."

The medic started to pull the sheet back over Frenchy's face. The widow checked his movement. She stared at the body and after a long moment sighed, "He was the handsomest man I ever met." She again bent over and kissed his lips. "Goodbye, my darling. *Szeretlek.* Already I miss you. I feel so . . . so cheated!"

When she stood up, for the first time a single tear overflowed her right eye. As she swept it away with her finger, her whole frame trembled. She leaned on Joe for support as they walked toward the door.

Chaplain Colson said, "Mrs. Villerouge, I think you'd feel better if you took a sedative and went home to rest. While we're here, you could—"

"Chaplain, I am pregnant! I take no drugs until the baby is born!"

"I've never heard of such a thing."

"In the Soviet Union, I saw the babies born to women who were drugged in the hospitals. No arms . . . mindless . . . deformed. I take no chances!"

"Certain precautions are necessary, but I've never heard of this sort of thing. I'm just a Chaplain and not a doctor. Mrs. Villerouge, in light of the hour and the trauma you've suffered, might I suggest that I call on you tomorrow afternoon? I'd like to help you through this as quickly as possible. Ensign, I could take you back to the Duty Office or drop you off at the fleet landing."

"Thank you, sir, but I have Frenchy's car and I need to return it. I can take Eva home too."

Eva said, "I would prefer to do that. I need someone to talk to before I go home."

Once Joe and Eva were on the road with only the glow of the dashboard lights lighting their faces, he remarked, "This is a nice car. A fifty-six Chevy?"

"No, it's a fifty-five. It arrived maybe two weeks ago. And now I've got to figure out what to do with it and where to go."

"Is it paid for?"

"I don't know. Frank was going to explain all this to me, but there were too many other things going on. Joe, I need help, your help, to sort all of this out. I trust you. You will help me, won't you?"

"As much as I can. Eva, you said something tonight that has stuck with me . . . about not being the person I thought you were. I indulged in a bit of reverie and thought about the day we met. I thought you were one of the athletes."

"Yes, I have thought about that day too. It was your words and your pass that put me in the place that I could not say no. To you, I owe thanks for the only moments of true happiness I've had in my life."

"You said something about secret police. Did Frenchy know?"

"I tried to tell him the night before we married. He didn't want to know. I think he suspected. He asked me if I wanted a fresh start in a free country. I said yes. To stay married, I would have to be his full-time wife and mother of his children . . . no cloak-and-dagger business . . . those were his words. His belief in America was so strong. He was on the side of right. The Soviets are evil. He was my knight in shining armor. I told him I never wanted to live in darkness again."

"Live in darkness . . . How did it all start?"

"In 1952, I tried out for the Olympic gymnastics team. Strictly by terms of the competition, I shouldn't have been allowed to go, but the girl who bested me was arrested for something. Later I found that my uncle arranged it all. The price for my competing was to join the AVH as an informer. I was to find out if anyone was planning to defect. I . . .

I served them well. Four were kept from escaping because of me and were put in Soviet custody in Leningrad on the way home. After the games, I was chosen for special training in the Soviet Union, near Kiev. I spent the next two years perfecting my English well enough to pass as an American. I probably know more trivia about the United States than you do; and if I work hard at it, I can just about completely lose my accent. They taught me everything from assassination to sexual seduction. After my graduation, I went home for two or three months. They encouraged me to marry, but I didn't want to. I was assigned to work with the Russians in Berlin."

Joe parked the car close to the edge of the parking lot above the fleet landing. The headlights illuminated the float below them until he turned them off. A single landing craft with its high bow ramp door was tied up there, and a lone sailor peered out of the control station aft of the open hold. The edge of the world could have been in the swirling mist beyond the shore. Huddled around the guard shack at the top of the gangway leading to the float was a bedraggled group of sailors.

Joe asked, "Then Commander Cannon was right when he thought he knew you?"

"Yes, seeing him scared me. I had been posted to West Berlin, posing as a footloose American girl of Hungarian descent. It was two years ago, and we were directed to work our way into some sort of sensitive job. I was teaching at a private elementary school for American and English children. We flocked around the American officers in hopes of compromising some of them. My partner and I met him at a party. I went with his friend. Both of them were married and were loud-mouthed drunks . . ."

Eva looked out the window for a long minute before saying, almost as if talking to herself, "He was drunk. Even in death, I could still smell the alcohol."

"Who? What?"

"Frank drank too much. He was drunk. That's what it was. I should never have let him leave the house."

"We had to go. Don't blame yourself. We all have `ifs' to live down. *If* I could have grabbed the gun off the table . . . but I froze just long enough for Brown to pick it up. *If* I could have hit Brown's arm when

Frenchy's gun didn't fire . . . I want to make it up to you. How did you get from Berlin to Melbourne?"

"Long story. They pulled me out—didn't say why—and assigned me as a beacon in Bremerhaven."

"Beacon? What's that."

Eva looked away. After a long pause, she explained, "A beacon acts as a control gate for other agents. They were mostly German prostitutes. In early September, they spirited me across the border into East Germany in the back of a truck. I was enjoying my first vacation when the uprising began."

"Join the AVH and see the world?"

"Yes, but not as I would have liked. As summarily as I was sent to Bremerhaven, I was ordered back to Hungary. I entered Budapest just after the Russian tanks. I was in the first cadre of AVH personnel to go into their headquarters. Suddenly I was made to change roles from collecting information to state security. The Russian bastards! What they did sickened me."

Joe held up his hand. "Should I be hearing this? Have you told the intelligence people here?"

"Yes, I told them everything. If you are around me in the future, you will hear terrible things about me. Let me admit now, I did what I was told because I feared them. It eats at my soul to this day. I was looking for ways to escape when I asked about security for the Hungarian team in Melbourne."

"And Frenchy never knew this, did he?"

"As we agreed, I never told him, but he may have heard some of it anyway. He knew more than I wanted him to, thanks to the NSA interrogators. They made it very clear in Hawaii that I had compromised a very valuable man. They even told him how I betrayed my own mother."

"Betrayed your mother?" exclaimed Joe, feigning surprise as if he hadn't already heard this from Frenchy.

She looked out the window for a long time, then swallowed before continuing in a tear-choked voice, "It was his reaction that made me realize how truly big a man he was. They had picked us up at Hickam and drove us to their office. I waited hours while they interrogated him, and just about made up my mind that we should part because it would best for him. Afterward he came into the room and walked toward me. In Russian, he said, `They told me about your mother. How old were you when they made you soil the memory of her?' I told him seven or eight. He closed me in his arms and, still speaking Russian, said, `Like Pavlik Morozov, they committed the crime and then exalted you in public, but left you to carry the enormous guilt for their cruelty.'"

"Who was Pavlik Morozov?"

"I had to ask Frenchy. He was a Russian boy under Stalin whose denunciation of his father led to his father's execution. Frank didn't judge me. He knew their system. He accepted me just as I was. He asked me if I wanted to stay with him, and I said yes. Then he told them that he meant to stay married to me and that he wouldn't accept orders where I couldn't be with him."

She looked at Joe through tear-filled eyes. "It was the end of his career. He never asked me any more about my previous life, and I never told him. I am ashamed of the life I led. This is the payment I get for the terrible things I have done. He paid for my errors."

"Eva, I can understand how you feel like you do. What happened to Frenchy was at best an accident and at worst, poor judgment. It had nothing to do with you. Speaking of poor judgment, how could they have let you go out with us in Melbourne?"

"Poor judgment? Oh, no! They had every reason to trust me. My mother was just the first; spying has been a way of life for me. I was probably the only one there trained to do the job they wanted. Remember when Piotr the interpreter apologized that he couldn't escort you after all, and I volunteered? That was actually the plan from the start. Just before you arrived in the cafeteria, my commander—who was really a Russian, not a Pole--told me to turn on the charm and find out all I could about Frank. They're very interested in people who speak fluent Russian."

Joe said, "I made a commitment to my friend Frenchy, so it matters little to me what they trained you to do in Melbourne or wherever."

Eva shook her head. "You are a silly boy on his way to serious trouble. I don't know why I let you play out your scheme in Melbourne as I did when I accepted your pass. It was extremely foolhardy. Maybe I was thinking that if I were caught, I could say I was trying to put myself in a better position to compromise him. Our timing at the gate was pure luck. Or maybe they just let me through. I'll never know."

"I guess not."

"And Frenchy . . . what a man! I couldn't keep my hands off him. By the next morning, I never wanted to leave his bed. I had never met a man so handsome. He could make love in three languages. He proposed and I accepted. The rest you know."

"That's quite a story!"

"Yes. Joe Xylos, you know things about me now that Frank, my husband, never did. You have a way about you. I feel very comfortable with you."

"Thank you, dear Eva. I'm sure that had there been time, both of you would have opened your hearts more. I feel honored that you shared this. Your secrets are safe with me. Frenchy and I talked about the communists quite a bit. He really knew his stuff."

She nodded. "Yes, he knew more about Lenin and the party than most of the political officers I knew. I was afraid to talk about it too much for fear I'd say too much. Now it's too late."

"Eva, I hate to leave you feeling like this. I don't know if I'll be coming ashore again before we sail. I've got to find a boat to take me out to the *Beaverton* before they hold quarters. Even if I get there in time, I've got to arrange for someone to take my duty so I can give that statement. I suppose I'll lose a day's liberty in Hong Kong too. Please keep in touch. I want to help."

Joe opened the glovebox and dug around until he found a piece of wrinkled paper. In the darkness he scribbled for a moment and handed it to her. "My address. Please let me know where you'll be. I'll write. I promise."

She took the paper in her hand and studied it in the growing light of dawn before pushing it into her purse. "I don't know where I'll go. I'm lonely for home. If I were to return to Hungary, I'd face prison or worse. There have been arrests in Germany because of me. Even in America, I'm not sure I'll be safe. If they could kill Trotsky, what trouble would they have with me? Joe, I have no place to run. I'm scared!"

"Eva, why not go to where Frenchy's folks live? At least until your baby is born."

" Why would they want to have me around? If not for me, they would still have a son."

"He was their only child, as I recall. Your baby will be all they have left . . . their only grandchild. Give them an opportunity to know you. My guess is that they will welcome you with open arms. Sure, you'll do okay. Now I've got to find out when they're going to start running boats. I can see the colors of dawn out there."

CHAPTER 23

Joe Is Injured

Joe gave the Chevy's door a hard push and took a step out. Perhaps the ground was uneven, or some loose wash gravel acted like ball bearings beneath his smooth leather sole. As the door slammed shut, he had a lightning jolt of pain from the ankle he had injured on the float. He let out a startled cry and hit the blacktop like a case of eggs dropped off a forklift. He lay still for a moment, then rolled onto his side. He held the throbbing ankle as he slowly worked his way to his feet while brushing dirt and mud from his coat.

He was tentatively testing the injured ankle when Eva got to his side. She pulled his arm over her shoulder and put her hand around his waist. He sensed the softness of her breast in his side as well as the strength in her arm.

As the slight officer made a half-hearted attempt to pull free, she said, "Joe, I've leaned on you tonight. Now it's your turn to lean on me. Let me get you to a doctor."

"Thanks, Eva. I'll be okay. It's just a bad sprain. There's no time. I have to get back to my ship. We have a quack on board, and they'll take good care of me there."

Some twenty minutes later, Joe negotiated a ride aboard a landing craft, an LCM from the USS *Skagit*, which would get him to the *Beaverton* en route to its own anchorage. After being helped aboard, he sat on the LCM's deck with his feet hanging over the side into the well deck as the boat pulled clear of the dock. He watched Eva standing by her car in the purple-turning-to-orange light of dawn until she was swallowed up in the mist.

Once they were clear of the shore, there was a fresh wind blowing.

It forced the fog to retreat into fingers between patches of water that formed a brocade of abstract patterns reflected off the brightly hued mists. The light salt spray was cold and refreshing. For a time the *Beaverton* was plainly visible ahead; then it faded as the fog shifted.

Joe was dozing when he heard, "Sir, we're approaching the *Beaverton.*"

Painfully he pulled himself to his feet as the LCM came alongside the forward port accommodation ladder leading to the quarterdeck. The landing itself was smooth and, with help, Joe pushed off with his sore left leg. Just then, a wave lifted the boat and he landed poorly on his good leg. He saved himself from falling by grabbing the handrails and kept gripping them as, slowly and gingerly, he put his right foot on the first step to begin his ascent.

The coxswain began backing the LCM under the accommodation ladder. Hearing shouts from above and sensing danger, Joe stopped on perhaps the third or fourth step up as the craft kept coming back, bringing its high bow ramp ever so close to the metal frame of the ladder. At what seemed the last second, the rounded corner of the ramp appeared to clear the ladder.

Then a wave slapped the side of the LCM, causing the ramp to strike the ladder a solid blow. The impact threw Joe hard against the inner handrail. The outer frame was instantly bent in, causing the bottom dozen wooden steps to pop out of their sockets and fall into the water below.

Somehow the unlucky Ensign managed to hold onto the inner handrail as his feet swung wildly in the air. He barked his shins on the inner support and finally slid clumsily down the rail to the sea-splashed lower platform. There he sat, the cold seawater on the metal platform quickly soaking through his coat and trousers. He looked out to see the large bow ramp, with the large letters "SK" painted on it, disappearing into the mist. Above him, he could hear all manner of confusion and profanity. As for himself, his whole left leg was a throbbing sea of pain that radiated from his ankle.

The OOD, Lieutenant Tumwater, gingerly tested the upper platform and, finding it safe, shouted, "Mr. Xylos, are you all right?"

"No! My left ankle hurts like hell! I need help."

"We'll get you up as quickly as possible."

Joe looked up to see the ship's rail lined with faces looking down at him. A moment later, a light line with a large loop tied into the end was lowered.

He heard the familiar voice of Boatswain Tallfeathers bellow, "You people stop standing around, get over here and stand by. Lieutenant, I suggest you step back onto deck. If that platform collapses, you'll be the man overboard, sir."

With the loop under his shoulders, Joe was hoisted up and pulled onto the main deck. The Corpsman, who had been summoned by the ship's general announcing system, took one look at the ankle. It was now swollen that the distended flesh overhung the shoe top. He ordered Joe placed on a stretcher.

By the time the ship's doctor, Rufus Johnson, had read the X-rays and determined that Joe's injury was a torn Achilles tendon, the exhausted and sedated Ensign was fast asleep on the examining table.

While the Corpsman was applying a walking cast, Rufus took a call from XO Longstreet. "I want to see Mr. Xylos in my office as soon as possible. There's some things I have to ask him."

Rufus replied, "Unless it's critical, I don't want to awaken him. The man was totally exhausted and showed signs of shock. He was out before I finished examining the ankle. It looks like a bad sprain compounded by a partial tear of the Achilles tendon. I prefer to give him a few hours rest before he's moved."

"Just as long as he doesn't vanish again, it can wait."

"You don't have to worry about that. He can't even walk without crutches."

"Good, I've got to get ready for Captain's mast anyway."

Just short of noon, Joe was shaken awake to find his roommate, Lawyer Sawyer, standing over him, wiping the lens of his thick glasses with a tissue.

Sawyer tossed the tissue toward a trash can as he exclaimed, "Joe, Joe! What in the name of blazes have you been up to?"

"What? Oh, it's you, Carter. Where am I, anyway?"

"You're in sick bay. When the XO personally comes to Boys' Town to conduct a bed check, something big has happened. What did you get into, anyway?"

"I don't feel up to talking about it now."

"Am I going to be on the opposite side of the table from you, old buddy? They've been in and out of our room a half-dozen times between midnight and reveille. What's up?"

"Carter, Frenchy's dead. He was shot by . . . by a crazy seaman. I was there. If I hadn't frozen, I would have had the gun. It wouldn't have happened. I was just too slow. They must want a statement. Oh, my leg! I feel like I was run over by a truck! Could you ask them if I could wait until later? I feel rotten." Joe sagged back onto the mattress.

Behind them, the door swung open hard and bounced off the rubber stop on the bulkhead. The XO bellowed, "Boy! What in the name of heaven have you pulled this time? ONI wants to talk to you . . . bad. They've been on the radio since the middle of last night. I don't like my sleep being interrupted to make me produce my black sheep Ensign for an interview with ONI. They're saying you eluded them."

Raising his plaster-covered foot, Joe asked, "What? Who was chasing me, Sam Snail?"

"Damn, boy, this is no time for smart remarks. You're in deep trouble. You're the only officer I've had under me that I'm constantly giving warnings to before I talk to him. I don't like it one bit. I want to let you know that you don't have to make a statement . . . and if you do, it could be held against you . . . ."

"Commander, I've been nursing this sore ankle ever since Mr. Leach maneuvered me into stepping into a hole in the float when we went ashore last night. I've not moved fast or far, but not once has anyone asked me to make a statement."

"The boat crew said there was a shootout out by White Beach. An officer was killed. I saw your clothes. They're soiled. And there's blood on your cuff. The chart says you've got bruises and chewed-up knuckles. I'd prefer to let ONI hear your story."

"XO, I didn't kill anyone! I tried to keep it from happening."

Joe retold the happenings of the previous night. When he had finished, the XO, who had seated himself on the foot of the bed, said, "There's no way on earth that I would knowingly walk unarmed into a room with a man holding hostages. What on earth prompted you to take it upon yourself to confront that man?"

"Commander, I thought all night about that. I guess the only words I can find to describe why I walked in there are, I had to. Did you ever read Dante?"

"No."

"In one place he said that the hottest places in hell are reserved for those who preserve their neutrality in a crisis. Frenchy was in no position or condition to go in there. He and I were the only ones there. The man hadn't shot anyone by the time we arrived. If I had been given just another half-minute, my friend would be alive and that pathetic kid wouldn't be facing a murder charge. I was an arm's length away . . ." Joe wiped the tears from his cheeks. "I failed him."

"Boy, you have a way of making me feel humble. That is not a privilege that should be accorded greenhorn Reserve Ensigns. The Captain gave you an endorsement on your request for Submarine School that surprised me: he said he'd rather have you serving under him in wartime than in peacetime. I'd say from your story—if it holds up—that his judgment is good. It dawned on me while you were talking that if I let you off the ship, they could well keep you here indefinitely while the lawyers play their games. That boy is facing a general court-martial. You can count on another stay on Okinawa for the pretrial hearing and more time for the trial. If I leave you behind, you could be here until after we get back from this WESTPAC tour. My trouble is that I'm committed to the shift of division officers, which calls for you to be put in as Second Division Jay Oh. Captain Sam wrote as fine an endorsement as I've seen. To be honest, Xylos, since you're a Reserve, I don't see much chance of Sub School taking you. I'm betting that when your boss gets out this summer, you'll be qualified enough to relieve him."

The XO tapped his fingernails on the hollow brass rungs at the foot of the bed before continuing, "Boy, maybe you'll get lucky and that nut will plead guilty and save us all a lot of trouble . . . And, Doc, putting the cast on his foot is convincing. Good thinking!"

Rufus laughed. "XO, Joe is fit for light duty only, maybe watches in Combat."

"Xylos," said the XO, "I want you to stay right here in sick bay until after the investigator has taken your statement. We'll provide him with clerical backup."

Turning at the sound of the door opening behind him, the XO concluded, "Ah, I see they've brought you a luncheon tray. Come on, Mr. Sawyer, Doc Johnson, it's time we got to the wardroom."

⋯⟢◉⟣⋯

Close to three that afternoon, Joe was awakened from a fitful sleep by a pudgy hand shaking him. "Ensign Joseph Xylos. Wake up, Mr. Xylos."

As he raised himself up to his elbows, a beer-bellied man in his mid-thirties, wearing a faded brown corduroy suit and a thin green necktie, extended his hand. "Sir, I'm Agent Detwilder, ONI. We've been trying to find you since last night."

Joe rubbed his eyes. "Well, here I am. What do you want, a statement?"

"Yes. At this point, it approaches being a formality. I've talked to everyone else who was there. I have a clear picture of what happened."

Joe recounted the evening as the man took notes and asked a few clarifying questions along the way. Once the last notes were taken, Agent Detwilder asked, "Are you planning to go ashore again to see Eva Villerouge before the ship sails?"

"I can't even put any weight on my foot. The ship's leaving tomorrow. I'd like to, but I'm staying aboard."

"What sort of relationship do you have with Eva Villerouge?"

"Relationship? Meaning what?"

"Meaning . . .Well, why did you run off to her place as soon as Lieutenant Villerouge was murdered?"

"Are you insinuating that there's something between Eva and me?"

"You did go directly to her house, and you said the two of you talked until you caught the *Skagit*'s boat. It left the fleet landing just after six fifteen this morning. The question has to be asked."

Joe looked at the green bulkhead at the end of his bed for a long minute before drawing in a deep breath. "Have you ever created something special out of the ordinary and felt good that you had a part in it?"

"What are you saying?"

"I did. I was in on it right from the start. I gave her my pass so she could sneak out of the Olympic Village. I was there when they were married. When I visited their home here on the island, it had a feeling of warmth, of love. Last night I sat across the room from the two of them and watched the glow in her cheek . . . the satisfaction in his eyes . . . the happiness. I patted myself on the back for my small part in bringing them together. You couldn't imagine how sick I feel. Every time I close my eyes, I hear Frenchy's gun 'click' while that damn crazy sailor was picking up the pistol. It's always in slow motion. I did nothing! Absolutely nothing until he turned his gaze toward me just as he pulled the trigger. I froze for that instant! I have to live with that the rest of my life. Frenchy was my friend!"

"And Eva?"

"I told her I'd look after her."

"Look after her?"

"Don't read the wrong things into it. She towers over me, physically and mentally. I'm not her type. What I see in her is a very frightened and lonely woman in a foreign land. She was my good friend's wife. I had a hand in bringing them together. I have an obligation to extend a hand to her, one human to another. My father used to read from the Bible, 'What you do for the least of these, you do for me.' Ideally I would have liked to stay here until after the funeral."

"There will be a memorial service tomorrow afternoon. I understand that she will accompany the body back to the States. I hope I didn't offend you with the last questions. I think I have a much clearer understanding of what motivated you than I had before. Although it's not my business to do this, I'm going to suggest that you be recommended for some sort of decoration. If Lieutenant Scoggins had shown the courage you did instead of crapping his pants, this wouldn't have happened."

"Don't be too hard on Scoggins. If that guy had stuck the muzzle of that forty-five down my throat, I might have sung a different tune. Thank you for the kind words. I don't feel like a hero. All I did was to save my own life. My friend is dead."

The agent gathered up his notes and shook Joe's hand before leaving.

Late in the afternoon, Rufus Johnson released Joe from confinement in Sick Bay. Slowly, using crutches, he made his way to his room. Once he had changed into wash khakis, he sat down on the chair in front of the desk and propped the throbbing leg up on an overturned wastebasket.

He opened the stationery box that his aunt sent him before the trip. The top of the stack swelled above the sides as the weight of the lid was removed. Awkwardly, he placed a clean piece of paper on his desk. After staring at the cubbyholes in the desk for some minutes, he wrote, "Dear Eva" to begin a sentence, then tore it up. He made two more tries before beginning again,

Dear Eva,

I just returned to my room from sick bay. I won't be going fast or far on these crutches. The doc has put my ankle in a cast. He said that I tore my Achilles tendon. Nothing is broken, but a lot is twisted and terribly sore. I put my leg up and the throbbing physical pain dies away, but there is another ache that tears at my being. It's an old familiar companion that followed me after my father died. Even though I had plenty of time to prepare for it then, those first few days afterward were hell.

And I now think of you, knowing that you too must bear it. I wish I could be there to help see you through the next few days. Your loss, my loss, grieves me. My friend, my shipmate, gone forever and with him, not just the spark of his life, but the fire of the love that I watched grow from our chance meeting to the happiness that was so apparent as we visited yesterday.

The agent told me that you will be going back to the States with Frenchy's remains. I don't know what awaits you. I want to let you know that you're not entirely alone in this. You are in my thoughts and prayers. Please write.

Frenchy was a good friend, my mentor. For his sake, I will always be available, a shoulder to cry on, and to the extent I have them, resources to tide you over.

Sincerely, Joe.

At dinner, Joe gave the letter to a shipmate to mail ashore. He watched the movie and then made his way slowly back to his stateroom. He thumbed through magazines, reading words but not absorbing content, until well after midnight when he painfully made his way to bed.

Morning found him sitting at the breakfast table with his shipmates, who felt almost as bad as he did thanks to their hard drinking on their last night ashore. By noon their hangovers were mostly gone and life had returned to routine as the cruiser pitched and rolled gently, pointing its bow south toward the Formosa Straits. Joe felt almost as bad at day's end as he had in the morning.

At lunch the following day, the Operations Officer, Commander Wyman, placed a message on the table next to Joe, saying, "Xylos, the Old Man asked me to give you a copy of the news item here. The Captain is relieved that you won't be going back to testify at the court-martial."

Joe picked up the mimeographed sheet, recognizing it as a fleet news broadcast. A third of the way down the page was a paragraph that read,

NAHA OKINAWA. SEAMAN THOMAS BROWN, WHO WAS CONFINED TO THE ARMY STOCKADE WHILE AWAITING COURT-MARTIAL FOR THE MURDER OF NAVY LIEUTENANT VILLEROUGE, COMMITTED SUICIDE BY HANGING HIMSELF FROM THE BARS OF HIS CELL."

The Ensign laid the sheet down beside his plate and stared at it before saying in a flat monotone, "The poor kid . . . Well, he got what he wanted."

Commander Wyman snapped, "The poor kid! Is that all you can say? That vermin shot a United States Navy officer! Don't you have any feelings for Frenchy Villerouge?"

"Feelings? I haven't slept soundly since it happened. Frenchy was a friend . . . a good friend . . . no, a *damn* good friend. And I hurt all over because he's dead and his bride is a widow. She'll have a baby that will never know its father. If only I had moved just a little faster . . . if only Frenchy hadn't barged into the room unarmed before I had the gun in my hand!"

"Unarmed?"

"He pointed an empty forty-five at Brown."

Joe's voice dropped as he tossed the paper toward the center of the table. "But this, I think, was what Brown wanted all along. He wanted to die. And he would have that night, if Frenchy had remembered to load the stupid gun. Up until just before Brown started to hand over the gun, I would have cheered to see him shot. In the end, what I saw was a frightened kid who was sick in the head. He needed help. I've been thinking about how the system broke down because he wasn't surveyed. There is one side of me that says Brown got what he deserved. He killed my friend. But another sees him as a moth drawn to a flame and thinks about the grief and shame his parents must feel. Nothing will ever bring Frenchy or that sick kid back."

"Joe, that wasn't the response I was expecting. You always surprise me, such empathy for the kid's family. Yes, we all share your loss. Lieutenant Villerouge was an outstanding officer. Aren't you relieved that you'll not be going back to Okinawa?" The Ops Officer leaned over the table to retrieve the mimeographed sheet.

"Yes, sir, I am. I want nothing more than to put this all behind me. The place holds no happy memories for me. Thank you for showing me the message. I apologize if I carried on too much. The whole affair was a big shock to me . . . and I haven't gotten over it."

Resting a hand on his shoulder, the Commander said, "I understand. You weren't carrying on, mister. Seldom have I seen such maturity in officers far your senior. I appreciated hearing your thoughts. Now enjoy your lunch."

CHAPTER 24

Xylos to Second Division Jay Oh

After the special sea and anchor detail was secured, Harry Leach strolled into Boys' Town, where Joe reclined with his foot resting on a pillow at the foot of his bed.

Although Joe's only movement was to lift his eyes from the page of the book he was reading, Leach said, "Stay where you are, Mr. Xylos. I'd like to take a moment to talk with you."

The chubby officer pulled a chair away from a desk and pushed it down the narrow passageway between the bunks. He positioned it facing Joe and heavily dropped himself on the seat so that his beefy arms rested on the back.

Joe stared at Leach while he blankly looked at Joe. He cleared his throat, then began, "Mr. Xylos, some time ago, I suggested to Commander Longstreet that if you were ever to be switched out of the Engineering Department, that you work for me in the Gunnery Department."

That's not what I heard, thought Joe. *It's going to be an interesting time until either he gets reassignment orders or I do.*

"Yes, we've had our differences. But I've come to know that you have an indomitable spirit, and I respect you for that. You've made me realize anew that a book cannot be judged by its cover. I had quite a talk with both the Chief Engineer and the Main Propulsion Assistant last night at White Beach. They made me feel that getting you is a prize. If you had a chance to talk to the man you're relieving, you must know you'll have your work cut out for you. And I know you're up to it."

"Thank you, sir. I'm sorry that I'll be laid up. The doc is talking about six weeks before I'm fully returned to duty."

"Six weeks, eh? I guess I've got no one to blame but myself for this one. And I apologize for what happened at fleet landing. I never intended for you to be injured like this. Joe, I've got to say that you take it as well as you dish it out."

Joe sat up and extended his right hand, which the Lieutenant shook vigorously. He smiled. "Thank you, Mr. Xylos. It's a pleasure to have a man working for me that doesn't carry a grudge. Well, I've got to get moving. I hope that leg feels better fast."

"Thank you, sir."

After Leach left, Joe mulled over his words and compared them to the comments made by Lieutenant (junior grade) Jules Corwin, whom he was about to relieve as Second Division Junior Officer. Corwin was ecstatic over becoming the Fourth Division Officer. He made no bones about Harry Leach, whom he regarded as an alcoholic sadist.

As for Outside White, the Second Division Officer and running mate of Harry Leach, Corwin described him as a "marine species of bear," who hibernated whenever the ship was underway and roamed only when it was in port. Although he was one of the five officers qualified as an Officer of the Deck Underway, White did very little other than the minimum required of him, which was to attend quarters in the morning and stand his watches. If the ship was underway more than eight or ten days in a row, he became an insomniac and wandered about the division spaces, nitpicking. During these brief periods of hyperactivity, he would undo most of the decisions the division's Jay Oh had been forced to make due to his absence.

Outside White's greatest claim to fame was a letter of reprimand, which he had framed and hung on the inside of his locker door. He got it for calling President Eisenhower, pretending to be the Vice President. Unfortunately for White, Vice President Nixon was in Los Angeles on an unpublicized trip, and the call drew the immediate attention of the Secret Service. Before the letter announcing the crew change was signed, Outside White proudly showed the letter to Joe and retold how he had let "The Man" know he was a failure who didn't deserve a second term. He loudly announced that it would earn him entry into the inner circles of Boston Democratic politics and possibly a strong position in helping Senator Kennedy run for President.

The third leg of this crew change was a very quiet officer whom Joe hardly knew: Lieutenant (junior grade) Tyler Cobb, the 4th Division Officer. He was in the zone for promotion to Lieutenant and had yet to attain qualification as an OOD Underway. Joe was surprised to find that Cobb was a Naval Academy graduate. He had put in a request to change his designation to Engineering Duty Officer and would relieve Joe as the Main Engines Officer. As the process of relieving began, Joe found Cobb to be a detail-oriented and meticulous individual with a keen intellect. His only failing was to constantly smoke a pipe filled with a mixture that smelled to Joe almost as bad as burning tires.

The transition was quickly and smoothly made. The weeks that followed went slowly for Joe as he recuperated. He stood, or rather, sat his underway watches in a corner of the Combat Information Center. Otherwise he kept busy doing paperwork both for his division and for Lieutenant Leach, who was the ship's Training Officer. In spare moments, he wrote brief notes to Eva, which he put in a single envelope on the last night before the mail went off the ship.

The *Beaverton*'s next two ports were Keelung and Hong Kong, China. The ship anchored out in both ports. Joe elected to remain aboard rather than risk stepping from the accommodation ladder to the boat and chancing further harm to his ankle. He was still on light duty and was excused from deck watches. The Communicator, who had the duty of decoding messages, was pressed into in-port watch in his place; so, to compensate, the injured Ensign was assigned to in-port communications watches and message decoding duty.

By choosing to remain aboard, Joe was drawn into the small circle of married officers who remained aboard and therefore out of "harm's way" (the shoreside whorehouses), so to speak. Prominent among them was his roommate, Lawyer Sawyer.

The mail awaiting him in Hong Kong included his first letter from Eva, thanking him for his concern and telling of her safe arrival in Frenchy's hometown of Richford, Vermont.

By the time the cast was removed and Joe regained most of his muscle tone, the *Beaverton* was alongside at Subic Bay, Philippines, where she would remain for a fifteen-day upkeep (routine maintenance). This was the first time Joe was out of the Engineering Department during an upkeep. The prospect of a time for some true rest and recreation was banished when he got a memo from the XO notifying him that he was given the collateral duty of Ship's Softball Officer. He would be in charge of the intraship tournament, which would be played daily from 1300 hours (one p.m.) until no earlier than 1600 hours (four p.m.), and the *Beaverton*'s intership games, which would be played from 1600 hours until darkness. The memo directed Harry Leach to excuse him from all in-port watches and duties between noon and the beginning of the evening watch.

Not being very athletically inclined, Joe groaned silently, but when the others in the bunkroom made envious noises, he decided not to complain. On the first day, he found out why. The ball diamonds were across the street from a beautiful sand swimming beach and close to a small Officer's Club. The ship's recreation fund provided all the equipment, including beer. Division officers were responsible for the conduct of their people, and Shore Patrol was assigned in sufficient numbers to keep order. Over the fifteen-day upkeep, only three games with other ships were scheduled.

Joe found after the first day that he need only be present to start the games and to gather and count the gear at the end. Other than that, he could swim close to shore, sit in the sun, read, write Eva, and drink free beer. After seeing the players off to the ship with gear in tow, he walked a short distance up the beach to the Officer's Club, where he had dinner on the days he didn't have the duty.

One day, as this idyll was drawing to a close, he was sitting on the beach, enjoying the last afternoon's sun stretching long shadows while the play went on behind him. Chaplain Finn approached, walking along the road from the direction of the ship. Joe looked up from the clipboard on his lap as the Father said, "I see you're enjoying your hardship tour out here on the beach."

"Hello, Padre. How was Baguio?"

"Wonderful. The golf course was a challenge, and the nights were cool. Joe, you're looking good. I'd say this place agrees with you."

"It's been an interesting vacation, but I wouldn't want to do it for a living."

"Good. I'm glad you feel that way. Rufus Johnson and I talked the XO into assigning you to this job."

"So I have you to thank for this! Why?"

"You hadn't been off the ship since Buckner Bay, and you've been a much-changed man. Rufus feels you're a bit too introspective, perhaps getting depressed. We're concerned about you." Reaching inside his sports coat, the Chaplain pulled out a pair of feminine-looking envelopes. "Mail's in. I took the liberty of bringing these along."

Joe took the envelopes. "Thank you. Good, here's yesterday's letter. They're from Eva, Frenchy's widow. I've been writing to her." Joe studied the pastel-colored envelopes for a minute. "Padre, I'm hurting. And I'm not sure I'm going in the right direction."

"How's that?"

"Eva. I began writing her because I felt responsible and wanted more than anything to comfort her. The morning I left her, she was downright paranoid that they would come after her next . . . all alone and extremely fearful. I couldn't visualize her being anything other than a friend. How could a sophisticated world-class athlete ever be attracted to a skinny lounge lizard like me? Well, I think it's happening. And I'm torn."

"What do you mean?"

"One side of me wants to go to my father and say, `I'm ready to settle down. Find me a good Greek girl.' Only my father is dead, and I don't know anyone whose judgment I could trust like I did his. And this woman is one of whom dreams are spun. The thoughts she shares in her letters make me feel we could make a lifelong commitment."

"What's the other side?"

"Guilt that I'm going after Frenchy's woman before he's even cold in his grave. The only picture I have of her is the wedding picture with my friend. I don't even look at it anymore. I remember the way she looked at Frenchy the day we met. She lit up the room. At first I felt disappointed that her light was for him . . . then, excited because we pulled off her defection. I still dream about sitting across the room and seeing the look of love in her eyes for him, the night he was murdered. I felt pride that I had a hand in bringing them together. And now . . . guilt, when I feel the hurt and loneliness that come out between the lines when she writes about evenings playing cards with the war widows at the church. If I had just been a little quicker—bumped the guy's arm instead of standing there like a statue and watching him blow out Frenchy's brains. Eva needs Frenchy. They really communicated, jumping from one language to another. It was like they were destined to be together."

"Does this come out in her letters?"

"No. In fact, there's a brightness to her words, a hope that lifts me up. I'm sorry to confess that she seems to be doing a better job of getting on with her life than I am."

"Joe, the loss of a friend, a shipmate, is always hard. Some people get over it far quicker than others. Some people bury their feelings and never work it out. If you'd like to talk about this more, I'm always available."

"Thanks."

Joe watched the Jesuit as he went over to the diamond and soon was playing in the outfield.

His attention was distracted from the game when three large olive-painted army trucks halted on the road at the edge of the field and quickly emptied of Filipino soldiers. All were well armed and dressed for combat. They hauled light mortars and machine guns with them.

Early in the afternoon, the Ensign recalled, a small boat had landed at the far end of the beach, discharging eight or ten ragged men who dashed into the jungle carrying a motley collection of weapons. The native lifeguard had said the men were Huks, communist guerrillas. However, other than watching them disappear into the foliage, no one had done anything until the three army trucks arrived.

About the time that the game was ending, the first sounds of distant small-arms fire echoed out of the jungle.

⋯⊷▦◉ ◉▦◁⋯

That evening, Joe was on the quarterdeck standing his usual watch as in-port JOOD, pleased that it was the evening watch, which ended at midnight, rather than the mid-watch, which began at midnight.

The booming sound of the well-amplified soundtrack of the evening movie had just ended to return the ship to the sounds of blowers, gurgling saltwater discharge lines, and cheerful voices of young sailors headed below. On the pier, a trio of besotted boatswains in dress whites plied a sinuous path toward the after brow. The only one he recognized by name was the ship's leading Master at Arms, Boatswain's Mate First Class Billy Bail. About two-thirds of the way across the sloping brow, Bail tripped, almost falling to his knees. His hat flipped off his head and struck the railing, then came to rest barely short of falling into the water below. As Bail picked up his hat, some loud laughter and shouted comments came from the fantail area. Joe was far enough away that only the modulations of the voices carried to him. The disturbance died down as quickly as it began. The Ensign, who had been standing at the top of the brow, turned and marched to the far side of the deck, his long glass tucked under his arm. He forgot the incident by the time he was relieved.

Two days later, he answered a knock on the bunkroom door to find First Class Machinist Richards standing there. Before he could say a word, Richards blurted out, "Mr. Zee, you gotta help me. I tried talking to that new Division Officer and he just don't believe that they're trying to railroad me."

"Railroad you? Who?"

"Yes, sir! You know I passed the Chief's exam last time, and if I get in trouble, all my hard work is gone down the drain. And I didn't do nothing wrong." The big man was wringing his hat as if he had just washed it.

Joe interrupted, "Richards, what's this all about? Who—?"

"It's those damn Masters at Arms! They don't like anybody of color."

"Come on in. Let me hear about it."

"Thank you, sir. I knew, I just knew, that you would give me an ear. God bless you, sir."

As he entered the room, he said, "The other night right after the movie, Bail, the Master at Arms, came back on the fantail and started kicking Starkings, telling him to 'get his black ass below.' It was obvious the man was drunk. I told him to cool off and I'd see that the kid went on down. The man turned on me and started swinging at me. All I did was give him a little push, and he fell on his butt. If he'd been sober, he would have kept his feet. There were two other deck apes with him, and I warned them not to try anything cute. Bail got up and swore at me. I helped Starkings pick up the blanket, and we left. All the way to

the ladder, the three of them called us race names, just trying to get a
fight going. Believe me, I had my hands full with brother Starkings.
The lad's got too much pride and not enough common sense. He wanted to tangle with the three of them. They jived us until we went below.
Yesterday morning I found out that Bail put me on report for assaulting
him while he was 'in the performance of his duties' as a Master at
Arms. After I tried to talk with Mr. Cobb, the Chief suggested that I
come see you."

Joe said, "Richards, I was the JOOD that evening and yes, I saw Bail
and two others come aboard. I think they're from the Third or Fifth
Division, anyway from back aft."

"Yes, sir, Lowell and Canning. They're his witnesses, and they back
him. They're both lying to cover his butt."

"I saw Bail trip on the brow and heard some comments from the
fantail. Did you say anything?"

"No! Starkings laughed at him and said a couple of words. After all,
Bail had put him on report last month for tripping on the brow, saying
that he was falling down drunk. Sir, the reason I came up there, was to
try to talk some sense into that kid. He feels that because he's colored,
everybody is against him. And that there's white man's justice and that
no colored man can ever get a fair shake. If they succeed with me, it's
going to be bad for every colored man. Could you speak for me at mast
and tell the Old Man something good about me?"

"I'll do more than that. Who else saw what happened?"

"I didn't pay attention to who was there. Besides, nobody is going to
volunteer to cross Bail. After all, he's like the sheriff of Dodge City."

"I think I may have a witness for you. Mr. White asked permission
to go up to the top of the crane right after the movie. He had to check
on something before they started hauling the boats out. Let me give
him a call."

"It's going to be my word against theirs. And Bail is the XO's man.
I don't have much hope . . . But if I could get away with a warning,
maybe I could make Chief."

"Richards, you're one of the finest Petty Officers on this ship. Say,
isn't Bail the clown that the Chief Engineer told you to escort out of
main control when he came down trying to put sea detail watch stand-

ers on report for wearing baseball caps?"

"Yes, sir, I think he was. I forgot about that."

After the black Petty Officer left, Joe called the log room and talked to recently promoted Lieutenant (junior grade) Larry White, whose version of the events coincided with Richards's. From his position on the ladder inside the crane's structure, he was unnoticed and yet close enough to hear all that went on. In his opinion, if anyone had violated the Code, it was the Master at Arms. Between Richards and Bail, there had been no contact other than Richards straight-arming the other man in self-defense. By the time White climbed down, everybody had left.

Using the book on Carter Sawyer's desk, Joe shopped through the index and read pertinent parts of the UCMJ, then began writing his rough draft of the charges, using some of the report sheets on his roommate's desk as a guide.

When Joe next saw Carter just before lunch, he asked, "What do you think about the problems between Bail and Richards?"

The sloe-eyed Southerner's eyes widened. "What's your interest in this?"

"Richards is a damn fine man, about the best PO in M Division. Do you remember the fight that night I had Shore Patrol?"

"Sure, say, wasn't he the guy that went in and busted heads?"

"Yes."

"Well, he tried to bust one head too many. Bail put him on report for assault and disobeying a lawful order, as starters. My recommendation as the ship's Legal Officer will be to remove one stripe. There are two witnesses."

"Lowell and Canning?"

"How did you know that?"

"I saw all three of them returning from liberty together. Bail tripped while coming over the brow. All three were drunk. That drew some comments from the fantail. Bail went back there, not in his capacity as a Master at Arms, but in a drunken rage. There he kicked a seaman by the name of Starkings. Richards intervened. That resulted in a shoving match between Bail and Richards, which ended when Bail landed on his butt. The seaman and Richards went below decks, leaving the other three topside."

"Sounds like you've been talking to that nigger."

"I have."

"It's his word against theirs. His chances of the Old Man believing him are between slim and none. Bail is an extension of the XO's right arm. Besides that, Starkings was up before the Old Man just a month ago.

◦◦▸▪◉▪◂◦◦

At Captain's mast, Captain Slaxman asked Richards, "Did you threaten Canning and Lowell?"

"If telling them not to start any trouble is threatening them, yes, sir, I did. I had my hands full because Starkings wanted to go after the Boatswain because after he was kicked, the three of them began calling names, and I mean dirty names. They were trying to get my goat and start a fight. As much as I would have loved to toss the three of them over the side, I knew I have too much to lose, so I dragged Starkings to the hatch. I took him back to his compartment. All the way, he was giving me this jive that I was yellow and had no pride in my race. I told him then, and I'll tell you now, that Boatswain Bail isn't worth working up a sweat over. I went to my compartment and went to bed. After quarters the next morning, I found out Bail put me on report. I tried to talk to him, and the man wouldn't talk. He said he'd have his say in front of you. Captain, I have worked hard for twelve years to get where I am. I just shipped over for another six years and I'm about to make Chief. I've swallowed my pride when they call me names and insult my race. I've never caused trouble. The Navy is about the finest opportunity a man of color can go after. Don't you see, I'd have too much to lose to get into something like this?"

"Had you been ashore earlier, drinking at the club?"

"Oh, no, Captain. I was in the Duty Section."

"Do you have any witnesses other than Starkings?"

"Yes, sir. Mr. Xylos and Mr. White."

Looking past the two men at the podium, the Captain said, "Mr. Xylos, did you see Richards shove Bail?"

"No, sir."

"Weren't you the quarterdeck watch?"

"Yes, sir."

Captain Slaxman pushed his bifocals all the way up his nose. "Then why did you take it upon yourself to write up my Master at Arms?"

"Captain, I saw Bail, Canning, and Lowell from the time they came onto the dock until they came aboard. They were loud. Bail wasn't steady on his feet."

"That's all?"

"Before they came aboard, yes, sir."

"And you did nothing?"

"I kept an eye on them. Although they weren't much of a credit to themselves or the ship, they weren't so falling down drunk as to warrant immediate action. I've seen members of the wardroom come aboard in worse condition."

There were snickers from the ranks pressed against the bulkhead.

"Then you wrote this up based on a report from the fantail sentry?"

"No, sir, I didn't learn about it until Richards told me. It was two days later, after we had gotten underway."

"And after two days, you elected to turn this man's defense into charges against the leading Master at Arms! Why?"

"Captain, first of all, I believe that either you're an agent who shapes events or you're an actor shaped by events. I verified Richards' story with an unbiased witness. I felt compelled to bring the countercharges that, had Richards filed them, would have been taken as a clever defensive strategy. Second, I owe loyalty to an innocent man who made my success in M Division possible. And third, and what should be important to you, sir, your Master at Arms force has a deserved reputation for treating colored men with open contempt. Consider Bail's own words today. How many times did Bail call Richards a nigger or refer to his race in less than a complimentary manner? Did you see Richards stiffen? You don't gain men's respect by treating them with contempt. Lastly, if I had done nothing and this fine man had been found guilty, I would be a party to an injustice."

Richards's hands trembled as he wiped a tear from his cheek and sniffled loudly. Bail looked down at his very well-polished shoes.

Captain Slaxman shuffled the papers in front of him before saying, "Thank you, Mr. Xylos. Mr. White, your statement says that you were up on the crane. Why would you be up there after dark?"

"The Chief Engineer's orders were to check the crane out after the movie because they had to lift boats aboard the next morning. There had been trouble earlier when the electrical cables to the worklight and the movie sound system got tangled with the hoisting cable."

"That's the system Lieutenant Kane left us with, isn't it?"

"Yes, sir."

"And you say that Bail rushed Seaman Starkings and kicked him. He turned on Richards, and Richards more or less straight-armed him. And Bail fell on his rear."

"Yes, sir."

"Did you see Richards strike or swing at Bail?"

"No, Captain. He bounced off Richards's hand and landed squarely on his butt."

"And what did you do?"

"Nothing. By the time Bail got to his feet, Richards had dragged Starkings to the hatch. The three Boatswains were calling them names like, 'Yellow-bellied nigger,' 'big-ass gingerbread baby,' for two. The whole thing was over almost as quickly as it began."

"How well do you know Richards?"

"I've stood watches with him. And like Joe, er, Mr. Xylos says, he is a fine man."

"Thank you, Mr. White. Mr. Moran, are you here to give a recommendation in favor of Richards?"

Chief Engineer Moran looked at the XO, who was shaking his head ever so slightly. Moran turned away from the XO and cleared his throat before saying, "Captain, Richards is one of the finest men in my department. He passed the Chief's exam with flying colors. The Navy would be the loser if he isn't promoted. On the other hand, I know that Bail has an outstanding record both in the Second War and Korea. I would ask that the whole thing be dropped as a personal dispute that got carried too far."

The Captain studied the papers on the podium for a moment, then began writing. When he looked up, he said, "Richards, Starkings, I find that there is no credence in the charges against you. I'm certain that, had this not involved a member of the Master at Arms force and a man who works very closely with the Executive Officer, Commander Longstreet would have cleared this at screening mast. Richards, it is a rare occasion for me to face a man of your caliber across this podium under such circumstances. You come well recommended. I hope the next time we meet will be to effect your promotion. As for you, Starkings, had the circumstances changed ever so slightly, I would be inclined to take action against you. However, in light of the fact that Bail wasn't acting in an official capacity and in doing so, assaulted you, and that you didn't let yourself be drawn into a fight, I'm dismissing all charges. As the saying goes, we can't go on meeting like this. Don't let me see you up here again. Is that clear?"

The youngster sighed, then exhaled, "Aye, aye, sir!"

Richards and Starkings saluted and filed out with the crowd of witnesses. Following their departure, the proceedings continued. The XO pleaded for Bail. After the CO went on at length about how and why their conduct could not be tolerated, Bail and his two friends were reduced in rank by one pay grade. The XO was directed to find a new Leading Master at Arms.

⋯⊷⊷◉ ◉⊶⊶⋯

The XO published a new memo based on instructions from the Secretary of the Navy and the Chief of Naval Operations. It proclaimed that conduct or actions that create racial disharmony would not be tolerated. At the next Gunnery Department meeting, Lieutenant Commander Craig Compton, the Gunnery Officer, read the memo in a monotone voice and dealt copies of it around the room. Harry Leach scanned his copy and, when he saw Joe looking at him, balled it and tossed it into the wastebasket.

As the meeting ended, the fat Lieutenant whispered, "Mr. Xylos, how does it feel to have created enough ruckus that the XO felt compelled to write a memo?"

"Humbled, that what I said was heard."

"It's only a 'protect your ass' memo, nothing's going to change. A few of the monkeys like Richards will slip through, but by and large, they are an inferior race."

"Lieutenant, you really don't believe that, do you?"

"Believe it! I've seen empirical evidence with my own eyes. Do you know why the South is so backward?"

"I didn't know it was."

"Trust me, it is. I was born there. The color of the labor force is black, and they are shiftless and ignorant. The economy goes no higher than the intelligence of the workforce."

"Sir, your logic reminds me of the entomologist who was trying to prove the theory that grasshoppers hear with their legs. He trained a grasshopper to jump on the sound of a mechanical snap. One by one, he tore off the legs until he pulled off the last one. And when he made the snap, the creature didn't move. He concluded that it was now deaf."

"Very funny, but what has that got to do with anything?"

"Look at what they have, lousy schools, lousy job opportunities, even denied decent public transportation. You say it's because they're inferior, it becomes a self-fulfilling prophecy. I say that give them the same breaks you give everybody else and given time, they'll be anybody's equals. Richards is what many of them are capable of becoming. His language is rough, and his pronunciations are off enough, to show that he is self-taught. The exciting thing is that his success is contagious. These other kids come aboard and see how he's succeeded, and they have something to shoot for."

Leach said, "Richards may have made a big impression on the Old Man today. There are a whole bunch more who remember him and you from the Yellow Dragon. They've had plenty of time to think during every in-port evening, thanks to the Old Man's Sundowners Club. There isn't a Boatswain who's not saying to himself, there but for the grace of God go I. Bail served eighteen and a half honorable years, fought in two wars, and for a few seconds lost his temper. That will cost him thousands of dollars over the rest of his life. He'll never make First Class back before he retires next year."

"That's tough. I'm glad I'm not in the Captain's shoes and had to make that decision. It wasn't a lapse of a few seconds. My gut feeling is that Bail was in the wrong job. It was a mindset; the guy has it in for anybody who's got dark skin. During the mast, every time he used the word 'nigger,' he'd look out of the corner of his eye at Richards. The man knew what he was doing. He had an out, just drop his case on the colored guy. Can you understand by what reasoning he would press forward after Richards told him he had a witness?"

Leach shrugged. "Yes, Bail ruled with an iron fist. What he failed to account for was facing off against a Reserve Ensign. I have to hand it to you, mister. Where did you learn all this stuff?"

"Right here on the *Beaverton*. I learned the legal stuff from listening to Carter Sawyer. But the right and wrong of it, I learned from you."

"Really now, what the hell are you talking about, mister?"

"Lieutenant, never had I been crapped upon because I'm Greek until I met you. You put me in a black man's shoes."

"I've come to respect Greeks, Mister Xylos. But if I were you, I'd tread very lightly and remain alert. Pray that you are accepted into Submarine School. Be advised that Commander Compton feels he was taken in that swap of musical chairs between departments."

"Thank you, sir, for the warning. I'll take it to heart."

CHAPTER 25

Joe Heals

The *Beaverton* passed through Bashi Channel in the Philippines, where she joined many of the other ships of the Seventh Fleet for a major exercise off the east coast of Luzon. Joe's general quarters station was as a director officer for the anti-aircraft battery, which consisted of three-inch guns. For the first time in his life, he stayed in the sun so long that he was sunburned.

Once it was over, there were more exercises as they headed north from summer's tropical heat into cooler springlike waters. One afternoon, they paused off a small island for a shore bombardment exercise. Perched in his small director control tower, Joe was very pleased that his turret, Number Two, had a higher rate of fire than the other two turrets. Following general quarters, Outside White bragged long and hard to anyone within earshot about how he had finally gotten the bugs worked out of the gun crew. Harry Leach openly speculated that Number Two turret would keep its white "E." Not one word was mentioned about the hours Joe had spent running loading drills or that there were no breakdowns during the firing as had occurred on turret Number Three.

Over the next few days, they steamed toward Japan in circles and squares, with the top of a white snow-topped Mount Fuji just above the horizon whenever the weather cleared. There was an air of expectancy as the days sped by, until at last they were headed for the last port visit of the cruise—to Yokosuka again.

After a picturesque entry into Tokyo Bay, past the small islands near the Yokosuka Navy Base, the *Beaverton* tied up in mid-afternoon beneath the huge hammerhead crane in Dry Dock Number Six. Joe supervised his men, who handled Number Two line. Soon after the sea and anchor detail was secured, he changed out of uniform and went ashore. He carried the samurai sword, still wrapped in the cloth it had been stored in since Fumiko gave it to him.

At the foot of the brow, he saw a very muscular young Ensign wearing a dress khaki uniform that was just tight enough to give the impression that he had outgrown it since it was issued. As he approached, the man asked loudly in a strong Southern accent, "Is this the USS *Beaverton*?"

"Yes."

"Good. I've had to wait here for ten days. What a dump! Other than drinking good Southern bourbon at the club, there was nothing to do. It'll be good to be around good solid Americans again."

Joe extended his right hand. "I'm Joe Xylos, Second Division Jay Oh. Welcome aboard!"

The new man said, "I'm Ensign Paul Lawson. Glad to meet you, boy! Where do I go to check in?"

Joe pointed back to the quarterdeck where Outside White stood. "Report in to the OOD there. He'll get you signed in and have a messenger take you below. I doubt if there will be anybody to assign you to anything, so once you get your gear stowed, you could go ashore. The odds are good that most of us will rendezvous at the club around dinnertime. I'm sure someone will take you out and show you the sights. There's really lots to do here, and the natives are friendly."

"I walked around town the first day I was here. It smells bad, and besides, I don't trust these slanty-eyed bastards one bit."

Joe shrugged his shoulders and watched the new officer's retreating back for a moment before walking toward the head of the dry dock. At the gate he hailed a cab and, pulling the now worn sheet of paper from his wallet, showed the driver the directions to Fumiko's place. The cab shot from the stall like a horse from the starting gate and began the ritual weave through the afternoon rush-hour traffic. The sights along the way were familiar, and soon he found himself standing on the gently arched bridge and looking up the trail that snaked between the houses. The browns of winter had been replaced with the greens and cherry pinks of spring.

At the door to Fumiko's, Joe knocked. After what seemed an eternity, a man, still kneeling inside, slid the door open. Joe saw in the man's square jaw, broad shoulders, and powerful muscular arms . . . Captain Slaxman.

The young man narrowed his eyes and, hardly moving his lips, said, "She gone States to be with husband. Not here."

"Then Fumiko is all right?"

"Yes. Why you say Fumiko, and not Fuji-san like others?"

"That was the name she used. You must be Shige, her son?"

"So! How you know my name?"

"She told me about you. I have something here that I don't feel right about keeping. She gave it to me."

Shige looked at Joe's parcel. "Please come in. Put shoes in box."

Joe hesitantly took the covered sword in the long narrow wrappings and placed it on the floor as he took off his shoes. The covering slid back from the hilt.

"My father's sword! I thought she take it to America! Why you have it?"

Joe took a position kneeling just inside the house. He put the sword on the floor between them. "We had a very emotional parting last January. She insisted that I take the sword with me. It must have great meaning to you and your family. Please take it."

"Very strange. She give away many things in days before she leave." Although his face remained impassive, his voice choked. "Thank you for your honesty. Yes, this sword mean very much to me. It belong my father, who die in the war."

"You call him your father, Shige?"

He put his hands on his knees, straightening his arms, and with his head somewhat lowered, looked through his eyebrows at Joe. "So she tell you too about her dishonor. Yes, yes, I will always remember him as my father. He raise me as his own."

"Yes, I understand. Shige . . . Shige, did she ever tell you anything about your birth father?"

"Other than he was American . . . a naval officer who disgrace her . . . very little."

"Would you like to meet him?"

The man inhaled audibly through his mouth. "Why should I? He not care. He use her, like all the others."

"I don't think that's a fair assessment, although I understand why you'd say that. He never knew she was pregnant. He's my commanding officer, Captain Sam Slaxman. He is a fine man. I'm sure he would like to meet you."

Shige waved his arm in a circle. "Why should I? I have everything I need. What good could come of it?"

"You don't have a father. He doesn't have a son."

Shige slowly stood up with the sword in hand and walked across the room to the shrine, where he knelt in front of the samurai armor. He polished the scabbard and the hilt of the sword with the cloth before gently placing them on the lacquered stand. He clapped his hands and then bowed, touching his head to the floor.

After about five minutes, he sat up and pivoted to face Joe. "I would like meet him at least one time. Yes, tonight?"

"I don't think so. I'll have to talk to him. Perhaps for lunch aboard ship. Would you like that?"

"Maybe, yes. I have to work the next two days, then I am off for two."

"Fumiko said you are married. I'm sure he would like to meet your wife."

"Eeeoooo . . . I not think she understand so easy."

⊷⫸⊙ ⊙⫷⊶

Just short of noon on the third day following, Joe guided Shige Saito from the quarterdeck to the captain's in-port cabin. The steward ushered them in and seated them in the overstuffed chairs along the outboard side of the room.

Captain Sam Slaxman entered, paused at the door, then strode boldly with a frozen smile to greet his visitors. Shige bowed and very hesitantly extended his hand to shake the Captain's. Once the introductions were completed, Joe asked to be excused, but the Captain motioned for both of them to join him at the table.

The meal was served and eaten with very little conversation. Shige was obviously uneasy as he waited for the other two to take a utensil before he imitated their actions. Slaxman looked at him through his eyebrows as he ate. Once or twice, he spilled a dribble of soup down his chin, which he caught with his napkin.

Upon the arrival of the coffee, the Captain said, "I've wanted to meet you from the moment your mother told me of your existence. I've always wanted a son. My two children back home are both girls."

Shige nodded.

"I feel cheated, not having had the opportunity to be a father to you."

"I had very good father before he go away to war. That is the memory I hold in my heart."

The Captain stared into his half-empty coffee cup as he began, "I'm thankful for that. I was a heel in the way I treated your mother, Fumiko. It wasn't until after she left New London that I realized what a great blunder I had made. Had I known her condition, I wouldn't have hesitated to marry her. The memory tainted the early years of my marriage. I don't think I put it fully behind me until Pearl Harbor was bombed."

"Ah, so!"

"Shige, I would like to keep in touch with you. And ask your forgiveness for my conduct those many years ago."

"Captain, no need to ask forgiveness. I never feel you do me harm. You gave me life and for that I am thankful. It was my mother. You one of many. She always a butterfly, beautiful, tasting sweet nectar of almost every flower. In the beginning, I thought it is through necessity because times so bad. Later, I knew it something else."

Joe asked, "Shige, when did you first suspect that the Colonel wasn't your birth father?"

"His last visit. A very bad argument. I heard him say he not my father and he not sure if my brother was his. I thought he going to kill her. After the war, after I mourn his death, she tell me I am half-American. She tell me your name once or twice, but I chose to forget it. Now that you ask to meet me, I will choose to remember it, but I must keep my name. In Japan, Saito good, but never Slaxman."

Nervously, Shige folded and refolded his napkin. At the end of his words, he stood and bowed. The Captain rose and bowed in response to his son, then said, "Shige, may I have your address?"

The young man took a rice paper sheet, on which he very neatly wrote the address with a calligraphic flair, and placed it on the table. Then the older man passed his son a three-by-five card with his own mailing address. He handed Joe a new Nikon camera. "Mr. Xylos, would you take our picture?"

After capturing several father-and-son poses on the deck outside the cabin, Joe took Shige back through the gates, where they parted after the young man bowed four or five times. Finally he stepped across and shook Joe's hand. It was only then that he broke from his almost grim, blank expression to smile and say, "Thank you."

Late on the last afternoon in port, Joe spent the time shopping with Doc Rufus Johnson, Outside White, and Ensign Paul Lawson, who was his new roommate. White and Rufus insisted that they stop by the Tradewinds for the "happy hour" show. This was an entertainment that most of the wardroom had raved over from the start, but one that Joe had never seen. Paul weakly protested about the decadent East, but finally joined them, swearing that he wasn't buying any Oriental bimbo cherry drinks. The signboard at the club's entrance announced that there were a dozen girls in the show.

As soon as the short but very muscular major domo saw Rufus, he smiled and bowed. "Doctah-san! Wer-come. I have you prace reserved. Prease come."

Rufus pressed a hundred-yen note into his hand, and the man guided them to a ringside table. A waitress dressed in a teddy, net stockings, and high heels took their order.

Paul mumbled, "She dresses like she's working in a brothel."

Rufus took a sip from his drink while watching the nicely rolling gait of the retreating woman. "Paul, don't get any ideas about her. She's in the floor show. And you won't get to first base with any of them. If you want some action, come on back about ten. The late-night girls here will take you home if you're halfway decent to them."

"Not me! I'm not about to expose myself to only God knows what sort of plagues and decadence they spread."

"Paul, you've been watching too many World War Two movies on TV. They have a very old and refined culture."

"They must be filthy, from the way this country smells!"

Joe said, "Actually these people are very clean. We ought to show you a Japanese bath on the way back."

"I can't believe that I wouldn't be exposed to some rare oriental disease that will hound me for life."

Rufus puffed up. "Hell, don't let that stop you! Anything they've got, I can cure."

Paul wrinkled up his nose. "Doctor, you're disgusting! I have the sweetest girl, Mabeline, meeting me in Hawaii. I wouldn't . . . "

Joe said, "I identify with that, Paul. Why don't you just sit back and enjoy the floor show? Here comes the master of ceremonies."

The show began and quickly became a procession of bumps and grinds over a trail of discarded garments. As in the show at the B Division party, each dancer soon was naked as she circled around the floor. After five dancers, an elderly man set up an easel in the center of the small stage at the far end of the room. The emcee asked for a volunteer to pose for him. Two of the scantily clad waitresses led a blushing young man from a table in the back of the room and seated him facing the audience. Just after he sat down, a willowy woman, whose modesty was partially protected by an array of gossamer veils, silently stepped from behind a curtain and took a pose, behind him and unseen by him, atop a small column with her slim arms held over her head.

The artist through sign language directed his subjects to adjust their position. The young man, now very intent, followed as best he could to an undercurrent of laughter. With a minimum of strokes, the artist outlined the form of the woman on his sheet. And with a few more strokes, he colored it in to an ever-rising level of laughter and noise.

When the artist was done, he bowed and helped the young man to his feet. He guided him to view his work. The room broke into applause as the old man handed the youngster the sheet he had just drawn while pointing to the figure atop the pedestal.

One of the dancers helped carry the easel offstage. The veil-shrouded dancer leaped from the pedestal and very gracefully moved across the open floor with moves that almost looked like modern dance, but with the grace of traditional Japanese dance. As she twirled and sinuated, the veils unraveled one by one and fluttered to the floor until only one remained.

Several times, she twirled along the circumference of the dance floor. The third time, she stopped in front of the *Beaverton* table and focused on Joe while slowly pulling the veil between her legs and wetting her lips. Joe recognized her as the bashful dancer from the B Division party. He exclaimed, "The Lady in Red! Toshiko!"

Toshiko pulled the veil behind his head as she climbed up on the table. For a moment she curled into a ball, and then she stretched out in time with the music. With her arms around Joe's neck, she said, "I rook you everywhere. I want tank you for arr you did. Mieko go America, Ras Vegas. Maybe you herp me, no?"

She kissed Joe full on the mouth and pulled him toward the table. Joe heard the sk-r-ritch sound of a match being lit. Toshiko stiffened as laughter rose behind them.

She looked over her shoulder. Right behind her was Paul Lawson, touching a lighted kitchen match to a cigar. Her leg straightened almost by reflex, and she hit Paul squarely in the chest. The impact threw him and his chair back and over into the aisle. In almost the same motion, the dancer did a somersault and landed on her feet a yard away. She was instantly crouched in a fighting stance with arms bent, palms up. "What you do?" she yelled. "You right match on my butt!" Toshiko held that pose for a moment, then swirled across the floor in graceful turning motions, picking up all her veils except the one that remained around Joe's neck.

Paul gained his feet just after she disappeared. He shouted, "Get that bitch! She kicked me!"

Joe jumped up with the veins in his neck bulging, his fists doubled. "Lawson, you dumb, bigoted son of a bitch!"

Rufus stepped between them. The heavyset major domo grabbed Paul by the arm. "You reave. I carr Shore Patroh."

Outside White said, "Don't worry. We're all leaving. And I want to apologize for him. What a dumb stunt!"

As they walked toward the door, Joe pulled the veil from around his neck and handed it to one of the waitresses. "Would it be possible for me to give this to her?"

"You give her? She no here. She go. Boy-san make big troubre! You reave before Shore Patroh come, *ne*?"

He placed it in her hand, saying, "Please give this to her. I would like to apologize. Tell her she has a class act. *Daijoubu desu ka*?"

The woman smiled, revealing a string of gold lined teeth. "Okay. You her friend?"

"Yes. Tell her we're leaving tomorrow."

"Everybody know *Beaverton* go Rong Beach tomorrow."

By the time Joe stepped through the door, Rufus had flagged a taxi. Once they were inside and headed toward the base, Paul said, "That degenerate was sticking her juicy twat right in my face."

Rufus said, "Paul, don't you ever pull a stunt like that with me around. If there had been Shore Patrol there, you'd be on your way back in a paddy wagon right now. That was so dumb!"

Outside White grumbled, "That goes double for me."

Paul said, "Look, I'll make it up to you in Pearl. Mabeline is going to be there and we'll have a party. Her sorority sisters will be coming along with her. These are real good-looking, white American women."

White said, "Paul, have you noticed that there aren't any *Beaverton* wives following the ship around out here?"

"Can't say that I have."

"There aren't any, and there's a good reason. You don't bring a sandwich to a banquet."

"I can't believe what you're telling me, sir. These people are moral degenerates. Can you name a place in the United States where a naked woman would be allowed to climb on the table where drinks are served? It's an invitation to spread disease."

Joe replied, "The Ace of Clubs in East St. Louis after hours. I worked there."

After a momentary lull in the conversation, Rufus said, "Joe, Joe Xylos, you are amazing! You stay aboard like you've joined the Padre in his celibate orders, then you go ashore and the women seem to fall all over you. How do you do it?"

"The dancer, you mean?"

"Yes, but that's only part of it. The last time we were in Yoko, you disappeared into the woodwork with the Original Fuji-san. I heard all about it from the Chief Staff Officer."

"That was different."

"Different! Here you are, sitting in a room with over a hundred horny males that would pay good money to get next to any of those dancers, and the best looking, most talented one in the show makes a run on you. I thought she was going to rape you."

"She's just a kid. She was one of the strippers at the B Division party. I think it was her first time. I gave her some tips, nothing I haven't done for other new dancers. I will say that she has put together a class act. The way she whips those veils around, you hardly notice that she's almost flat chested."

"But why you?"

"I put the other act in touch with a Stateside agent, and apparently she's playing Las Vegas. She combines a strip with a magic act, a very gifted performer. I think the honey wanted me to get her an audition, but now we'll never know."

White turned around from where he sat in front and said, "Joe, Harry warned me to be careful around you on the beach. He regards you as the original liberty risk."

"Me? Why?"

"How many people have gotten into deep trouble ashore with you? Look at Rufus here . . . the Tijuana jail."

Joe looked out the window, and his voice took on a weak monotone. "And then there's Frenchy rotting in his grave . . . and Eva carrying a baby who will never know his father."

Paul asked, "Who's Frenchy?"

There was a silence filled by the sputtering snap of the boxy Toyota's exhaust.

Joe spat, "The man who occupied your bunk. My friend and shipmate, who was needlessly murdered by a crazy sailor. There isn't a man in the wardroom who's fit to carry his bags. He was a mind, a talent that's lost from the world forever. And I just stood there and let it happen!"

Paul's voice dropped to almost a murmur. "Joe, I'm sorry. I didn't know."

⋅⊱══◉══⊰⋅

The next morning the *Beaverton* stood out of the harbor on schedule. Following sea detail, Joe visited his boss, Outside White, to have him sign some reports and to seek his agreement on a schedule for continuing training of the Number Two turret crew. All the time he was in White's stateroom, there was a gentle gurgling with each roll of the ship. Joe looked toward the sound. The source was a wall of the stateroom lined with cases of booze. As he finished, Joe asked, "How do you plan to get this past Customs?"

"Easy. Every bottle has a legal importer. The kids under twenty-one can't use the stuff, but they have the right to bring it into the country."

"I can't believe there are that many underage seamen. Sir, you've got enough booze here to drown an elephant."

"Ah, what a way to go!"

"And how are you going to get this hoard home to Boston?"

"My brother will be coming out with a delivery truck."

CHAPTER 26

Homeward Bound

The formation consisting of two cruisers, a tanker, and eight destroyers steamed across the blue Pacific to Hawaii in the warm days of spring without anything more than light squalls to dampen its passage. The entrance into the channel at Pearl past Ford Island and the sunken USS *Arizona* was done in postcard-perfect weather.

Like the trip west, the stay would be brief, only long enough to refuel, take on stores, and make some minor repairs. While the seamen were doubling the Number Two line, Joe stood by the edge of the deck and watched the greeters, both official and unofficial. He recognized two or three as wives, one of whom was the XO's. There was a group of six rather good-locking girls, all well tanned and wearing off-the-shoulder sundresses with brightly flowered leis around their necks.

There was a squeal from them, and one very shapely blonde waved and shouted in tones dripping with a Southern accent, "Paul! Paul, honey! Here I am, darling . . . ready whenever you are."

Joe looked down the deck to see his roommate waving back at them. He searched for the feminine voice he heard calling, "Joe, Joe Xylos" from the pier, and saw a vaguely familiar shapely blonde whose large breasts bounced as she waved at him. It wasn't until she was almost at the edge of the pier that he recognized Lyla Reeves, Rufus's date from the ill-fated weekend in Tijuana.

"Lyla, what are you doing here?"

"A little vacation. I flew out on United. Where's Rufus?"

"He's aboard. Come on board as soon as they clear the quarterdeck for visitors. I'll escort you to the wardroom, and we'll round him up for you. Lyla, I'm glad you're giving him another chance."

"Thanks, Joe."

Over his shoulder, Joe heard Rufus shout, "Lyla! Lyla, you could come!"

Before Joe could say a word to him, the doc rushed to the quarterdeck. He dashed to the brow just ahead of the sideboys who were forming for the Admiral's departure. He bounded ashore and swept Lyla into his arms, lifting her off the ground as the high trill of the boatswain's pipe sounded. Oblivious to the official party that walked past them to a black Navy sedan, Rufus and Lyla clung to one another.

After Joe watched their very passionate embrace, he checked the lines and secured his crew. On returning to Boys' Town, he saw that Paul Lawson had changed from his tropical whites into a light tan sports coat and brown slacks. His collar was smudged with bright red lipstick. The new Ensign asked, "Did you see my Mabeline out on the pier?"

"I don't know."

"She and five of her classmates are out here on vacation. We're meeting on the beach this afternoon. You're going to change and hit the beach now, aren't you?"

"Later. I've still got some loose ends."

"If we miss you on the beach, there's a party tonight. Here's the address. I passed the word around the wardroom. I'd like for you to come, roomie. An old teammate's giving them the run of his place. It's an apartment over a store down on Waikiki. You'll come, won't you?"

"Thanks, Paul. It sounds like a good way to celebrate our return to the land of the big PX. Where is this place?"

"Right on the main drag in Waikiki. They tell me you can't miss it. Don't wait until it's too late. We're going to be on the beach at Fort De Russy this afternoon. Come on down."

"When I can. I've got to proofread some reports for Harry Leach. The yeoman screwed up the last draft."

"Doesn't that guy ever let up on you? I was feeling sorry for myself that I got assigned to the Ops Department, but after seeing all the stuff you do, I count my blessings."

"It's really not all that bad. I've got to take care of Second Division and do most of the Training Officer's paperwork."

"Yeah, but you're an Ensign and the Training Officer is a Lieutenant.

I don't think Outside White knows what's going on in his division. People are always calling or coming here to ask for you. It isn't right."

"Oh, I don't know. That's why they have division Jay Ohs, to do the grunt work. If you're halfway smart, you'll work your boss out of a job. With Leach and White, it's easy because if I don't do it, it doesn't get done. Thanks for the invite, Paul. I need to get off the ship, and this is as good a reason as any. On the way west, we were in highest panic, getting ready for the Suez flap, so I didn't get time off to do much of anything. I'll see you out there later, buddy."

Over two hours later, Joe returned to his quarters with a stack of letters in hand. He placed them on his desk and opened the one with the earliest postmark first. As he read his way through the pile, he was distracted by a tirade from Carter Sawyer.

The Legal Officer threw a manila folder on his desk. "That damn bitch! Now I have to stay on board until the XO signs answers to these damn letters." His face was red, and his hands were shaking.

Looking up from his reading, Joe asked, "What's with you? I've never heard you swear before."

Carter swallowed, making his Adam's-apple cycle up and down. "I've got all sorts of problems. Lynda has screwed up my bank accounts. I'm overdrawn, and she passed bad checks at both the post exchange and the commissary. The worst of it is, when I called home, nobody answered."

"It's only three hours later since they're on Daylight Saving Time. Try back later after their dinnertime."

Carter pointed at the envelopes that cluttered the top of the Joe's desk. "How I envy your mail. I took one envelope to the post office for you, and she sends you one for every day we were underway. Lynda has written me only twice over the whole cruise—both times to complain about getting my money orders too late. You must really have something going with Eva."

"This is entirely a new experience for me. I've never carried on a relationship by mail before. She expresses herself very well. If you have a moment, I'd like to share this letter with you."

"Well, okay."

Joe read,

It's just after six a.m. I've been getting up early and watching the night turn to day. With the house so quiet, I've started each day reading and when you're at sea, re-reading your letters. Those twenty-two consecutive days of mail from Subic spoiled me. Earlier I wrote about the crocus pushing through the spring snow. Now they are in bloom and as I look out the kitchen window, the trees are budding. Life in this peaceful place is coming alive as this city girl has never seen it before. And within me, I felt the first twinges, I think. I am one with the earth. I feel complete and yet empty. Mama and Papa Villerouge are wonderful and full of love, but I fear the future raising the baby alone. Your letters are like a window on a beautiful rainbow that shines into my empty life. I would hate to think of life without them.

All my love, Eva."

Carter patted his roommate on the shoulder. "That was beautiful. I wish . . . Hell, I dread going back."

"Paul's invited the wardroom to a party. His honey is throwing it, and there are five, count them, five spare honeys with her. Why don't you come along?"

"No. No, I couldn't. It wouldn't be right."

"One other thing, Eva sent me a power of attorney so I can pick up Frenchy's car. Do you think it will pass muster?"

Lawyer Sawyer picked up the form and after brief study said, "Sure. It's a standard limited power. What are your plans?"

"I don't know. It all depends on whether orders for Sub School come through."

⊷━●─●━⊶

Late in the afternoon, Joe left the ship with Inside White and Tyler Cobb, who had taken over M Division from Joe. At Ty's insistence they took a cab to a Japanese restaurant, the Ishii Gardens. Much to Joe's surprise, the building could have been transplanted from one of the inns he had visited with Fumiko. Around them, loud American voices battered the rice-paper walls. When Ty gave his order in passable Japanese and the trio chose *hashi* (chopsticks) over silverware, service went from passable to superb.

When asked how his new job was going, Ty took a puff on his evil-smelling pipe and said, "I should have made this move over a year ago. I was going nowhere in the Gunnery Department. It's been down-right frustrating because Captain Sam only qualifies enough OODs to fill a one-and-five rotation. But having M Division has renewed my faith in the Navy. Henry Moran is a good man to work for. The one thing I get tired of hearing is that if my predecessor, who was only a Reserve Ensign, could do such-and-such in so many days, a regular Academy grad should do it in so many less. Joe, you've been a hard act to follow. I can't believe you got qualified as Engineering Watch Officer as quickly as you did. I busted my buns and just got my own watch after we left Yoko."

"It's hard to stand underway watches and do a lot of studying," replied Joe. "The one thing about being an Ensign and broke is that crawling around bilges in the evenings is far more intense than watching reruns in the wardroom. I'm glad it's working out for you. By the way, Ty, I never knew you were so deeply into things Japanese."

Ty looked around the all-but-bare room, then said, "Ishii Gardens is the last outpost of Japanese culture; I much prefer life on the other side of the Date Line. I've been selected for postgraduate school, so this may be my last trip. If my plans go right, I'll be an EDO on graduation. Maybe I can get shore duty at the ship repair facility in Yokosuka. Pearl wouldn't be a bad consolation prize either."

Inside White said, "EDO, Engineering Duty Only, those are the guys who never go to sea, right?"

Ty said, "There are some sea billets, and there's overseas shore duty. I was never cut out to stand on the bridge hour after hour."

Joe said, "We can shoot the breeze after we get going, but there's a party starting, and I'm dying to find out what kind of woman is attract-ed to young Ensign Lawson."

Larry White said, "It better be something special after all that crap he gave us in Yoko about polluting ourselves with degenerate, dis-ease-laden Orientals. And that line about the 'pure womanhood of the South.'"

Looking off into the distance, Ty said, "Little does he know. If I had the courage of my convictions, I would be bringing one back."

"This has the makings of a good old-fashioned *Beaverton* bash," said Larry. "I saw my alter ego, Outside White, taking a couple of cases ashore, so I know they won't be lacking for liquid refreshments. I've heard the tales about these bachelor orgies. And never had the nerve to take my wife. I'll go just long enough for a look and a few drinks. We'll be back in Long Beach in a week, and I'd rather not take any chances."

Ty said, "Friend, we aren't in the Land of the Rising Sun anymore. We aren't going to a skivvy house. They don't just flop on their backs. You have to seduce them."

"That's easy for you to say, but I'm married."

After a leisurely twenty-minute cab ride, the trio walked up a steep, narrow flight of stairs to a green door beyond which a stereo throbbed an earthy beat that wasn't familiar to Joe.

A tall, well-tanned blonde greeted them. She wore a blue patterned muumuu that billowed in the light breeze blowing out the door. Long, fine blonde locks that hung in the air like parts of a spider web partly hid one eye. She swept her mane back and over her shoulder with a jerking motion as Joe said, "We're from the *Beaverton*. Paul Lawson invited us. I'm Joe. This is Tyler Cobb and Larry White."

Almost exhaling her words, she responded, "Friends of Paul! I think everybody on the ship is here. We're all having a wonderful time. Come on in. I'm Solange."

The blonde introduced him to Al Mazini, a big, darkly tanned man wearing bright green-and-yellow Bermuda shorts. He said a quick hello, hardly breaking from dancing with a buxom brunette whose obviously bra-less breasts swung beneath her very thin T-shirt. When he tightened his arm around her waist, the bottoms of her cheeks peeked out from beneath the tail of the shirt. Solange explained that Al was officially the host. He was in the Athletic Department of the University of Hawaii as some sort of assistant football coach.

Around the room were more women, with at least two or three *Beaverton* men clustering around each of them. Larry whispered, "Paul Lawson is another man in the *Beaverton* tradition. The guy in Washington who assigns Navy jobs must have a special flag to identify them."

Ty sighed, "Something must have happened while I was away. I don't ever remember round-eyes like these."

Joe eyed the women one after the other, then said, "Don't kid yourself. Each one of those honeys is a baited trap waiting to slam shut on some unsuspecting bachelor. The trick is to taste the nectar before the flower closes around you."

Larry arched his eyebrows and smiled. "Joe, you talk a good line, but you sure passed the opportunities by on this cruise."

"Touche! You got me there. I'm no longer in the hunt." Joe pulled a beer from the cooler and worked his way across the room to where Harry Leach was talking to a short brunette. It was obvious from the way she pressed her back against the wall and kept looking around that Leach had not established a beachhead. The tubby Lieutenant blocked her from exiting the closed door that was just beside her.

As he drew near, Joe said, "Good evening, Lieutenant. Nice party."

"Hello, Joe. Melba, this is Ensign Joe Xylos, my Second Division Junior Officer. Joe, Melba Walker from Memphis, Tennessee."

"Hi, Melba. One bit of business, sir. Your reports were put into the XO's basket this morning. By the way, where's Paul?"

Leach said, "We put him in a cab and sent him back to the ship."

"Why?"

Melba, pressing her nose with an index finger and thumb, said, "He barfed all over Mabeline and the bed."

"Good grief! Poor Paul has done nothing but rave about Mabeline, and then he does this. Is she still here?"

The brunette pointed her thumb toward the wall behind her and giggled as she said, "She's in there getting cleaned up. We're cleaning up the bed too, so it's ready to use as soon as she gets herself put back together."

Leach momentarily stretched his mouth into a half-grin. The brunette grimaced and, turning away from the tubby Lieutenant, hooked one of Joe's arms. Brightly she said, "Want to go out on the terrace? You've got a nice tan for someone who wasn't on the beach this afternoon. Where were you?"

Joe stood looking toward Leach, whose bloodshot eyes registered only a blank expression. He poured half a glassful down his throat as Melba took Joe's hand and began pulling him toward the door. They stepped through onto a flat tar-covered roof. A refreshingly cool breeze momentarily caught her light muumuu, pressing it against a pair of very high, well-rounded breasts and framing the slim figure beneath.

Both cast furtive looks out of the corners of their eyes toward passionate sounds emanating from beneath a cover on a double-wide lounge chair where a couple were curled up. Behind them, the sound of the stereo throbbed in the tropical night air.

Joe and Melba continued to the front of the roof, where the street sounds balanced the party's uproar to make a general white noise. Releasing her hand, he leaned on the upraised roof edge and looked up and down the well-lit four-lane street in front of them.

Melba said, "You never answered my question."

"What?"

"Why weren't you on the beach this afternoon?"

"I had to take care of some paperwork for the boss. And then we went to a Japanese restaurant."

"Japanese restaurant? But you just got back from there. What's wrong with American food?"

"Nothing, but my friends wanted to go. You ought to try it, the Ishii Gardens. It was very good."

"You're different from the others. I can feel it. And not like your boss, the fat guy. What a creep! Glad I don't work for him. Thanks for rescuing me."

Joe swallowed the dregs of his bottle. "Didn't know that I did. But you're welcome. That's my specialty, rescuing damsels in distress. Tell me a bit about yourself, fair damsel. Do you live here, or is this a vacation?"

She tilted her head back and laughed. "Live here? I'd love to! No, we're here on vacation. We all lived in the same dorm at Tennessee and graduated midyear. This is the last fling before having to face the workaday world."

She took a bare foot and ran it up Joe's shin as she continued, "We're out here for fun and one last chance to be naughty."

Joe moved his leg.

"Are you married?"

"That's not a question to which you'll ever get a straight answer on the *Beaverton*. There was something else I was doing this afternoon. I was thinking about what I'm going to do with the rest of my life. I'm screwing up the courage to make a phone call."

"So you've got a girl back in Long Beach?"

"In Vermont. And I'm not even sure she'd be my girl. She's the widow of a shipmate."

She wrapped her arms around his waist. "Widow? There's a saying that a bird in the hand is worth two in the bush. We can still have a good time."

Joe looked back into the shadows, where the regular motions beneath the covers on the lounge chair caught his eye, before saying, "Melba, tomorrow I'll probably be kicking myself, but without pouring out a lot of ancient history, the answer is no. And no offense, please, it's definitely me, not you."

Her arms fell to her sides. Slightly sticking out her lower lip, the brunette said, "I was hoping you'd save me from the fat man. What'll I tell him?"

"Harry? Tell him to come back after he loses a hundred pounds. Say, there's Tyler Cobb. He's a bit shy, but he's a single john."

Joe waved to the figure standing in the open door. Ty strolled across the open roof toward where the couple stood. Melba lightly tossed Joe's empty beer bottle into the wire mesh trash basket standing at the curb below. It bounced off the inside and loudly disintegrated into a shower of shards, a few of which landed on the sidewalk.

She chirped, "My Daddy says I ought to have been born a boy so I could play basketball. Want to bet I can do it again?"

Ty said, "Basketball? Wouldn't make any difference. You're too short."

After making introductions, the brunette planted a loud, wet kiss on Joe's cheek and said, "Go make that phone call. And if there's nobody there, come on back for some real Southern hospitality."

He walked through the party and onto the sidewalk in the direction of Fort De Russy, where he'd been told there were pay phones at the Officer's Club. As the sounds of the party melted into the night noises of Waikiki, he heard two bottles crash into the sidewalk in front of the building.

After locating the phones, he realized that when it was ten-thirty p.m. in Honolulu, it was six hours later or four-thirty in the morning in Vermont. He loaded up on change at the desk. With pockets jingling, he paused at the door to the bar, but decided against waiting there for morning in the Eastern Daylight Time zone. He walked out into the warm night and sat down on a bench opposite the sand beach. There he remained in the half-light and watched the ocean. Frequently he checked his watch, then returned to his vigil.

Down the road from the fort, the party continued. Many of the revelers moved from the overheated confines of the apartment to the large, cool deck. Melba quickly attracted bettors who believed they could best her marksmanship over the trash can. The amount of broken glass on the sidewalk grew along with the thickness of the stack of bills in her hand.

⋯⋯◉ ◉⋯⋯

Citizens' reports of beer bottles being noisily smashed in the street brought the Hawaiian Armed Services Police, HASP for short, to raid the party at Al Mazini's. They poured up the narrow stairway, which was blocked by one man, Big Al himself. Right behind him were three of the girls. Loudly protesting that they had no authority to bother him, a civilian, Al forcefully opposed their entry by turning the lead man around and using him as a shield against the nightsticks of the others. In the dark, narrow stairway with its steep stairs, the five men learned what defensive linemen were taught in Coach Mazini's school of hard knocks. It was only after they fell back to the street that they were able to surround their adversary. Their swinging truncheons swiftly removed Al from the fight. One of the women snatched handcuffs from a patrolman. All three did their best to interfere with the arrest and continued until after Al was handcuffed and tossed into the paddy wagon. In the melee, nightsticks were tangled in loose muumuus or rough hands tore garments, which exposed bare flesh and resulted in more screams: partly nude females clawed and screamed as if they were about to be raped. More precious minutes were lost subduing them and tossing them into the paddy wagon, as well as assuring motorists who stopped that this was official HASP business.

The apartment in the moments following the HASP arrival was not unlike a nest of crabs uncovered under a rock at low tide. Doors banged open. People scrambled for clothes, with the instinct of self-preservation overcoming concerns for modesty. Out the kitchen window in back, down the creaking steel fire escape, and into the alley went one after another of the revelers. Some were barefoot. One paused in the shadows to don his pants. The first of the forces of law and order made it up the stairs to hear the metallic groans of the fire escape as the last escapees jumped and bounded toward the sounds of cars starting in the shadows.

They piled into the sedans like clowns at a circus. At one stoplight, six of them jumped into an empty taxi, and the load was again lightened into more cabs in front of the Reef Hotel. The Honolulu Police, alerted to the escape, pulled alongside one sedan with Melba and her friend Sandy riding in the front seat, but drove off satisfied without stopping them, missing the opportunity to find Ty Cobb on the floor in back.

When the Marine Major in charge arrived, one of his people came back down to report that the apartment was now empty. He returned to the paddy wagon to try and quiet the women, whose Southern-accented profanity and screams were proving to be a focus of the small crowd gathering on the street. He was relieved by the Honolulu Police, who put them into the back of a squad car and quickly drove them from the scene. The cops ignored Al's pleas to save him, a civilian, from abduction by the HASP.

With the disturbance below quelled, the Honolulu cops and the HASP searched the empty apartment. They examined a scattering of women's undergarments decorating one of the closets, a male sock on the kitchen floor, and some wet swimsuits and towels in one of the bedrooms. One suit was stenciled "LAWSON," and two of the white towels looked to be of military origin. Interest in further searching the rooms ended when one Shore Patrolman found the vomit-soiled bedclothes by sticking his hand into them. Partly filled glasses with ice cubes still in them were mute testimony to the swift departure of the occupants. The other clear evidence of any connection to the armed forces was a *Beaverton* cigarette lighter sitting on a pack of Marlboros.

The excitement ended and the lawmen departed, leaving the place in silence. Meanwhile, Leach and Mabeline were bundled together on the roof and escaped discovery. Well after the last of the HASP had left, they crept down into the darkened apartment and into one of the beds to complete what the raid interrupted.

Most of the escapees rendezvoused at the O Club at Pearl Harbor for one last drink before walking back to the *Beaverton* in twos and threes. When they got back, a quick muster showed that of those known to have been at the party, Harry Leach, Larry White, Ty Cobb, and Joe Xylos were missing. A quick call to sick bay revealed that Ensign Lawson was there, suffering from the combination of too much sun and too much beer.

⚓

It was fifteen past midnight, Honolulu time. Joe felt at peace listening to the chimes ringing in his ears as he fed each quarter into the phone. The harmonics had barely faded when he heard Eva's melodic voice. "Joe, Joe, is that you? Why are you calling now?"

"It's the middle of the longest, darkest night I've ever seen. I wanted to know if there's going to be a dawn."

"Yes, yes! A beautiful dawn. There was a very light rain during the night, and everything is so clean. The grass is getting green. You are so poetic . . . My dear friend, you bring me so much comfort. And light to brighten my days. It would have been so much more difficult without your thoughts and support."

"Eva, how are you getting on?"

"Fine.

"The power of attorney arrived in the mail today. Lawyer Sawyer says it's okay. I'll check with the people at the Supply Center about your car as soon as we arrive in Long Beach."

"Are you really calling all the way from Honolulu, Hawaii?"

"Yes."

"You are so clear. Almost like you were right here in Richford. When will you be back in Long Beach?"

"It won't be too long. I really can't tell you over the phone. Regulations don't allow it."

"Now, that I understand. The papers they sent me say that the ship carrying my car will arrive in Long Beach in early May."

"How about the insurance?"

"It's okay. Thanks for asking about it in your letter. The company is letting me keep the old policy, and they said it was okay for you to drive it across the country for me."

"It sounds like you've thought of everything. Eva, I've been giving you and me a lot of thought. I stopped at a party earlier tonight. My world has changed. I feel different. I left after just one beer and sat out by the beach thinking for hours. Eva, whether I take leave to drive back or I stop on my way to Sub School, I'd like to come courting. I don't want to rush the season, but I want to let you know that I want to be more than a friend to you and the baby."

"'Courting,' Joe? That's not a usage I know."

"Courting is the only word I could think of. To spend time together to get to know each other. No pressure, just to give us both the opportunity to decide if we want to go further. To give you time to heal and not feel rushed into anything. I promise I'll be on my best behavior. I want to be old fashioned like my father and save sex for after we're married, if that is to be."

"Oh, you want to date me! I don't know what to say."

"There's nothing you need to say. I want you to think about it. To get used to the idea. If it doesn't appeal to you, I'll understand. I never want to stop being your friend. If what I've said is awkward, please give me the benefit of the doubt. This is all new to me too. I've never said this to anyone, ever. I have to go. I'm out of time. I'll write."

"Thank you, darling Joe. You've given me a beautiful lift to start to the day. Goodbye."

CHAPTER 27

Frenchy's Widow's Dream

As Joe entered the Officer's Club bar, Larry White called him to his table. The XO, Stan Longstreet, and his wife Letty were sitting there.

As Joe slid into the seat, Larry asked, "Did you get through to her okay?"

"Sure did, and everything's coming along. She's felt the baby move. Hello, Mrs. Longstreet, Commander. It's a surprise to see you here so late, sir."

Longstreet said, "We're staying at one of the cabins. I reserved it on the way west. Very nice, actually. We just dropped by for a nightcap."

Letty said, "Joe, I didn't know you were married."

"I'm not."

She wrinkled her forehead. "Oh."

Larry said, "Eva Villerouge, Frenchy's widow, was pregnant when he was murdered."

"Oh, my stars! And you called her now! Why, it's the middle of the night in California."

Joe replied, "You caught me red-handed, Letty. However, the sun has just risen in Vermont, where she's staying with Frenchy's folks. She's all alone except for them. On the princely earnings of a single Ensign, a station-to-station phone call is all I can afford. My only choice is to call in the early morning there just after she gets up. Eva gave me power of attorney to pick up her car and drive it east. I need to be sure the insurance is okay.

Letty looked at Stan and asked, "Who is Eva Villerouge? And who is Frenchy? Stan, you don't tell me a thing. I didn't know we lost an officer on this cruise."

"Dear, I wrote you about the staff officer who married the Hungarian in Melbourne and was murdered by a sailor on Okinawa after he was detached. We put him up in the Jay Oh bunkroom with Mr. Xylos. Joe disarmed the man just after he shot Villerouge. I believe our own Joe Xylos will receive the highest decoration of any officer on this cruise."

She looked at Ensign Xylos. "Congratulations, Joe. Darling, I remember you wrote something about a marriage and sent me a clipping about a picket fence, but nothing about a murder."

Joe stared at the table before him. His voice was soft. "If Frenchy were alive, I would feel I earned it. The truth of it is that all I did was save my own neck. I'm no hero, sir."

Longstreet said, "Joe, none of us knows what he'd do, facing down an armed man who just killed someone. You have no reason to be so damn humble, boy."

Letty wrinkled her forehead again. "Stan Longstreet, you certainly gave me a different impression a short time ago."

"Letty—"

"You were sounding like Harry Leach . . . how you were apprehensive about Joe's knack for drawing trouble."

The XO studied the ice cubes in his glass. "Joe, I must confess and apologize. Earlier, I was relieved when you walked out of the club rather than sticking around. Call it self-preservation. It's been my observation that it's always somebody with you that falls in the hole."

Joe laughed. "Commander, what can I say? You're conveniently forgetting the six weeks I spent recovering from the torn Achilles tendon."

"That may be, yes, sir, that may be. It's just a feeling I have. Not long after you left the party, there were a couple of HASP people, a Marine Major and a Navy enlisted man, looking the place over very carefully. The thought crossed my mind that they were looking for you."

"Me! Why?"

"I don't know. It's just that you've made a number of my days memorable in ways I don't like to remember. If you know what I mean."

"Commander, I've hardly been ashore since Buckner Bay."

The XO smiled. "I know. I know. I've enjoyed the peace. Seeing you ashore tonight is almost enough to make me lie awake wondering what mess will explode in my face first thing tomorrow morning.

Joe frowned and shifted uneasily in his chair. *This has gone on far too long. What is he going to spring on me after breakfast?*

Longstreet put a hand on Joe's sloped shoulder. "I don't believe anyone in the Gunnery Department has said this. The Captain observed that Number Two turret has come a long way in the short time you've been up there. You do make a difference. They really shined during the exercises on the way into Yoko. What I appreciate the most is you managed to do it without any seamen asking for request masts on account of the kind of pressure old Boatswain Tallfeathers applies down on the shell deck. How did you do it, boy?"

"Discernible standards, sir."

"Discernible standards?"

"Yes, sir. The gun boss's memo established time spent on the drills as a standard . I made a minor modification: setting a standard that we achieve and maintain a loading rate roughly five percent faster than required to win an `E.' And I said nothing about how long it would take. I used some of my work study material and a lot of help from the old hands, those with World War Two experience, to teach the kids how to do their jobs right. Some of them resented the Boatswain's stopwatch, but I think the attention is making people work together."

"I've already heard about the stopwatch from the Chaplain, and I'd wondered where Tallfeathers got the idea."

Longstreet took a sip from his tall rum drink. After a pause during which he studied Joe, he turned to his wife and said, "Letty, if you told me after the Admiral's reception last fall that I'd be singing this man's praises, I would have told you to have your head examined. And if you'd said I'd have to ask him questions about what's going on with the Captain, I would have certified you nuts, but that's exactly what I'm going to do."

"Sir?" said Joe.

"Back in Yokosuka, he sent me to attend what was essentially a command performance luncheon put on by Commander Fleet Activities. I was the only XO there. Later I learned that he stayed aboard and had lunch with you and a guest."

"Yes, sir."

"Who was the young Japanese gentleman that you brought aboard to eat with the Captain?"

Joe fingered the napkin in front of him before asking, "I take it that Captain Slaxman hasn't chosen to discuss our meeting?"

"He has not."

"Sir, the matter was very personal, and I would prefer you to hear about it from his lips and not mine."

Stan cut the end off a cigar. "I halfway thought you'd say that. And I applaud you for your discretion, sir."

"Thank you, Commander."

"I hope you'll not take my question the wrong way. Captain Sam is as fine a commanding officer as can be found in human form. My job is to serve him and carry out his will. I have to understand what he thinks and wants. There have been some changes that have blindsided me since we left Yoko in January. For instance, the one that involved you and that oversize machinist. He's developed a real feeling for tolerance, race relations, that pushes right to the edge of Navy policy."

The XO rolled the end of the cigar in his mouth as if he were testing it. He put it in the crook of his finger as he continued, "The Old Man has an uncanny sense when it comes to judging people. Joe, what you stirred up with my Master at Arms distressed me terribly. I pleaded for Bail's stripe. The Captain told me to talk to two people. Both had been to mast; both were colored. One had passed the Chief's test like Richards, and both had been put on report by Bail. I talked to them. Suddenly I could see why there was so much open resentment by the colored who came up in front of the Old Man. My Leading Master at Arms was cooking cases! Informally I talked to witnesses and decided that there wasn't evidence enough to go forward. The Captain agreed with my recommendation not to carry the matter further. Bail will not get his stripe back, nor will he be recommended for re-enlistment. "

Larry asked, "What about those two men he railroaded?"

"We're doing what we can administratively to turn those cases around. Another thing . . . Captain Sam's feelings about swaps when we left for this deployment were uncharitable at best. Today, he spun me one hundred and eighty degrees. We have a storekeeper who put in a request for a swap so he could go back to WESTPAC and marry some Japanese girl. He had swapped his way onto the *Beaverton*. After

I checked 'no' on his application, Captain Sam personally made some calls today, and that Second Class is going to shore duty in Yokosuka."

Letty interrupted, "Really, Stan. That's miscegenation! I'm having a hard time seeing our boys marrying those Jap women after what they did us in the war—"

"Hell, woman, the war was over eleven years ago. And their women are attractive. Isn't that right, Joe?"

"Some of them certainly are."

"You took a bunch of leave back in January, didn't you?"

Joe hesitated before he replied, "Yes sir. It was an experience I'll never forget. I got to go to Tokyo and travel out in the country. We even stayed at traditional Japanese inns."

Letty said, "My, that must have cost you a bundle."

"We shared expenses, or I wouldn't have been able to do it."

Half-smiling, the XO lit his cigar. As he blew out his first lungful of smoke, he said, "I heard you climbed to the top of the original Fuji."

His wife said, "It must have been an arduous ascent with all that ice and snow in midwinter."

Larry suppressed a laugh, and Joe smiled. Longstreet smiled ever so slightly. "Now that's a sea story you don't hear too often. Of course there's something about a star and a single golden stripe that draws women like flies. If there weren't, there wouldn't be any happily married Commanders."

"Oh, Stan," sighed Letty. She was blushing, finally realizing that "original Fuji" must be code for a popular Japanese woman.

"Come on, Letty, dear, it's time to call it a night. Good night, gentlemen."

⋅⊷▣◉▣⊶⋅

Joe awoke to find Tyler Cobb standing next to his bed. "Come on, get up, or you'll sleep through breakfast."

Joe rubbed his eyes until they focused and shielded them from the bright incandescent light in the center of the passageway. "What in blazes are you doing here, Ty?"

"Shipmate, I came by to thank you for fixing me up last night. I don't think I've ever had such a fantastic night! Those two turned me every which way but loose."

"Two?"

"Melba and Sandy. We left the party together when the HASP came storming in."

"HASP?" Joe exclaimed. "They raided the party? Why? Have you gotten everybody bailed out?"

"Someone called in a complaint about beer bottles smashing in the street. As far as I know, nobody was arrested. Sean was the last out, and he said the place was empty. You should have seen us. Everybody piled into three cars. It was a panic! Getting back to last night, those two taught me things I never dreamed possible. I don't think I slept over an hour all night."

"You must be one buck well spent."

"I am. Believe me, I am. Little Melba was disappointed that you didn't come back. "

"I thought about it, but Inside wanted to come directly back to the ship, so we did."

"Well, how about it? Let's go back over. They're still at the motel. Sandy is more my type. I'm sure the Chief Engineer will let me off by ten. Okay?"

"By ten! How times have changed since I was a snipe! Thanks for the offer, Ty, but I don't think so. I talked to Eva last night, and I feel committed to her."

"Hell, she's on the other side of the world. This is the *Beaverton*, man! Nobody will tell her."

"You're right. I'm sure you're right, but I'd know . . . and that would be one person too many."

Across from Joe, a dark red arm moved and Paul Lawson slowly and painfully raised his bright red face from the pillow. He opened eyes that were only a degree less red than the skin around them.

As he stretched, he complained, "Damn, can't you people be quiet and let me die in peace?"

Joe asked, "How's the tummy, Paul? I understand you had an upset last night."

He moaned, "Ohhh, God, I lost her. Mabeline was mad as hell. I waited so long for last night . . . and then I threw up all over her."

Joe laughed. "Don't feel too bad about it. It goes with the territory. I barfed all over a guy in the O Club in Guam. It sounds like you're on your way to becoming a regular member in good standing of the *Beaverton* wardroom. You threw a party that drew the cops and—"

"You don't understand, I love Mabeline. She was my girl. I can't face her after what I did."

Ty laughed.

Joe said, "Paul, nobody I know of can control when or where they throw up. You were sick. It was an accident. You're not the first to mix too much sun with too much beer. Go out there today and beg forgiveness. If she's half the woman you say she is, she'll be full of sympathy. If she's not, you wouldn't want her anyway. And whatever you do, stay out of the sun and stick to Coke."

The lobster-colored Ensign slowly raised himself up to his elbows and rested his head in his hands.

Joe said, "Come on, Paul. Get up. There is another rule on this ship. If you don't make quarters, you don't get liberty."

"I don't care. I feel rotten."

"Get yourself vertical and take it slow and easy. Rinse your mouth out with water, but don't swallow any. Order some dry toast. Just take a sip or two with the toast. If you take it nice and slow, you ought to be back on your regular feed by lunch. But go easy."

Paul pulled himself to his feet and walked ever so slowly out of the room.

Ty waited until the door closed, then said, "After you left, Mabeline and Harry Leach were together. It was a case of the beauty and the beast. She is centerfold quality."

"He was with Melba when I came in, but that doesn't mean anything."

"After you left, the party moved out on the roof. Do you remember the loveseat-like lawn chair, a sort of double-wide chaise longue?"

Joe smiled. "The one with the spread on it?"

"Mabeline and Harry carried the cushion into the apartment, and that was the last I saw of them. Harry came aboard just ahead of me this morning. There was a spring to his waddle, if you know what I mean."

"That's pretty strong circumstantial evidence. Ty, I don't have the heart to tell Paul. Who knows, maybe she'll welcome him back with open arms. Would you check on Inside White? He had a few more than I did. I'll see you in the wardroom."

Half an hour later, Joe entered the wardroom. Eyes lifted from coffee cups and yolk-smeared plates to follow him until he sat down.

At the center table, the Operations Officer, the Chief Engineer, and the Chaplain rose from their seats and left, loudly talking about who caught the biggest fish the day before. The occupants of the outer port-side table whispered and watched them leave. One or two winced when the steward stacked the plates to remove them from the table. Joe nodded to them and got glares in return. He ordered breakfast and poured himself a cup of coffee.

Ty, wearing a lopsided grin, slid into the seat on his right. "Has a shave and a fresh cup of coffee cleared your head enough to change your mind about going ashore?"

"No."

Lieutenant Sean Perkins slid into the seat on the other side and jabbed Joe in the ribs. "You greasy little son of a bitch, why the hell did you call the HASP last night?"

Joe exclaimed, "What? I didn't call them! What on earth are you talking about?"

In a low voice, Perkins said, "You and your snipe friend left, and next thing we knew, they pulled up, sirens blaring. We damn near all got arrested last night. It was damn close! I could have lost everything, my career, my marriage. If it weren't for that crazy Al Mazini, we never would have made it out the window. I've never had much use for you, ever since you stuck that splintery fid up my ass."

"Sir?"

"You know, when you got me made Mess Treasurer with Harry Leach as Caterer. We were talking last night about all the bad luck people have with you on the beach. You're a damn liberty risk!

"Lieutenant, as I've told you before, you won the election fair and square. That was the majority vote of the Jay Oh caucus. As to who called the cops, it's hard for them not to be called when you keep breaking bottles on the sidewalk on the main drag of Waikiki. I heard them breaking almost all the way to Fort De Russy. If you're concerned about your marriage, then don't screw around."

"Look, smart ass, your bottle was the first one thrown."

"Oh, now, wait one bloody minute! It was that little brunette, Melba, who tossed it into the basket. Isn't that right, Ty?"

Ty looked from side to side, then smiled. "Well . . . that's right. Do you think little Melba caused all the trouble? I don't think she missed more than once or twice." He pointed at the others as he began to laugh. "Others of us weren't as accurate. It worked out okay, though, because she paid for the room with the winnings."

Perkins pounded his fist on the table, rattling the dishes. "Of all the damn fool stunts! I had no idea what was going on out there. It's only a matter of time until they come aboard and start asking questions."

Harry Leach had entered the wardroom while they were talking. He strode over to the table and whispered out of the corner of his mouth, "Sean, stop whimpering! If we keep our heads, nothing is going to happen. They don't know who we were. And Al Mazini isn't talking."

"Harry, we were worried sick about you! How did you get away?" exclaimed Perkins.

The chubby Lieutenant raised his eyebrows and smiled smugly. "Sean, I'm above running from trouble and smart enough not to put myself in compromising circumstances."

"But those HASP were swarming all over the place. Surely you didn't stay in the apartment?"

"Hell, yes, I spent the night there."

Perkins leaned back in his chair and looked down the table. His hands were shaking almost as much as his voice. "It's only a matter of time until they come out asking who was there. Why should we listen to you? You made a deal with them, didn't you, Harry?"

Blowing lightly on his big knuckles, the obese officer replied, "Do you think I'd do that to a shipmate? They never saw me: my companion and I were up on the roof. I must confess that there were a few moments of slight apprehension, but we managed to contain our passion, keeping out of sight until they all left."

Ty said, "Harry Leach! I've got to hand it to you, sir."

"It looks like most of the crew are here," said Leach. "Gentlemen, the best way to solve our problem is for everybody who was at the party to go ashore today and disappear. Leave as soon as you can. If you've got the duty, get a swap. Don't go near that apartment. Stay away from Waikiki. Come back late, the later the better, but don't miss movement. The *Beaverton* will be underway tomorrow at eight." He thrust his index finger at Joe. "No exceptions! That includes you and Inside White."

Leach took a seat at the head of the table and motioned to Paul Lawson, who entered taking little steps like an old man. After the sunburned Ensign eased himself into a chair, Leach repeated his instructions and then said, "I had a talk with Mazini. His attorney got a judge out of bed to issue a restraining order against the HASP."

Paul squirmed all the time Leach spoke until he couldn't wait any longer, then interrupted, "What happened to Al?"

"A knot or two on his head and a few bruises. He's all right. Three of the girls fared worse. This is the third time they've rousted him. He admitted that he had guests over, among them a teammate from the Volunteers, and that some bottles were knocked off the ledge, but maintains that the HASP didn't have cause or a warrant to enter his apartment. Now as long as we aren't questioned, he's home free. I'm sure we can count on his silence. Sometime today, they're going to come to the *Beaverton*. If no one is here to answer questions, the problem will blow away as the last line is taken in. The HASP can search this island from one end to the other come tomorrow morning. We must be on our best behavior today."

Joe asked, "Lieutenant, how do you know about this?"

"Al and the girls came back close to six this morning. We had a chance to compare notes and lay out a plan of action."

Paul said, "I don't want to go anywhere. I don't feel good at all. I want to go back to bed."

Leach lightly rested a hand on his shoulder, causing the Ensign to flinch. "Paul, Mabeline will meet you at Ewa Beach Park. Don't go near the apartment! And a little bit of advice. Keep that hide out of direct sun and go easy on the booze. Stick to shade and Shasta. With Mabeline, that shouldn't be too hard."

"Thank you, sir. I still don't understand what's happening. Why can't we go back to Waikiki?"

"After you left the party last night, it grew wild. All of your shipmates fled just before the cops and the HASP came. Nobody from the

Beaverton was caught. And no one need get caught if we keep our collective heads. Your friend Al is a true friend; he's going to take the heat. But for him to succeed, we've got to stay clear of him. As long as they can't tie him to anybody in the service, we'll be in the clear."

"But I left my swimsuit and towel out there."

"Come by my stateroom and pick them up. That goes for the rest of you. There was a pack of Marlboros and a lighter too. Let's everybody get to quarters. Keep your heads up, gentlemen!"

⊷⊙⊶

The officer's country was deserted by shortly after ten except for the Duty Section and the XO's office, where Commander Longstreet and his Administrative Officer, Lieutenant Barry Tumwater, had worked their way through the bulge of paper that was dispatched while the *Beaverton* was en route to Hawaii. What occupied the mind of the XO was the opportunity to spend a quiet afternoon and evening with his wife after their many months apart. However, after his lunch was interrupted by a Marine Major from the HASP, he couldn't deny that something was wrong.

After the exchange of greetings, the XO thought the Major's voice, deep and resonant though it was, had the tones of a man who was not asking, but begging, "Do you have a man aboard your ship named P. Lawson? We think he's a larger fellow, an officer. Do you have such a man?"

I've earned the time to be with Letty. I should have been informed if it was serious. The XO made an effort to look the Major in the eye. "I've received no reports. What has he done?"

"We were called by the local police about beer bottles being tossed off a second-story roof by military personnel. The civilian who resisted arrest has hired an attorney. We need to verify that there were military personnel there."

"Yes, we have a new Ensign, who reported aboard in Yokosuka, a Paul Lawson. His first duty station. On arrival, he was met by a group of young women. Was he involved in an altercation, a violation of the UCMJ?"

"I don't know. Is your Ensign a big man, blond hair, played football at the University of Tennessee?"

Stan deepened his Southern accent as he replied, "He is a good Southern boy, a very handsome young man, and I think he said something about being a Volunteer when I interviewed him just after he came aboard. What is the nature of his offense?"

An officer volunteered, "Pardon me, Commander, Lawson's on liberty. In fact, everybody but the Duty Section is ashore."

The Major raised his voice. "Everybody is ashore? Commander, what the hell is going on? I need to talk with him to unravel a very embarrassing incident. It involved a number of my people over in Waikiki last night. Would it be possible for me to talk with him today?"

"When he returns from shore leave, certainly," answered the XO. "All the wardroom is on shore leave except the Duty Section. This is our last day in port before heading home at the end of a long deployment. I was just about ready to leave myself. Major, I'll put my Master at Arms and personnel man at your disposal. Let's see what we can do to help you."

Ten minutes later, the Marine Major smartly saluted Commander Longstreet and eased his large six-foot-four frame into the Navy-issue chair beside the XO's desk. After lighting a cigarette, he said, "Let me share with you why I need to talk with your Ensign Paul Lawson. We received a complaint that a sailor in civilian clothes had barfed all over one of their cabs. The fare had been picked up at 1516 Ala Moana Drive. We had a patrol wagon in the area, plus an officer in a sedan. They saw a bunch of people who were in civilian clothes, but looked like military, tossing bottles off the roof of a store at 1516 Ala Moana Drive. The three from the wagon, followed by the two from the sedan, charged up the stairs to an apartment on top of the store. And here is where it all fell apart."

"How's that?"

"They met one Alfred Mazini, line coach for the University of Hawaii. With bare hands, he stood up and stopped five of my people. I have an airman in the hospital with a broken collarbone and numerous contusions. The marks are all from our own nightsticks. The officer, recognizing a stalemate, ordered his people back down the stairs. This brought Mr. Mazini onto the street, where we subdued him with force. There were three women on the stairs behind him, and they joined in the melee. They suffered injuries and torn garments. Unfortunately none of them were wearing any underclothing.

"My, oh my, *we*? Then you were personally involved?"

"Yes, sir, and the fracas quickly drew a crowd of spectators. The women were arrested by the Honolulu Police on a number of charges. The HASP and the Honolulu cops went into the apartment. No one was there, but there were ample signs of a hasty exit. The only piece of clothing we found that could be identified was a swimsuit with the stenciled name 'Lawson,' the same name given to the cab company. We need to talk to him."

"Why? Obviously he wasn't there."

"Yes sir, but this command is in boiling hot water. Mazini's attorney got a federal district judge out of bed last night to issue a restraining order. The best looking of the three, a tall blonde named Solange, bared a breast that had been solidly whacked with a truncheon. It wasn't a pretty sight. In my time in the Corps, I felt that I had my ass chewed by experts, but when that judge finished with me, I knew I had been reamed. I don't think he left a stone unturned, from the Magna Charter to the Nazi death camps. I never want to go through that again."

"Then your people were off base?"

"I have no doubt that they overacted in what they did to Mazini, and especially to the women. We can straighten out the way our people act. But I have a federal district judge who wants blood. I'm sure there were military people, people from your ship, at that party. I need to provide evidence that the HASP had probable cause to take the action they did. But I have to prove it."

"You need to know who was at the party, good luck."

"Commander!"

"I've been through this before with my 'bad seed,' a misfit draft-ee officer. Thankfully, he left the Navy when we were in Yokosuka." Mentally he added, *And I'm sooo glad to be shut of you, Milt Kane.* "However, I still have a resident Jonah who has the knack of igniting a powder train. On detonation, he has a history of being well clear and innocent when the inevitable explosion occurs. Last night, he was sharing a table with me and my wife at Fort De Russy." The XO stared his guest down before he continued, "Major, here is your problem in a nutshell. In order for you to get what you want, someone must come forward and say he was there. After he does that, Captain Slaxman is going to hang him by his thumbs. The net result is that everyone you talk to will say nothing."

"You mean this has happened before?"

"Regretfully, yes. Just before we left on deployment, the Long Beach police mounted a regular operation. Surrounded the place before they moved out. And for the first time, they got them all except one. Our Jonah was lucky enough to be across the street on the beach with a girl."

"Damn! I felt that it was a set-up deal. You see, this is the third time we've tangled with Mazini. They stopped him once, and he created a scene. And then he was arrested for violating a curfew that was imposed after the crew of the *Thetis Bay* went on a rampage on Waikiki. Mazini looks like he's in the service; I don't understand how he could have been deferred."

"Maybe the guy's a queer."

"Not likely. He always goes around town with two or three young things on his arm. His attorney is threatening a civil suit and undoubtedly significant damages. I'm not interested in rolling any of your people's heads. I just want to keep my own."

Longstreet relit the cigar that had been sitting in his ashtray. "You may not be interested in rolling heads, but I can assure you that I am. I'll be damned if I'm going to have to listen to any more lectures from my boss after he has had another audience with the Admiral because of this wardroom's drunk and disorderly ways. Major, my command duty officer will call you as soon as Mr. Lawson is aboard. You may have full access to him until we get underway. Press your investigation. Give me the names of any other individuals whom you suspect were at this party. Send me a report of this incident. I'll do all in my power to help you, son."

"Thank you, Commander."

"But don't get your hopes up, boy. I've never cracked one of these before."

CHAPTER 28

The Clap Epidemic

The next morning, just after the special sea and anchor detail was called, Joe watched a yellow Ford convertible screech to a stop on the pier. Paul Lawson reached across, cupping the blonde driver's breast in his hand, and gave her a long passionate kiss. He jumped from the car, sprinted across the short distance to the brow, and disappeared below decks.

As Paul sped by the bollards where Number Two line was secured, Joe gazed up to the port wing of the bridge where Harry Leach stood. Leach smiled and gave Joe a thumbs-up signal, then turned to face the pier and waved to the blonde in the convertible. She blew him a kiss before driving off.

Stan Longstreet stood at the edge of the "01 level," the deck just above the main deck, chewing the butt of his cigar. . He was puzzled about the exchange of signals between the blonde and Leach after the very passionate leave taking. Technically Paul was late returning aboard, but not by more than a couple of minutes. He wasn't the first officer to be brought to dockside in such a rush. His late arrival left no time to notify the Marine Major, which Longstreet figured was just as well: perhaps the whole thing would blow over with their departure. Longstreet made a mental note to have his Operations Officer give Ensign Lawson a good chewing-out.

After the sea detail was secured, Legal Officer Carter Sawyer passed Longstreet a copy of the previous day's Honolulu *Star-Bulletin*. In it was a three-line item about the incident with Coach Mazini and the HASP. There was no mention of the *Beaverton*, and for that the XO was grateful. The current day's paper had a quote by an obviously liberal attorney, and the tone of the story gave all the armed services a black eye, with the Marine Major as the main villain. Mentally the XO pictured Harry Leach running from the HASP, and he chuckled to himself.

After the sea detail, the XO met with Ensign Paul Lawson and got his story. Al Mazini, said Paul, graduated from Tennessee Tech a year ahead of him. Both played football, Al as a defensive guard and Paul as a running back. The Ensign had invited most of the *Beaverton's* junior officers to join him at the beach and later at the party at Al's apartment. He and Mabeline had reached the apartment ahead of the others and went to bed. He awakened feeling very sick. After he threw up, someone called a cab, which took him back to the ship. He got sick and threw up again in the cab. He didn't remember who was there. He was vague about who was on the beach in the afternoon. He had been in the bedroom with Mabeline until the cab arrived. One of her girl friends had helped him downstairs to the cab. He had no idea who came over to the apartment. He didn't learn what happened to his friend until he met him the next day. He wasn't there during the HASP raid, and he would say no more.

The XO informed Commander Wyman that if there was to be an investigation of the Waikiki incident, he would appoint him as the investigating officer. He didn't want to delve into it unless circumstances demanded. However, the speech he gave to the wardroom before the noon meal ruined more than one appetite. He concluded by threatening a fate worse than death to the first officer who was involved in any scrape with the law once they were back in Long Beach.

⊷⊷⊙⊜⊶⊶

From the second day out of Pearl, the atmosphere in the wardroom grew more and more tense and hostile. There were some waspish exchanges that just didn't seem right for the last days of a deployment. The XO dismissed them as symptoms of cabin fever, although it greatly surprised him that the bookish and professorial Tyler Cobb could build up such a head of steam. The reason for Ty's ill temper came clear in Boys' Town when he stood at Paul Lawson's bunk, which was right by Joe's, and shouted, "Pure Southern belles, horseshit! I've got the clap. Thank God I don't have a wife waiting for me."

All Paul said was, "I'm sorry. I guess you should have used a rubber."

After Ty left, Joe queried Lawyer Sawyer, who forecast that there would be an investigation when they returned to Long Beach. "I imagine," opined Carter, "that what the Marine Major is looking for is a way to get off the hook. A list of names would be enough."

Joe said, "Isn't that as good as a confession?"

"Not if it's limited to names. The HASP needs names of military personnel who were present to counter any legal action against them for trying to arrest Mazini. If there is an investigation, they're going to be questioned. But everyone is protected by Article 31."

"Carter, are you sure? I wasn't there for the grand finale, but I don't want to have to fight my way out of another *Beaverton* screwup. I've got too much to lose."

"Hell, Joe, you're one of the few straight arrows. Remember, you were with the XO when this all happened."

Joe got back to Paul and relayed what Sawyer said. He assured him it would be all right and the furor would die down once the list of names was provided.

⊷▭◉ ◉▭⊶

On the afternoon of the fourth day out, Doc Johnson placed a green can of "crab powder" on the XO's desk, saying, "This is yours, Commander. Use it often and liberally."

Wrinkling his brow, the XO said, "What? Why would I need this?"

"For the first time this cruise, XO, we've got a serious public health problem in the wardroom. Thirteen crab lice infestations and one case of the clap. One of them shares your head."

"Thank you, doctor. Thirteen cases, ouch! Are any of them married?"

"Yes, sir, including the clap case."

"Would this have anything to do with the party in Waikiki that nobody from the *Beaverton* attended?"

"Unfortunately, yes. Commander, it's going to be a bad day in Long Beach for a number of our married officers: some deservedly and others who have the ill fortune to live next to someone who has crabs. Boys' Town appears to be the worst hit. I'm issuing crab powder to every officer on board."

"Would you say that all thirteen brought the crabs on board?"

"Eleven for sure, sir. It's like that notorious outbreak at Olongapo a few years ago, all over again. There were seven women, all of whom were infested. From prior experience, I predict this clap case will be the first of many on this cruise."

"Damn!"

"Two claimed that the women didn't want to use condoms. Judging by the number of contacts per woman, it was an orgy. Thank goodness Lyla came to Hawaii or there, but for the grace of God, go I."

"Wasn't it you who said, 'Anything they've got, I can cure?'"

"I can, but my worst fear is that we'll arrive in Long Beach before it incubates. Could you, in a low-key way, pass the word to the department heads about the necessity of immediately seeking treatment, more or less retelling the policy that we put out to the crew at the beginning of the cruise?"

"I'd be glad to. Thank you, doctor."

"One last item, Commander. I'm convinced somebody up forward is sitting on a case of the crabs instead of reporting for treatment, because the two people who came down with crabs today were only lightly infested and definitely weren't at the party."

"Rufus, that's a good report, boy. Sounds like you have a handle on this situation. Keep me informed."

The tension continued to build. Harry Leach barely kept himself under control when someone called the *Beaverton* a "crab town." Sean Perkins, whose macho attitude was his calling card, seemed out of place sitting in his chair in the wardroom with tears streaking his cheeks.

The air of expectancy was mixed with an air of dread with each turn of the ship's screws. The crabs marched invisibly from bunk to bunk. Or maybe from toilet seat to toilet seat. The married men seemed to move about in a cloud of crab powder and were mavens of cleanliness. Henry Moran groused about the high usage of fresh water and threatened water rationing to ensure an adequate supply for field day on the day before arrival at Long Beach.

The butt of their anger was Paul Lawson. He withdrew into silence toward everyone but Joe, whom he cursed and threatened.

The countdown to the end of the deployment continued. Joe was in

Combat on the four-to-eight watch when the radarman announced that he had picked up land, mountains along the California coast, on a long-range scan. As they plowed eastward, the ship was rolling in seas that were heavy for so late in the year. As the watch ended, he read a message that directed the formation to lie to in the lee of Santa Catalina Island for final preparations prior to entering Long Beach the following morning. He made his way to the wardroom through knots of sailors who grumbled over the delay.

Through the afternoon, all hands were busy holding field day, the term for a maintenance session to bring the flagship up to its sparkling best. By the time the boatswain's pipe sounded to secure the ship from field day, everything was in place for a triumphant entry the following morning with awnings stretched over the quarterdeck.

Joe returned to the wardroom to wash before the evening meal. Walking down the darkened space between the bunks, he heard a groan from Paul, whose body was balled into fetal posture beneath his bedspread. Joe turned on his bunk light and looked across to catch a momentary glimpse of his roommate's reddened eyes and tear-streaked cheeks before he buried his head under the covers.

Xylos placed a hand on his back, softly saying, "What's wrong, Paul?"

"Go away."

"It sounds like you're hurt. Come on, tell me."

"I can't."

"Paul, Tyler Cobb told me he caught the clap from that girl I introduced him to. Do you have some signs?"

"Shut up."

"You can't hide this stuff. Besides, the longer you go without treatment, the worse it becomes."

He pushed his head farther under the covers.

"Paul, we live too close together on this ship. Either you take yourself down to sick bay or I'm going to ask Rufus to make a house call. Look, we both know where you got it. Not getting it treated isn't going to change things between you and Mabeline. Stop kidding yourself. Cut your losses. She's not your one and only if she gives you something.'"

Paul flipped the covers back from his head and turned over. "You damn little greaseball! If I didn't hurt so much, I'd break your skinny neck. You're the one who talked up the idea of the list of names. I betrayed my best friend, Al Mazini. It's your fault!"

Joe backed away, then walked to the phone where he dialed Rufus Johnson.

Just before dessert, Rufus entered the wardroom and paused by Joe to say, "You were right, Lawson was loaded with crabs. I hope he's the last."

⋅⊷⊷⊙ ⊙⊶⋅

Joe took his place on the quarterdeck as the JOOD beside Lieutenant Perkins as OOD. Dour and grumpy, Sean said, "I feel like a man given a one day's reprieve before hanging. Duty on the first day will buy me a little time. If I'm lucky, she'll be on the pad. If I'm not, it's going to be the end."

"Do you still have crabs?"

"I wish it was that simple. Damn coed gave me the clap!"

"Ohhh! How long will it be before you're cleared up?"

"I don't know, but I'm not going to take any chances. Damn that stupid Ensign!"

The air had been scrubbed so clean by a predawn squall, which accompanied the passage of a cold front, that the mountains surrounding Los Angles were visible for the first time since Joe came aboard. He welcomed temperatures so cool that the material of his dress white uniform felt a little light.

With the aid of tugboats and, later, the crew heaving on the mooring lines, the *Beaverton* inched the last few yards until it was tied up portside to the USS *Toledo*. What had been indistinct faces in the crowd could now be picked out as loved ones, who waved and shouted across the lessening distance. It was Joe and Sean's headache to pick out the official visitors among the crowd of wives and children, because it was their duty to see that VIPs were announced as they strolled onto the *Beaverton* from the *Toledo*. A Navy band clustered on the level above the main deck, looking somewhat like Salvation Army veterans but playing with stentorian authority. Their repertoire of Sousa marches built the excitement of the homecoming for the first two times they were played. By the third time, they were reminding everyone of how long it was taking to double up the lines and secure the sea detail.

While family and loved ones poured over the after brow, the pomp and circumstance of arriving and departing flag officers held the officers' wives on the sidelines until after the last wail came from the boatswain's pipe and the sideboys returned to their benches. Joe took his usual position on the starboard quarterdeck, where he gave signals to the Boatswain who announced the official visitors over the ship's general announcing system.

With the initial rush of people, a man wearing a somewhat wrinkled business suit found his way to Joe and said, "I'd like to see your Legal Officer, a Mr. Sawyer."

"May I tell Mr. Sawyer the nature of your business?"

"It's privileged information that I can only discuss with him."

"Very well."

Joe directed the messenger to call the wardroom and returned to the port side. About five minutes later, Carter stepped onto the quarterdeck. "Who is this Tom Sayles, Joe?"

"Didn't say. Some civilian attorney, I guess. He asked to see you. I assume it's about one of your problem children."

"I haven't even seen my wife, and these guys are showing up—"

Sayles all but vaulted across the deck. "Mr. Sawyer, Mr. Carter Sawyer?"

"Yes . . ."

"I have a summons here for you." He shoved the envelope into Carter's hand and fell back.

"You can't deliver this here. Not on board. Not like this. What's this all about?"

The man let his voice drop almost to a whisper. "It's regarding a divorce action. What the hell, all you guys screw around overseas. And no doubt the little lady didn't like it."

Carter swallowed two or three times as he blinked away tears. He drew his hand back, folding it into a fist, paused, then crumpled the unopened envelope with the other. The man backpedaled toward the brow until Carter turned on his heel and walked away with his shoulders bent.

The agent turned to find himself facing Joe, who pushed the end of his long glass into the man's stomach. "You know better than to deliver a summons on board! If it were up to me, I'd heave you over the side and let you swim back. Do you get paid extra to rub salt in the open wounds?"

"No offense, I thought—"

"You didn't think! Take this message back to Lynda. She's tying a can to one of the few decent married johns on board. He remained one hundred percent faithful on this cruise. Of all the people on board, he least deserved this. Now get out of my sight!"

Sayles raised his hands, palm up, as if testing for rain. "How the hell should I know? I'm just doing my job. Obviously the lady wants out."

About an hour later, a sailor, with a small boy of three or four clutching his hand, said, "This little fellow is lost. He says he is Freddy Gibbons, but we don't have anybody on board by that name. The Boatswain said to bring him here and ask that you pass the word on the 1 MC for his parents."

The small hand clutched Joe's with a warm, sweaty grip that was slightly sticky from the lollipop whose stick dangled from his mouth. They stood in the athwartships passage between the port and starboard quarterdecks as the pipe wailed over the loudspeaker and the gravelly baritone of the Boatswain announced, "Will the parents of Freddy Gibbons lay up to the starboard quarterdeck? He lost you."

Joe stood facing the brow. Until this moment, he had enjoyed the cool breeze that funneled through the passage. Then he saw Eva step from the brow onto the teak deck. *What? Is this a dream?* He was acutely aware of the chill playing down his back and across his neck when he first saw her. She had one arm raised to hold the front brim of a large white hat, turned down to shade her eyes. She wore a white high-waisted dress that accentuated her full, high, cantaloupe-sized breasts and her watermelon-sized tummy. She had lost little of her athletic grace with her pregnancy. Before she passed into the shade beneath the awning, the long, curled, blonde locks framing her face sparkled in the bright sun.

Their eyes met. Her steps across the deck seemed like slow motion. Halfway across, she pushed her hat back so that her eyes caught the light and turned from brown to green when she passed through a finger of sunlight beaming through a seam in the canvas awning. Eva fell into his arms, leaning over and resting her head on his shoulder. Her hug was so powerful that it almost squeezed the breath out of his lungs.

At his side, Freddy said, "Hey, mister. This ain't my mother. I want my mother."

Falling back, she looked down as Joe said quickly, "Don't worry, he's not mine! Part of the job: lost children. Watch out for the lollipop. He got separated from his folks."

Eva laughed. She put a hand behind Joe's head and kissed him lightly.

From the corner of the quarterdeck, Harry Leach snapped, "What the hell are you doing, Mr. Xylos? You are on watch! Your job is not to personally greet the crew's dependents, but to facilitate their meeting their loved ones."

Eva said, "He is my good friend."

Leach stared at her belly, snorted, and walked away shaking his head.

After they embraced, she said, "I had to come. Hold me . . . I feel empty . . . so alone."

"Later . . . Harry's right. I am on watch and must play the role. Eva, I never dreamed that you'd be here! I'd like to be with you. Would you mind waiting for me in the wardroom? It won't be too long until I'm relieved."

"You're not angry that I came?"

"Surprised, yes. Angry, never . . ." With a hand signal to the seaman standing nearby, Joe said. "Messenger, take Mrs. Villerouge to the wardroom."

Once in the wardroom, Eva sat on a couch that was squeezed between the outboard dinner table and the bulkhead. She picked up a magazine from the end table and began to thumb through it.

After Eva had almost finished her second magazine, Leah Leach rose from a table halfway across the room. She maneuvered between tables with a coffee cup rattling on its saucer until she sat down next to the blonde. "I don't believe we've met before. I'm Lieutenant Harry Leach's wife, Leah."

"Hello, I'm Eva Villerouge."

"Villerouge? Is your husband new on board? I don't recognize the name."

"I have no husband on board. I—"

"Really! And who are you here to meet, your brother?"

Eva pushed a finger into the hollow of a curl and stretched it fully until it swung free and recoiled itself. She lowered her eyes and after a pause that Leah would later describe as "pregnant," said in a low, melodic voice, "No. I'm here to see Joe Xylos. He asked me to wait here until he is finished with his watch."

"And where did you meet Joe?"

"In Melbourne."

Leah eyed the front of Eva's dress as she held out the coffee cup. "Really. Would you like a cup of coffee?"

"No, thank you. Not while I'm pregnant."

"Really?"

"Would you give a baby a drink from your cup?"

"Of course not!"

"Then why should I do that to my baby?"

"That's novel. Where did you get that kind of idea?"

"I must be careful. This child is special."

"The first one always is. And I suppose that you're here, expecting that Joe will marry you."

Eva looked away, and her eyes momentarily clouded. "Someday, when the time is right, I . . ."

"Someday. Someday! You don't have that much time. Were I you, I wouldn't count on that unprincipled greaseball. He is a walking example of the lowest human common denominator. He is trouble with a big capital tee. You know, the first time I met him, he was with this harlot who rubbed herself with an ice cube that she put into MY drink."

Eva said, "How embarrassing."

"And he has been into one scrape after another. Did he ever tell you about leaving Captain Nuslund's daughter to rot in the Tijuana jail?"

"No."

"Before the ship left, he was into one scrape after another. And from the things Harry has written, it was even worse overseas. I understand that after he was involved in the death of an officer on Okinawa, he was kicked out of the Engineering Department where he had been a division officer and placed under Harry as a junior division officer. And the troubles he's caused my husband! How they can they let an Ensign, and a Reserve Ensign at that, get away with all that he has? Poor Harry. He's leaving the Navy at the end of next month, not even sure that he'll be getting into the Reserves. Why would you ever want to tie up with him? He is an albatross if I have ever seen one."

Eva opened her purse and pulled a worn white envelope from between her wallet and compact. She frowned as she began, "I can't understand why Joe would get in trouble over Frank's death. Everyone said he was very brave . . . a hero. He was a good friend to my husband and after his murder, a comfort to me."

"You mean that you're the widow and you . . . Oh, forgive me. I had no idea. It's just that Joe has such a reputation. He worked in burlesque brothels and even brought a stripper to an Admiral's reception. You will forgive me?"

Eva, pointing at her expanded belly, laughed for the first time. "Did you think? . . . Oh, no, Frank and I found out I was expecting right before it happened. Joe was the first to know."

"Really . . ."

"He and Joe were good friends. Joe was best man at our wedding. I've never heard these stories you told about him, but I've seen him in action. I wouldn't be here today if it weren't for what he did for me in Melbourne. He put his life on the line to stop this crazy man, to keep my Frank out of danger when he was drunk. But Frank tried to play hero with an unloaded gun and got himself killed. Before I left Okinawa, they told me that Joe would be recommended for a medal for his bravery."

"A medal! I never heard anything about that. Eva, be careful. He lives right on the edge. I don't know how many people have come into grief by just being around him. He's really big trouble, As Harry says, 'a liberty risk.'"

Eva removed from the envelope a sheaf of lined paper, which was worn and the top piece tearing along one of the folds. She studied the writing as she said, "I have no reason to doubt what you say about Joe. There is another side to him. It's the side I know. I'm all alone in this country . . . in this world, and he reached out to me. Over these months, he has filled my mailbox with beautiful thoughts and concern for me. I was a stranger, and he has made me welcome. His words have been a balm for the open wounds of my loss."

Leah drew her little finger along her eyebrow and then played with her coffee cup. "I had no idea."

"Here let me read this, I don't think Joe would mind:

Dear Eva,

We are scant days from leaving Yokosuka and turning east across the Date Line. This evening I went to the club with Carter and the Chaplain. We took in a movie on the base. It was a musical with Gene Kelly. Afterward we walked back to the ship through one of those warm spring evenings that make you wish to have a girl in your arms. I believe I said as much and the good old Padre reminded me that I had, over these past months, become a member of a select minority who weren't spending the nights on the beach. And he's right, because for the first six weeks after we left Okinawa, I wasn't getting about well enough to go ashore. And by then, maybe it was because we were at Subic and more likely because I have come to see the world through different eyes. Following Frenchy's death, I said I'd take care of you and I still mean it. Only I have to be realistic. I remember the day we met. You only had eyes for Frenchy and I'll never speak four languages and look like a matinee idol. My hope is that we can always be friends because I would be honored to be an uncle to the child you carry . . .

Love, Joe."

Leah dabbed her eyes. "That was beautiful. And you came here because of this letter?"

"The letter and then the phone call from Hawaii . . . all the way to Vermont. He called me at six in the morning, asking me if there was light at my end of the tunnel . . ."

"Vermont? Where in Vermont?"

"Richford. It's close to the Canadian border. I was staying with Frank . . . ah . . . Frenchy's family."

"Frenchy Villerouge . . . The name is sort of familiar. What did your late husband do in the Navy?"

"He was a Lieutenant, a line officer. I'm not sure what he did on the *Beaverton* before we met, but after we married, he was the White Beach Officer on Okinawa."

"You must be mistaken. There was no Lieutenant Villerouge on this ship."

"He had a special job on CINCPAC Fleet staff in Hawaii."

While the women were talking, Filipino stewards cleared the tables in the center of the room and spread fresh white linen tablecloths. While they were still setting the table, a short, somewhat overweight steward walked forward, pounding a small mallet on a set of gongs.

Leah jumped to her feet at the first tone. "Noontime already! I've got to wash up. Please excuse me."

⊷━◉━◉━━⊷

Everyone was seated at the table, with Harry Leach at the head, when Joe walked in. He slipped easily into an empty chair halfway down the table. He gently squeezed Eva's hand, and a slight smile colored his lips. "A morning in the sun sharpens the appetite, and delightful feminine company makes the first meal in port special. What special consolation prize is being offered to the Duty Section today?"

Leach, with his head down, glared at Joe through his eyebrows. "Mr. Xylos, we are having chicken a la king. And I'm at a loss as to why you would be so damn happy when you have the duty on our first day in port. It's downright annoying! Surely it couldn't be the presence of your . . . er, ah . . . companion?"

Joe pulled a printed letter from inside his whites and passed it to his boss. "Sir, some days were made for smiling. Let me give you the good news that you will have at least a few days' peace before you are detached at the end of June. Here are my orders for Sub School. I've got to be there by 8 July."

The Lieutenant's bearpaw hand snatched the letter from the table. "What! Shi—! Figures . . . Well, congrat-you-lay-shuns, Mr. Xylos."

"Thank you, sir."

Leach tossed the letter back on the table, where it landed with its corner in a butter dish. Between clenched teeth with his lips barely apart, he muttered, "They must be desperate to take schlock like him."

Joe smiled and, raising his water glass, said, "Thank you, sir. I certainly appreciate the continuing vote of confidence you so nicely voiced. And having served in your shadow, I've come to appreciate some of the good things in life you've brought to this wardroom . . . like crab . . . a la bungalow."

Paul Lawson, who was seated alone at the far end of the table, dropped his fork loudly on his plate. A number of the chairs around the table creaked. Leach nearly choked on his coffee, spraying droplets over the rim of the cup.

He was still dabbing his lips when Leah said, "Harry, why, that's one of your favorite dishes. Do you mean that you put it on the menu here? It must have cost a fortune to get fresh crab flown in. You never told me."

Lieutenant Perkins gave a thumbs-down gesture. "It wasn't fresh, it was canned."

Joe said, "Yes, but it had promise that even lousy canned crabs couldn't disguise. Now that we're back in the States, I'd hoped we'd get some fresh crabs on board and give it another try."

A voice at the far end of the table muttered, "That's all we need, are more fresh crabs."

Leach wiped his forehead with his napkin and, with his voice squeaking, said, "Steward, would you clear the table and bring the dessert?"

Leah smiled at her husband and said, "Harry, give everyone a chance to finish their meal."

"I lost my appetite."

"Darling, I had no idea that crab a la bungalow was still on your mind. Do you remember when we had it the first time when we were in Norfolk?"

"Yes."

"Harry, I'll stop by the fish market in San Pedro on the way home. We can have it tomorrow. It'll be just like it was after our honeymoon."

The steward who cleared the Lieutenant's place began laughing, but cut it short when Leach growled, "Santos!"

The room grew so still that the white noise of ventilation fans and machinery became noticeable. A number of the others at the table glared at Joe, who chose to ignore them. One or two left before dessert was served.

After the meal, the wardroom emptied except for Joe and Eva. She said, "There was a lot of hidden meaning in that 'crab a la bungalow.' You hit a raw nerve with a number of people. Why?"

Joe nodded. "I apologize for not being on my best behavior. That muttered insult and tossing my orders into the butter has been the real Harry Leach from the day he laid eyes on me. I thought I had him turned around, but for last couple of days, he has been impossible. I suspect that he's one of the people who brought a plague of crabs aboard in Hawaii."

"Oh, my!"

"I should have been more mature, more understanding. I'm glad you were here to give me perspective. I'll apologize."

"Joe, it wasn't Harry alone. Many of the others reacted to the word 'crabs.' I don't understand. Why?"

"We've had a rather heavy infestation. What's life if you can't laugh at yourself?"

Moving away from him, she said, "You mean . . . body lice?"

He laughed. "Yes. And Paul Lawson, who's occupying Frenchy's bunk, has been sitting on a case until last night. I don't know if I'm infested, but if you get too close to me, you'll smell the DDT powder. Don't worry, I'm not about to do anything that would put you in a position to cause you to worry."

"Then you don't find me attractive?"

He took a sip of now-cold coffee. "Very attractive, Eva. And I'm very pleased. You could have knocked me over with a feather when I saw you on the quarterdeck. I feel like the man who wanted a 'mail order bride' and she arrived before he posted the letter. On top of that, she was far prettier than his wildest dreams."

"Joe, how can you say that? I'm gaining so much weight, and I've lost my shape."

"Eva, you glow. Motherhood becomes you."

"You say that just to make me feel better. Thank you. But 'mail order bride'? Am I to be bought? They never taught me about that. What do you mean?"

"No, you're not for sale. The term comes from the old West, where there were many more men than women. After the men had staked a homestead or settled in, some of them advertised for a woman to marry them. My grandfather sent back to Greece for a bride. It was a completely arranged marriage. They met on the day before the wedding.

Over these months that we've written back and forth, I tried to picture you in my mind's eye. With each of your letters, I've felt closer to you. I can't say what exactly made me feel the way I did. Only knowing you from words on paper is not enough. During the watch this morning, I've been wrestling with the fear that I said too much . . . talked you into doing something way too soon. I would have driven directly to Vermont and spent my leave with you. Why did you come? Is there something wrong between you and Frenchy's folks?"

"No. It was Richford. I never felt at ease there. Frank's parents were wonderful to me. But I was afraid I'd end up like those other widows . . . raising a child all by myself . . . all alone except for an affair with some married man. After you called me from Hawaii, I felt very lonely. It's always when I feel alone that I hurt the most. I told my friends about your call and how much I wanted to meet your ship, but there obviously wasn't time to arrange for travel papers."

"Travel papers? We don't have that sort of thing."

She laughed. "I know, I know. But they have placed restrictions on me because of my background."

"I've never heard of such a thing! Who? They have no right!"

"Joe, it is for my protection. They told me that they have information that my death has been ordered."

"They can't just come into this country and kill people."

"They can go anywhere. I must be cautious. I have to check in with the local FBI office. They assigned me a 'control,' to whom I report. I misunderstood that I needed the equivalent of a passport to come here. It's hard to believe that I could travel thousands of miles without an internal passport. When I called and asked permission, the man simply asked if I had enough money to get back. And when I checked in with the Los Angeles office, they found me a place to stay. Everyone is so nice. I can't get used to all the freedom."

She looked away and played with her empty coffee cup for a moment before continuing, "The hardest part was breaking the news to Papa Villerouge. I didn't know what his feelings would be. You've written me an awful lot of letters, and I shared them with Mama. Fortunately he wasn't surprised. He told me that Richford wasn't a good place to find a good man. But he wants to be a grandfather. I told him that he and Mama are the only family I have. I promised him that I would return to Vermont. He paid for half of the tickets out and told me to write if I needed money to come home."

CHAPTER 29

Joe Proposes

Joe awoke on the second morning in port to find his roommate, Carter Sawyer, sitting at his desk unshaven, with big dark circles under his bloodshot eyes.

Drumming the eraser of a wooden pencil on the desk, Carter mumbled, "I called and called. Finally, just after two a.m., he answered the phone."

"Who?"

"How the hell should I know? The man sleeping in my bed with my wife!"

"Carter, she has filed for divorce."

His voice broke. "I know. I know . . . But I loved her. You know, that son of a bitch warned me not to stop sending her my paychecks . . . or they would have a judge order it! Can you imagine, the SOB is screwing my wife and thinks I have an obligation to support them. What is the world coming to?"

"Pretty sick. Well, that's California for you."

"Sick! Why, in Florida, I could have them run in for adultery. It took every bit of self-control I had not to hang up on him. And after having to listen to him cry about how short they are and about having to hang around the house this weekend because they are going to have a garage sale, she never did come to the phone. To top it off, he laughed up a storm when I told him I want my car back."

"Holding a garage sale? I don't know much about divorce law, but it sounds to me like you ought to get out there and find out what is going on."

"Joe, I can't believe this is happening to me. What did I ever do to her to cause her to treat me this way? You're right, I'm going to call a taxi after quarters."

Joe rolled out of bed and pulled his trousers on over the skivvies he had slept in. As he walked toward the sink, he said, "I think you need help. Maybe Eva could give you a ride."

"Oh, no, I wouldn't want to impose. After all, she came a long way, and this is your first day together."

"Carter, we had plenty of time together yesterday to get caught up. Let's see, your place over in Huntington Beach is close to the ammo depot . . ."

"Yeah, but I don't want to drag you into this."

"Carter, giving you a ride isn't dragging me into anything. Besides, it wouldn't hurt to have some backup."

⇥▪◉ ◉▪⇤

Shortly before ten, Eva, with Carter and Joe as passengers, pulled into the driveway of a two-story townhouse. The faded yellow stucco was streaked with brown water marks that amplified the powdery dirt on either side of the walk. Here and there, spidery patterns of Bermuda grass stretched out in spirals around barely green weeds.

"What happened to the lawn?" Carter said to himself. "Didn't she water it?"

He hesitantly opened the car door. With the dejection of a condemned man on his way to the gallows, he shuffled slowly to the front door with his head down and shoulders rounded. He cleaned his eyeglasses, held them up to the light, and wiped them some more before putting them on. He waited almost a minute before stealing a glance at the couple in the car. He stood tall, adjusted his sports shirt around his belt, and knocked on the door.

After what seemed an eternity, the door swung open wide and Joe saw Lynda Sawyer for the first time. She was a little shorter than Carter, but had a well-rounded figure, which her shortie nightgown did little to hide. Her hair, a bright red, tangled rat's nest, fell to her shoulders around a round, freckled face.

With tones that emphasized her Southern accent, she snapped, "You little turd! You've got your nerve, calling in the middle of the night and then showing up out here at the crack of dawn."

"Lynda, it's almost ten. And where is your modesty?"

Closing the door slightly, she said, "Go to hell!"

"Please, darling, we need to talk. Why have you done this to me?"

She pulled a filter-tip cigarette from a pack and placed it in the corner of her mouth. "Talk to my attorney. He knows. I told you I wasn't going to sit around seven months for you while you're off playing sailor boy. And all you talk about is going back to those god-awful swamps. Why, the thought of those enormous bugs is more than a body could bear."

"I didn't have any choice. I have to serve."

"You have to serve. Bull! Look at Dennis McKay, he went in the Reserves and he was out in six months. No, you never heard me."

He half-raised his hand. "I hoped you could understand. At least give me a chance. I thought we could have talked this out. I still . . . I still love you."

She lit the cigarette and blew a cloud of smoke upward. "Lawyer Sawyer, you've had your chance. I've got me a real man, and he knows how to show me a real good time. And he isn't afraid to spend real money either."

With each word, it seemed that Carter's shoulders grew rounder.

After a pause while she deeply inhaled the cigarette in her small mouth, the redhead continued exhaling smoke with her words. "God, I don't what I ever saw in you. No, I don't. Well, is that all you've got to say? We're going to the beach today. Why don't you be a good little boy and get the hell out of here?"

"I need to get my things."

"Your things? It really isn't convenient to have you wandering around my house right now. Like I said, we're getting ready to go to the beach."

"Lynda, cut the crap! I'm not here to cause a scene or start a fight. I need the civilian clothes I left behind. Your boyfriend said something about a garage sale. What are you selling? I have a right to get my things. And I want my car."

"Your car? How are we going to get around? Gunther, dear!"

A tall man stepped up behind her. His receding dark blond hair was streaked with lighter sun-bleached strands. The heavy muscles in his chest rippled as he slipped a light nylon robe over Lynda's shoulders . He was naked to the waist, wearing a pair of faded, patterned Bermuda shorts. He towered over both Lynda and Carter.

Gunther leaned his well-tanned hairy arm against the door jamb and thrust out his square chin on which blond stubble caught the sunlight. "Little man, the lady has made her position clear. She wants you out of her life . . . yesterday! Now why don't you do the smart thing and get in the car and leave before I roll you up into a ball and dribble you out to the curb?"

"Lay one hand . . . just one hand on me and I'll have you thrown in jail, you bastard! I have witnesses. And I know criminal prosecution."

Gunther tensed the muscles in his arms and narrowed his lips, showing his nicotine-stained teeth. Lynda, who had retreated behind the hulk, touched his arm and said, "Be careful, darling. He may not be much of a man, but he is one hell of a lawyer."

Carter took a step toward the door. "I have a right to my property. Let me in!"

Gunther put a hand up. "If you want your junk, it's in the garage. Nobody would buy most of that crap anyway. But you're not taking the Buick, understand? Her lawyer says you've got to agree to a property settlement."

He stepped past Carter and flicked the garage door up, opening it in one fluid movement. Inside, hanging on ropes, were a few shirts and jackets on wire hangers. On each was a piece of masking tape with a price written on it. Farther back were a stack of texts and lawbooks and, on a table, a number of seventy-eight RPM records, similarly marked.

"You're selling my stuff! You have no right! . . . "Where's my tux? And my camel's-hair coat?"

Lynda stood in the middle of the door with her arm bent. She held her cigarette between her thumb and index finger. "It went last week. Some guy put an ad in the *Times*, advertising for a tux. He bought a bunch of those old records too."

"Who?"

"Charlie something or other. How should I know? We cashed the check right away."

Carter began shuffling the records on the table. "Where are my Glenn Millers?"

Gunther said, "He took a bunch of those off our hands too. Who'd want a bunch of old scratchy records anyway? He gave me twenty-five cents apiece."

"For two bits each! Those were collector's items! How could you?"

Lynda lit another cigarette off the half-smoked butt of her last smoke. "Old lo-fi scratchy junk. Who cares? Got back from Vegas and we were broke. We needed the money because your last paycheck arrived a couple of days late. The lawyer says you have to support me just like you were doing before I filed. You're a lawyer, so you don't have to be told."

Carter stood with fists and his jaw clenched. His red eyes narrowed and the sinews in his cheeks worked before he spat, "Bitch!"

Joe, approaching from behind, said, "Don't say anything, Carter. Come on, I'll help you load your stuff into the car before you lose control."

Lynda arched her eyebrows as she looked around. "Joe, Ensign Joe Zilch, isn't it? You two losers are a pair. Leah Leach told me all about you. And who's your friend in the car? Another chorine from a strip joint?"

"The name is Xylos. If you can't handle it, just call me Joe. The lady in the car is Eva Villerouge. She's the widow of a former shipmate."

"Well, pardon me!" she said, smiling and looking at her lover.

Joe pointed at Gunther. "You, give me a hand and we'll be out of your hair that much quicker."

"Look, shorty, you don't give me orders."

"Lighten up, buddy. This is their problem. The sooner he has his stuff, the quicker you and I can get on with our day. How about it?"

The stud looked at Joe with a blank expression. "Well, all right, but the car stays. Remember, I'm no swabbie you can push around." He gathered up an armload of clothes while Joe gingerly stacked records and carried them toward the car. Eva opened the trunk.

Once the goods had been laid within, Joe extended his right hand. "My name is Joe Xylos."

"Gunther Wilkoski."

"What do you do, Gunther?"

"I'm between situations right now. I'm a member of the Screen Actors Guild. I'm what you would call a stunt man. I've been doing quite a bit of driving for the TV shows. And I did surfing scenes in *Beach*

Boy."

"That's great. I was in show business before I joined the Navy."

Gunther hollowed the vowel as he said, "Oh?"

"I was the emcee in nightclubs and strip joints while I was in college. And of course, some people never let me forget it."

Gunther squinted as he said, "That doesn't sound like much."

"No big money for sure, but it paid the bills and got me through college. Where do you go to the beach?"

"Down at Huntington Beach. I like to surf, and there's still some good waves."

Carter joined them with a stack of books. Soon the car was loaded. The three of them piled in as Lynda returned wearing a modest two-piece swimsuit. She leaned over, displaying her ample, freckled cleavage above the flowery top of the suit. "Thank you, Carter, for not making a big scene. And honey, you've got to talk to my attorney because the finances are a mess."

"I don't understand. I sent you every nickel I could."

"Well, you've got to talk to him. Lawyer fees and all. You understand. No hard feelings . . . okay?"

"What do you mean, the finances are a mess? You've been the one taking care of the bills. I don't like this. I don't like this one bit."

"Like I said, I don't want to see you or talk to you. Talk to my attorney. Joel will set you straight."

They backed out of the driveway with Lynda and Gunther standing near the well-polished chromed rear bumper of Carter's car. On Joe's directions, Eva headed back toward the Long Beach Naval Shipyard where the *Beaverton* was moored.

Once they were well on their way back in the stop-and-go traffic on Westminster Boulevard, the lawyer said, "She has no right to that car. My Daddy gave it to me the fall before we met. It is my car and registered to me! It still has Florida plates on it, and I intend to get it back."

"If it means anything, they're going to Huntington Beach. Did you notice the surfboard tied to the carrier on top of the car?"

"Was that what it was? You know, at this moment, I don't give a damn. It's over. I shouldn't have tried to hold on." And then, laughing hollowly, he added, "And I sure as hell shouldn't have lost any sleep because I caught the crabs off a toilet seat!"

Later, after Joe and Carter lugged the goods aboard the ship, Joe and Eva stayed aboard for lunch before heading for Torrance and the apartment she had rented. Joe drove because the Hungarian émigré was unnerved by the L.A. traffic.

Eva broke the silence by saying, "I didn't want to give Carter any false hope. That Gunther, or whatever his name was, will be gone as soon as the money runs out. He's living on her money."

"Oh, I don't know. He said he was a stunt man. It's not a nine-to-five job. They make a good wage."

"Then why doesn't he have his own car?"

"What makes you think he doesn't?"

"The surfboard on top of the car and the way he guarded it. When he leaves, I'll bet the car goes with him. He's bad news, Joe . . . conceited. . . doesn't give a hoot for anyone but himself. I've seen too many of them."

"Eva, you sized them up far quicker than I have. What makes you so sure?"

"Experience, darling. In my old life, I looked for people like them. With a little money, time, and sympathy, they could become very useful . . . It's too bad about your friend Carter."

"Yeah, it's tragic. He was true and sent home every dime that he could. There are a whole bunch of other people on board who richly deserve to be in his shoes."

⋅⊱━❁━⊰⋅

Sitting with a city map in her lap, Eva guided Joe through heavy traffic and past the foul-smelling oil refineries and the seemingly endless miles of road signs, stores, and stoplights until he made one last left turn off the Pacific Coast Highway onto a narrow street whose curbs were hidden behind parked cars. She directed him down a sheltered alley, which was blast-furnace hot in the afternoon sun. He was sweating by the time he parked the Chevy on a badly cracked concrete slab beside a freshly whitewashed stucco apartment that had small patios with rusty wrought-iron railings.

This would be the first of his almost-daily trips. He said little about it to anyone other than Carter, and only the most observant noted that Joe had a life off the *Beaverton*. Most days, Eva picked him up in the afternoon at the head of the pier. Once clear of the base, they disappeared into the anonymity of the rush-hour traffic.

To any casual observer in Torrance, they were a happily married couple. While she fixed dinner, he sat on the small deck by the living room and read the evening paper. On a few evenings, they went out to a movie or walked along the beach. Each evening, sometime after ten and before midnight, she drove him back to the ship.

Eva remained at home on his duty days except one Saturday evening when she came aboard for dinner and the movie. Invitations to parties by the wardroom bachelors were nonexistent thanks to Joe's reputation as an albatross of doom. Little attention was paid to him by the married officers, who were either enjoying a happy return to the hearth or were preoccupied with worries over whether returning from an extended deployment with an active case of gonorrhea would be enough to sink their marriages.

On Joe's part, his physical attraction grew for this woman who gently touched him and laughed at his old comedy routines. Yet there was a reserve, an almost compulsive sense of order and self-discipline, that made him feel as if he was courting a Marine drill sergeant. Whenever they were out, she had a catlike presence and spoke in guarded whispers. Her eyes always moved. She seemed physically tense, ready to strike. At the apartment, her words expressed a fear of strangers.

Eva would later recall that over the first two weeks, Joe had a way of filling every moment with laughter and attention. He was genuine and caring in doing little things for her. She felt that life was beginning anew.

Yet she wasn't sure of herself or of how Joe felt. He seemed to have a fixation on his shipboard roommates' problems, which he reported each day. Paul Lawson was about to be given a letter of reprimand for concealing a case of gonorrhea. His self-confidence was fast ebbing because of constantly being the butt of many jokes and learning that Harry Leach had spent the night with his girl Mabeline. Lynda Sawyer was overdrawn at the bank and bounced a check at the Navy Exchange. Carter was fighting a court order to give her three-quarters of his pay, and his attorney fees were sinking him further into debt.

Eva sensed an emotional veneer in Joe that held her at a distance, as if he was beginning to draw away from her thanks to his shipmates' turmoil. She filled the days that they were apart with solitary exploring trips, from the tip of the Palos Verde Peninsula through downtown Los Angeles to Beverly Hills. On one of these adventures, she found a lone picnic table at the end of a street overlooking the beach in Redondo Beach. Nearby was a crude fire pit made of broken pieces of concrete and rocks.

Excited about her discovery, she packed a newly purchased picnic basket with dishes from a nearby delicatessen and surprised Joe with a Memorial Day outing. They sat side by side as close as they could, as the chilly late afternoon sea breezes raised goosebumps. Freshets of wind made patterns on the water and foamed the crests of the waves that slammed against the bluff. Unruly updrafts inflated Eva's loose maternity blouse like a hot-air balloon, then collapsed it. Later, the stiff breeze made her silken hair stand up almost straight before it moved on to leave them in a temporary eye of calm air.

Following a particularly heavy gust, Eva put the last of the leftovers into the hamper and lifted it off the table. She grimaced and drew her hand toward her back. "I'm not in good enough condition to have this baby. My back is killing me."

After swallowing one last piece of dark Russian bread, he said, "Now that's something I can treat. Get up on the table and I'll give you a back rub."

"Out here in public?"

"Sure, out here. I'm not going to rub anything but your back, so you won't have to get undressed. Come on, hop up there."

After he helped her lie on her side, Joe began massaging her back, taking directions as to where the pain was. With each stroke she made little contented sounds, almost as if she were purring.

In time she indicated her satisfaction and sat up facing him. They kissed. Eva wrapped her long legs around him in a scissors and drew him as close as she could. He responded, running his hands up and down her back and then hugging her.

As their lips parted, the widow said, "Joe, you have set me ablaze. I want you. Please, let's go home."

Joe smiled and slowly released her, and she him. He sat on the table next to her. Taking her hand in his, he said, "I would like that. Yes, I would like that very much . . . But there is another side of me that wouldn't. And I suspect it's true of you too."

"What side? What do you mean? Is it because I carry this child that you find me unattractive?"

"No. It's who you are and who I am. It has to do with trust."

"Trust? I trust you, Joe."

"And I trust you . . . but you and I are birds of a feather. We're users, people users . . . and we've been used. From the time I started college and later working in the clubs, I was like a kid locked in a candy store . . . the women who passed through my life. I was never honest with myself or anyone else. It caught up with me. Last winter in Yoko-suka, for a fleeting moment, I fell in love with a woman old enough to be my mother. I didn't see it at the time, but she did me a great service. In a single night, I felt like old Scrooge being taken out to see the future. As a young woman she had been used badly . . . forced to marry a bastard of a husband . . . yet retained a charm and beauty that any man would seek. Inside, she is a mess. It really hurt when I found out she was married to an Air Force Colonel."

"I think you said something to Frank that night about her."

"Yes, I probably did. After he was shot, I thought about her life and promised I would take care of you. I mean it in every sense of the word. If I could do it as your husband, it would be the answer to my wildest dreams."

"You still feel you are performing some sort of duty?"

"No and yes. I enjoy your company, and I'm tantalized by your touch. I feel we've become more than pen pals . . . good friends. Yes, fate was my matchmaker. I don't want to throw you any curve balls. And I'm not sure either of us could think straight after spending the night together."

"With this bulge between us, you mean?"

"Yes. Your kiss a few minutes ago was more than enough to ring my bell."

She lightly touched him. "And you're no piece of wood either."

"Thanks, Eva. I've spent countless hours thinking about what you said the night Frenchy was killed . . . about a sadist who took an innocent little girl's mother out of her life and then gave her credit for turning herself into an orphan . . . who twisted the evil of betrayal into a virtue. And an uncle who sent her off to spy school, where it became a profession. You wouldn't have defected if you were comfortable with that picture."

"I never thought about it this way. Joe, I defected because of what the Russians did to my people. I regret the things I did to help them."

"There must have been some point, some event that was like the straw on the camel's back. What was it?"

Eva's eyes filled with tears, and she leaned against Joe. After a loud sniffle, she whispered, "Anna Fuchs . . . It was wrong. It could have just as well been me, or anyone."

"Anna Fuchs? What happened?"

"She was a young girl, maybe seventeen or eighteen, just an ordinary teenager. They had been working on her for some time when I was asked to be a 'gentle persuader,' the good guy. Her face was swollen so badly from the beating that she could hardly see. They burned her hands to try to get information."

"Why were they doing this?"

"A Russian tank had been destroyed, killing the crew. They found a scrap of paper in the pocket of an abandoned jacket not far from the scene. Other than saying she knew nothing about the incident when she was arrested, she said nothing through days of brutal torture. I showed her the note and asked her why she would deny that it was her phone number written on it, pleading for her to cooperate before they came back and beat her again. Her only words were, 'I know nothing. Check the records.' I did. They had reversed two numbers; she was innocent. I showed them their mistake and asked that she be taken to the hospital. Instead they took her back to her cell, where she died during the night, because the damn Russians felt that if the others saw her, they wouldn't resist. I'm so ashamed that I didn't have her courage. You are the only person I have ever told this to. I don't know how anyone could want me, knowing all that I've done."

"Eva, that's just the point. We need to put our pasts behind us. You and I need to build our lives on a foundation of trust and respect. I've been on a ship of fools, most of whom don't keep their vows. Carter is a victim, as are many of the wives. From what I've seen of life, the world isn't any different from the *Beaverton*. I don't want to be like them. I want us to know that trust, not betrayal, will be what keeps us together. I want you to feel good enough about us that you make a commitment we'll keep for life."

"Yes."

"Yes?"

"I thought you were asking me to marry you. And I said yes."

"I didn't know I had gone that far. I've gotten way ahead of myself. I'd like to do things the way my father would have done. He wasn't as particular about who I would marry as how I would marry, before God, and making a commitment to Him that it would be for all time."

"In a church? Me? I've only been in one church in my life and that was a tour of St. Basil's in Moscow. Must I become a religious person?"

"I would feel that we're not just play-acting, but starting our lives together the right way. Darling, I don't know what the rules are. As you've noticed, I don't go to church. It's just right that a man and a woman marry in the sight of God. I think religion is something that's strictly up to you. Papa used to say that with belief comes forgiveness. In his last days, he used to talk quite a bit about a Greek word, *meta-noya*, the change from within. How do you tell what's on the inside, anyway? Does this change your answer?"

"To the question you didn't know you had asked? I'm not sure. What if they won't marry us because I'm godless?"

"There must be somebody who'd do it. You and Frenchy didn't have any trouble finding someone."

Eva pointed down to the beach and the surf. "And afterward, we'll make love down there, just like in the movies."

Joe shivered. "Do that, and you'll get a case of raisin toes."

"Raisin toes?"

"Yea, all wrinkled from the water and purple from the cold."

She laughed. "That's why I love you. In a nice sort of way, you're very funny."

CHAPTER 30

At the Commissary

Friday morning, Joe left the ship shortly after quarters thanks to Commander Longstreet's decree that all those who stood duty the first day in port would have a four-day weekend over Memorial Day.

Armed with a shopping list Eva had given him the night before, when she had suggested that he take her car back to the ship, Joe waited in the commissary parking lot for the doors to open. Shortly after he arrived, Lynda Sawyer drove by in the same faded blue Buick he'd seen a few days earlier. She parked some rows away.

It took Joe another five minutes to realize that he ought to call Carter and let him know. Here was a possible opportunity for Carter to reclaim his old Buick. He walked past her car to the pay phone that stood next to the building.

After two tries with busy signals, he finally got through. He heard the familiar voice, "This is Mr. Sawyer. May I help you?"

"Hey, old buddy, she's here in the commissary parking lot."

"Who, Lynda?"

"Yes, Lynda . . . and driving the Buick."

"Is that why you called me?"

"Why, yes, Carter, I thought you wanted to do something to lay claim to it. Here is your chance."

Joe waited so long for a reply that he thought the line had gone dead. Finally his roommate's slow, deliberate reply began, "Why, yes, I do have the papers showing separate ownership. My attorney suggested what I already knew . . . that I ought to settle for the car in exchange for paying off the better part of the debt she has run up. What has me the most concerned is that she's writing rubber checks too. The thing I

"

have disliked the most since I've been abroad has been all those damn bad-debt letters. And now Commander Longstreet is having me write a reply to the Commanding Officer at Nellis Air Force Base because she wrote a sum of one-hundred-twenty-three dollars and twenty-three cents worth of bad checks over two days. After all the help I gave the local ONI with that despicable car dealer, J. J. Caruthers, they owe me a favor. I wonder if they'd sweep her in for a little interrogation. It might scare some sense into her head."

"Carter, I know you're ticked at her. Before you start schemes to have her run in, I suggest you consider your priorities and what you are trying to accomplish. Time's a-wastin' as you have so often said. The commissary opens in ten minutes. When I hang up, I'm going over and be sociable. Who knows, I may stall her for a few minutes."

"I've got to hand it to you, Joe. You're always thinking. Thank goodness you're on my side."

"Carter, I'm not involved. Whatever you do is up to you, okay?"

Joe hung up the phone and walked slowly back toward his car. He stopped in front of the old Buick. "Why, Lynda Sawyer, what are you doing here so early?"

"I should ask you the same, Joe. You look so handsome in that khaki sailor's costume. And happy too."

"Thank you. I believe my mother was the only other person to call me handsome. It's a uniform, an officer's uniform. There is a difference."

"Well, when we went to the party last fall, Rufus Johnson, your doctor, kept calling it a 'costume.' Now there is a real handsome man. And so eligible! And you, Joe, I saw you go by on the way to the phone booth. Why, you've been smiling like the cat that swallowed the canary. What are you up to?"

He smiled broadly. "I guess it's something I can't hide. Yesterday evening, I asked Eva to marry me . . . and she said yes."

"You mean the pregnant blonde in the car the other day?"

"Yes."

"Boy, it took you a bit long enough to screw up your courage! Now, didn't it?"

"Actually, I feel like I'm a little ahead of the season."

"Joe, you are something else. What is she, four or five months along and you are just getting around to thinking about giving the child a last name?"

"Lynda, I thought you knew. Eva is widowed. The child is hers and Frenchy's. He was murdered just after they found out she was pregnant."

Carter's wife pulled a cigarette from a pack in her purse and tapped it on her thumbnail before lighting it. "Joe Sigh-most, you are weird! Here we are in Southern California and it's full of absolutely beautiful women, and you pick a big, fat pregnant one. What makes her so special?"

"Special? It's hard to put into words. When Frenchy married her, I felt she would be the standard against whom I'd measure the women I met. I saw her as a very loving person who brought great happiness to my friend. And as close as I have ever seen it, the perfect woman . . . brains, beauty, athletic skill . . . a Helen of Troy, an Aphrodite, all rolled into one. I've been in touch with her since Frenchy died. I planned to pursue her, but not until later, after I went back East. To my surprise, she was on the dock when we tied up. And I want to be a father to her baby because Frenchy was a good friend."

"Carter wrote about it. Wasn't he the guy who died rescuing a bunch of hostages? How did you get involved?"

"Yes. I was one of the hostages. The guy was going to shoot me next."

"And he died saving your ass, so you're going to take care of her. That's quite a story. Knowing you don't miss an angle, I'll bet he left her with a bundle of money."

"Actually, the only things she's gotten have been the government benefits and his car. The benefits go away when she remarries. His parents were still the beneficiaries on his life insurance. We're both poor as church mice."

"Well, I know all about that. I've been married to a church mouse for too damn long. Let's get over there, they've opened the doors."

Joe opened the car door for her. "Good. Lynda, you've shopped here before, right?"

"Sure have."

She alighted on small high-heeled feet. The redhead smoothed her tight skirt, which somewhat hobbled her knees, before reaching back into the car to pick up her large leather purse and a folded piece of scrap paper.

As Joe shut the car door, he said in a flat voice, "I've never been in a commissary in my life. And I don't want to waste half a day finding my way around. Could you show me where things are?"

"Why not? Let's see that list." As she scanned it, she read, "Fresh carrots, cabbage, peas, potatoes, garlic, flour, milk, Polish sausage, two pounds of ground beef. And then you're to stop at the Best Bakery for one loaf of bread. It's too early for the peas. You get a much better deal buying canned peas. And you can't get a better price on bread than here in the commissary."

"Eva doesn't like this bread. She says it tastes like chemicals."

"Ah, so she's still sick in the mornings?"

"I don't think so."

"You don't think so? Why do you think she sleeps in while you shop?"

"It's not quite that way. I borrowed her car last night to go back aboard. It's easier for me to stop on the way back rather than have her make a round trip."

"What, you slept on board?"

"That's right."

"You're weird. Why, even Carter and I lived together for a term before we married."

"Lynda, the more I learn about you, the more I ask myself what you ever saw in Carter in the first place. The two of you are like night and day. How did you ever get together?"

"I'm a practical woman, Joe. He had a car and I had an apartment. He was a ticket out of north Florida, and I'm not going back."

They entered the store. Joe fumbled with his wallet when asked for identification, then grumbled, "Why do they need to see an ID card when I'm in uniform?"

She laughed. "Maybe they think you rented the costume. Here, let me see your list again."

They passed the meat section. She dropped a pair of ribeye steaks in her basket. Joe got the ground round.

When they arrived in canned goods, she said, "Here are the canned peas."

While she loaded up on brand-name foods and gourmet soups, Joe carefully studied the rows of canned peas. He picked up the first can and carefully read the label, then the next, until he arrived at one that had no label. After turning the can over in his hand a few times, he asked, "How do I know these are really peas?"

"Numbers on the lid. They're standard Navy issue."

"How do I know what's inside the can besides peas?"

Lynda smiled. "Goodness, Joe, you eat peas on the ship, don't you?"

"Well, yes, but . . ."

"For crying out loud, these are the same peas."

"But Eva is very serious about what she eats. I don't think she trusts all the chemicals we put in the food."

"Chemicals? Oh, come on. If they didn't put preservatives in the food, we'd all be in danger."

Hefting the larger unmarked can in one hand and a Del Monte in the other, he said, "The price is less on the plain one, but I wonder if I wouldn't be getting more peas than we can eat."

She laughed, "I've never seen a man like you. Where did you get such ideas? Haven't you ever heard of leftovers? You do have a refrigerator?"

"Well, yes. But she should be having a balanced diet."

With each item, Joe compared sizes, figured costs per ounce, and asked question after question. After they had gone through the fresh produce department, where Joe examined most of the stock and made selections only to put each back and then take yet another, Lynda said, "I have never seen such a worry wart of a time waster of a man. How do you ever make your mind up?"

"It's not easy when I have so many things to choose from. On the ship, they put a plate in front of you. If you don't like it, you don't eat. Well, if I'm going to be given a choice, I ought to look at the alternatives, don't you think?"

"I think you're making a day's work out of a short shopping list. And I can't waste any more time with your silliness."

She pushed the cart past him. After quickly gathering the remaining items, she headed for the checkout line. Joe joined the queue with a single cart separating them. After the groceries had been checked through and bagged, the clerk called out the total.

She wrote the total on the check. As she handed it to the clerk, Joe asked in a voice that could be heard in the back of the store, "Oh, Lynda, did you remember to put some more money in your account to cover those checks you bounced at Nellis?"

The redhead's face first grew pale, then flushed. The clerk held the check up, looking from Joe to Lynda and back to the check.

Finally Lynda cleared her throat, saying, "Ignore him. That's my husband's roommate. He is one of the world's premier practical jokers. He's always pulling some stupid stunt like this. On second thought, I might be short. Let me pay with cash instead." The clerk was reaching for her microphone as Lynda snatched the check. "Give me that! I've got cash enough to pay."

She reached into her purse and, after rummaging for a moment, took out a roll of bills. Still glaring at Joe, she peeled off a pair of twenties. "Here, give me the change."

The bag boy followed her out of the store while Joe awaited his turn. The woman ahead of him had a full cart, and the clerk was about a third of her way through it when Lynda came charging in through the exit door. She stopped at the end of the checkout counter, blocking the bag boy. With fists clenched and her face almost as red as her hair, she screamed, "You bastard!"

The clerk reached for the microphone as she watched a mischievous grin spread across Joe's face. "Why, Lynda," he said in mock surprise, "what's come over you?"

"You know damn well! You set me up, stalling me while that little four-eyed rat stole my car!"

"Stole your car? Who stole your car?"

"Carter! You called him, didn't you?"

"Did you see him take it?"

"You put on that show, stalling me, didn't you?"

"Come on, Lynda, I noticed you were getting your share of the laughs at my expense while I was finding my way."

"Damn . . ."

The clerk waved her hand between them. "Lady, I don't what your problem is, but you are disrupting my station. This is no place to have an argument."

An older Chief Petty Officer, threading his way through the carts and patrons, asked, "What's going on, Mabel?"

The clerk said, "I don't know. This woman here started to pay with a check until the Ensign asked her about an overdrawn account. Then she paid with cash. Now she's back screaming about her car being stolen."

Stopping next to Joe, the Chief asked, "Excuse me, sir, could you tell me what this is all about?"

Joe said, "She and my roommate on the ship are splitting up. He told me she had overdrawn their checking account. Look, I'm a Division Officer, and I know how serious it is when someone writes a rubber check at the commissary. When I saw her start to pay with a check, I was concerned, that's all. And Lynda, if I embarrassed you, I'm sorry."

Her fists were still clenched, as were her teeth as she spat, "Why no, Ensign Zilch, you didn't embarrass me . . . much!" She pivoted on her heel and disappeared through the door.

The Chief said, "In the future, sir, if you have information of this sort, please let us handle it. If she is passing worthless checks, she should be stopped. If you're wrong, that woman could put you in a mess of trouble."

"Thanks, Chief, As a Division Officer, I'm very much aware of that."

When Joe came through the exit door, Lynda rushed toward him from where a lone cart loaded with bags stood. "You lousy little son of a bitch! You were in on it! Where did he take the car?"

"Lynda, I have no idea. I was in the store the whole time."

She tried to kick him but missed, sending her shoe flying past him, "Damn! That little jellyfish doesn't have the backbone to take my car. You put him up to it. Admit it!"

"Lynda, I called him and told him you were here, but believe me, I didn't suggest that he take the car. I figured he'd come into the store and confront you about the car and the bad checks. I admit that I stalled you to buy him time to get here."

Half hobbling and half jumping on her high-heeled foot, she worked her way over to the shoe. "You've really screwed my life up. We've got to be on location outside Flagstaff by Monday noon. If Gunther gets his hands on him, he'll turn him into hamburger. And does that man ever have a temper! Oh, what am I going to do?"

The bag boy, ahead of him by perhaps five yards, asked, "Sir, which one is your car?"

"The Chevy with the red bottom and the white top. Lynda, I'm not going to get in the middle of this mess between you and Carter. However, you are afoot and I'm willing to give you a lift home. It'll save you cab fare."

She slid her foot into the shoe and turned back toward her loaded cart. After she took a couple of steps, she called out, "Do you mean it? I've got steaks and ice cream in here. Damn him!"

"Sure. Let me call Eva and tell her I'll be late getting home."

Lynda didn't thank Joe for the ride. Gunther's profanity-laced diatribe had her full attention before Joe backed out of her driveway.

Joe spent the rest of the weekend uneventfully. He returned to the ship Monday morning to find Carter sorting through a pile of file folders.

"Carter, I never thought you'd have the nerve to just take the Buick. What did you do with it?"

"What do you mean, nerve? Boy, that's my car and it's paid for!" His eyes twinkled through his thick glasses. "It was kind of exciting and satisfying. It's in locked storage. Before I came back to the ship, I told the Long Beach police what I did, showing them my Florida papers. Like I figured, they didn't want to get involved. Now if she reports the car stolen, nobody has to ask me about it."

⋅⋗▸■◉ ◉■◂⋖⋅

While Joe went about his day's duties, Eva drove directly from the shipyard to Lomita, which wasn't far from her apartment. After searching for almost half an hour, she found St. Matthew's Greek Orthodox Church. The building was new and didn't have the old, neglected look of the Orthodox churches she had seen in Russia.

Much to her annoyance, she found the front door locked. Peering in the windows, she concluded it was deserted. She was unlocking her car when a graying man wearing a cream-colored sport shirt and nearly matching Palm Beach slacks appeared at the door of the house next to the church. As she was sliding into the driver's seat, he called out, "Madam, please wait. Are you looking for someone?"

"Yes, I'm looking for the pastor."

"I'm Father Michael Makridakis, the priest here. And pardon my dress, I usually don't have appointments on Monday mornings. What do you wish to see me about?"

As she walked toward him, she almost whispered, "About getting married . . . Father."

"What did you say?"

"I need to get married."

"But you don't look Greek to me. Are you Russian?"

"No! I'm Hungarian." She flavored her answer with an accent.

He stepped back from the door. "Come into my study. Please sit down. I don't believe I've ever seen you at my church. What is your name?"

"Eva. Eva Villerouge."

"May I get you a cup of coffee, Eva? I mean *real* coffee from Greece."

"Thank you, no. I'd prefer some water, if you have it."

He momentarily left the room and returned with a small tray on which were pungent coffee in a demitasse and water in a much used, scratched-up glass. As he served her, he asked, "And which one of the young men in the parish wishes to acknowledge you as his wife?"

"Joe. Joe Xylos."

"Xylos is certainly a Greek name, but I don't think that he has ever been to church here. Is he from Los Angeles?"

"No. He's in the Navy. He's an officer on the USS *Beaverton* and has orders to Submarine School in New London. He has to be there in early July."

"And you want to make sure that he marries you before he leaves town?"

"Exactly, I knew you'd understand."

"When did you first meet your Joe Xylos?"

"Last December."

His focus went to the mound in her belly. "I see . . . and when is the baby due?"

"September twenty-fifth."

"Well, we have some time. I gather that you are not of our faith?"

"No."

He waited for her to say more before he steepled his fingers. "And where have you gone to church?"

Eva bit her lip and looked down at the floor. "I don't . . . I made a tour of St. Basil's in Moscow . . . once."

Leaning forward as if getting ready to stand, the priest said, "St. Basil's? Is this some kind of joke? That is now a museum in Moscow. Wait, I thought you said you were Hungarian."

"I am. I was sent to Moscow as a child just before the Great . . . ah . . . World War Two."

"Then you grew up as a communist, an atheist?"

"More or less."

"I can't just marry anybody! You have to be of the faith."

"Please. No, this is no joke. Joe wants to marry in your church. It's very important to him. Yes, I will become a religious person."

He laughed. "Religious person? That's a new one!"

"I'm serious. I wish to have religion in my life. It will make Joe happy. I want to have a good life, especially for my child. I need him very much to be a father to my baby. He is a very good man."

"Very good man, indeed. The church is a moral institution, the rock of our Greek culture. Your circumstances are difficult. Would you agree to raise your children in the Greek Orthodox faith?"

"Yes, I would."

"And would you accept religious instruction? Baptism?"

"Whatever you require, yes. I said I wish to become a religious person."

"Did Joe talk to you at all about our faith?"

"Not much. Only that he wants to marry in the sight of God and make a commitment to me for life."

"Well, at least he has a belated sense of responsibility. Eva, I believe you are serious, but I'm not going to agree to perform this marriage until I've had the chance to talk with the two of you. I'm not going to hold out any hope that I will. But I'm not saying I won't, either." As he rose, he extended his card to her with a flourish. "Here is my card. Call between nine and two, Tuesdays through Fridays. You know, you don't sound like a Hungarian."

She remained seated, wrinkling her forehead as she took the card.

She studied the card, saying, "I went to school with Americans in Moscow as a child and have studied English for many years."

"Tell me, where did you, a lifelong communist Hungarian, meet a young Greek-American naval officer?"

"In Melbourne during the Olympics. He was one of the people who helped me defect."

His eyes widened. "Oh, I see. I see. The Olympics last fall. That's perfectly understandable. And you . . . Well, we'll discuss that the next time we meet, when you bring your Joe Xylos. Xylos . . . That is not a common name. Oh, so many good Greek names are shortened and bastardized in this country. Here you are in a new country. . . alone . . . and about to become a mother for the first time. Eva, thank you for having the courage to come here."

He smiled and placed a hand lightly on her shoulder. "I've sworn to uphold the rules, but rules can bend. Call me for another appointment soon."

She flipped her long, curly, blonde locks back over her shoulders and extended her hand. "Thank you, Father. I am serious about this."

⇢⊶⊷⊷⊶⊶

The misadventure at Pearl was a bad memory that wouldn't go away. Sean Perkins, who had predicted that his wife would not understand, proved correct; he was the first to move aboard after she turned him out of their apartment.

Tyler Cobb shared with Joe the letter he got from his date on Waikiki, in which she apologized for what she did to him. She identified the source of her infection, as well as all the others, as Al Mazini, with whom they had stayed for five days before the *Beaverton* arrived.

Sandy's letter told more. In the tradition of the protective parent, Solange's father had gone on the warpath, starting with a letter to the University of Hawaii. The letter demanded Mazini's removal because, besides his daughter, the seventh female infected had been a student, a senior. He also wrote his Congressman about the HASP, enclosing a glossy photo of Solange's bruised breast. The part of the letter that sent ripples of fear through the *Beaverton* group was the news that all the women had been asked to give statements to investigators regarding the incident.

Commander Wyman was officially appointed to conduct the investigation. None of the principals would give him any information on the grounds that they would be incriminating themselves. What information he gleaned was from the three who weren't there when the HASP arrived: Joe Xylos, Larry White, and Paul Lawson. From them, he knew who had been there before the HASP arrived, but could not answer the most elementary who, what, when, where, and how of the incident itself. The only person he could positively place at the apartment after the incident was Harry Leach, because he had brought Lawson's swimsuit back. He assumed, however, that Leach had not been a part of the incident because the HASP had searched the apartment and reported that it was empty. The Lieutenant was too fat to either run or hide. Wyman was told to keep the investigation open, pending receipt of the other statements and copies of the reports from Hawaii.

CHAPTER 31

The Nuptials

Joe would have met with Father Makridakis earlier, but he had the duty Monday evening. On Tuesday afternoon, he and Carter spent a long, painful hour in the XO's office explaining what had happened at the commissary the previous Friday morning.

Commander Longstreet had received phone calls, first from Lynda's attorney and then from the local Congressman's office, alleging that Joe and Carter had conspired to steal the woman's car and that the Navy was allowing them to hide it somewhere in the shipyard. For the better part of the hour, the Legal Officer told the XO that what had happened was none of the Navy's business. His answers danced around the point, never admitting that he took the car or that he even knew where it was.

The XO at one point told Carter he was going to make him the Assistant B Division Officer and was going to call BUPERS (the Bureau of Naval Personnel) and have Joe's orders canceled. Carter argued about basic property rights under the Constitution while Joe protested that he had nothing to do with the car's disappearance. Carter came strongly to his defense, saying that Joe wasn't involved and had in fact acted as a good Samaritan to give Lynda a ride home.

Longstreet ordered them both to prepare written statements and not to leave the ship until they personally delivered them into his hands. The next day, the XO went golfing right after quarters and didn't come aboard until Thursday morning. Carter was content to wait until summoned, but Joe insisted that they call for an appointment. He didn't think his answer to Eva's question about getting cold feet had satisfied her.

While awaiting the appointed hour in the Personnel office, Joe was glad he had put the statement in a manila folder because his sweating hands had already soaked the folder. Finally the yeoman told them Commander Longstreet would see them. The two Ensigns stepped into the XO's office braced for another bout of verbal inquisition.

As they approached his desk, Stan Longstreet was talking on the phone. He smiled, showing his nicotine-stained teeth, and set the receiver gently in its cradle. "Well, boys, do you have those statements ready for me?"

Each handed over his folder. The XO read Joe's statement first and casually tossed it on the desk blotter as he began perusing Carter's. As he finished the body of the statement, he muttered, "Just like a damn attorney, you took three pages to 'state all the relevant facts,' and in total, you didn't say a damn thing. And what's this, a copy of the title to the car? And of course it's in your name."

"Yes, sir."

"And enclosure two is a draft of a letter to our beloved Congressman answering the query from his local office. Well, let's see if it passes muster."

He held Carter's draft well away from his eyes and read it while puffing gently on his cigar. Finally he tossed it across the desk. "Damn, Carter, you write enough of these letters to know better. You are correct in saying that the Navy's policy is to remain uninvolved in the domestic disputes of its members. And that the documentation provided by Mr. Sawyer shows that he is the sole owner of the automobile in question. But there isn't anything about Mrs. Lynda Sawyer."

"What do you mean, sir?"

"Let's start with the bad checks from Nellis Air Force Base. There's more, there's a young loan officer at the Bank of America who may lose his job because he approved three loans for her to buy new refrigerators in less than six weeks. And Kahn's Fine Furniture is after her because they're holding a time purchase agreement for $3,000 worth of furniture that has disappeared."

"Three . . . thousand . . . dollars' worth of furniture! I never agreed to buy any furniture, let alone $3,000 worth! But what has that got to do with my car?"

"It seems that sweet Lynda Sawyer has been buying new goods for nothing down and then selling them for all she can get at garage sales, telling buyers she has to sell because of a pending divorce."

"But how did her creditors find out?"

"Luck. Pure luck. The first refrigerator that she sold broke down, and the buyer asked for a service call because it was still under warranty. And when they asked him to bring the delinquent monthly payments up to date, he said, 'What payments? I bought this for cash.' I thought you took the car because you had a suspicion about all this."

"No, sir. I acted on impulse after Joe told me she was in the commissary."

Longstreet pointed the cigar at Joe and snapped, "Mr. Xylos, lightning strikes around you so often that I would swear you use ozone as an aftershave. I don't know if I'll be relieved when you're detached or have cause to lie awake nights wondering where you've left the mines planted."

"Commander, I don't know what you're talking about."

"Boy, you have been given an opportunity that very few Reserve officers are given, Submarine School. One more incident . . . just one more incident, and I'm going to the Captain with a strong recommendation to ask BUPERS to cancel those orders. I don't give a damn how innocent you are!"

He chewed on his cigar, then turned back toward the other officer. "Sawyer, I can't think of an officer in the wardroom who less deserves the hand she dealt you. I'm sorry. Detective Ramirez from the L.A. County bunco squad will be down late this afternoon with copies of the documents. He wants to talk to you. On second thought, I'll draft the letter. I'm sure that when that legal barracuda that she hired reads my reply, he'll think twice before writing his next letter to Congress. Well, that's all for now."

Joe asked, "Commander, then can I assume that this satisfactorily clears all this up and that I can request shore leave?"

"That's correct, Mr. Xylos. But do you remember what I said?"

"Yes, sir."

⋯⊷◉⊶⋯

Thus it was a chastened and almost shell-shocked Joe Xylos who followed Eva into Father Makridakis' office just after five p.m. Thursday afternoon. After the introductions, the three of them arranged themselves around a small round table. Eva sat forward in her chair, nervously moving the half-full glass of water around the tabletop. Joe leaned back, almost far enough to raise the front legs of his chair off the floor, while he sipped strong coffee from a demitasse. The clergyman sat forward, his brawny arms resting on the table as he studied the couple.

Father Makridakis looked through a small book, whose cover was so worn that grey cardboard ears poked out of the corners. He stopped at a page marked by a small green ribbon, then leafed on to a second and a third before he put the book down. He looked from one to the other before speaking, as if these were the first words of a sermon. "Marriage is a very serious sacrament. I never like to rush into it."

Joe said, "I feel the same way, Father. And perhaps we are a bit ahead of the season. Yet, I feel that necessity demands we act now."

"The time to ask a blessing on the crops is before planting the seeds and not at the harvest. There are some questions I must ask. Is either of you now married?"

"No."

"No."

"Good. Has either of you ever been divorced?"

Eva shook her head. "No."

Joe answered, "I've never been married."

"Well that certainly removes the major obstacles. Joe, are you baptized into this church?"

"Yes. It was at St. George's on Staten Island, New York."

"New York? You don't talk like you're from New York."

"After my father was crippled in the war, we moved to Missouri."

"What does he think about you marrying this woman, who isn't even Greek?"

Joe smiled at Eva and ran his hand gently along her arm as he replied, "If he were alive, I believe he would have chosen her for me."

"And your mother?"

"She preceded him. I took care of him after she died. We became very close."

"I'm sorry you lost your parents. Were you ever confirmed?"

"Yes, Father. In Saint Louis. This is my church."

"I have the feeling that you don't go to church very often. Am I right?"

Joe placed the cup on the table. "You've got me there. I haven't been since I was in high school."

"Why?"

"I worked my way through college working nights. Sundays were the only days I could sleep in. And after my mother died, I spent the time with my father because he was alone and couldn't leave his wheelchair."

"And what sort of work did you do?"

"I was the master of ceremonies, the announcer, in nightclubs . . . strip joints."

The priest sat straight up in his chair. "And after a life like that, why do you want to be married in church?"

"It's *because* of a life like that . . . of what I've seen and experienced, that I want to be married in the sight of God."

Father Makridakis took a sip from his coffee cup as if the brew were too hot. He savored it while seeming to study the book open before him. Pointing his finger at the prospective bridegroom, he said, "Joseph Xylos, you seem to have all the answers. Tell me why I should risk marrying you, an apostate, and an atheist woman whose only visit to a church was a tour of a desecrated one in the Soviet Union? What kind of chance will this child have to be raised in the faith?"

Eva asked, "And what sort of chance does he have to be raised in your faith if you turn us down?"

"That's the question I have been asking myself. I don't like the corner you're pushing me toward. It's as if the church is blessing immorality. The two of you live your lives free of God's influences. Then you get up one morning and decide to get married in sight of God, as you put it . . . come down here for a ceremony, then go home to bed that night as if everything is all right."

Joe raised his hand. "You're right that there has been a lot in my life that I've done wrong. Yet . . . Father, I don't like the picture you paint of me. Apostasy is a renunciation of faith. I think it's fair to say that you don't know me. My father died a diabetic and blind. I was his eyes. I read him the Bible. He loved Saint Paul. I read him Plato. We had lively discussions. You can't be around a man day in and day out as he makes peace with himself and his Lord and not be touched. It's because of him that I came to understand the importance of making a commitment and sticking with it. Neither Eva nor I have a family. Both of us have suffered terrible losses of those closest to us. We're from different worlds, we need every bit of help we can get. Please don't use the past to deny us our future."

Father Makridakis sat back in his chair and took another sip from his cup. "This coffee becomes bitter when it's cold. Joe, I'm not used to such maturity when counseling a couple under your circumstances. Eva told me that the Navy is sending you to the East Coast and that you wish to be married before you go."

"Yes, Father. I'll be detached on Monday the seventeenth."

"I want to talk to the two of you again. . . . at least one more time. And you, Eva, I'll need to see you at least twice and more if time permits. Don't forget to come to church Sunday. People in this parish like to know who I'm marrying. Let's see, today is the sixth. Would the twelfth be a good day?"

"That's my last duty day."

"Thursday and Saturday are out," said the priest. "It's either Friday or Sunday afternoon."

Eva answered, "I have a doctor's appointment. Joe has to check out because the ship leaves Monday. Sunday afternoon is perfect. Father, when may I come for my first lesson?"

"That was a good question. My approval is still conditional. Tomorrow in the early afternoon. Is that convenient?"

"Yes. And thank you for giving me a chance."

⋯⊙⋯

The days passed quickly for Joe Xylos until he had stood his last duty day and was cheered at "happy hour" Friday at an informal "Hail and Farewell" party at the Officer's Club. Father Makridakis held the nuptials on Sunday afternoon. The marriage ceremony was a simple one, held without the usual fanfare or music. Best man Carter Sawyer and Father Makridakis's wife were the two witnesses.

Afterward, the couple cut a small cake in the church's meeting hall while the wedding party stood around drinking coffee. During a lull in the conversation, the priest's wife asked, "Eva, have you decided on a name for your baby yet?"

After swallowing a bite of cake, she looked at Joe for a moment before she said, "After his father, Francois Henri Villerouge, if it's a boy. And Frances Henrietta Villerouge, if it's a girl."

"Really! I thought you had never been married?" queried the priest in a loud voice.

Joe put his arm around her waist. "Of course, Eva was married. She—"

The priest, with his eyes bulging, interrupted, "This cannot be! I asked you both if you had been—"

Eva smiled and raised her right hand with two fingers extended. "You asked two questions. Are we now married? Had we been divorced? I answered you truthfully, 'No.' I remember it very clearly. You never asked if I was a widow. If you took Joe to be the father of my baby, that was far better than the alternative of raising this child alone."

The priest pointed first from Joe to Eva, then back again. His face reddened, and his voice rose to a sharp pitch. "But I assumed that the two of you had . . ."

The blonde put her arm around her husband's waist, pulling him closer to her. "Joe could have, if he chose. I wanted him because that was what has always been expected of me. At first I felt rejected, and I probably would have left except I didn't think I could drive across country by myself.

Father Makridakis looked down and shook his head.

Eva said, "He never drew away from me. His words and his every action let me know that he cared. He won me with trust, respect, and love. His Greek filial love came first, with a hint of the *eros* to come. As I thought about the lectures you gave me, Father Michael, I have come to cherish him even more. He didn't take advantage of my vulnerability, but gave me time to come to grips with the reality of my Frank's murder."

"Murder!"

"Yes, by a crazy sailor on Okinawa right after I found out that I was going to have this baby."

The priest's wife said, "Eva, why, you have been widowed such a short time! I'm surprised you could rebound so quickly. How can you be sure?"

The blonde paused, then looked at Joe. "I don't know if I'll ever be sure. I do know that this man I married today will never be jealous of Frank's memory. He has promised to take care of me and this child. His idea of marriage is of each of us making a commitment to each other upon which we'll build our love. Under the circumstances, I don't think I could ask for more."

Father Michael pulled his finger around his clerical collar. "I don't know if I would have been as quick to approve this match if I'd understood your true circumstances. There isn't a compelling reason to rush into it. I almost feel as if I've been tricked."

Carter, who had stood back from the others, broke his silence. "Well, Mr. Preacher, you're no different from any other mortals who've been along the road my old shipmate Joe Xylos has walked. He has a way of getting things done, making things happen. And right now, you may be having misgivings for having listened to him. It's been my experience that you'll be patting yourself down the road."

"But . . ."

"Let me give you an example. He got me to take my car from my faithless wife who's divorcing me. I want to tell you that he caused me a whole mess of trouble. And more than a little for himself, which kept him from meeting you for a couple of days. Well, I found out that if I hadn't taken it, she and her boyfriend would have taken it out of state and may well have sold it by now. They did some crazy things that make them fugitives from justice. Things may be bad, but without him, they'd be far worse."

Father Makridakis shrugged his shoulders. "Carter, that may be. As Joe's best man, you were very persuasive today. The vows have been made, and I haven't grounds to take them back. Whether this marriage has been entered into advisedly, only time will tell. As for you, Joe, I should have listened better. You gave me clues. Rather than being an amoral hustler with a golden tongue and a belated guilty conscience, I'm surprised to find you to be a mature man, willing to take on responsibility for another man's child. I was hard on both of you. Why didn't either of you object to what I said?"

Joe pulled his earlobe. "Well, Father, the reason is that you weren't all that far from the mark for both of us. Angels didn't follow in our footsteps. Eva defected because she couldn't live with what was required of her. Thank you for giving us the chance. If fate allows, we'll be back to baptize the baby here. Fair enough?"

"Yes, certainly. God bless you both."

⋅→╞═◉ ◉═╡←⋅

The next morning, Joe parked in one of the few parking places on the pier and left his bride in their fully packed car. Nearby, the *Beaverton* stirred from the quiet of the night into the preparations for getting underway.

Eva, dressed in a maternity blouse and shorts, stepped out of the car. She leaned her elbows on the roof and watched her husband walk up the brow and out of sight. After scratching her head and again feeling the grit of beach sand from the night before, she pulled a clear plastic hairbrush out of a vanity case sitting on the pile of goods in the back seat. She bent over and began to vigorously brush her hair, just as Leah and Harry Leach drove up to the foot of the brow.

Leach leaned over to give his wife a perfunctory kiss, but she pushed him away. That startled him because he had been staring at Eva from behind. Breaking his gaze, he began to button his khaki blouse with one hand while pulling a small cloth suitcase out of the back seat. He caught his wife's eye for a moment, but she turned her head away. He looked down to the ground and heavily lifted his foot onto the brow. With his characteristic waddling motion, he made his way upward, every so often glancing back at Eva's long, well-shaped legs. It was only when the high-pitched wail of the boatswain's pipe cut through the myriad noises and the word was passed, "Now man the special sea and anchor detail!," that he picked up speed and focused his full attention on the task at hand.

Leah wheeled into the space next to Eva and leaned her head out of the car window. "Eva, I can tell you've been up to something."

"What do you mean?"

"Back when Harry was a Firstie at the Academy, I used to ride the bus back to Baltimore Sunday evenings and wonder just how many others had spent Sunday afternoon like Harry and I did. There is a certain look of satisfaction that a woman can't hide. Don't let that little twerp use you, Eva."

"Twerp? Do you mean Joe?"

"Who else, darling?"

"Leah, I resent that! Joe and I are married."

Wrinkling her nose and squinting her eyes, Leah exclaimed, "What? Married to him! When?"

"Yesterday afternoon. The trip across country will be our honeymoon."

"Eva, I wish we could have talked. It's too soon after your husband's death. You need more time to sort this out. Six months or a year from now, you'll be better able to decide that the man you're marrying is one you can live with."

"Live with? Perhaps I asked myself the wrong question. Leah, I asked myself if Joe was the man I couldn't live without. I thought about it long and hard. A man like Joe comes along once in a lifetime. He is the first man who ever wanted me for what I am and not for what I look like. He wrote me a letter every day since Frank died. In the beginning, they weren't mushy love letters, but a hand reaching out to say he cared. He cares about the child I carry."

"Eva, it's so soon. You need time . . ."

"The time since my husband's death seems like an eternity. The time I spent with Frank's folks in Richford made me realize how easy it is for time to pass me by. There were three women who befriended me there. They were widows like I was. I became the fourth for bridge. All of them lost their husbands in the war. They had their children, who were almost grown, and no one else. Oh, one of them had an affair going with a married man. The local people pretty much decided their lives by the time they finished high school. I saw myself alone with a child to raise far from my own people, and my prospects limited to affairs with a string of strangers. Then Joe called from Hawaii."

"And have I heard about that! Joe walked out the door, and no sooner did he leave than in came the Shore Patrol! Did you hear about the party and all the trouble?"

Eva paused, then said, "Yes, but that sort of thing doesn't interest me any more. Joe called me very early in the morning just after I woke up. He asked if the sun was there to shine on the light of his life because it was so dark in the middle of the night where he was. He said he'd drive to Richford on his way to Sub School. The next words he said, I'll remember for as long as I live. He said he'd like to 'court' me when I felt right about it. I didn't give him an answer. At lunch that same day, I told one of my friends what Joe had said and that I'd think about marrying again when I stopped hurting inside. She said she had been alone for fourteen years and she still hurt. She said it hurts a lot less when you're not alone. And that it's far easier to get a man to marry you before the baby arrives. Frenchy's dad gave me the money for the plane fare."

"At the Hail and Farewell, Joe kept it a secret."

"I wanted it that way. Marrying when you're six months pregnant carries an immoral stigma. Besides, we decided at the last moment."

"I see. Well, congratulations. I'm more than surprised that you'd decide so quickly. Still, you hardly know him . . ."

"Leah, I've known him for longer than I knew the father of this child."

"And from the way you glow, he must make you very happy."

"Yes. After the first night of marriage to him, I feel like a fine Stradivarius being played by a master."

Leah pushed open her car door and stepped onto the pier. "Eva, I apologize for the way I talked about your husband. You told me about a side of him I didn't know existed. My first encounter with Joe was not at all pleasant. And looking back on it, Harry started the trouble. In fact, Harry Leach never has had much good to say about him."

"I can believe that."

"Since returning from the deployment, all I've heard has been how this one skinny Reserve Ensign was singlehandedly responsible for ending a promising career. Never mind that Harry was passed over the second time before he ever met Joe Xylos. Never mind that Harry drinks until he passes out and is always screwing around with the girls. I've had it up to here with that fat jerk. Harry never will admit he has made a mistake and blames me for not being a good hostess. Well, I never did like buttering up some snooty bitch just because she was lucky enough to marry some guy who made Captain. Officer's Wives Clubs, Navy Relief, gossip—that's what it takes to get ahead. Oh, I don't need to tell you, you've been there. Coming back for seconds tells me you'll be a good asset to Joe's career."

"No, I am the kiss of death to a Navy career. They fired Frenchy from his job and took away his security clearance because we married. Joe will probably lose his."

"Really? I never heard of that happening before. Why?"

"I was an officer in the Hungarian AVH."

"AVH?"

"State security . . . the secret police."

"Oh, my! You don't talk like a foreigner."

"I was trained in the Ukraine for two years."

"Then you're a communist?"

"I used to say I was. Looking back, I don't know if I ever was. I went along because it was the thing to do and because my uncle was a power in the party. In the end, I had become ashamed of what I was. I am ashamed of what was done to my country. I felt used . . . dirty. Since my liberation, I have had to make a conscious effort to trust people. The whole time I was with Frank, I kept trying to figure out who the informers were. I was sure the Chaplain was some sort of political officer. It wasn't until after Frank was murdered that the warmth, the friendship, and yes, the love of these people overcame my fears and suspicions. I like being a Navy wife. In Richford, Frank's parents were wonderful in spite of their loss. Other people there were good to me, but I felt so . . . so alone. The open border to Canada surprised me, in spite of all I had been told in training. And living so close to it made me fear that someone could sneak across and either kill or kidnap me."

"This is a free country. You don't have to worry."

"That may be, but last night we had a brush with the border police."

"Border police? You mean the Border Patrol?"

"Yes. We were down on the beach together. Now I had spent hours there earlier, watching, and never once did I ever see a uniform. And then there in the dark, I saw them coming with their flashlights. We didn't even have a chance to go down into the water and wash off the sand."

Leah laughed. "Eva, what were you doing on the beach?"

Eva's eyes sparkled as she softly said, "We're married. So what difference does it make?"

"Did you get arrested for skinny dipping?"

"No. I used my training. We hid among the rocks until they went the other way and then climbed up a trail to the car. We got back okay, but I'm still brushing the sand out of my hair. Joe thought it was all very funny, but I didn't want to take any chances."

Eva tossed the brush into the car and began to do stretching exercises.

Leah watched the other woman's almost masculine-looking muscles rippling in her calves and arms in silence for a long minute before saying, "I'm going to miss the Navy. I can't say I'm going to miss that fat jerk."

The blonde paused in her exercises. "What are you talking about?"

"I told him to get out and stay out."

"Why?"

"He humiliated me. I've put up with his games for years. Last fall, he embarrassed the hell out of me when he shacked up with Miss Finland after the Miss Universe contest, but the latest takes the cake. That fat bastard gave me the clap! And he didn't tell me about it. The Public Health people told me because my 'sex partner' had been treated! Can you imagine?"

Eva struggled to keep a straight face. She paused long enough for the muscles in her cheeks to relax before saying, "I never heard of such a thing."

"Oh, we've had a pretty open marriage, and maybe that was a mistake. But this, along with his insistence on going back to Virginia, was more than I could take. Eva, I've been working for three years to build up my real estate business. I can't afford to go back to Virginia. I made more in commissions during the first three months than Harry made all last year. He just flipped when I suggested that he stay home and take care of the children."

Leah shaded her eyes and looked upward toward the bridge of the *Beaverton*. Then, pointing upward, she almost shouted, "There he is now! Look, on the bridge. He so loves to run the ship. He had his own command once, the USS *Fusillade*, an LSMR, but he lost it. Got drunk and missed movement. It's been downhill from there. Well, I hope he makes it through the day. He was so hung over this morning that I barely got him dressed in time."

The general announcing system sounded two bells followed by the words, "Ensign departing!" The pipe wailed.

Eva and Leah turned to see Joe shake hands with the black Chief nearest the side—the newly promoted Richards—and salute smartly, then walk down the brow, followed by a Filipino steward lugging a suitcase. After Joe unlocked the trunk, the steward carefully laid the suitcase inside.

As he closed the lid, Joe said, "Thanks, Diego, for carrying the bag down for me."

The steward smiled. "It was my pleasure, sir. You one damn fine officer, sir. Good luck in submarines, okay?"

"Okay."

Joe put an arm around Eva's waist and said, "I've got my orders, and I hope I didn't forget anything."

Then, looking at Leah and pointing toward the wing of the bridge where Harry Leach stood, he said, "Well, Mrs. Leach, the cruiser *Beaverton* is safe for another week with Lieutenant Leach at the conn. You can go home. He has the first watch, so I don't think he'll sneak off this time."

"Harry wouldn't miss this week for the world. It's his last one. I wanted to be here to see him go out this last time."

"And hopefully, it will be a good week. I was tempted to stay to have the satisfaction of being there for the gunnery shoot. Number Two turret has an `E' on the line with the exercise this afternoon. Now if you'll excuse me, I'm going over to help on Number Two line."

Soon, the crane removed the brow and the nylon mooring lines were singled up with only an eye to the bollard around which they were secured. The Captain and Harry Leach watched as Joe and a seaman lifted off the eye of the Number Two line and tossed it over the side. The end fell on the camel, the wooden float that separated the ship from the pier. The seamen on deck hauled in on it until the eye passed through the chocks and lay on deck like a dead nylon snake.

After the other lines were hauled aboard and with the tugs throwing up wakes, the first backing bell was transmitted to the engine room.

The line handlers walked toward the head of the pier. Still standing at pierside was one couple. The Captain briefly trained his binoculars on Joe, who was holding Eva's hand. He muttered, "What's the country coming to? Officer's ladies don't wear shorts. Who's he with anyway? Damned if she doesn't look pregnant. "

Leach scanned the pier before saying, "That's Frenchy Villerouge's widow. You remember the guy who was murdered by that crazy seaman in Okinawa?"

"Oh, yeah. What's she doing here?"

"I guess she's settled here. She's been around since we got back from WESTPAC. I suppose Mr. Xylos has something going."

The Old Man adjusted his metal-rimmed sunglasses. "He may, and again he may not. That incident certainly was a watershed for that young man. He has been a straight and sober young officer who has stayed out of trouble. These last months certainly vindicated my judgment. I'm sorry to lose him. I know you've had little use for him. Yet, admit it, Harry, he bailed you out of a mess of trouble in Second Division. You may yet go out in a blaze of glory this week. Number Two turret should keep their 'E.' The breeze is setting us nicely off the pier, you can go to two-thirds anytime."

"Aye, aye, sir. All back two-thirds. We do have a chance as long as I get a good fire control solution. No, he wasn't all bad."

CHAPTER 32

Sweet Old Bob

The pomp and circumstance of the change of command was over. Guests, official and otherwise, had departed. At the relieving commanding officer's insistence, Captain Sam Slaxman had acquiesced to having the reception held in the wardroom. It had been a short one. Wives and sweethearts had retreated to their cars to await their loved ones in the late afternoon sun.

XO Longstreet stood beside the new CO, Captain Robert Pinkney, as they watched Captain Sam drive away in his black 1938 Ford coupe. In contrast to him, his relief was tall, lean, with distinguished white sideburns. Where Slaxman was ruddy with a light beard, the new man was pale and had very dark whiskers that gave him a five o'clock shadow even right after a shave. Although his orders read that he was detached from duty at the Bureau of Naval Ordnance, he had spent his career in destroyers and openly regarded submarines and submariners as "the enemy." This often-expressed opinion chilled the cordiality of the turnover.

The new CO grumbled, "A four-striper who's drawn sub pay for just about his whole career, and he drives a prewar Ford! Talk about cheap! I doubt if he'll make it across the Mojave Desert."

The XO said, "Actually, he's probably put enough into that coupe to buy a new one. With the Captain's family back on the East Coast, working on that car has been his hobby ever since we returned from WESTPAC. Last month, he put in a new transmission over at the base hobby shop."

Pinkney's voice rose an octave. "Do you mean the commanding officer of a ship of the line crawled around in the grease pits over at the hobby shop?"

"Yes, sir, he did. And was in a better mood the next day for doing it."

Pinkney shook his head. "Here are all these kids who can't afford to have their cars worked on, and he's taking up a stall when he could pay to have the work done. Commander, have all the officers assemble in the wardroom. I wish to speak to them. Their shore leave is canceled until I pass the word."

"I beg your pardon, sir. There are a number of wives waiting on the pier, and it's fifteen thirty, and—"

"Commander Longstreet, I am well aware of the time."

Empty coffee cups and glasses, as well as the depth of butts in the ashtrays, were ample evidence that the wardroom had been waiting some time when, at twenty minutes after four, the new CO stepped to the podium. He searched through a manila folder filled with papers and news clippings until he found a pair of sheets from a lined pad. He stretched himself taller, throwing his shoulders back and lengthening his neck slightly. Uniformly, the eyes that met his were hostile. Most officers sat with their arms folded.

After looking around the room from face to face, he broke eye contact and began, "Gentlemen, as you must be aware, even my wife calls me 'Sweet Old Bob,' and to those of you who don't meet my high standards, you'll quickly understand why. It is my firm belief that high moral standards are what have given this nation the edge in the wars we have fought. And it is my intention to stiffen the crew's moral resolve and end the decadence that has made this ship an embarrassment to the fleet. It is my firm belief that the wardroom sets the tone for the rest of the ship."

He opened the folder and took out a clipping, which he held away from his body as he read, "San Diego *Union*, September 24, 1956, dateline Tijuana, Mexico." He paused and scanned the assembly before he continued, "'Among the unfortunate victims of the early September raid on the gambling casino were Mr. and Mrs. Martin Sarkian, owners of the Best Way Laundry. Coincidentally, Best Way had a contract with the Tijuana jail and it was Sarkian's decision to hold the jail's laundry hostage that helped speed the release of the Sarkians and numerous others. Among the recent returnees was a local schoolteacher, Tammy

Nuslund. Miss Nuslund said that an Ensign Xylos bailed out a call girl and his two shipmates from the USS *Beaverton*, a Long Beach cruiser, but left her to rot. Chivalry and good judgment must have been left in San Ysidro!'"

The tall Captain looked around the room from face to face. "Xylos, where is this Mr. Xylos?"

Rufus Johnson, who had risen from his seat and was walking toward the door with his fists clenched, barked, "You don't have to worry about him, he's in Sub School, sir."

"A sub-ma-reen-er! Sounds like one of them. Thank you, doctor." Rufus was almost to the door when the Captain loudly called, "Where are you going, mister?"

"Out! Out to cool off before I say or do something that both of us will regret."

The door to the wardroom would have slammed had it not been for the hydraulic door closer, which arrested its swing.

"Sweet Old Bob" turned to his XO, his voice going up a couple of octaves. "No one walks out on me! Tell that man to report to my cabin! Who the hell does he think he is?"

Longstreet blinked, then, in his slow Southern drawl in almost a whisper, said, "Captain, I would hope you could meet with him in private. He deserves an apology. The so-called 'call girl' is his bride. They married in August."

There was a scattering of snickers that rippled into nervous laughter.

The new Captain held the folder up. "Gentlemen, what I have to say is no laughing matter! There are more of these reprehensible news items. 'War of the Worlds in Belmont Shore'; 'Picket Fences in Melbourne'; fights and college pranks in the Officer's Clubs in Guam; riots in Yokosuka; and on and on. Does it stop when we get back? No, there's an ongoing serial in the Honolulu papers about just a two-day stopover. Now, an officer's wife tells the papers that she was driven to a life of crime because her estranged husband, an officer aboard this ship, refused to support her."

His voice got even higher and his mouth wider. "There is a common thread to this, the name of this ship . . . *Beaverton* . . . *Beaverton*. I am here to put an end to this infamous theater. Gentlemen, during my command, this kind of news shall not happen. Because if it does, heads will roll! Do I make myself clear?"

The white noise of the shipboard equipment was broken by a faint creaking in a chair here and there. The assembled officers sat impassively, most with arms still folded across their chests. The XO said, "Certainly, Captain. Isn't that right, gentlemen?"

There was a faint murmuring of "ayes" from mouths that hardly moved.

The Captain laid the folder aside and went on to another subject. "This ship is reasonably clean, but that isn't good enough. It must shine! We are the flagship, and we shall look like the flagship. During the coming deployment, Commander Seventh Fleet will be riding aboard for six weeks. We will be ready and will look the part from the top of the mainmast to the double bottoms. My belief is that if a ship looks good, it will be good. Every Saturday morning until I am satisfied, there will be material and personnel inspections. In preparation for this Saturday's inspection, field day will be held starting tomorrow at eight and will continue until eighteen hundred. This ship will shine!"

Pointing at Longstreet, he screamed, "You and that quack in my in-port cabin as soon as possible!"

Five minutes later, Captain Pinkney stood on the far side of his dining table with Doc Johnson and the XO standing on the other side. The new CO said, "Whatever possessed you to run, doctor? Is that how you will face the enemy?"

Rufus's jaw tendons worked and his lips moved before he said, "Lyla and I had to grovel in the mud to get out of that damn Mexican jail. To have the falsehoods we were forced to admit under duress thrown up again, is more than I can stomach. And thank God for Joe Xylos! A better shipmate I've never had. An apology would convince me that the insult to my wife was a thoughtless one. Yes, sir, I apologize for leaving as I did."

He reached a hand out to the Captain, who looked at it and paused before screaming, "You challenged my authority as commanding officer!"

Rufus snapped, "You insulted my wife! I was hoping there would be some attempt to mend fences, an apology."

"Come, doctor, how was I to know the wh— woman was your wife? I simply read the news clipping. If you have a beef, take it up with the paper."

Longstreet said, "Captain, please for a moment look at this through the doc's eyes. Every officer in that room knows who the woman was, his wife. We all know that this is a very tender subject with Rufus. I don't see how you could have possibly known, sir. I would have liked to have the opportunity to allow you to give him a public apology, but he left too quickly. Now isn't too late."

"I don't know if I should shake hands with a man I'm about to put in hack."

Staring the Captain in the eyes, Rufus barely moved his lips, muttering, "I'll appeal!"

"You'll lose."

"You won't win, sir."

The minutes ticked by in the quiet room. The Captain's lips thinned and he barely showed his teeth; then he slightly smiled as his right hand went out. "Doctor, I would be getting off on the wrong foot with you. Don't think you're setting a precedent with this conduct. Go on ashore and enjoy your wife's company while you can. We'll be going west all too soon. And yes, you can expect a notation of your conduct on your next fitness report."

"Thank you, Captain. I'm sorry I reacted as I did."

The XO remained after Rufus left. When the doctor was out of earshot, "Sweet Old Bob" shouted, "Commander, don't you ever suggest that I apologize. You back me, understand? The man who apologizes admits he is weak. I will not be humbled."

"Yes, sir."

Stan Longstreet was dismissed by the Captain after six p.m., his ears ringing from the bombast that had followed. He stopped in the wardroom to announce the beginning of liberty for the officers. He went ashore and slid behind the wheel of his car.

Letty said, "Didn't he know the wives were left sitting on the pier for almost three and a half hours? What was that all about?"

Longstreet stubbed into the ashtray the stump of the stogie he had almost chewed in half. After tossing his cap into the back seat, he gripped the steering wheel and stared down the road in silence for a while. Then he said, "Yes to your first question. And to the second, I really don't know. By the way he carried on in front of the wardroom, I thought I was going to be fired. In fact, for most of the time we met, I had the feeling he was ready to call BUPERS. But in the end, he expressed a need for us to work together during the transition before my relief arrives in December."

"What happened?"

Exhaling the last vestiges of a lungful of smoke, he said, "He called a meeting of the wardroom and let us cool our heels for the better part of an hour. The first words out of his mouth so stung Doc Johnson that he walked out of the room."

"How?"

"I'm positive that it wasn't intentional. He read aloud the article about the Tijuana jail incident last September. He made his point, but I fear it cost him dearly."

"Why should that keep everyone on board all this time?"

"He and I met in his stateroom until just a few minutes ago. At his insistence, the wardroom had to remain on board until it was over. That man is a screamer! I don't mind getting chewed out for what happened today, but to be dragged over the coals for every sin that has been committed since this ship was commissioned . . ."

"Stan, I don't ever recall hearing about this."

"I kept a folder of news clippings, good and bad, for Captain Sam. Captain Pinkney went over every bad clipping with me. I wonder if that was his plan before Rufus stomped out. And the look on the faces of the wardroom! That man has lost every one of them. I don't envy my relief. I've never seen Rufus Johnson with his dander up before. He stared him down. I thought the doc had cut his own throat. Thank you, Lord, for giving the Captain that small opening to save his face."

While he was talking, she pulled a tan envelope out of her purse and removed a single sheet. With it fell a three-by-five card and a Polaroid photo. As she unfolded it, she said, "It's time to stop thinking about work. Joe Xylos mailed a letter to the house. Let me read it to you."

"All right."

"Dear XO and Letty,

*Eva had the baby on the 17th at 1430, a boy, Francois Henri Vil-
lerouge, Jr. Both are doing very well. The time since the* Beaverton
*arrived in Long Beach has been the happiest of my life. I feel a great
fulfillment in sharing my life with my wonderful Eva. We are learning
to love each other, getting closer every day.*

*We're in quarters on base, a cramped one-bedroom apartment,
which we were lucky to get. Eva thinks it's a palace. It's within walking
distance of everything. . . . Sub School is going very well. I'm standing
sixth in the class, thanks to support from Eva. Actually I'm playing
hookey from studying by writing this letter. With her, you don't study
until you get the homework done, you study until you know it all. . . .
We have been regular homebodies. No parties and haven't even been
to the club, except for one command performance reception. I know
you'll find it hard to believe, but no one around me has gotten into a
scrape since we arrived. I saw the article in* Navy Times *about Captain
Slaxman's orders to be Deputy CNO. He's a prince among men. The
new CO will have a hard act to follow. . . ."*

Longstreet muttered, "That's for damn sure."

*"I've written a letter to Captain Sam, telling him of the news and
thanking him for this opportunity. I owe him and you more than I can
ever repay. Enclosed is a picture and a card with our address. I hope
this finds all of you on the* Beaverton *enjoying fair winds and following
seas.*

Sincerely, Joe."

Longstreet sighed, "There's the Dutchman's breeches, the first
glimpse of blue sky I have had all day. Sixth in class! Not bad, not bad.
Let me see that picture. Sort of looks like Frenchy. I wonder when they
got married. Thank you, dear. Sam was right about that young man.
Let's stop on the way home for some Chinese take-out food. I'm too
hungry to wait for you to cook."

◦→═◉═←◦

The *Beaverton* anchored late in the afternoon of 7 November. Without even checking the incoming mail, Stan Longstreet followed what
was becoming a shipwide practice: go ashore when there was any opportunity. The next morning, the item on top of the mound of correspondence was a light-pink box that was about a twelve-inch cube. On

it was a pattern of shields, which he immediately identified as nearly a double for the ship's insignia. He pulled out his special-issue Zippo lighter with the insignia on it and closely compared the two, noting three significant differences. Most obvious was that the three eight-inch projectiles looked like inflated torpedoes. The second was that the limbs making the "V" at the top were legs, at whose juncture little was left to the imagination. The last was that the word on the second banner was "SHIELDS" instead of "USS *Beaverton*." He opened the big box, spilling numerous little red boxes onto the table. On one side they had the same shield trademark and on the reverse, a silhouette of a *Baltimore*-class cruiser and the words "Ticklers For Eager Beavers."

He picked up one little red box and muttered, "This is a joke." The weak laugh that croaked out of his throat was not convincing. He removed a high-quality bond sheet from a business-size envelope nestled among the condom boxes.

Out loud he read,

"Dear Captain Pinkney:

We at the Shield Rubber Company congratulate you on taking command of the cruiser, USS Beaverton. *One of our dealers in Topeka, your hometown, sent us the picture of you shaking hands in front of your ship's bronze seal. We couldn't help but notice the extremely close resemblance your very handsome seal bears to our registered trademark, which we began using in 1935. Our attorney told me that the keel to your ship was laid in 1943.*

He suggested instituting a lawsuit, but I'm not in business to make him rich. Captain, imitation is the highest form of flattery. And we here at the Shield Rubber Company, a small business in the Midwest, marketing our very high-quality product in vending machines in the best bars and night clubs, are flattered that you would choose to model the great seal of the cruiser USS Beaverton *after our trademark.*

We wouldn't think of asking you to change or stop using your current seal. It must have cost a king's ransom in taxpayer's dollars to cast that bronze shield. If you did change it, no doubt our taxes would have to go up.

In fact, it is only if you do change, that we will object. Our public relations firm has prepared a hard-hitting campaign for that contin-

gency.

There are very good business reasons for our acquiescence. The Los Angeles manufacturer's representative that we recently signed on has landed a contract to place our vending machines in Navy and Air Force Clubs from Seattle to San Diego. We are in the vanguard in the fight against venereal disease.

Since conventional advertising isn't available to our industry, we have consistently had success penetrating new markets by wide use of free samples. Concurrent with posting of this letter to you, every ship in the U.S. Pacific Fleet will receive a sampler pack for free distribution or sale in the ship's store. The box you received should have more than enough for one for each Beaverton sailor. We have no objection to the excess being sold in your ship's store. Captain, we've adopted you. . . .

Cordially, Vincente Costello."

Behind him, he heard a snicker. He turned as Lieutenant Barry Tumwater, with his face contorting between a grin and an attempt to look serious, said, "Commander, I've always wondered why they gave us the radio call sign 'Rubber Duck.' How do you think the Captain is going to react?"

Longstreet swallowed. "I imagine . . . he'll . . . he will go high order no matter how we break it to him. You know, looking back on it, that beaver wasn't so ugly."

Tumwater handed the XO a large thick envelope. "Commander, here is some more bad news."

"What?"

"The statements from the women who were at the party on Waikiki last May."

"What took them so long? I thought we had that all settled last summer. What could they add?"

"Just about everything. Commander Wyman's investigation didn't get very far, except to confirm who was at the party when the HASP arrived. The official interest ended when that Mazini fellow was fired by the university and he dropped his suit against the government."

The Commander chuckled. "That man, after infecting seven women, was in no position to expect them to cover his butt."

"The contents, if they ever leaked, would harm these officers terribly. Parts of these statements aren't the kind of thing I'd want my kids reading. It's no wonder we had a clap epidemic. Captain Bob will skewer everyone they've identified. The one you ought to read is Melba Walker's."

Longstreet moved the box aside and took the onionskin sheets that Tumwater handed him. As he read, Tumwater said, "Commander Wyman never focused on Joe Xylos because he wasn't there when the HASP came. The first thing she says is that it was Xylos who encouraged her to throw the first beer bottle into the trash container on the street.

"Note, Xylos did not throw a single bottle. Hrrumph, just like him."

"And she fully implicated Mr. Cobb, Outside White, and the Navigator as poor shots whose bottles fell wide of the mark. Check the last page. That's far more graphic than anything you'd see in *Playboy* . . . the detail she goes into about all the things that went on between her and Mr. Cobb and the third female."

As the XO read, he said, "Oh, shit! What on earth possessed this woman to commit this sort of thing to writing?"

"As fine an example of 'hell knows not' as I've ever seen."

"Could you imagine a woman sitting on a witness chair in open court giving this kind of testimony? Regarding Xylos, does anyone else back her?"

"When Commander Wyman had the duty Saturday, I asked him about Joe. He told me that Inside White and Xylos were the only ones who acted like they had nothing to hide. Both cooperated fully. Nobody else, either here or among the officers, even mentioned Joe's name. There were some bad feelings between the revelers and Joe. Sean Perkins, for one, claimed Joe was the one who called the HASP. Maybe this was the reason."

"I was with him that evening. He was sober as a judge. Yes, Joe is capable of getting something started and walking away, but his mind was back on the mainland. He was preoccupied about Eva, really subdued. I take this as sour grapes. "

Tumwater repeated, "Captain Bob will skewer every one of them."

"Hardly. Xylos and Cobb are in school. Harry Leach and Wayne

White are out of the Navy. The Navigator has been passed over for Commander. There are three broken marriages, including Harry's. The affair was reflected in the last fitness reports. I'm sure Captain Pinkney will get upset, but the instructions are clear about such matters. It all happened on Captain Sam's watch."

"Commander, these statements are terribly defamatory. We should treat them as if they are top secret."

"Concur. Call the Legal Officer and have him come to my office to review this material. There's too much here that would ruin reputations if leaked. And please assemble the pertinent directives so I can brief the Captain."

"Did you forget that the new Legal Officer is still in Justice School?"

"Tell the Chief Engineer that I have to borrow Mr. Sawyer again. At least he can give me straight answers."

"Aye, aye, sir."

The gongs sounded on the announcing system, followed by the words *"Beaverton,* arriving!" The XO pulled his hat on and went to the quarterdeck. Captain Bob was coming aboard.

The Captain's face had more color in it that morning than anyone could recall seeing. It was mostly red as his head appeared above the deck at the top of the accommodation ladder. His thin lips quivered as he went through the piping-aboard ceremony on the quarterdeck. Once clear of the columns of sideboys, he pitched a little red box sidehand at his XO as his voice filled the quarterdeck. "Commander Longstreet, whose idea of a joke is this? They have made a laughingstock of me and my command."

Longstreet snagged the box like a shortstop, asking, "Where did you get this, Captain?"

"From the Chief Staff Officer! And I had to take a ribbing from Llewellyn on the *Toledo*! The Shield Rubber Company! Really, this has to be some sort of bad joke!"

"I'm afraid it's not, sir. We have a whole box of them, plus a letter from the president of the company. I'll bring them to your cabin as soon as possible."

Captain Pinkney pointed at the bronze insignia. "How long has this been the ship's insignia?"

"Oh, I don't know. I think it was right before we deployed last time that we held a contest."

From the back of the quarterdeck, Father Finn said, "That's right, sir, I judged the entries."

The Captain screamed, "Contest? Who's responsible for this?"

"I am, Captain. I chose this handsome design over all the other entries." Father Finn held the box up as he continued, "But I've never been in the market for these. I remember it very well. It was the only entry submitted on posterboard. Come to think of it, the three projectiles looked more like torpedoes."

"Who submitted this entry?"

"We gave Saul Fineman, the Quartermaster, a twenty-five-dollar savings bond."

Captain Pinkney pointed a finger at the XO. "Commander, get that man! You know what to do."

"Aye, aye, sir."

Father Finn raised his hand. "Captain, let's not act in haste. There may be a reasonable explanation. Besides, this is a beautiful work of art and probably the finest example of naval heraldry in the Pacific Fleet. Let's not give in to owners of the devil's factory."

Just over two hours later, Lieutenant (junior grade) Carter Sawyer joined the XO in the Captain's in-port cabin. Both of his sleeves were wrinkled from cuffs to mid-arm from having recently been rolled up. His unbuttoned collar was stained with sweat, and his tie failed to bring the ends of his collar together.

Bob Pinkney's eyes jumped from side to side, and he rubbed his hands as if they were cold, while Carter and Longstreet filed in. Zeroing in on the young officer, he said, "Well, Mr. Sawyer, it looks like you're finally getting your hands dirty. How is the work progressing on Number Two boiler?"

"Yes, sir, I am. We're well into removing the old bricks. It's really neat to stand inside and see all those hot water pipes, Captain."

"And what role did you have in this affair?"

"No role, sir. The XO asked me to look at the letter he got from the rubber company."

Longstreet said, "Since his relief is away at school, I asked Mr. Sawyer to stand in. Besides, he's the only real lawyer we have on board."

The CO straightened his back and stretched his neck like a giraffe reaching for an overhanging branch. "After he laid waste a day's work for my Number One special court, I am well aware that he is a real lawyer. He is well practiced in the use of legal technicalities to effectively jam the smooth working gears of our military justice system."

Carter, with his characteristic half-open eyes and a slight smile tugging his lips, said, "Sir, you give me undeserved credit. The machinery was already broken. I only did my job as defense counsel to point out the breakdown."

"Breakdown! Every one of those men was guilty."

"Well, that may be, sir, and again it may not. The President of the Court certainly made a mockery of the basic concept of the presumption of innocence when he told the Master at Arms to 'bring in the next guilty bastard.'"

"Enough of this. Commander, what did you find out?"

Longstreet threw a worn, empty condom box on the table. "QM Two Fineman admitted that he used the Shield Company's trademark as the inspiration for the insignia. He says he didn't copy it. Here is the box."

"Then it's obvious, we're the copycats. I'll have to tell the Admiral. Thank goodness this thing was adopted before my watch. I've never heard of the Shield Rubber Company. Where did he get this box?"

"Ensign Xylos gave it to him along with enough hints to submit a winning entry."

"Xylos again! He's a bad dream that comes back for re-runs. Well, I can't think of a better place in the Navy for people like him than in submarines. This time we'll cook his goose and that copycat Quartermaster too. I'll deal with Fineman at mast."

Carter said, "Captain, I'd advise against acting in haste. As much as this has embarrassed you, Fineman has not committed a criminal act."

"I beg your pardon!"

"You can't take away a man's liberty because you don't like his artwork. It's all a part of the Constitution that we swore to uphold and defend."

"Wait a minute, Mr. Sawyer! Plagiarism must be conduct contrary to good order and discipline."

"Then why aren't those guys who sell the rubbers screaming that you violated their copyright? They could get plenty of publicity out of the litigation. But if they did that, you'd be on solid ground."

Stan Longstreet held his Zippo lighter beside the condom box. "Captain, I see two possible reasons why they aren't doing anything. The first is that Fineman changed the thing just enough that their lawyer isn't sure they have a case. After all, trying to convince a jury that two fingers, complete with fingernails, held in a 'V' is the same as the frontal view of a naked woman would take tremendous skill. The second is that this is the company's first attempt to sell their rubbers to military activities in the West. You don't get contract renewals by suing your customers."

The CO waved a condom box. "I'm still a laughingstock. There are ways we can make Fineman pay dearly without bringing him to mast. That damn Xylos! Somehow, I'll have his ass."

The lawyer said, "Captain, life would be hell without a sense of humor. Oh, there will be a few words for a few days, but most people don't buy rubbers in the men's room when they can get them in the exchange for a whole lot less. This will all be forgotten well before the ship returns from the next deployment."

"Forgotten? 'Ticklers for Eager Beavers,' not by me! That cast piece on the quarterdeck must have cost an arm and a leg."

The XO said, "That's right, sir. It is irreplaceable. We could never get another like it on this side of the Date Line."

Captain Bob asked, "Stan, how did you get that job order through?"

"I didn't ask the Engineer. But I understand that we traded a substantial number of gallons of paint."

"Paint . . . Would that be white house paint?"

"I don't know, sir. Why?"

"Do you remember the white paint I found during the very first zone inspection?"

"Vaguely, yes, sir."

"Since it was house paint, I directed the First Lieutenant to turn it in to Supply."

"That makes sense. This isn't a wooden ship."

"It seems that all twelve cans were from a lot that was stolen from the supply depot on Guam. A total of sixty-two five-gallon cans disappeared from a lowboy while the *Beaverton* was alongside. I had a call from an ONI investigator, and they are after blood."

"Why didn't they talk to me? What's so special about this paint?"

"Apparently it was the depot's entire allotment. There's a rather extensive list of other missing items. Cumshaw is one thing, but I gather they defined it more like pillage. XO, the void that paint was in belonged to M Division, and the infamous Mr. Xylos was the M Division Officer when the ship visited Guam."

The XO said, "Yes, sir. Like I've told you before, Xylos was regularly at the edge, but beyond the reach, of trouble. He is a bright, promising officer and doing very well in Submarine School. In the letter he sent me recently, he said he's standing sixth in his class."

Carter said, "Captain, we've been talking about that paint in the log room. Nobody remembers seeing it around before the inspection. Just because you found paint down there, who's to say that Joe had anything to do with it? Besides, Joe took leave and more or less disappeared into the woodwork with some Japanese honey."

The XO nodded. "That's right, I remember. He was shacked up with The Original Fuji the whole time."

Captain Bob steepled his fingers and leaned back. "I remember her from when we came in off the line during Korea. If you weren't at least a Commander, you couldn't even afford to buy her a cherry drink. I've never heard anyone say that this fellow is independently wealthy. I wonder where he got the money. Selling paint, perhaps?"

Carter shook his head. "Captain, you don't know Joe Xylos. He'd never buy sex."

"Mr. Sawyer, I may not know Ensign Xylos, but I do know The Original Fuji and she does no charity work. Working behind the scenes, he duped Fineman into submitting the entry, then released some of the paint that he had his men steal to trade for that insignia. And taking leave with Fuji is as fine a cover as I've ever seen."

"Captain, I'm not going to be a party to this railroad you're building. Joe Xylos is one of the finest men I have ever known." Carter tossed a legal-size folder on the table.

"Railroad? You must be good friends with Mr. Xylos. Is that correct?"

"Yes sir, we lived in Boys' Town for the whole cruise. I heard Captain Slaxman say Joe was the kind of officer he would like to go to war with. That's pretty much the way I feel too."

"Mr. Sawyer, loyalty to a shipmate is understandable. Thank you for taking time away from your pressing duties in B Division. Your counsel will be weighed before I make my decision."

Carter nodded, stood to full attention, and turned to leave. "Thank you, Captain."

After he left the room, Captain Pinkney said, "XO, have Commander Wyman call me before he talks to Boatswain Bail in the paint locker. I'm sure Mr. Xylos will be rightfully surprised to find himself caught in a web of his own making. I intend that he fully pay for the embarrassment he has caused this command."

CHAPTER 33

Second Thoughts on Security

Through the warm days of July and August, Eva took numerous solitary walks through the submarine base at New London, Connecticut, during the afternoons while Joe was in class. In the beginning, she walked from her apartment just south of the base golf course to the North Gate and back. Then she began exploring, extending her adventures into the wooded and hilly areas along the eastern fence. She attracted little attention. Male eyes would be drawn to her pretty face, then fix for a moment on the pregnant bulge in her middle before moving on.

In mid-August, news traveled around the base about four enlisted men who were caught riding their motorcycles through an illegal postern gate cut into the chain link fence in a hilly area that was obscured by a stand of trees. A week later, PFC Robert Durinmeyer, USMC, was found derelict in the performance of his duty as gate sentry at the North Gate by the CO Marine Barracks. The evidence was a pair of Polaroid photographs showing him seated on a stool, slouched over and apparently asleep.

Four days after Joe's first underway on the USS *Milkfish*, Eva's control, FBI Agent Martin Pugsley, shipped a small sheet metal box to FBI headquarters in Washington, D.C. Pugsley reported that Eva found it in a dumpster at the head of the pier where the *Milkfish* moored. It contained carbon paper sheets with Secret text imprinted on them.

In early September, Commander Casey Collins, the XO of Submarine School, while driving back to his office from lunch at the Officer's Club, saw a cloud of ashes raining down on the road ahead. It was a sight he had seen many times because they came from a trash incinerator on the lower base. What caught his attention was a long-legged and pregnant blonde, who was waving an open book through the ash cloud raining down all around her. Thanks to her strikingly beautiful face and golden hair, he easily remembered that he'd seen her walking around the base before. The last glimpse of her in his rear-view mirror froze in his memory; it reminded him of some sort of pantomime. Pulling into his parking place at the office, he thought fleetingly that she could have been catching the ashes in the pages of the book. He dismissed the thought, concluding that she probably was trying to keep them out of her hair.

Later he penciled a memo to his boss about the steps he had taken to assure that the carbons used in typing classified correspondence were treated with the same caution as the correspondence. He was pleased that none of his people were as careless as the USS *Milkfish*, whose classified carbons had been found mixed with ordinary trash in the dumpster at the head of the pier.

Casey Collins was on the stage when most of the New London officers were gathered in the base auditorium to hear Admiral Hyman G. Rickover, known as the "Father of the Nuclear Navy," speak at the dedication of the Nuclear Power School. The Admiral was late. The room was so hot and humid that Collins felt it was more like a day in August in Charleston than New London in October. To fill the empty minutes while awaiting the Admiral, the schedule was changed so that the Commanding Officer U.S. Submarine School could present a Navy and Marine Corps Medal to a Sub School officer student. He was familiar with the name only because it was last on the alphabetical list.

Collins watched the short, slightly built, round-shouldered officer make his way from the second row to the stage. As he stood in front of the commanding officer, Captain Brent Gilmore, who was a large-boned six-footer, the young officer even looked smaller, almost effete.

The Commander let his mind wander as the Captain began reading the citation. The first words he caught were ". . . with great disregard to his own personal safety, unarmed, entered the Duty Office near White Beach, Buckner Bay, Okinawa, where an officer and four enlisted men were held hostages at gunpoint. There Ensign Joseph Xylos, United States Navy Reserve, confronted Seaman Thomas Brown, a man who was five foot eleven tall and weighed one hundred ninety-five pounds. Through moral suasion, he had all but convinced Brown to surrender his firearm when another officer burst into the room, intent on rescuing those present. Brown shot and killed the officer. Ensign Xylos engaged in a physical struggle with Brown during which the weapon was discharged twice before he knocked the pistol from the seaman's grasp. He denied Brown the opportunity to regain possession of the gun until others present joined with him to subdue Brown. Ensign Joseph Xylos, United States Navy Reserve, is hereby awarded the Navy and Marine Corps Medal for courage well beyond the call of duty that saved the lives of the other hostages present."

As the Captain shook Joe's hand, he said, "Congratulations, Mr. Xylos. Judging from the size differential, that was a tremendous feat, disarming a man so much larger than you. I take it that you've practiced judo or karate."

"Thank you, Captain. No, sir, I have awfully big adrenal glands."

There was a slight ripple of laughter as Joe stepped to the microphone. His voice croaked as he said, "I would like to accept this medal on behalf of my friend, Lieutenant Francois Villerouge, who gave his life trying to save mine. My reason for going into that building was to keep him out of harm's way. The world and yes, the Navy are poorer for his loss. Wearing this medal will always be a reminder that I failed. Thank you, Captain."

Collins noted unchecked tears running down Joe's cheeks as he passed him. The words of his last sentence and the show of emotion surprised and remained with the Commander.

Joe's steps on the hardwood echoed off through the huge room as he returned to his seat, while on the far side of the stage, Admiral Rickover, dressed in civilian clothes and accompanied by the Atlantic Submarine Force Commander, entered as if on cue.

It was no surprise to Collins when the Public Affairs Officer reported that Xylos had refused to discuss the affair with his journalist for publication in the base newspaper.

On the Monday before Thanksgiving, Commanding Officer U.S. Submarine Base sent a message that tersely announced that the incinerator in Building 43 was not designed or intended for the destruction of classified material

On the Friday after Thanksgiving, Commander Collins was called to the commanding officer's office. Captain Gilmore, like Sam Slaxman, had been a World War II submarine skipper and had the decorations to show for it. His chest was a clutter of ribbons adorned with stars and clusters. Though now somewhat portly, he was a handsome man with a thick, full head of dark hair.

Collins was introduced to Commander Jack Tinker of the National Security Agency. The guest was slim and wore an expensively tailored business suit. Collins felt the man gave him a cold look not unlike that of a hangman about to put a rope around the condemned man's neck. Seated against the wall was Martin Pugsley, a man of medium build whom Collins knew well; Pugsley had been a torpedo mate under Collins in the closing days of World War Two. Today he looked tired, with deep, dark circles under his eyes. He moved the top of a wooden pencil through his fingers like a string of worry beads.

After the formalities, Tinker said, "As I was telling your boss, the illegal burn facility has been the latest in a series of security problems reported by one very observant lady. And it's going to cost at least two more officers their careers."

Then, looking over his shoulder toward Pugsley, he added, "And not do much to advance the career of her control."

Commander Collins said, "Control? What has this got to do with us?"

The CO said, "Casey, just as this Sub School officer's class convened, I had a call from Washington informing me that an individual formerly involved in intelligence activities was married to a member of the class . . . that she was under possible threat of death . . . and that being housed on a military facility would be in the best interests of all concerned. According to an agreement with the FBI and the NSA, the number of people who know of her existence has been severely restricted. As CO Sub Base, I was to make sure that she and her husband were assigned to quarters on base and that her background remained undisclosed. I was assured that she was not a threat to our security and that her fears of serious threats to her personal safety were well grounded. The lady in question is Mrs. Eva Xylos, formerly of Richford, Vermont.

I met her once at a reception for the new Sub School class. She is physically a very striking woman. She speaks with a very flat midwestern accent and told me that she was born in Ames, Iowa. And now I find that she is a Hungarian who spent a good part of her childhood in the Soviet Union. She was a trained covert operative. And the people who grant the clearances knew of this all along!"

"But how could this be? How could her husband pass a background investigation?"

"That's a question I've been dying to ask. Well, Jack?"

Commander Tinker replied, "This is a problem that has sort of grown like Topsy. Xylos' background check was completed well before his orders were issued. Personally, he's clean as a hound's tooth. They married on the Friday before he detached on Monday. To her credit, she notified us as soon as they got off the road in Vermont, well before he reported in off leave. We discussed our options with the Sub Officers desk in BUPERS and concluded that if he completed your curriculum, he could be assigned to an old submarine incapable of special operations."

Captain Gilmore snorted, "Xylos is one of the star performers in this class. I've tracked him personally."

"When the Agency granted a waiver, we felt the rewards outweighed the risks. She was part of the Hungarian Olympic Team, performing essentially a minor internal security function for them. Her debriefing greatly helped our side. She volunteered information that solved the murder of a Hungarian nationalist last summer, plus some leads about low-level espionage of some Army operations in West Germany. She has a deep hatred for the Russians. Stalin murdered her parents when she was a child; and she had a front-row seat to the repression following the invasion of Hungary. Compounding all the trauma of what happened earlier, her first husband was murdered on Okinawa early in the year. This summer, some ham-handed goons from the Hungarian U.N. delegation were intercepted in Montpelier, Vermont. From them we learned that they want her back, dead or alive. Rightly or wrongly, we concluded that keeping her with her husband on this military base was in the best interests of all concerned."

Captain Gilmore asked, "Jack, isn't the care and feeding of defecting agents somewhat beyond your charter?"

Tinker paused, then, looking directly at the Captain, formed each word carefully in his reply. "Ordinarily, yes, sir. But she defected directly to us. Her first husband was one of ours. Frenchy Villerouge was one of the premier artisans of our trade, from collection to deception. We will long feel his loss . . ."

Collins snapped his fingers. "Villerouge! Of course! She didn't waste much time rehitching her wagon! That must be some story, her marrying Xylos right after her old man got blown away. He was crying when he left the stage after getting his medal for that. It was very moving. He got very high evals from his underway. What's changed your mind about him?"

Tinker pulled three glassine folders from his briefcase. Scattered inside were a number of black-printed five-letter code combinations and one red-printed serial number. The borders were all charred into irregular shapes.

As he fanned them out, he said, "She collected these samples on the upper base. We've found numerous other pieces caught on branches and even in the gutters on the BOQ. But this is the only serial number, and she found it. It was for a key list that the USS *Blowfin* reported destroyed last September."

"Holy mackerel! Wait a minute! Is she a big tall blonde? Pregnant?"

Agent Pugsley brushed his sideburns back as he said, "She delivered in September."

Gaining eye contact with his commanding officer, Collins said, "I'm sure it was in September that I saw a pregnant woman in the middle of a cloud of ashes on the sidewalk between here and the O Club. After I drove by, I thought she might have been catching ashes in an open book. I guess I should have stopped and questioned her. It never dawned on me what she was up to. Right out there in broad daylight. That takes balls!"

Then he pointed at the glassine folders. "But these are shards. There's nothing here that could be used to break messages. How did you catch her?"

Pugsley said, "We didn't. The truth is that she is a colossal pain. There hasn't been a week that's gone by that she hasn't reported something else wrong with your security. Holes in the fences, sleeping sentries, people coming ashore unchallenged from boats on the river, classified carbons, inattentive topside watches, doors left open and unguarded, people talking about submarine schedules and operations. And then she brought me all these little bits of burned paper, upset as hell. I'll admit I took an extra day or two to forward them to Washington. I had to make sure they were all packaged properly. You don't treat material like this casually."

Collins said, "Martin, from the reports and messages going around this base, it sounds like she's doing us a service."

The CO, drumming his pencil on his desk, asked, "Jack, if she's so damn harmless, how come she was sweeping up bits and pieces of crypto key lists? And if she's been doing this since September, why did it take until today for you to come to this office?"

Commander Tinker wrinkled his brow into well-creased furrows, bringing his receding hairline closer to his eyebrows. "As to your first question, Captain, the only time she gathered up any pieces was before she had the baby in September. Pugsley's incident report was the same date as the burn report. She swore that all were picked up in broad daylight, standing on the sidewalk not far from the BOQ. Like your XO, the traffic drove by, totally ignoring her."

"You didn't answer my second question."

"It's another case of the spooks not talking to each other. The FBI made a routine query to the NSA about the key list. We took our sweet time answering it. The Bureau was looking to collect brownie points, but instead we are all wading in brown doo-doo. If we had understood the source of the residue, we would have been here long ago to shut down the incinerator. To tell the truth, it was our lady agent who got the wheels moving. Following her control's instructions, she stopped collecting samples from the stack, but then right after Veteran's Day, she saw another plume. She wrote a letter to the Director of the FBI. That shook the tree. My boss and J. Edgar Hoover both are very upset that she is even here or on any other military installation. Isn't that right, Pugsley?"

The agent nodded while staring blankly out the window.

Tinker shuffled the glassine sheets as he continued, "I'm not going to say anything more than there are very serious national security implications that she had sufficient knowledge to come very close to IDing the key list from those shards. We aren't in the habit of letting the Bureau run our ship. Let's say that there's more than serious concern that her husband's waiver should stand."

"Concern! Did she hold out on you?"

"No, I spent a number of hours questioning her. It looks more like we didn't ask her the right questions. And again to her credit, she was the one who brought this to our attention."

"Could she have learned this since she defected?"

"Not likely. If she could walk aboard any boat or into a secure office while six months pregnant and waddle off with the secrets, we've got real big problems. While the incinerator is a serious breach, there are very serious implications of extremely serious problems elsewhere. That's more than I should have said."

Collins asked, "What do you want us to do?"

"Find a way to ease this young man out of here without making a single ripple in the pond."

Captain Gilmore said, "I've been puzzled as anything over the Force Commander's continuing emphasis on security. It's obvious that we're too damn lax. She ought to be commended, but instead our reaction is to boot her husband out of Sub School. You don't solve problems by keeping your head in the sand. This smells too much like a cover-up to me."

Tinker said, "It may look that way, but we're doing nothing more than being cautious. She could just as easily slip back over to the other side."

The Captain raised his arm. "We have more problems. Let me put another variable into your equation, Commander: Admiral Rickover. The day he was here to open the Nuclear Power School was the day I presented the medal to Ensign Xylos. He was very favorably impressed. His people have already asked for the Ensign's school records for review. He stands sixth in the class. Has an engineering degree. They'll want him."

"We can finesse that easily. Xylos won't apply."

"He doesn't have to. He will be invited. And when the Admiral finds out that you essentially positioned a very obviously skilled agent on this base concurrent with the opening of his school, he will be very upset."

"Look, they aren't going to be interested in him until he finishes his submarine qualifications. And he'll never get that far because you're going to drop him. I see no need to act in haste. We've got to go about this in a manner that won't draw attention to us or her. This whole matter must be handled with tact. If not, this young woman isn't at all bashful when it comes to making complaints."

Pugsley said, "You can say that again. She's working on a letter, let's call it a treatise, about how to make your facilities secure."

Gilmore said, "After the glitches she brought to our attention earlier this year, like that hole in the fence, maybe we need some guidance."

"Yes, she found the hole. And if you put her ideas into practice, you wouldn't have enough money left to run the fleet. And the first time somebody was juiced touching the fence or had his foot blown off by a mine or was shot from a tower, there would be hell to pay. There is one thing going for us."

"What's that?"

"She is none too happy about the prospect of Xylos going to sea."

Tinker said, "Joe Xylos has been a pleasure to work with. He readily agreed to every restriction, including serving only to the end of his obligated service. The Navy is the net loser on this deal because like you said, he's the kind of guy Rickover ought to be taking into his program."

Captain Gilmore said, "Gentlemen, as much as I would like to continue this conversation, many of us have a train to catch. Tomorrow it's Army versus Navy, and we have a large party catching the 3:23. Commander Collins is taking a week's leave to house-hunt in Norfolk in preparation for taking command of Submarine Division Sixty-two." The Captain paused and looked directly at Tinker before he said, "Sir, I feel very ill used by the way you played cloak-and-dagger with this command. With the opening of the Nuclear Power School, security concerns cannot be taken lightly. There is little or nothing that can be done today without attracting undue attention. And the easiest way to buy time to make this a smoothly executed action, is to bump the decision up the chain of command. I can't second-guess what my boss will do, but if I'm not mistaken, you'll have to explain all this to your Director. I'm sure we'll have this wrapped up by the time you return, Casey."

Commander Collins asked, "Should I bring Cal Norcross into the loop?"

"No, I'll do it once we have clear direction. Commander Tinker, this command is an innocent bystander to this fiasco. Do I make myself clear?"

Tinker said, "Very clear, sir. Please accept my apologies for not spelling out her exact circumstances." Then, looking at Collins, he said, "And please, not a word to Xylos. And, oh, yes, beat Army!"

⋅⟩═◉═⟨⋅

The following Tuesday afternoon, near the end of the school day, Joe Xylos sat across the desk from Commander Calvin Norcross, the Director of Officer Submarine Curricula. To his question as to what was so important that he had been pulled out of class, the Commander told him he would find out as soon as he gave him his Article 31 warning. While the officer, who was infamous as the Submarine School hatchetman, thumbed through the hardbound UCMJ rulebook, Joe asked, "Does this have to do with the *Beaverton*?"

Norcross nodded, then read the warning in a flat voice. By the time he was finished, the Ensign had pulled a letter out of an envelope and pushed it across the desk. He said, "I thought so. Is it related to the items mentioned in this letter?"

Commander Norcross rolled his half-smoked filter-tip into the corner of his large mouth and held the letter almost to arm's length as he focused on it. "Why, yes. It sounds like you've been waiting for the other shoe to drop, mister."

Joe studied the big man, who was chubby in the way that former football players become when they go to seed as middle age approaches. He had a large oval head with high cheekbones and a large mouth. Pointing toward the letter, the young officer said, "Not until this arrived, when my old roommate wrote that the new CO said he was going to 'have my ass.' Frankly, I'm at a loss as to how any of this involves me."

"Apparently he feels you violated the Code."

"If this is about the ship's insignia and the paint, neither was my responsibility. I was a snipe and not responsible for either area."

Joe looked the man in the eye and recalled the description of one of his classmates as being like looking at a blue-eyed Chinaman because his eyes were so narrow. As his inquisitor read through the letter, he asked, "Mr. Sawyer doesn't sound like he has much use for his commanding officer. What do you think?"

"You can read what you want between the lines, sir. I know Carter to be a straight arrow. He is also one hell of a sharp attorney. As for why he's now the Assistant B Division Officer and not the Legal Officer anymore—maybe that's your answer."

Commander Norcross pulled a stack of papers held together with a paper clip from inside a large manila envelope, After looking at one sheet after another, the big man drew a lungful of smoke from his cigarette and mumbled, "Let's start with the last item chronologically. Do you recall the incident at 1516 Ala Moana Drive?"

Puzzled, Joe asked, "Where is Ala Moana Drive?"

"Come on, it's the big wide street in Waikiki. Don't play dumb."

"Dumb? I was only there once, sir. If you're talking about the incident last May in Honolulu, when this crazy civilian held off the HASP while the *Beaverton* crowd escaped, I heard about it. But I wasn't there."

"Are you sure you want to make that statement?"

"Commander, I stopped at the party only long enough to have a beer. I chose to leave because it was quickly turning into a classic *Beaverton* bash. I wasn't in the mood for an orgy or for taking a chance that there'd be trouble with the law."

"So you got out of there one step ahead of the HASP?"

Joe shook his head. "No, sir. I walked out the front door and strolled over to Fort De Russy, where I waited until it was after six a.m. Eastern Time. I called Eva, my wife, only she wasn't my wife then. I sat out on a bench and wrestled with myself about how to approach her, letting her know I wanted to date her and yet not being too pushy. Frenchy had been murdered back in February."

"Murdered? Who's Frenchy?"

"Her husband. My roommate. That's why I was decorated."

"Oh, yeah. Well, was there a witness? Were you with anyone?"

"Not the whole time, but the XO, Commander Longstreet, saw me come into the club after I spoke to Eva, and we talked. My roommate Larry White was there."

The Commander pulled an onionskin thermocopy from the sheaf. "How about Miss Melba Walker?"

"Who?"

He pushed the sheet to Joe. After reading it, Joe shrugged his shoulders and replied, "There was a brunette who made an offer, which I declined. I don't remember much about her except that she threw my beer bottle into the trash basket on the street. I introduced her to my roommate Tyler Cobb, and she gave him a full boat, the crabs and the clap."

"Did you challenge her or bet that you could make more baskets than she could?"

"Absolutely not! I didn't throw any bottles."

"The woman says you encouraged her to throw it."

"Somebody needs to talk to Lieutenant Jay Gee Tyler Cobb. He bragged that she paid for a room for them with all the money she won betting on her aim with the bottles. He woke me up the next morning and thanked me for fixing him up with her."

"Can you think of any reason why she wouldn't be telling the truth?"

Joe smiled. "For starters, she was soused. Next, she's probably mad as hell over getting the clap too. Maybe her pride was hurt because I refused her offer."

"And I suppose you were sober?"

"Yes, sir! I'll never let myself get into the condition I was the night Frenchy was murdered. If he had been sober, he wouldn't have gone in there with his piece empty. If I had been sober, I would have reacted and knocked the gun aside and saved his life."

"You're referring to when you got the medal?"

"Yes, sir. I'm no hero. They gave me that for saving my own ass."

The Commander paused and inhaled on his cigarette. He watched the cloud of smoke he exhaled curl up toward the ceiling, then said, "For as short a career as you've had, Mr. Xylos, you have some very interesting items in your record. Take this letter of appreciation from the Los Angeles office of the U.S. Marshal. How did you play a key role in breaking up an interstate car theft ring?"

The Ensign shrugged his shoulders. "There was a crooked car dealer, J.J. Carruthers, who stole the Chaplain's car. There was a call from the wardroom's central casting, and I accepted the role. With the help of the Feds, we set up a buy across the Nevada border. I didn't do much, and we got his car back."

"What happened to them, the guys who stole the car?"

"Carruthers lost his dealership and the whole bunch went to prison."

"Mr. Xylos, you seem to take a certain pleasure in standing in harm's way—from dodging bullets in Okinawa to dodging the HASP in Honolulu."

"I don't know what you're getting at, sir, but if you're trying to put me in the same frying pan as those guys who stayed at the party, then I suggest it's time to confront my accusers. I did nothing illegal that evening."

Norcross said, "Ensign, I have never seen a piece of correspondence like this before. And I'm not at all sure what motivated them to put this together. There are two more items." He pushed a red condom box across the table. "I have to ask you what this reminds you of."

Joe picked it up with his index finger and thumb. As he held it out, he smiled broadly. "The last night before I went to OCS. The Velvet Glove in North Glenn, Colorado, and the B-29."

"Velvet Glove? B-29?"

"The tassel twirler. She was in the same show in two or three towns with me over the years. She invited me back to her dressing room between shows. I bought a box in the men's room."

"Same show?"

"I worked my way through college as the emcee in a number of night clubs."

"This sort of thing happen often?"

Joe paused, then asked, "Looking for something interesting to do after you retire, Commander?"

There was a slight upward turning of Norcross's lips, and his eyes twinkled for a minute, before he said, "Let's stop playing, Mr. Xylos. Do you see any resemblance between the shield on that rubber box and the *Beaverton*'s insignia?"

"Yes, sir. Some."

"Then it was your idea to use this condom company's trademark as your last duty station's insignia?"

"No, sir. The sailor who later won the competition asked me what heraldry was. I gave him the box as an example. I could see the resemblance, but I didn't think it was an exact copy." Laughing, he continued, "The *Beaverton*'s radio call sign is 'Rubber Duck,' and the first time I saw that big bronze shield on the quarterdeck, I cracked up. But no, I could never take credit for it. The kid who drew it did a beautiful job."

Laughing also, the Commander exclaimed, "Rubber Duck! You've got to be kidding, mister. It takes a warped sense of humor to pull a stunt like this. Did you ever tell anybody about the resemblance?"

"No, sir. I didn't think anything was wrong with it."

"I see. The last item is undoubtedly the main reason for this letter. What role did you have in taking sixty-two five-gallon cans of white latex house paint from the pier at Agana, Guam?"

"No role in taking them, sir."

"What knowledge did you have of the theft?"

"Probably as much as anybody else on board. Did somebody really take it all? Commander, the First Lieutenant had told me he was short of inside white, the kind of paint we used in Engineering spaces. He used to issue paint in little soup cans, so we could only daub it here and there. As a result, my spaces looked like white polka dots on pale nicotine yellow. Like everybody else on the ship, I saw a whole trailer of paint sitting on the pier; and I told my Chief that we ought to be in good shape after we got underway. I heard about the paint after we got underway. I'm sure that some found its way to my division because most of the after engine room turned yellow not long after it was painted. Beyond that, I know nothing."

"Weren't you curious as to where that paint came from?"

"Not enough to ask."

"How about the whereabouts of the rest of the paint?"

"It could have been anywhere. There were other ships tied up while we were there."

"Then you're telling me that you don't know how the twelve cans Captain Pinkney discovered came to be stored in the void that was assigned to your division?"

"Commander, the paint was still on the pier at the end of my quarterdeck watch. I was moved from M Division not long after I applied for Sub School. I believe there have been two people in the job since I left. Why me? Why now?"

"While you were in Yokosuka, didn't you take leave and spend most of your time with one of the most expensive prostitutes in Yokosuka?"

"I won't dignify that with an answer. I've never paid for a piece of ass in my life."

Waving the sheet from the record, Norcross said, "You took the leave! I've been to Yoko and The Original Fuji doesn't take charity cases!"

"Commander, I don't know who wrote up these questions, but they're nothing more than a witch hunt. They are very hurtful to my reputation and especially so to my companion. I ended the relationship on the last night of my leave when I found out she was married to a retired Air Force officer. She is a troubled woman, no matter what you've heard about her. I wouldn't want to see anything more jeopardize her marriage or her emotional stability."

"Then where'd you get the money to finance all that time on the beach?"

"I've never found it necessary to buy what is so freely given. In fact, we split the expenses, with her picking up the better part of it."

Norcross put a filter-tip into his mouth backwards and, just short of bringing his lighter to its tip, stopped and reversed ends. He inhaled deeply, lighting the tip to a red-hot glow, before slowly exhaling. As smoke trailed out both nostrils and his mouth, he said, "And I suppose you're going to tell me you had nothing to do with the cans of paint bartered for the brass insignia?"

"I didn't know about the insignia until I came back off leave. M Division took care of main engines, not the quarterdeck, sir. How could there have been enough paint on that truck to paint the better part of the Engineering spaces, finance a fling with my companion, pay for the casting of such a large shield, and still have twelve cans left over?"

Putting his chin almost against his chest, the Commander asked, "Companion! Do you really expect me to believe you spent two weeks with Fuji for free?"

The corners of Joe's mouth turned up slightly, and his nod was barely perceptible.

Norcross shot the sheets across the desk to the partly filled outgoing basket. "Wear that medal with pride, son! You earned it. If what you said is true, this is a bunch of crap. I don't know what's going on in your last command, but this is ridiculous. I'll have the yeoman type up my conclusions for your signature. Get the hell out of here. And mister, don't let up on the hard work! You're slipping; you're down to seventh in your class."

"Aye, aye, sir."

CHAPTER 34

Eva Versus the Commander

Eva answered the phone on the third ring, "Hello."

A male voice said, "Hello, Eva? Eva, from the Hungarian Olympic Team? Is that—"

She slammed the receiver back on the cradle as if the message had heated the plastic to flesh-searing hot, crying, "Joe! Joe, it was one of them! They've found us!"

Joe rose from the table where he was studying. As he approached his wife, her complexion took on the pallor of a cloud of chalk dust.

She folded into his arms, her body shaking, and said in a small high-pitched voice, "I'm scared, darling. What can I do? I could be brave alone, but what about Francois?"

"Let's call Pugsley."

"Pugsley! Do you really think he would do anything after what went on this last week? It's his own fault for sitting on my report."

"Please, Eva, relax. You've had a tough week with all those hours of questioning."

"Two days of grilling because that fool couldn't recognize a major security breach when it was dumped in his lap. They came here thinking I'm some kind of double agent. I was scared, real scared, and now this."

The phone rang again. Joe lifted the receiver. "Hello."

"Hey, Joe, old buddy. Good to hear your voice. We were cut off just a minute ago. Damn phone company!"

"Rufus? Doc, is that you? Where are you? Did you just call?"

"Yes, I'm in Greenwich. Lyla has some relatives here, and we're visiting."

Joe put his hand over the mouthpiece. "Eva, the last call was Doc Johnson, the quack on the *Beaverton*. We're okay."

She stepped free of him, turned away, and dabbed a tear from one eye.

Joe touched her shoulder gently as he continued to speak into the phone, "Thanks for the invitation to your wedding. I would have loved to have been an usher."

"I understand. We're going to be arriving in New London late Friday. Are you busy Friday evening?"

"Not really. Would you like to drop by?"

"Drop by, hell! We want to take you and Eva out to dinner at the club to celebrate her anniversary of freedom."

"With a new baby, we haven't been going out."

"Typical father of a firstborn. You've got to give the mother a break from the house. You don't want to burn her out, do you?"

"We feel comfortable sticking close to home."

"Ask her, Joe. I know it's tough to run a household on an Ensign's pittance. We want to take you out as a way of saying thanks for keeping us in contact after Tijuana. It would mean a great deal to us to do this for you."

Joe asked, "Rufus wants to take us out to dinner at the O Club Friday evening. What do I tell him?"

"And I hung up on him! Oh, no! Joe, I'm so embarrassed. Yes, if it wouldn't be too late. We would still be on the base if we're at the club."

"What about Francois?"

"I've been watching Thelma's baby during the day while she shops and, remember, they brought her over when they went out for their anniversary. I think they'd be happy to return the favor. I'd like a night out."

"Rufus, we can do it. Now tell me, what are you doing in this part of the world?"

"I'll be in the next Sub School class. I'm free of that hellhole of a ship!"

"The *Beaverton*?"

"The new CO is 'Sweet Old Bob' Pinkney, and he lives up to his name. I'll tell you all about it later."

"I'm dying to hear. Lawyer Sawyer sent me a letter just before I spent the afternoon answering a bunch of stupid questions about the new *Beaverton* insignia and the paint that was stolen from Guam."

Rufus laughed. "The Shield Rubber Company has adopted the *Beaverton,* and they keep the ship supplied with free rubbers in little red boxes that say 'For Eager Beavers.' Ess Oh Bee will keelhaul you if he ever gets his hands on you."

"Me! Why?"

"I'll tell you about it Friday evening. Want to start with happy hour?"

"Not really. Let's make it about seven. That will be late enough to have the baby down."

"Spoken like a true married john. We'll meet you in the bar at seven and then have dinner. See you Friday, shipmate."

⋅→▪▬◉ ◉▬▪←⋅

More than a few heads turned as Joe and Eva entered the bar about ten minutes of seven. Joe wore a light grey wool suit, a black shirt, and a silver tie. Eva towered over him by almost a head. The backless cocktail dress she wore clung to the curves she had been working hard to recover since the baby was born. Their entry produced a momentary drop in the noise level generated by the hangers-on from happy hour.

Among those taking a break from their labors at the bar was Commander Cal Norcross, whose eyes hardly strayed from Eva. As he surveyed the swell of her milk-laden breasts while she seated herself on the far side of the bar, he said to the officer next to him, "Can you imagine a big, passionate woman like that wasting herself on that little runt?"

The friend grunted as he fished for the orange section that evaded his tongue in his almost empty glass. "He dresses like some petty hood. Yeah, she is some beauty."

"The way that woman walks, I'll bet she'd turn you every which way but loose. And him . . . He's such a runt, I'll bet he has to tie a board across his back to keep from falling in."

The friend said, "That's Joe Xylos, the guy who got the hero badge. He's a cocky little fart. That's the first time I've ever seen his wife. She is a beauty, Cal."

"Yes, I know. I had him in my office earlier in the week. Hmmmm."

After seating his wife at the one empty stool toward the middle of the bar, Joe ordered two sodas with a twist of lime.

The bartender's eyebrows rose as he repeated, "Two sodas with a twist of lime?"

Joe said, "That's right. I'm driving in the front seat and she's driving in back."

Seven o'clock came and went, as did a number of his classmates, all of whom were bachelors. Between conversations, Joe glanced at his watch. Eva's eyes searched the room, stopping on each face long enough to study it, then going to the next. When she came to Norcross, he looked into her eyes and smiled. She returned the gaze without expression, then looked at his friend before breaking away to take part in the nearby conversation.

As soon as the couple next to Eva left, Commander Norcross and his drinking buddy slipped into their seats. Norcross said, "Good evening, Mr. Xylos. I believe this is the first time I've seen you at the club. I don't believe I'd had the pleasure of meeting your beautiful wife."

"Honey, this is Commander Norcross, the Officer's Curriculum Director with whom I met Tuesday. Commander, my wife, Eva."

She smiled as the Commander took her hand and gently kissed it. He said, "My friends call me Cal."

The conversation was about to resume when a Filipino waiter called out in a heavily accented voice, "Telephone call in the office for Ensign Joe Xylos."

Watching out of the corner of his eye as Joe walked toward the door, Norcross leaned over and asked, "Eva, what special occasion brings you to the club tonight?"

"We are meeting friends from Joe's last ship."

"The *Beaverton*. Joe must have told you about the interrogatory we have to answer."

"Very little. He never talks about his work."

"You could help make sure that this doesn't in any way harm your husband's standing here at Submarine School."

"And how could I do that?"

With his left hand, he pulled out the cigarette that hung from the corner of his mouth as he exhaled and said, "Just take a few minutes to go out to the parking lot and look at my new Volkswagen camper bus."

His right hand was now resting on Eva's knee. She gazed into his bloodshot eyes. Norcross would later swear that there was a very slight smile touching her lips. In a low, almost embarrassed voice Eva said, "Cal, I'm a very happily married woman. Move your hand."

He smiled and pushed his fingers up her thigh past the top of her stocking. His first notice that she was reacting was in the instant he felt her thigh muscles tighten. He broke eye contact when her left hand clamped his uplifted left wrist with a grip that crushed his watch painfully into the tendons. She jerked his arm across in front of her, rolling him toward the bar. By reflex, he bent his arm and tightened his biceps to check her movement. Eva drove her right hand in a karate-like chop into the high side of his elbow joint and slammed it hard on the edge of the bar. The cigarette flew from his fingers and spread a trail of ashes as it careened down the bar before coming to rest under the rim of a bowl of peanuts.

Eva's moves tipped over her barstool. It bounced painfully off the shins of a nearby drinker who sloshed over his glass onto the bar, trying to avoid it.

The blonde, whose high heels were on the floor standing neatly next to the brass rail, stepped behind Norcross. His stool had fallen the other way, its legs clattering noisily against the brass rail. The big man held his injured elbow for an instant until Eva said, "If you ever—" He pivoted to his right, swinging his arm like a boom. She ducked and caught the arm, turning him almost through two hundred seventy degrees before she planted a foot in front of his and tripped him. He fell so hard on her overturned stool that drinks on the bar beside him splashed onto the smooth bar top.

Norcross moaned for an instant, but didn't move. The whole incident was over so quickly that those nearby were still standing like mannequins in a display while the long-legged blonde smoothed her stockings, then stepped into her heels, picked up her purse, and walked out through the hole they made for her.

The silence continued until the tap, tap of her heels on the hardwood floor ended and she stepped onto the carpet outside. Eva paused, half-turned, and looked back at those in the room. As Commander Norcross slowly got to his knees, she turned and disappeared from view. He sank into a sitting position by the brass rail with his shoulders resting against the bar. A small trail of blood oozed down his chin from the lip that split when his face hit the floor.

Weakly he said, "It hurts when I breathe. Somebody help me."

Back in the crowd, a woman's voice said, "So old lecherous Cal finally got thumped by a jealous husband for making a pass. Looks like he did a number on the SOB."

A male voice replied, "Husband, hell! It was that big blonde that came in here with the little guy. The way she looked back, it was almost like she was challenging him to step outside and finish it off. I sure as hell wouldn't want to meet *her* in a dark alley."

With somewhat of a drunken laugh, the female voice said, "A woman! Well, all the more power to her."

Joe had just hung up the phone from talking to Rufus when he heard the very short-lived commotion. He met Eva on the stairs. Although there wasn't a hair on her head out of place, he sensed by the way her nostrils flared and the catlike way she moved two steps at a time, that the trouble had involved her.

"What happened, Eva? I heard a big thump on the floor."

She stopped, grabbed the rail, and bit her lower lip. "Oh, my husband, you are going to be very mad at me! Please forgive me. I just knocked your school director onto the floor. I think I overdid it."

"Overdid what?"

She swiftly went down the steps separating them and pressed herself against him as she said, "You are the only man in the world that I ever want to touch me."

Joe's voice rose. "He made a pass at you?"

"He invited me to come outside with him and ran his hand up all the way to my panties. I told him to stop, but he didn't."

"The son of a bitch!" Joe tried to break free of her arms.

"I hurt him very badly," she said. "You can do nothing but cause trouble now. Let's get out of here."

Above them, a voice shouted, "Call the ambulance. He's having trouble breathing."

Relaxing in her grip, Joe said, "Eva, you weren't kidding. No, we aren't leaving, because in my experience, the guy who leaves the scene of the brawl is the one who gets blamed. Please let me go. I've got control of myself. I'm not going back to kick him when he's down. We're going to find the manager and tell him why we aren't ever coming back to his club."

"But Joe, he is a Commander, a senior officer. He said something about those questions hurting you."

"I don't care if he's one of the Twelve Apostles. Nobody paws my wife!"

"Maybe I shouldn't have worn this dress."

"There's nothing wrong with the dress. It's tasteful and stylish; it's you. There's everything wrong with using his position to do what he did."

"I have made a terrible mistake. I used my training. Everyone noticed me."

Taking her hand, he said, "Eva, self-defense is no mistake. People will always notice you. You are special. Let's ask the cashier where we can find the manager."

After they talked to the cashier, who pointed them in the direction of the bar, a somewhat plump, buxom redhead in a black knit dress stopped in front of them. She said to Eva, "I'm Dagmar Holmes. My husband is Lieutenant Barney Holmes. You did something tonight that about half the wives on this base have wanted to do."

Joe extended his hand. "I'm Joe Xylos, and this is my wife, Eva. What do you mean?"

"That man makes a habit of free feels and whatever else he can get away with. I put up with it when he was my husband's CO. Now that he's at Sub School, he thinks he's a kid in a candy store. I heard that when he swung at you, you ducked, and he was so drunk he fell on the barstool. Serves the scum right."

Looking at Joe and wrinkling her forehead, Eva said, "I did more than duck."

Three Navy Corpsmen carrying a stretcher passed by them heading into the bar. Dagmar took her husband's arm and left. In the lull, Joe said, "I almost forgot. Rufus had a flat tire. They were calling from the other side of the bridge. They'll be here in twenty minutes or so."

Joe found the club manager on the edge of the circle of spectators surrounding the open place where the Commander was being tended to. Putting his hand around the man's elbow and leading him to one side, the Ensign spoke in a low, tense voice. "Sir, I'm very unhappy about what happened to my wife tonight. I've worked in the entertainment and hospitality industry prior to joining the Navy, and it was only in the most disreputable dives that a man couldn't leave his wife alone for the short time that I was called away to answer a phone call."

The manager jerked his arm free and turned around. "I'm very sorry about this incident, Mister . . ."

"Xylos."

"Xylos. It appears that you don't have to worry about your wife taking care of herself. Commander Norcross is seriously hurt. He doesn't understand . . ."

Eva stuck out her chin and jabbed with her index finger like a pointer. She let her voice rise as she spoke. "Doesn't understand? Doesn't understand! From the moment my husband and I came into the bar, he stared at me. Then he sat down next to us and when Joe went away, he put his hand on my leg. I told him to move it, and he pushed it all the way up to my panties!"

The manager stepped back from her and paused. Then, as if measuring his words, he replied, "Perhaps you didn't understand his true intentions."

She swung her head, shaking her long blonde curls out in a swirl. "I had no doubt about his intentions. If he ever lays another hand on me, I'll break his neck."

The manager pulled one side of his bow tie. He looked up at her out of the corner of his eye as he said, "I believe you mean that, ma'am. The Commander should certainly have learned a lesson tonight. I'm sure he'll steer clear of you in the future."

Joe said, "This is our first visit to your club, and it has been most unpleasant. We came here tonight to have dinner with friends. We won't be staying. I don't feel that you particularly cater to the married officer and his family."

"That's certainly not the case. Under the circumstances, I understand how you must feel. The patronage of all officers is encouraged. Please accept our apologies. Have your dinner tonight as guests of the club. I am terribly sorry about this incident."

Joe smiled and shook his hand. "Thank you very much, sir. Your apologies are accepted."

Eva was giving her statement to the duty officer when Rufus and Lyla arrived. Joe explained what had happened while they waited in the dining room for Eva.

She appeared in the doorway, talking to a Lieutenant Commander with a yellow brassard on his arm, and began pointing to people sitting at a number of tables. The officer seemed embarrassed as he walked over to each table and spoke with those seated. Eva stood just inside the door with her arms folded just below her breasts. After speaking to the last of them, he escorted her to the table where Joe and their friends sat.

After the men had risen, the officer said, "Mr. Xylos, you have a remarkable wife. She remembered just about everyone who was in the bar, and where they were when the incident took place."

As the short Ensign pushed his wife's chair in, he said, "She is remarkable in more ways than you'll ever know. And that's why I love her. Thank you, sir, for all you've done this evening."

Lyla exclaimed, "How did you get yourself back in shape so quickly? You hardly have any tummy at all."

"I work out in the gymnasium every day," said Eva. "They have a complete set of equipment. It's been years since I've been able to practice like this. I'll never be as good a shape, though, as when I was a teenager."

Rufus leaned back in his chair as he recalled, "I remember the night a year ago that you and Frenchy walked into the party in Melbourne. Two very handsome people, and you looked like you belonged together. If anything, you are more alluring and glowing tonight than you were that evening. I never had the opportunity to say how sad I felt at your loss and how pleased I am seeing you and Joe together here tonight."

She took Joe's hand in hers, and for a moment her eyes clouded. She swallowed and said, "This man . . . This man, who has taught me the meaning of trust and love." She looked into Joe's eyes. "Maybe I shouldn't be telling this. When I met Joe in California, I expected to become his lover. After all, that is what every other man demanded of me. But not Joe. He said there would be plenty of time after we were married. I decided at first that he wasn't a very passionate man, but maybe he would be good to me. Then I began to have backaches, and he rubbed my back. I thought I was going to go out of my mind with passion. I begged him."

Joe slightly colored. "Eva, darling . . . "

"You kept your word. With you, my life started anew. I can hold up my head. And I can tell my son to be a man like his father. That fat man was trying to rob me of my happiness. There is no man in the world that I want besides you."

Lyla said, "That's beautiful, Eva."

"Without him, I don't know where I'd be. He has endured my bad days . . . comforted me and consoled me in my loss. He's helped keep alive precious memories of Frenchy, my Frank. I see him every day when I'm with the baby, the turn of his mouth, his hands that are just like Frank's. I'm still not completely over him. Being around Frank was like the feeling you get right before a summer thundershower when the air seems to be full of electricity. And physically beautiful like the sun shining on the billowing tops of the clouds in the late afternoon."

Eva looked at Joe as she continued, "I don't know what force drove me to run to California to meet the *Beaverton*. Or why Joe put it in his mind that he wanted to marry me. I think maybe it was God's hand starting to guide my life. But since then, I've come to know a different kind of love, one that's steady and warm, caring. I feel immersed in its essence . . . marinated in a passion that grows with every day we are together. This man, whom I hardly noticed on that fateful day I escaped to freedom, is the one I now know is the once-in-a-lifetime opportunity every woman seeks, my Joe. I worry that I'm not worthy."

Joe patted her hand. "This blind pig who has cornered the market on truffles isn't going to complain. Eva, I am indeed the lucky one."

She sniffled, then continued, "That evil man, his hand was like something reaching from my past, pulling me away from all that I love. What would you have thought if you had seen him compromising me?"

"There would have been fireworks, I guarantee. However, I wouldn't have hit him."

"Even now I still feel threatened . . . dirty. I didn't think clearly. I'm sorry, Joe. I should have simply walked away. Instead, I have caused more trouble. I am very worried. The man is powerful and will seek revenge. And no one will help us."

Rufus said, "Nonsense. That guy fell on his own sword. The Navy doesn't put up with this kind of thing. Commander or no Commander, he cooked his own goose. What I can't understand is why anybody would step so far over the limits to tangle with a world-class athlete, especially a Hungarian woman of your background and training."

She put her index finger across her lips, then said, "No one knows. Please don't say anything about my past. Everyone here thinks I am an American."

"What?"

Joe whispered, "We are under FBI protection because the people from the other side are after her."

"Eva? Who? Why? You were just a translator. Why would they want to do that?"

Eva whispered, "I'm not who you think I am. I had a very different past. After the last interrogation, I'm afraid it has harmed Joe's career."

Joe patted her arm. "I have the best of both worlds. You know I agreed to serve in the Reserves. And thanks to standing sixth in the class, I got my first choice, the *Bowhead* in Pearl."

Rufus raised his glass and said, "Congratulations, Joe. Pearl, hey, hey! And to you, Eva and your first year in freedom! And may all of Hungary someday be as free."

As they raised their glasses, she whispered, "Not so loud. I tell them I was born in Iowa."

Lyla and Eva began talking about babies and little Francois in particular.

Joe asked, "Doc, why did you decide to come to Submarine School? I thought you were getting out."

"Well, I was, but Captain Sam set it up so I could go through the escape tank in Pearl when we were there on our honeymoon. I'm qualified to go from one hundred ten feet via submarine rescue device. I was still intent on getting out when the Old Man was relieved, but one meeting with Sweet Old Bob and I knew I couldn't work for him. The ass called a wardroom meeting right after the relief ceremony, keeping everyone there for hours while the wives sat out on the pier wondering. He insulted Lyla and me."

Lyla said, "Rufus was so mad when he left the ship that evening, I thought he was going to burst a blood vessel."

"I called the detailer the next day to see if I could get in the next Sub School class and told him why. Let me tell you, SOB just about exploded high order when I submitted the request for Submarine School. He tried to browbeat me out of my decision. And he gave me a lousy fitness report. All of his comments were about the first day, when I walked out of his meeting."

"Rufus, you walked out? I don't believe it."

"He dredged up that Tijuana thing and called Lyla a whore. If I hadn't left the room, I would have punched him out. I will write a rebuttal; I don't feel I have anything to lose. Besides, he let it be known that a request for submarine duty is the equivalent of professional suicide."

"How can he do that?"

"I don't know. And I think the way he carries on has contributed to the exodus of talent. The Chief Engineer is retiring. Carter Sawyer got fired as Legal Officer because the Los Angeles *Times* wrote up Lynda's crime spree and identified her as the wife of a *Beaverton* officer."

"So that's why he's B Division Jay Oh now. I don't understand. Why do his wife's antics have anything to do with Carter's job performance?"

"SOB's rule of thumb is that an unfavorable news article about the *Beaverton* is an automatic ticket to Purgatory. Guilt or innocence, that's irrelevant."

"My goodness. How is Carter taking it?"

"Your old roommate is doing okay, but I'm sure the Old Man is regretting his decision."

"How's that?"

"Carter is a much-sought-after defense counsel. He got a whole day's worth of special courts thrown out because the President of the Court told the Master at Arms to 'bring in the next guilty bastard.'"

"Carter, the hard-nosed prosecutor?"

"Not only that, the Old Man was having kittens because Carter was the defense counsel for a snipe and got him off even though he drove the Captain's gig all over Long Beach harbor in the fog. SOB even had a regular JAG officer as the prosecutor."

"Who was the snipe?"

"A Guamanian kid. It wasn't open and shut. He was the engineman and chose to sleep on the boat. He said he woke up to find that the boat had broken free of the boat boom. He started it up and tried to find his way back, but he was lost in the fog."

"I suppose he ran it up on the rocks."

"No, he just drove it in circles. And the stories that the fantail sentries told apparently didn't survive Sawyer's cross-examination. The jurors on the court said that the JAG guy didn't prepare his case very well. Carter had him for breakfast. I felt kind of sorry for him because old slow-talking, sleepy-eyed Carter Sawyer can be easily misjudged."

"It must be hell for Carter in B Division. Putting him there is like asking a two-toed sloth to count to five on his toes."

"I don't know about that. He seemed relieved at not having to work with the Old Man. He's getting pretty short. He's counting the days until he goes back to `lawyerin'' in Florida."

"What about Lynda?"

"She's out there somewhere pulling a scam. They've hauled her in a number of times, but they always let her go. I really feel for Carter."

"Carter said in his letter that everybody who can is getting off."

"I'm one among many. Reliables like old Lieutenant Barry Tumwater wangled a staff job ashore. Boatswain Tallfeathers, who'd been on board since the ship was commissioned in World War Two, swapped for an amphib out of San Diego. When Corpsmen volunteer to serve with the Fleet Marines, things are tough."

"Good grief. What's the new guy's background?"

"In destroyers for a while. I heard he's spent years in D.C. in some weapons procurement job. I think he's in over his head and is afraid to admit it."

Joe told about the interrogatory and asked Rufus what he knew.

Rufus answered, "The guy has a phobia of adverse publicity. The XO kept a scrapbook of all the times the *Beaverton* was in the news during Captain Sam's tour. At the first meeting, Pinkney carried on a tirade. I told you already about the article on the Tijuana incident. Of course, the picket fence escapade in Melbourne was high on his hit list. Both articles involved you. I have the feeling that if you had been at that first meeting, he would have verbally skinned you alive."

"Why should that old stuff concern him? It happened long before his time. Besides, I wasn't guilty of anything!"

"He wanted to make a point, I guess. The straw that broke his camel's back was the publicity about the condoms."

"You mean the Shield Rubber Company trademark?"

"Yeah. He even sent a letter asking that the ship's radio call sign be changed from 'Rubber Duck.' I'm sure if that man could lay hands on you, he'd have your skinny little butt."

"Hey, I had nothing to do with the thing. I gave an old box to some Quartermaster, who drew it. And he's trying to make a federal case out of it?"

"Fineman's a real nice kid. The old man busted him to third class for something that happened on the bridge . . . and had him transferred to some ship out of Norfolk that goes to Antarctica. The Captain believes you are the consummate practical joker. He says that you inspired the kid to submit the entry and then cumshawed the patterns made for the plaques and the big quarterdeck insignia using the paint you stole in Guam."

"That's crazy. I hardly had enough time to do my own work, let alone pull something like that. Besides, I was on leave most of the time we were in Yoko. Where did he get that idea?"

"First off, sea stories get better with each telling. Since you weren't there to defend yourself, you became a convenient patsy for certain individuals from both the wardroom and the deck force to blame for their own misdeeds."

"Deck force? Why?"

"Boatswain Bail, who's now in charge of the paint locker, and his buddies are still worked up over Richards making Chief."

"The man deserves it. Now I understand. Since the paint was found in an M Division void, they're hoping to hang something on him. How do they know Bail didn't plant the paint down there? He's cooked up charges before. That lying bigot has the credibility of a used car salesman."

"Hey, our boy Bail got his stripe back! And, I might add, over the protests of the XO."

"That's crazy. I suppose the rubber company is suing the Navy."

Rufus laughed. "That's the funny part. Tumwater told me SOB is afraid to do anything because the rubber company promised to unleash some kind of public relations campaign if the ship changes the insignia. And its legal eagles are questioning whether the insignia infringes on their trademark. Meanwhile Shield is selling rubbers in boxes imprinted with the silhouette of the *Beaverton*."

"I saw one."

"When I left, the Old Man instructed my relief that he would have his head in a basket if he passed out as much as one box of Eager Beavers. When I left the ship, there were boxes and boxes of them in the storeroom, but he's forbidden them to be sold on board. They're only sold in vending machines at the Enlisted Men's Club. And the more he makes an issue of them, the more coveted they become. From a public health standpoint, those rubbers are a breakthrough. I think there are more sailors carrying a box of Shields than carry a Zippo with a ship's insignia."

Joe laughed.

"The whole thing would be forgotten by now if the man only had a sense of humor. And he is serious about coming after you. There are some in the wardroom who think you'd make a good scapegoat."

"Why me? I was detached last June."

"There are still some open wounds from the mess on Waikiki. Captain Sam came down hard on that whole crowd. Sean Perkins is in the middle of a messy divorce. I know you didn't have anything to do with it, but Sean still thinks you called the HASP. Like I said, the sea stories bring you into that disaster, as well as just about every other caper during the cruise."

"It's crazy. I stayed out of trouble after we left Long Beach."

"Friend, you have a reputation on the *Beaverton* that is bigger than life. You are the original liberty risk. And Captain Bob has hung on every word. They say the only reason you got Sub School was because you have something on Captain Sam."

"Oh, come on."

"You bet. I had a go-around with him in his cabin just before I left.

He as much as said that Captain Sam put you up to setting up all these things that have ruined his command tour. The man called me 'perfidious' for going over to the Dreaded Enemy."

"Dreaded enemy? We're in the same Navy, for crying out loud! And how can he judge me for things that happened before he came aboard?"

"I don't know. Just before I left, there were rumors that they were going to make you the subject of an investigation."

CHAPTER 35

The End of the Line

FBI Agent Martin Pugsley entered the empty Submarine School conference room late Tuesday afternoon. He walked around the ornate conference table and admired how the diffused rays of a weak December afternoon sun reflected off the glass top. As a World War Two veteran, he was impressed by the tradition on display there—including the oversized cast gold dolphins, the insignia worn by officers qualified in submarines, and the wood-paneled walls on which hung row after row of plaques bearing the insignia of many submarines, submarine commands, and various submarine support ships and activities.

After thoroughly inspecting the room, he couldn't put off his task any longer. He slouched in one of the soft leather-backed chairs and lit another filter-tip off the butt of the one he'd been smoking. At last, he opened the folder to focus on what brought him to the sub base: his charge, Eva Xylos. He again looked at his watch, tapping the crystal to make sure its hands weren't frozen. He was distracted for a moment by a gurgling sound from the silver-painted steam radiator. It looked like a museum piece, with ornate cast-iron feet and valves. The radiator's relief valves began to hiss, quickly making the room heavy with the feeling of rusty water vapor. The air seemed so supersaturated that it felt like it was going to start raining stale tobacco juice and burned coffee.

Pugsley was relieved when Jack Tinker came through the door and seated himself at the head of the table. He observed that Tinker was wearing yet another expensive, custom-tailored dark blue business suit, but with the same dark red and navy blue patterned tie he had worn to the last meeting. Pugsley's eyes focused on the gold cufflinks on Tinker's heavily starched shirt as Tinker riffled through file folders.

He wondered how Tinker could be so calm and detached with bridges burning behind him and disaster ahead. Yet he sat with the confident expression of a poker player with a pat hand, while nursing a steaming cup of coffee. The way Tinker averted his eyes and maintained silence made him feel more strongly that somehow it would be he, Martin Pugsley, who would be the only one to take a fall because of Eva's capers on the submarine base.

Pugsley rubbed his hands nervously. "Aren't you going to tell me what your boss found out?"

"No change."

"Damn, Jack, I thought the Navy people were going to run with all that stuff Xylos' last ship complained about."

"The *Beaverton* has a whole basket of dirty linen, but none of it belongs to Xylos. My boss had a long talk with his old CO, Sam Slaxman. His opinion is that the whole mess is more of a reflection on the prejudices of his relief than on Xylos."

"Prejudices? Masterminding the theft of hundreds of gallons of paint, who is he kidding? And what about the plagiarized insignia?"

"I had a long phone call with the resident agent in Long Beach. They are certain that a substantial amount of the missing paint left Guam on the *Beaverton*. But nobody will admit seeing the paint come on board and after all this time, the only paint around was the twelve cans they turned in. Xylos is in the clear."

"How could he be? They found them in his part of the ship."

"Xylos was in the Gunnery Department when he was detached. The ONI has a statement from two seamen proving the paint was placed in the void during the night prior to the inspection. The man who told them to hide the paint there was the Boatswain in charge of the paint locker."

"Why would he do that?"

"The agent told me it was probably a grudge, at a minimum, up to possibly racial hatred. The Boatswain earlier had been caught attempting to cook up charges against the leading Petty Officer of M Division because of his race. Although young Mr. Xylos had left the Engineering Department, he stood up for the machinist, bringing the charges that ultimately caused the Boatswain to be fired from his job as Leading Master at Arms and lose a stripe. I think the man should have been given a court."

"Let me tell you, Jack, you'd better do something, because this whole thing is on the edge of blowing up. It's only going to take one phone call from that wife who talked to Xylos on Sunday to put this right in the middle of Congress."

"Are you talking about Kari Hedren, Representative Rivers' niece?"

"Of course. You would never have known about this without your phone tap."

"We have a federal court order. Certainly, there's no question about the risks to national security here."

"True, but ordinary citizens aren't too happy to have their conversations recorded. Martin, it's obvious to me that the man who would be the loser is Norcross." Pugsley rolled his eyes. "As I recall her words, she promised Xylos she would tell her uncle if anything bad happened to him as a result of his blowing the whistle on this masher."

"That's all the more reason for playing this absolutely by the book and taking no action that can't be backed up."

"Jack, don't let some false sense of loyalty to cover for a fellow officer blind you. Your butt is hanging out in the wind! And it's going to get blown away if you don't do something. So he wasn't involved in the paint theft? But he was up to his eyeballs in that insignia thing. It sure makes sense to use it as the hammer to give them some plausible justification for kicking him out."

"Martin, I'm not going to throw good money after bad. The patterns were made on an approved job order. The quarterdeck insignia was poured on another approved job order using metal provided by the *Beaverton*. They may have traded paint for scrap metal, but it's impossible to prove. Xylos was on leave, and the whole thing was done by other divisions. Captain Slaxman is old school, loyalty up and loyalty down. I can't fault that. Joe Xylos is no villain. However, he has something else going for him."

"What's that?"

"Captain Pinkney, the new *Beaverton* CO, has little use for submariners and is very outspoken on the subject. His tour is not going well. Captain Sam feels that the man is trying to use Xylos as a pawn." Tinker smiled for the first time. "Pinkney has been pissing up a rope and is paying for it. My boss didn't share any details with me other than to say that one of Slaxman's submariner friends blocked the *Beaverton*'s request to change their radio call sign from 'Rubber Duck.' With a ship's store full of Eager Beaver rubbers and a call sign like that, you have to have a sense of humor get through the day. I understand that Pinkney doesn't. Say, I thought Eva Xylos would be here by now. I know she's been called."

For the fifth time in almost as many minutes, Pugsley pulled his coat sleeve up and again checked the time. "That damn woman! Maybe she has done us a favor and cut and run."

"That's wishful thinking, Martin. It's not likely."

They both turned their heads as there was a bump against the heavy oak door, followed by a rattling of the doorknob as someone seemed to struggle with it. The door opened an inch, then paused, and they saw Eva leaning into it with her shoulder. On one hip sat Francois, his blue eyes curious as to what lay beyond. On the other hip was an overstuffed diaper bag whose strap dug into her square shoulder. Two or three stray locks hung down in front of her ears, confirming that her ponytail had been hastily pulled back. She wore a tan gabardine coat with two rows of brown buttons and a belt snugly tightened around the waist.

The eyes that met theirs were red and almost at the edge of tears. They moved quickly from one man to the other, then behind the door and around the room. Her arm had a slight tremor that spread to her chin.

Both men rose as Eva took her first steps into the room. She halted halfway to the table, her voice breaking as she said, "Will I have an opportunity to see my husband before you take me away?"

Tinker motioned her toward a chair. "Why do you ask that?"

The tall blonde eased the heavy bag off her shoulder. "Because the man said that I'm on my way out."

"What man?"

"The man who called me and said that I was to report to you in this building in this room immediately. When I asked him why, he said it's over. They don't want commie spies here. He repeated that I'm on my way out. It's because of last Friday night, isn't it?"

The FBI agent asked, "What took you so long to get here?"

"I had to get my things together. The diapers were still wet, and I had to wait until they went through the dryer. I wasn't prepared. I guess I should have been. Frenchy was wrong. You are no different from the Russians. No warning, just tell me to go."

"Eva, take a seat at the table. We want to ask you some questions."

She dropped the bag noisily onto the floor; laid her baby on the table; and took off his snowsuit. She sat him up facing her and paid more attention to her baby than to the others in the room.

Francois grinned and made a small happy sound.

While she settled herself, Tinker lifted a dark brown briefcase onto the table. He snapped open the latches one after the other. He rummaged through the case, then dropped a large brown envelope onto the table.

On seeing the envelope, Eva drew Francois across the table to her and asked, "What reason do you have for separating me from my husband?"

Spinning the envelope slowly with his hands, Tinker said, "So far, no one has asked you to leave him. Eva, there are a couple of reasons we've asked you to come here today. Take a look at this."

The NSA officer pushed the large envelope down the table. Pugsley twisted his lips into a grimacing grin as he removed the contents: a pair of mugshot-style black-and-white photographs of Eva in an officer's uniform, and a single sheet of paper with an address and phone number written in almost calligraphically perfect penmanship.

The FBI agent inhaled a lungful of cigarette smoke before asking Eva, "Recognize these?"

"Yes, official AVH photos. They were taken on my return to Hungary just over a year ago. And that's the Villerouges' Vermont address and phone number. Where did you get these?"

"Where should we have gotten them?"

She drew Francois against her breasts as her voice took on a brittle tin-like tone. "How should I know? Here? Here in New London? Oh, no, they're this close! Is that why you sent for me the way you did? And I took my time getting here!"

Tinker said, "They were intercepted by Customs at the Canadian border, at the Richford crossing, the Monday before Thanksgiving. The men who had them were from the Hungarian embassy in Ottawa. Look at the sheet. Do you recognize the penmanship?"

"No. Who? What were their names?"

"We'll tell you later."

She studied the sheet of paper with the Villerouges' address and phone number. In a voice that was almost too quiet to hear, she asked, "Did they harm Frank's parents?"

Tinker played with his cup, rotating it around on its saucer, as he said, "Eva, this kind of cat and mouse game is new to me. I've heard all sorts of theories. Can you give me an explanation?"

"They have no scruples. They want to kill me, my baby, destroy all that I love. What did they do to Frank's parents?" She rocked Francois hard, nervously twisting at the waist. His loud wail drowned out the first of her sobs.

"The Villerouges are okay. As you know from previous meetings, you've come to the attention of people all the way up to the top."

Pugsley added, "Yeah, you and your damn letter."

Eva's voice took on a nasal tone. "My letter? Don't blame your bungling on me."

Pointing to the photos, Pugsley rebutted her. "Come off it. You can't blame this on me!"

Tinker chimed in. "There are too many questions without clear answers. The Montpelier intercept last June, and now this. No one in Washington knows for sure why they came as they did. They weren't armed. Maybe they *wanted* to get caught, to bring you under suspicion. There are also worries that you may be a sleeper, a spy put in place to come out in the open when they need you down the road."

Her voice broke as she said, "It would be foolish to arm a spotter. The pictures probably were for a contact in Richford. The actual killing would be well planned and every attempt made to make it look like an accident or death by natural causes. I fear for Mama and Papa Villerouge. You think I am a sleeper?"

"That's one theory."

"Mister Tinker, sleepers enter your frog pond without making a ripple. I arrived with a splash, remember? Don't you understand? They want me dead!"

Over Francois' unhappy squeals, Jack Tinker said, "Maybe you threw us a few bones to distract us from something far more important that you've already lifted from right under our noses. After all the holes you've poked in our security and all the hell you've raised, maybe you're one of the most effective agents they've ever sent over."

Eva leaned back in the chair and began to unbutton her white blouse. Soon her baby was quietly nursing. She looked up to see the two men's eyes averted from her. She took a deep breath before quietly saying, "I would never do anything to cause me to be separated from my baby and my husband. Why are you doing this to me? I hate the Russians! Why should I help them? It is a citizen's duty to report serious shortcomings. I have done nothing more than any patriotic citizen should do. I only wish to be a good American."

Pugsley leaned across the table. "I would think that after fourteen hours of serious interrogation, you would stop the bull."

Her eyes narrowed. "Serious interrogation! Don't make me laugh. That may have been your intent, but it was, in truth, an investigation into your inability to perform your very simple duties. What I heard in the end were compliments for my concern for security and, yes, my tenacity in the face of complacency."

The NSA officer shook his head slightly. "Eva, you must agree that your knowledge of cryptographic publications puts you into a different category than how you were initially classified."

"Mr. Tinker, I held nothing back when I was debriefed in Hawaii. After last week, it was very apparent that no one was listening. I'm pleased that my concerns are at last being taken seriously. Are you now buying into Pugsley's theory that I must be a spy because I would not ignore a very serious continuing breach of your security?"

"That's not it."

"If it's not, then why must I be threatened with arrest, or is it deportation? How can you give me this taste of paradise and yank it away from me? I love Joe! It's that man, that vile drunk, isn't it? Norcross is a disgrace."

Tinker talked loud to be heard over the baby's cries. "Please calm down. This has nothing to do with Norcross. Eva, no one is asking you to leave your husband. You were the one who suggested it."

Her eyes flashed as she looked at Pugsley. "If I was the one to suggest it, you have taken all too long to let me know I was mistaken. What else could be meant when I'm told that I'm on my way out, calling me a commie spy? Then accusations! If this is your idea of a joke, it's sick! Why are you treating me this way?"

The man from the NSA said, "I apologize, the notification was handled poorly. The yeoman shouldn't have summoned you as he did. That was my fault. The real reason is that Joe's security clearance has been yanked. What I was trying to convey were not accusations, but valid reasons for making this decision. He is being dropped from the school because he's ineligible for duty on any submarine."

"Dropped for lack of security clearance? It's because I reacted too strongly to that man."

Tinker raised both hands. "Not true! Eva, after our meeting on the Friday after Thanksgiving, I tried to convince the school to drop your husband. They refused to make a move until directed in writing. I certainly don't blame them. Then all hell broke loose when news of those Hungarian clowns from Ottawa came tumbling down. I thought those pictures would speed up the process. Instead, more meetings, more delay. To top it off, the incident last Friday at the Officer's Club caused more handwringing and delay when your husband instigated more complaints against Norcross."

"Until Sunday morning after chapel," said Eva, "Joe was more concerned that I might get in trouble. After all, the man was drunk. Bonnie Holt congratulated me for what I did to Norcross. We learned that there were many others whom he touched, that no one in the married officers' quarters went to happy hour on Friday anymore. Most wouldn't even discuss it. Only Dagmar Holmes and Bonnie agreed, but were afraid to lodge a separate complaint. So Joe took it on himself. He became very angry when I tried to change his mind."

"Eva, speaking of anger, couldn't you have just as easily pushed Norcross's hand away?"

She shrugged her shoulders. "From the moment I saw him on the floor, I knew I had made a mistake."

"Then why did you react so violently?"

"It was like a flashback to my old life. I've seen that look in men's eyes too many times. Whatever I said or did wasn't going to stop him. I remembered what Joe said right after the baby was born."

Pugsley asked, "What was that?"

"About a week or ten days after I came home from the hospital, I had a terrible day. I never felt so bad, so blue, in my life. I hardly remember much about it other than sitting on the bed and looking at the wedding pictures, Frank's and mine. He was the most handsome man I ever met. He wasn't perfect, but he loved me."

Tinker nodded. "Frenchy was special people."

She looked out the window and swallowed. "Joe came home from classes and found Francois in the crib, wet and crying. I was vaguely aware he was home, but I didn't move. Nothing had been done all day. I had never even gotten dressed or made the bed. I heard him muttering when he changed the baby. I was sure he was going to be angry. And I didn't care. When he saw me, the look on his face changed, softened. He put Francois on my breast. It was then I became aware how hard my breasts were and how much they hurt. Poor little Francois, I had even forgotten him. He struggled and finally started getting milk. My Joe sat down next to me and put his arm around me."

She wiped a tear from her eye. "After a while he said, 'It must have really hurt today. I've had days like that.' Afterward I felt a warmth, a glow from his being there, like Frank was telling me to love this man. Joe later said, 'I don't mind sharing you with the ghost of my good friend, but I could never share you with anyone else.' From that day on, we've grown much closer."

Tinker looked at his watch. "Then you were worried that Joe would be jealous?"

"Not as much as fearing that I would repay his trust with betrayal."

"I understand. Thank you for sharing that with us. Cal Norcross made a pass at the wrong woman. The close ties that have grown between you and Joe confirm the need to keep him away from any classified material. The opportunity for blackmail or worse is too great. Surely you must understand that there are events, decisions beyond your control, that you both must live with."

"Meaning?"

"Eva, in a few minutes there is going to be a meeting in this room with you, Joe, and the Executive Officer. I don't know how it cannot be painful all the way around. Your husband came here highly regarded and has made an outstanding reputation for himself at this school. Joe has worked hard to stand so high in his class. They went to bat for him last week. Bringing Commander Norcross's vices to the Old Man's attention must give him a following among the married officers. After last Friday night, it would be too easy to assume he's being dropped because of the incident at the club. Nothing is further from the truth. It has everything to do with your background."

"They promised he could serve. Why must he be kicked out of submarines now?"

"We've been over that ground. You were no bit player in Germany."

"I never pretended to be. I gave a full accounting at my debriefing."

"If the papers were to write about what happened to you at the club, we would be concerned for your safety."

"Who would write about such a little thing?"

Tinker said, "A shattered elbow and two broken ribs is not a little thing, especially when done by a woman who didn't even muss her hair. It sells papers, believe me, especially if your true background is leaked. We promised to keep you safe. We need your understanding and cooperation, and especially your husband's. In addition, I'm concerned about the careers of some very fine officers whose reputations could be unnecessarily damaged because of my poor judgment."

"So you wish to save Norcross?"

"He did himself in. I believe the Executive Officer can best explain. We need your understanding and support. Could I count on you to believe that what's being done isn't because anyone is trying to cover anything up or to get even because of what happened last Friday?"

"Are you still going to send me away from my Joe?"

"No, Eva, we aren't that kind of people."

Still keeping the same impassive expression, she nodded. "We will be together, yes?"

"Yes. Will you help us convince your husband?"

She settled back in her chair a little. "As much as I can. Don't be surprised, Joe is unpredictable. I don't know what he'll do. As for me,

I'll be happy to go wherever he goes. That is a wife's duty, is it not?"

"I would think so. Thank you, Eva. I believe I hear the Executive Officer outside the door right now."

Commander Casey Collins entered through the door behind Eva. He was wearing a pair of dress blues whose fabric was shiny at the elbows and the seat of the pants. The gold stripes were aged somewhat, but not quite dull. Under his arm was a stack of manila file folders.

He smiled and slightly bowed as he was introduced to Eva. His eye contact with her was uneven as he let himself focus on the back of Francois's head.

He paused a moment longer, then pointing at Eva, said, "You're the woman I saw working out on the uneven bars at the gym two weeks ago. Your baby was watching you from a little seat on the floor."

"Yes, I have been working out most afternoons. Francois is a good audience."

"I had never seen such a high-quality routine since college. My daughter Wendy said you're the best gymnast she has ever seen."

"Please, I'm not all that good anymore. This is the first time in years that I've had access to facilities. Really, I'm very rusty. I've been casually working out to get back in shape after Francois."

"Casually? Wendy thinks you train for very serious competition. The gymnasts were disappointed that you weren't interested in helping to coach their team."

"I have given them pointers, but coaching, no. Participating in competitions . . . that's too easy a way to attract attention."

"I understand."

He walked to the head of the table, and both Tinker and Pugsley rose. Following greetings, Tinker walked to the wall near the window and Pugsley took a seat on one of the metal chairs along the other wall. He sat erect with arms folded across his belly, and yet another cigarette hung from his lips.

Collins opened the top folder and pushed a mimeographed piece of paper down the table. As it stopped in front of Eva, she backed away. "That is an official message, isn't it? Are you trying to trap me?"

"Mrs. Xylos, please don't worry. The message is unclassified. Regretfully, it's a message that I must give to your husband. The first paragraph says it all. His orders to the *Bowhead* have been canceled, and his clearance for access to all classified material has been revoked. The reason, which is not in the message, is that he married you . . . and your background in Soviet-bloc espionage activities makes the risk of compromise too great."

"You wait until graduation is ten days away to make this decision. It's to cover up for that drunken boor Norcross. You're too much like the Russians."

Collins looked at Tinker. "I thought you were going to talk to her."

The NSA officer shrugged his shoulders. "We have."

"Please, Mrs. Xylos, don't jump to conclusions!"

"Conclusions! What else am I to conclude? Friday I used my training to defend myself and Tuesday . . ."

"That's not the case. Look at the top of the piece of paper. See the six numbers together? The first two are the date, and the remaining four are the time."

"Yes, and it confirms what I said. . . . last Friday at 2112 hours. The message was sent while we were eating dinner. All it took was a phone call."

Collins rose from his chair and took the message from her hand. "No, it wasn't. The date-time group is in Zulu Time."

"Zulu Time? What do Africans have to do with . . ."

"All message traffic uses Greenwich Mean Time for reference, what we call Zulu Time. Greenwich is five hours ahead of Eastern Time, so it was 5:12 in the afternoon. Look at the rubber stamp mark. It wasn't received here until Saturday morning at 1:14 a.m. local time."

"Why the delay from five in the afternoon?"

"Since it was Friday afternoon, there probably were a ton of messages with higher precedence. It required special handling. And I didn't see it until just before ten yesterday morning."

"Norcross threatened me if I didn't go with him. He must have known about it."

Collins's face reddened. "Commander Norcross has never seen this message. The timing of the incident was most unfortunate. Yes, an unfortunate coincidence."

Eva sniffled, then paused before saying, "Please forgive me. I wasn't trying to pry. How you run your messages is not mine to know. I am trying to understand this nightmare. The Commander threatened the others too, if they as much as breathed a word."

"Don't worry about Commander Norcross. He has yet to report for duty following his injuries last Friday evening. There will be no cover-up of the incident at the club. He is being relieved of his duties as Curriculum Director pending his retirement. It was his choice rather than face an investigation of his conduct. He served his country honorably for over twenty years, but this incident dashes any hope of future promotion. I hope that satisfies you and your husband."

"Yes. Joe was intent on protecting me, nothing more."

Collins looked at his watch. The room fell silent except for the sucking and swallowing sounds of the infant.

Pugsley lit another cigarette off the end of the one in his mouth. After a long silent minute or two, the door banged open. Joe stood in the open doorway wearing dress blues and carrying a couple of books and a blue three-ring binder.

The XO pointed to the chair next to Eva. "Mr. Xylos, please have a seat at the table next to your wife."

At the sight of her husband, Eva's eyes overflowed. The catlike tension in her posture visibly softened.

As Joe took the few steps from the door to the table, he asked, "Eva, what's wrong? Why are you crying?"

"They ordered me to come here. I was frightened."

He almost tripped over the full diaper bag on the floor. "This is loaded up like you're taking a trip. What's going on?"

Sniffling, she replied, "The man said I was a communist spy and I was on my way out. It . . ."

Joe turned to face the FBI agent as his voice rose an octave. "Pugsley, what the hell are you doing, terrorizing my wife?"

Pugsley pulled the cigarette from his mouth and pointed toward Tinker. "Not me. He's the one who set up this meeting."

"Wait a minute, remember Montpelier last June. The threats against her life . . . concern for her safety. There would be no Navy contact with Eva, only through you. Strict—"

Eva said, "It was the yeoman."

"Yeoman! Good grief, *everybody* knows."

Collins said, "Mr. Xylos, please sit down."

Then, seeing the pair of glossies, Joe froze and looked at Eva. The color drained from his face. As he gained eye contact with her, she sobbed, "It's not what you think. They took these from men who were looking for me. They want to kill me."

Jack Tinker shook his head. "We don't know that for sure."

"If you don't know for sure that they weren't, then why are you upsetting my wife?"

Casey Collins stood up halfway. "Please, Mr. Xylos, sit down! I called the meeting. The pictures are another issue."

Joe sat at the table, and Francois released his grip on Eva's nipple and reached out toward him. The Commander's brow furrowed deeply as the infant was transferred into his stepfather's arms. His jaw dropped when Joe burped the baby.

The XO snapped, "Can't your wife burp the baby?"

"She can, but he'll probably cry because I'm around."

Collins muttered, "Damn married Reserve Ensigns!"

Joe's eyes fixed on the photos, then traveled to read the message. He pointed toward the mimeographed sheet. "Is this the reason for the meeting?"

Collins nodded. "Mr. Xylos, this isn't the way I wanted to handle this matter."

"Sir, I don't understand. When we met with the people in Vermont before Sub School, I specifically asked about security clearances. I was told it would be no problem as long as I wasn't involved in special operations. Commander, we made no secret of our marriage or Eva's background. And she has stayed within the instructions about reporting in. We've hardly gone off base, mainly because of fears about people looking for her. We've maintained the cover per instructions. Nobody in my class knows about her background unless you told them. Does it have to do with all the security screwups she has found? Or Commander Norcross?"

"Mr. Xylos, I have never before asked for a wife to be involved when dropping an officer from Submarine School. In light of the unfortunate timing of the incident last Friday, I feel that it is necessary to clear the air. Commander Norcross will not relieve me as Executive Officer. He has been relieved of his duties pending retirement from the Navy. This would have happened independent of this message. Higher authority has determined that your security clearance for access to any and all classified and, especially, cryptographic materials must be revoked because of your wife's background in Soviet-bloc espionage. It is a decision that I mistakenly fought because of my understanding of the criteria for your clearance and, more important, your exemplary performance."

Tinker moved from the wall as he said, "I would liken Eva's actions to Lady Godiva's ride through Coventry. She's drawn too much attention to herself."

"Attention? Protecting herself from being put upon by—"

"Her letter to J. Edgar Hoover focused attention at the highest levels on the two of you. That, combined with other disclosures, collapsed your whole house of cards."

In a small voice Eva said, "I'm sorry, Joe. I should have known."

The Ensign said, "Darling, you should never feel bad about doing what is right."

The NSA official stopped behind the XO and continued, "Her letter flagged the fact that your wife has the ability to identify sensitive cryptographic material, putting her in a far different category than what we had earlier established. What had been evaluated as a routine defection of a bit player has been re-evaluated. The consensus is that the risk is too great."

Joe studied the message while the NSA officer spoke, then flipped it down the table. "Commander, they did you no favors. Paragraph One cancels my clearance, and Paragraph Two says, 'Utmost discretion must be used during out-processing so as not to draw undue attention to Ensign Xylos' wife.'"

"I'm aware of that."

"This class graduates in ten days, sir. I don't care how you try to paint it. Nobody is going to believe my departure isn't tied to Commander Norcross. It has taken close to three weeks or a month for other married people to leave after being dropped."

"We could have you on your way by dark, mister."

"I'm sure you could, sir. And it would look all the worse if you did. If the Bureau acts with its accustomed speed, we could spend Christmas here too. That would be the safer course for all concerned."

"What are you getting at, mister?"

"My gut reaction is to bail out today, leaving someone else to pack us out. For Eva's sake, I fear publicity. And if your yeoman knows about her background, how many more people do?"

"We are better than that, Mr. Xylos."

Eva pointed at Jack Tinker. "He let the cat out of the bag. I have been compromised, and I'm scared."

While Joe rocked the sleepy infant in his arms, he said, "If you can confirm that he's the only one to learn about Eva, I'd prefer to continue in class until my orders arrive. My wife will remain inside the apartment until we leave."

"What! Without a clearance, you can't be enrolled."

"I'll turn in all my classified books today. Tell me which classes I can't attend and I won't."

"Xylos, I'm at a loss to understand your logic. Give me one good reason for this course of action."

"Damage control. If I graduate with my class, there will be no opportunity to draw more attention to Eva or create the appearance of retaliation for what I did about Commander Norcross. It will be months before anyone will be aware that I didn't go to the *Bowhead.* And you won't have another mess in the papers like when Rhea McTavish sued the Navy last summer for not letting her into the exchange in slacks."

"And what do you gain by this?"

"Sir, we have no place to go. Oh, we could camp out in a cheap hotel, but I'd rather not waste leave or money. More important to me is recognition for what I've earned. I want my resume to read 'graduated sixth or seventh in the class,' not 'attended.' And if I must be in the Reserves, I want to be in a submarine unit. I can't conceive of anyone taking me after I was dropped."

Commander Collins steepled his hands. "I can't conceive of a unit taking an individual who can't qualify for an active duty billet. Yet, what do we lose by this arrangement? It would certainly quiet any rumors."

Tinker said, "Xylos, how are you going to explain this meeting to your classmates?"

"Simply, it had to do with Commander Norcross. He is being removed from his position pending retirement."

Collins nodded. "Ensign, I have the feeling you are trying an end run on me. I talked to your old XO on the *Beaverton* this morning. After what he told me about what went on around you, and realizing what happened since you came here, don't think that I'm not going to expedite your orders."

A flicker of a smile crossed Joe's lips, and his eyes danced for a moment. "That could be the very reason you should let me stay. As I recall, the big trouble generally happens after I leave."

"You'd better not push things too far, or you might find yourself spending the rest of your active duty time on an unaccompanied hardship tour."

The square-shouldered blonde stiffened in her chair, then snapped, "You can't do that! I was promised that my husband would not be separated from me."

Joe rested his free hand on her shoulder. "Don't worry about that, darling. We're going to be together for a lifetime. Commander, can I plan to graduate before you move me to a duty station where my family is safe?"

"Yes, Mr. Xylos, the two of you are free to go."

The door was still swinging shut behind them when Tinker said, "You've got to give that young man credit. Thinks on his feet. He played a losing hand perfectly. He calmed her right down when he said, 'You should never feel bad about doing what is right.' I liked that."

Collins demanded, "Tinker, what does that woman mean that she was promised?"

"It was the only condition she asked for. And it didn't cost us a dime. Of course, one could argue that the promise applied only to her first husband. But I wouldn't advise it."

"Why not?"

"I learn from experience. I'm not sure how much of a career I have left after her letter to J. Edgar."

"Don't feel like you're the only one to ride a splintery fid today. My orders to COMSUBDIV SIXTY-THREE are being canceled, and I will be here through another winter, pending selection and transfer of a new XO. Damn Cal Norcross! We had just put earnest money on a house in Norfolk last Friday."

Pugsley rubbed his chin. "Yeah, you're lucky. I'd resign from the Bureau if I weren't so close to retirement. It's a bone sticking in my throat to be assigned as field agent in Bettles, Alaska. Do you know where that is?"

"No."

"North central Alaska, just north of the Arctic Circle. My kids will have to attend boarding school in Fairbanks. I'm not even sure if I'll find a place for my wife."

Tinker said, "That ought to put enough distance between you and Eva."

"She's been an enigma from the start. On one side, she is a loving, almost submissive housewife, wrapped around that runt's little finger, fearful of almost everything and everyone. On the other, she is tough both physically and mentally. She's always been difficult. Usually you can feel an intensity, an anger that broods just below the surface. Norcross is lucky she didn't break his neck."

Collins chuckled. "A shattered elbow and two broken ribs without as much as ruffling a hair. The woman is an amazon."

"Yet she sat at the end of the table here today all teary eyed, acting vulnerable and afraid. That woman! The contempt I've had to endure! It wouldn't surprise me a bit if she makes a break for it and goes back to the other side."

Tinker said, "That little exercise she pulled with your duty officer last Friday night fully demonstrated how sharp her observational skills are. She placed and described just about everyone who was in the bar when the incident occurred. The reevaluation by the people in McLean is that she may well be KGB, Directorate S."

Casey asked, "Directorate S, what's that?"

"They infiltrate Soviet-born agents into the West, using assumed identities. Eva is amazing. She has an ear for language that is unbelievable. Already she sounds like she's a native New Englander. She speaks Russian with a pure Moscow dialect. They've verified that as a child, she attended school in Moscow's Sokolniki district at one of the elite schools for the party big shots. They're not even sure she isn't Russian, because she speaks both Hungarian and German with a very slight Russian accent. Yet her reaction to those pictures was pure terror. Whether the terror was that she was about to get caught or that they had sent someone to zap her, remains to be seen."

Pugsley said, "She is a remarkable woman. Listening to her, I would never guess she was foreign. What I don't understand is how she could have been involved in so many activities and be so young."

Tinker said, "I can. I think they selected her when she was a child in grade school. And raised her up to do their bidding. I, for one, am extremely impressed with her capabilities. Before she crossed over, she delivered. What bothers me is, after all the disclosures she's made, what are the hole cards that she's taking with her? One analyst theorizes that she was a KGB sleeper plant in Hungary, whom they redirected to the West."

Collins said, "Like she said, if she is a sleeper, why are they trying so hard to get in contact with her?"

"The two operations mounted by the Hungarians have been pure comic opera. The usual thing that happens when an individual defects, is that the family that's left behind suffers. Her only living relative is an uncle who has been promoted since her defection. He is very close to Janos Kadar. I, for one, feel that the nation will be a more secure place with Mr. Xylos out of the Navy and his wife without access to any of our bases. There would have been orders to that effect included in that message had the drones in BUPERS not insisted on a pound of flesh from Xylos for his time here. We may yet win that one."

The NSA officer looked out the window and followed the progress of the short round-shouldered ensign and his tall square-shouldered wife as they walked to their red Chevy. Joe still carried the well-wrapped baby in his arms as clouds of steam marked their every breath. After she slid into the car's front passenger seat, he kissed her. She put her hands on both sides of his head and prolonged the embrace before taking Francois into her arms. Joe walked around the car, his shoulders more rounded and his head hanging down. As he opened the driver-side door, he looked up at the window where Tinker stood and shook his head before disappearing from view. Eva too saw Tinker in the window. She smiled and waved to him.

The NSA officer cut the syllables as he snapped, "Now what on earth has she to smile about?"

Behind him, the XO grumbled in a flat voice, "We've all been taken for a ride, gentlemen. The only time she wasn't acting scared, but instead showed anger, was when I suggested an unaccompanied tour. I've concluded that what has been really motivating Madame X's zeal to improve our security and moral standards, is nothing more than the strong primordial desire to have her man in bed next to her every night."

CHARACTERS BY CHAPTER IN
ONE HELL OF A SHIPMATE

CHAPTER 1 - *Long Beach*

Joe Xylos - Ensign US Navy Reserve - Boy's Town

Harry Leach - Lieutenant- Senior Watch Officer, SWO - Main Battery Officer

George Speed - Lieutenant (jg) - First Lieutenant

Sam Slaxman - Captain - Commanding Officer

Milt Kane - Lieutenant - Main Engines Officer, M Division

Wayne White - Lieutenant - 2nd Division Officer - 'Outside White'

Barry Tumwater - Lieutenant - Personnel Officer

Stanley Longstreet - Commander - Executive Officer

"Lawyer" Carter Sawyer - Ensign - Legal Officer - Bull Ensign - Boy's Town

Cyrus Penelton - Lieutenant (jg) - Assistant CIC Officer - Boy's Town

Bos'un Tallfeathers - Second Division - Bos'un

CHAPTER 2 - *Long Beach*

Joe Xylos - Ensign US Navy Reserve - Boy's Town

Larry 'Inside' White -Ensign - A Division Officer - Boy's Town

Promoted to Lieutenant (jg) while in Yokosuka

Cyrus Penelton - Lieutenant (jg) - Assistant CIC Officer - Boy's Town

Harry Leach - Lieutenant; Senior Watch Officer,SWO - Main Battery Officer

Sam Slaxman - Captain - Commanding Officer

Mike Wyman - Commander - Operation's Officer

Rolan Swenson - Lieutenant (jg) - Mess Treasurer - Boy's Town

Todd Morgan - Lieutenant (jg) - B Division Officer

Henry Moran - Lieutenant Commander - Chief Engineer

CHAPTER 3 - *Long Beach*

Joe Xylosb- Ensign US Navy Reserve - Boy's Town

Harry Leach - Lieutenant- Senior Watch Officer, SWO - Main Battery Officer

Henry Moran - Lieutenant Commander - Chief Engineer

CHAPTER 7 - Long Beach

Joe Xylos - Ensign US Navy Reserve - Boy's Town

"Lawyer" Carter Sawyer - Ensign - Legal Officer - Bull Ensign - Boy's Town

Cyrus Penelton - Lieutenant (jg) - Assistant CIC Officer - Boy's Town

Milt Kane - Lieutenant - Main Engines Officer, M Division

Rufus Johnson - Lieutenant - Ship's Doctor

Larry 'Inside' White - Ensign - A Division Officer - Boy's Town
Promoted to Lieutenant (jg) while in Yokosuka

Father William Flinn Lieutenant - Chaplain - 'Father Bill'

Stanley Longstreet - Commander - Executive Officer

CHARACTERS ASHORE-Chapter 7-

Tammy Nuslund - Cyrus date Tiajuana

Ole Nuslund Captain- Joe left his daughter in Tiajuana jail

 J.J. Carruthers, the Chrysler dealer

Chief Dilpikil in Fox Division - auto stolen by JJ Carruthers

Paul Mellon, a federal marshal

CHAPTER 8 - Long Beach & Hawaii

Joe Xylos - Ensign US Navy Reserve - Boy's Town

Harry Leach - Lieutenant- Senior Watch Officer, SWO - Main Battery Officer - Public Affairs Officer

"Lawyer" Carter Sawyer - Ensign - Legal Officer - Bull Ensign - Boy's Town

George Speed - Lieutenant (jg) - First Lieutenant

Sean Perkins - Lieutenant - 3rd Division Officer - Elected Mess Treasurer

"Frenchy" Francois Villerouge - Lieutenant - CINCPACFLT Staff - Boy's Town

Rolan Swenson - Lieutenant (jg) - Mess Treasurer - Boy's Town

Stanley Longstreet - Commander - Executive Officer

Barry Tumwater Lieutenant - Personnel Officer

Joe visited USS Bocaccio [SS 223]

CHARACTERS ASHORE-Chapter 8

Mrs.Leah Leach Harry's wife

CHAPTER 9 - Crossing the Line

Joe Xylos - Ensign US Navy Reserve - Boy's Town

Stanley Longstreet - Commander - Executive Officer

Harry Leach - Lieutenant- Senior Watch Officer, SWO   Main Battery Officer

George Speed - Lieutenant (jg) - First Lieutenant

Milt Kane - Lieutenant - Main Engines Officer, M Division

"Frenchy" Francois Villerouge - Lieutenant - CINCPACFLT Staff

CHAPTER 10 - Melbourne

Joe Xylos - Ensign US Navy Reserve - Boy's Town

Stanley Longstreet - Commander - Executive Officer

"Frenchy" Francois Villerouge - Lieutenant - CINCPACFLT Staff - Boy's Town

CHARACTERS ASHORE-Chapter 10

Peotr Waluski, official interpreter for the Polish Olympic team

Eva Atvar, a Hungarian Interpreter

CHAPTER 11 - Melbourne

Joe Xylos - Ensign US Navy Reserve - Boy's Town

Stanley Longstreet - Commander - Executive Officer

Alex Frisch, & Murray Allen - Boilertenders from Beaverton

CHARACTERS ASHORE-Chapter 11

"Felicity Freeman - Australian girl friend of BTs

Mrs. Lionel Collings-Cartwright - Australian hostess

CHAPTER 12 - Melbourne

Joe Xylos - Ensign US Navy Reserve - Boy's Town

Henry Moran - Lieutenant Commander - Chief Engineer

Cyrus Penelton   Lieutenant (jg) Assistant - CIC Officer - Boy's Town

Larry 'Inside' White -Ensign - A Division Officer - Boy's Town
> *Promoted to Lieutenant (jg) while in Yokosuka*

Harry Leach - Lieutenant- Senior Watch Officer, SWO - Main Battery Officer

Stanley Longstreet - Commander - Executive Officer

CHARACTERS ASHORE-Chapter 12

Mr. Brian Fitzhugh - Australian host

CHAPTER 13 - Melbourne

Joe Xylos - Ensign US Navy Reserve - Boy's Town

"Frenchy" Francois Villerouge - Lieutenant - CINCPACFLT Staff - Boy's Town

Henry Moran - Lieutenant Commander - Chief Engineer

Sam Slaxman - Captain - Commanding Officer

Harry Leach - Lieutenant- Senior Watch Officer, SWO - Main Battery Officer

CHARACTERS ASHORE-Chapter 13

Peotr Waluski, official interpreter for the Polish Olympic team

Fitzhugh - Australian hosts

Melissa Peters - Australian party "Coming out" object

Mrs. Eva Villerouge

Mr. Brian Fitzhugh - Australian host

CHAPTER 14 - Guam

Joe Xylos - Ensign US Navy Reserve - Boy's Town

Frenchy" Francois Villerouge - Lieutenant - CINCPACFLT Staff - Boy's Town

Sam Slaxman - Captain - Commanding Officer

"Lawyer" Carter Sawyer - Ensign - Legal Officer - Bull Ensign - Boy's Town

Lieutenant Leach - "Leftenant Koala,"

Henry Moran - Lieutenant Commander - Chief Engineer

Stanley Longstreet - Commander - Executive Officer

CHARACTERS ASHORE-Chapter 14

Mrs. Eva Villerouge

Commander Betty Gates - stationed with Frenchy earlier

CHAPTER 15 En route Yokosuka

Joe Xylos - Ensign US Navy Reserve - Boy's Town

Henry Moran - Lieutenant Commander - Chief Engineer

Harry Leach - Lieutenant- Senior Watch Officer, SWO - Main Battery Officer

Wayne White - Lieutenant - 2nd Division Officer - 'Outside White'

Barry Tumwater Lieutenant - Personnel Officer

George Speed - Lieutenant (jg) -First Lieutenant

Stanley Longstreet - Commander - Executive Officer

Father William Flinn - Lieutenant - Chaplain - 'Father Bill

COL Delbert C. Sullivan, USAF - Spouse of Fumiko

Mrs. Eva Villerouge

CHAPTER 19

Joe Xylos - Ensign US Navy Reserve - Boy's Town

Sam Slaxman - Captain - Commanding Officer

CHARACTERS ASHORE-Chapter 19

Ole Nuslund Captain- Joe left his daughter in Tiajuana jail

Fumiko - "Original Fuji" Tanaka - Joe's companion

CHAPTER 20

Joe Xylos - Ensign US Navy Reserve - Boy's Town

Harry Leach - Lieutenant- Senior Watch Officer, SWO - Main Battery Officer

Richard R. Richards - First Class Machinist, assigned Shore Patrol at Division Party

CHARACTERS ASHORE-Chapter 20

Commander Howard Cannon claimed to have met Eva in Berlin

CHARACTERS and evidence ASHORE in Okinawa-Chapter 20

"Frenchy" Francois Villerouge - Lieutenant -White Beach Officer

Frenchy's red and white 1955 Chevy.

Mrs. Eva Villerouge - wife of "Frenchy"

Willyam"Scoggins" - Lieutenant - Duty on Okinawa

Tom Brown - Seaman Apprentice - Crazy sailor who murders Frenchy

Hostages at base duty office

Bob Munday - Commander - Executive Officer at Okinawa

CHAPTER 21

Joe Xylos - Ensign US Navy Reserve - Boy's Town

CHARACTERS ASHORE-Chapter 21

Chaplain Colson - Okinawa based Chaplain

Tom Brown - Seaman Apprentice- Crazy sailor who murders Frenchy

Hostages at Okinawa base duty office

Bob Munday - Commander - Executive Officer at Okinawa

"Frenchy" Francois Villerouge - Lieutenant   -White Beach Officer

Mrs. Eva Villerouge - wife of "Frenchy"

CHAPTER 22 CHARACTERS ASHORE

Joe Xylos - Ensign US Navy Reserve - Boy's Town

Seaman Apprentice Tom Brown - Crazy sailor who murdered Frenchy

Willyam"Scoggins" - Lieutenant - Duty on Okinawa

Hostages at base duty office

"Frenchy" Francois Villerouge - Lieutenant –DEAD

Chaplain Colson - Okinawa based Chaplain

Bob Munday - Commander- Executive Officer, Okinawa

Mrs. Eva Villerouge - widow of "Frenchy"

CHAPTER 23

Joe Xylos - Ensign US Navy Reserve - Boy's Town

Barry Tumwater Lieutenant - Personnel Officer

Rufus Johnson - Lieutenant - Ship's Doctor

Stanley Longstreet - Commander - Executive Officer

Bos'un Tallfeathers - 2nd Division Bos'un

CHARACTERS ASHORE-Chapter 23

Mrs. Eva Villerouge - widow of "Frenchy"

Agent Detwilder, NIS; Naval Investigal Service

CHAPTER 24

Joe Xylos - Ensign US Navy Reserve - Boy's Town

Harry Leach - Lieutenant- Senior Watch Officer, SWO - Main Battery Officer

Stanley Longstreet - Commander - Executive Officer

Jules Corwin - Lieutenant (jg) - 4thDivision Officer

Wayne White - Lieutenant - 2nd Division Officer - 'Outside White'

Father William Flinn - Lieutenant - Chaplain - "Father Bill."

Larry 'Inside' White - Ensign - A Division Officer - Boy's Town

Tyler Cobb - Lieutenant (jg)- Relieves Joe of M Division - jo

Clarence Compton - Commander - Weapons Officer

Richard R. Richards - First Class Machinist,

Billy Bail - Boatswain Mate First Class- leading master at arms,

Starkings, - Fireman - kicked by Bail

Lowell and Canning, Seamen

Letty Longstreet XO's wife

CHAPTER 25

Joe Xylos - Ensign US Navy Reserve - Boy's Town

Paul Lawson - Ensign - Reports aboard in Yokosuka - Boy's Town

Wayne White - Lieutenant - 2nd Division Officer - 'Outside White'

Rufus Johnson - Lieutenant - Ship's Doctor

CHARACTERS-Chapter 25

Shige Tanaka - Father=Capt.Slaxman + Mother=Fumiko

Frenchy" Francois Villerouge - Lieutenant –DEAD

Eva Villerouge - Atvar, a Hungarian Interpreter

CHAPTER 26

Joe Xylos - Ensign US Navy Reserve - Boy's Town

Stanley Longstreet - Commander - Executive Officer

Paul Lawson - Ensign US Navy Reserve - Boy's Town

Harry Leach - Lieutenant- Senior Watch Officer, SWO   Main Battery Officer

Wayne White - Lieutenant - 2nd Division Officer 'Outside White'

Henry Moran   Lieutenant Commander - Chief Engineer

CHARACTERS-Chapter 26

Lyla Johnson - Rufus Johnson wife

Mabeline - Paul Lawson's girl

Lynda Sawyer - Carter Sawyer's wife

Eva [Atvar, a Hungarian Interpreter] Villerouge - widow

Solange - Party girl Waikiki Blonde

Al Mazini, Paul Lawson's friend- coach at Univ Hawaii

Melba Walker from Memphis, Tennessee - party girl - brunette

CHAPTER 27

Joe Xylos - Ensign US Navy Reserve - Boy's Town

Larry 'Inside' White -Ensign - A Division Officer - Boy's Town - Promoted to Lieutenant (jg) while in Yokosuka

Stanley Longstreet - CommandeR - Executive Officer

Sam Slaxman.- Captain - Commanding Officer

Lieutenant (jg) Tyler Cobb - Relieves Joe of M Division

Paul Lawson - Ensign - Boy's Town

CHARACTERS-Chapter 27

Eva [Atvar, a Hungarian Interpreter] Villerouge - widow

Letty Longstreet XO's wife

Bos'un Tallfeathers - 2nd Division Bos'un

Melba Walker from Memphis, Tennessee - party girl - brunette

and Sandy

Mabeline - Paul's girl

CHAPTER 28

Joe Xylos - Ensign US Navy Reserve - Boy's Town

Paul Lawson - Ensign - Boy's Town

Harry Leach - fat - Lieutenant -SWO Main Battery Officer

Stanley Longstreet - Commander - Executive Officer

Henry Moran - Lieutenant Commander - Chief Engineer

Rufus Johnson - Lieutenant - Ship's Doctor

Lawyer" Carter Sawyer - Ensign - Legal Officer - Bull Ensign -   Boy's Town

Mike Wyman - Commander - Operation's Officer - Investigating Officer

CHARACTERS ASHORE -Chapter 28

Al Mazini, Paul Lawson's friend- coach at Univ Hawaii

Mabeline - Paul Lawson's girl

Lynda Sawyer - Carter Sawyer's wife

Eva [Atvar, a Hungarian Interpreter] Villerouge - widow

Leah Leach - Harry's wife

Ole Nuslund Captain- Joe left his daughter in Tiajuana jail

Frenchy" or Frank Francois Villerouge - Lieutenant - deceased

CHAPTER 29

Joe Xylos - Ensign US Navy Reserve - Boy's Town

Lawyer" Carter Sawyer - Ensign - Legal Officer - Bull Ensign   Boy's Town

Paul Lawson - Ensign - Boy's Town

Harry Leach - Lieutenant- Senior Watch Officer, SWO   Main Battery Officer

CHARACTERS ASHORE

Eva [Atvar, a Hungarian Interpreter] Villerouge - widow

Lynda Sawyer - Carter Sawyer's wife

Gunther Wilkoski - Lynda Sawyer's boy friend

Mabeline - Paul Lawson's girl

CHAPTER 30

Joe Xylos - Ensign US Navy Reserve - Boy's Town

Stanley Longstreet - Commander - Executive Officer

Lawyer" Carter Sawyer - Ensign - Legal Officer - Bull Ensign - Boy's Town

Rufus Johnson - Lieutenant - Ship's Doctor

"Frenchy" Francois Villerouge - Lieutenant –DEAD

Sean Perkins - Lieutenant 3rd Division - Elected Mess Treasurer

Lieutenant (jg) Tyler Cobb - Relieves Joe of M Division

CHARACTERS ASHORE

Eva [Atvar, a Hungarian Interpreter] Villerouge - widow

Lynda Sawyer - Carter Sawyer's wife

Father Michael Makridakis - Greek Orthodox priest in Lomita

Melba Walker from Memphis, Tennessee - party girl - brunette

CHAPTER 31

Joe Xylos - Ensign US Navy Reserve - Boy's Town

Lawyer" Carter Sawyer - Ensign - Legal Officer - Bull Ensign - Boy's Town

Stanley Longstreet - Commander - Executive Officer

Harry Leach - Lieutenant- Senior Watch Officer, SWO   Main Battery Officer

Sam Slaxman - Captain - Commanding Officer

CHARACTERS ASHORE

Father Michael Makridakis - Greek Orthodox priest in Lomita

Detective Ramarez from the LA County bunko squad

Eva [Atvar, a Hungarian Interpreter] Villerouge - widow

Leah Leach - Wife of Harry Leach

CHAPTER 32 Sweet Old Bob

Sam Slaxman - Captain - relieved Commanding Officer

Robert - "Sweet Old Bob" Pinkfney - Captain - Commanding Officer after Sam

Slaxman

Stanley Longstreet - Commander - Executive Officer

Rufus Johnson - Lieutenant - Ship's Doctor

Wayne Wyman - Commander - Operation's Officer - Investigating Officer

CHARACTERS ASHORE-Chapter 32

Joe Xylos - Ensign US Navy Reserve - detached duty at Submarine School

Letty Longstreet XO's wife

CHAPTER 33 New London - SUBMARINE SCHOOL

Casey Collins - Commander - Executive Officer of Submarine School

Admiral Rickover - Head of Nuclear effort

Brent Gilmore - Captain - CO Training Command New London Submarine School

Jack Tinker - Commander - National Security Agency

Martin Pugley - FBI agent - Eva's Control

Calvin Norcross - Commander - Submarine School - Director of Officer Submarine Curricula

Joe Xylos - Ensign US Navy Reserve - detached duty at Submarine School

PFC Robert Durinmeyer, U.S.M.C. - Asleep on post at North Gate

Eva [Atvar, a Hungarian Interpreter] Xylos - Married to Joe Xylos

CHAPTER 34

Eva [Atvar, a Hungarian Interpreter] Xylos - Wife of Joe Xylos

Joe Xylos - Ensign US Navy Reserve - duty at Submarine School

Martin Pugley - FBI agent - Eva's Control

CHARACTERS-Chapter 34

Rufus Johnson - Lieutenant - Beaverton Ship's Doctor - Detached

Lyla Johnson - Rufus wife

Robert "Sweet Old Bob" Pinkfney Captain - Commanding Officer after Sam Slaxman -

Dagmar Holmes. Wife of Lieutenant Barney Holmes, Sub School student

CHAPTER 35 - SUBMARINE SCHOOL

Martin Pugley - FBI agent - Eva's Control

Jack Tinker - Commander - National Security Agency

Casey Collins - Commander - Executive Officer of Submarine School

Joe Xylos - Ensign US Navy Reserve - duty at Submarine School

CHARACTERS ASHORE-Chapter35

Eva [Atvar, a Hungarian Interpreter] Xylos - Wife of Joe Xylos

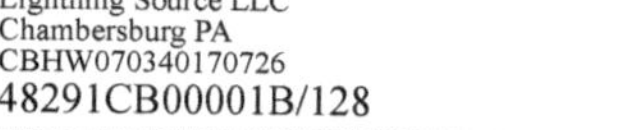
9 781942 661498